RAPT - The Price of Love

Everhide Rockstar Romance Series – Book 3
by
Tania Joyce

EVERHIDE
ROCKSTAR ROMANCE

For lovers of true passion.

Chapter 1

GEMMA

My wedding day was the one day I didn't want to be in the spotlight. I wanted to be away from the crowds, the fans, the paparazzi. No cameras. No security. No craziness. I wanted to get married on a private island in Belize, to Kyle—my rock, soulmate, and fellow Everhide bandmate. With only our four best friends present. Perfect.

But in the past two weeks, Kyle had hinted at changes. The pressure had mounted to turn our simple beach ceremony into a gala event. I didn't want fanfare. Even wedding dress shopping had turned into a frocking nightmare.

Kara, my best friend and stylist, had dragged me into Nina's Bridal Atelier, a glitzy, strictly by-appointment-only boutique in SoHo. Surrounded by gilded mirrors, damask-covered chairs, and crystal chandeliers, I tried on my seventh wedding gown. I glanced at my watch. My pulse hit overdrive. This was taking too long. I needed to get to rehearsal.

"Kara, please stop." Summoning my sweetest smile, I ran my clammy hands over the lace bodice of the exquisite wedding dress Kara and Nina, the head designer, had slipped me into. The gown weighed a ton. The top gaped. Pearl-colored beads and sequins snagged my calloused fingertips. Clutching at handfuls of the silky princess skirt, I twisted the fabric from side to side. The tulle underskirt itched my legs. I didn't care if this was the most popular style worn in Manhattan. It wasn't something I'd wear. "I'm not getting married in anything like this. It's not me. Let's go with something that says more rockstar, less prissy princess."

"Gemma." Kara thrust her hand on her hip. "You've got to try different styles to see what you like. You can't go with the first dress you put on." She flicked her hand toward the pale cream sheath hanging on the change room door. With Swarovski rhinestone straps crossing the open back, the silky gown looked like it should be at Agent Provocateur not in a fancy bridal shop.

That was why I liked it; it was sexy and seductive, and screamed *smoky siren.*

"Yes, I can." I tugged at the neckline of the gown I had on and jutted my chin toward the sheath. "I love that one."

Kyle wouldn't care if I turned up in a burlap sack. But if I had to go through with the fiasco of a ceremony, I wanted to wear something I liked. I loved dressing up in designer clothes. It was my job to rock up a storm on stage, walk red carpets, and attend performances and award shows. If my heart wasn't so set on a beach wedding, I'd be happy to throw on a simple dress, head down to the Marriage Bureau with Kyle, and sign the paperwork.

A quick press release from Kate, our publicist, could announce Kyle and I were married.

That would put a stop to the media wolves trying to pry the wedding details from us during our appearances. Put a halt to the influx of letters and social media posts from fans that ranged from ecstatic well wishes to tear-filled, heartbroken devastation. Some bordered on crazy. Managing our correspondence kept Bec, our personal assistant, and our administration team constantly busy. At least it gave Kyle, Hunter, and me one less thing to worry about with our hectic schedules.

Kara placed her hands on my forearms, her eyes shining brightly. "You're one of the most influential women in the world. Everyone will want to see photos of your special day. Nina will be inundated with orders for the 'Gemma Lonsdale' wedding dress.

You can't wear something off the rack that costs six hundred dollars. It's my duty to make sure you shine."

I wriggled the skirt sitting uncomfortably on my hips. The wedding would mean more to me if it *didn't* make headline news. I'd had enough of my personal life splashed across the Internet to last a lifetime.

"I will shine. But not in a dress like this." Maybe Kyle and I should elope. That would make life easier. Likelihood of that happening?

Zero.

Kyle insisted on a ceremony. For me, marriage was about the two of us committing to each other. It should be private, not a show for everyone we knew and the world to feed on. I didn't want our plans to change. I'd rushed out the door this morning to avoid more heated wedding conversations. The whole thing had become stressful.

Nina's heavy cat-lined eyes glinted as she grabbed a veil and pinned the comb into my hair. "Gemma, I can make you anything. You're marrying the man of your dreams. Don't you want the most divine dress?"

"I do. But I need something practical for the beach. I'm sorry. I'm not feeling this one." I glanced at the price tag on the dress. *Twenty-four thousand dollars!* My breath stabbed my lungs. *Definitely not feeling it.* Just because I could afford any dress, custom made or designer, there was no way I'd spend that amount of money on one gown. Not ever. Growing up less than poor in the back streets of Montgomery, New Jersey, had forced me to fight for what I wanted. It had given me motivation to make something of my life and follow my love for music. I respected and appreciated everything I'd achieved in my short twenty-six years. I didn't take any of my fame or fortune for granted.

"Fine. You don't like that style." Kara flipped her golden-brown ponytail over her shoulder, turned on her high heels, and walked over to the dress rack to grab another gown. She held it out toward me. "Try this one."

I glared at the A-line creation. What was Kara thinking? We

normally agreed on fashion. Kara knew what I liked, but not today. "No way." I shook my head as I stepped out of the princess dress and handed it to Nina. "I don't do strapless."

A playful sparkle shimmered in Kara's eyes as she wrinkled her nose. "I know. It's just for fun. Please put it on."

I sighed and snatched the dress from her clasp. I'd do anything to get out of here as quickly as possible. "This is the last one." I slipped it over my head, wriggled and zipped it into place. I groaned and yanked the gaping bustline higher. "This is so wrong. I don't have the tits to hold something like this up." I'd need Victoria's Secret to custom-make me the ultimate mega-boosting padded push-up bra if I were to fill out this gown.

Pinning in the back of the dress, Nina winked at me via her reflection in the mirror. "It's nothing a bit of customization can't fix. But I must say, this design suits your petite figure."

Kara flapped her hands in front of her face. Tears welled in her eyes. "Oh, Gem. You look so beautiful."

I kicked my feet against the long, silky skirt. *Swish. Swish. Swish.* The dress was made for someone six-feet tall, not five-foot four. "Kar, it's a nice dress. But it'll be too hot. This heavy skirt is too much."

Despite the air-conditioning, perspiration dampened the small of my back. I clutched at the thick material. My patience had worn as thin as the old Bon Jovi T-shirt I'd worn today.

Nina stood back and admired her creation. "I can change the fabric from satin to silk. The lace is a simple overlay we can remove. It's about finding a style you like."

"I have. It's hanging over there." Frustration clipped my voice as I pointed at the sheath again. I'd had enough of wedding dress shopping. I contorted and twisted my arms behind me, trying to reach for the zipper. "I'm done. No more. Can you get me out of this thing?"

After Nina pulled the dress over my head, I spun to face Kara. I didn't want to hurt my best friend's feelings, but a line had to be drawn. "I love you and appreciate your help and everything you're doing. But no more dresses." I strode over to my clothes and pulled on my old T-shirt.

Kara followed me, her dark blue eyes hooded. "Gem, what's wrong? You love trying on clothes."

"I do, but not wedding dresses. I don't have time to fuck around." I feigned a smile. "I've gotta go. The guys will get shitty if I'm late." Could I get to Brooklyn in less than fifteen minutes? *Nope.* Damn it.

"Gem," Kara pleaded. "It's less than six weeks till your wedding. We need to work on the design today, so I can organize fittings to fit in with your busy schedule."

"You're not listening." I snatched my frayed denim skirt off the floor. I could have a crowd of sixty thousand people hanging on my every word, but no, not Kara. "I have to get to rehearsal."

Kara's shoulders slumped. "Gem, please let Nina design a dress for you?"

I sighed and zipped my skirt. I flicked my hand toward the sheath again. "Nina has designed it. It's right there."

I wished I could get swept up in the wedding excitement, but I couldn't. My experiences had just left me jaded and cynical. I'd been to too many of my mother's gaudy affairs. Janine, my gold-digging, fame-riding mother, was onto husband number five. She'd only want to come to my wedding to take photographs, and sell them to the highest tabloid bidder . . . like she'd done before. I had no father to walk me down the aisle. I didn't even know where he was. He'd taken off without a word when I was twelve. Family who were supposed to love me had used me, broken my heart, or left. It had hardened me, given me thick skin, kept me guarded.

I threaded my belt through the loops on my skirt and buckled it into place. "Kar, be happy. I've found a dress." I didn't have time to traipse all over Manhattan to every bridal shop and try on gowns. Kyle and I didn't want a spectacle of a wedding with a large group of friends, distant family members, and colleagues. I didn't need an over-the-top dress. I wanted to avoid anything to do with seating plans, dietary requirements, and decorations. Nope. The whole wedding thing wasn't for me.

Small and intimate. No stress. No hassle. No fuss. That was

what I wanted.

But it was Kyle's day too.

What we'd planned was perfect.

Shit. What could he possibly want to change?

I didn't want to upset or disappoint him. I didn't want to cause a rift between us. Living with him was incredible. Our life, awesome. Fucking up what we had terrified me. I was terrified he'd leave if things got tough . . . like my dad did. That void had never healed. Never faded.

Kara drew her shoulders back and sucked in a deep breath. "Gem, you're a rock goddess. You should have something designed that is unique and amazing." She turned and helped Nina stuff the strapless dress into a clear plastic garment bag. "I'm sorry, Nina. Let me talk to Gem. I'll see if I can change her mind."

With a hard yank, I pulled my hair-tie free, ran my fingers through my long hair, and retied my ponytail. I hated it when people talked like I didn't exist or thought they knew what I wanted. It made my blood boil. "Kar, that won't be necessary." I jammed my feet into my Vans, my heels thudding against the carpet. "I've tried on some gowns. I know what I like. I've made my decision."

Nina glided over to the slinky gown hanging on the dressing room door and slipped the silk of the skirt through her hands. "It's a beautiful dress, Gemma." Her tone was soft and floaty, like chiffon. "It's perfect for a beach wedding. I'm honored you've chosen one of my designs for your special day."

"Thank you, and you're welcome." I threw her a *I'm-so-over-wedding-plans* smile, then turned on a sympathetic one for Kara. "Be happy, Kar. It's one item off the wedding plan to-do list." *A list I wished didn't exist.*

She lifted her chin and eyed the gown like it had been mass-produced for a budget online outlet. "Gem, are you sure?"

I, unlike Kara, didn't care where the gown came from or what designer label was sewn into its silky lining. It was what I loved and wanted to wear.

Kara's brow furrowed like the satin ruching on the third dress I'd tried on. "But that dress is so plain and simple and—"

"It's exactly what I want." I stepped forward and caught her hands. "Don't be silly. You know I'm chill. Please don't turn this into a big deal."

"It's your wedding." Kara swept her bangs out of her eyes. "It's supposed to be a *huge* deal. It's about you, the dress, Kyle, the suits, the dinner, the cake, and the venue."

"Nope. It's just about Kyle and me. No hype. It's what we want." *Providing Kyle's changes don't get too outrageous.* "You can go wild when you get married. Okay?"

Kara pouted and sulked like a little girl being told she couldn't dress up as a princess today. "I don't think Hunter is a put-a-ring-on-it type of guy."

"You never know. But yeah, don't hold your breath." I giggled. Kara had been dating my fellow band mate for three months and they'd moved in together one week ago. They both deserved some happiness after their hellish year. I rubbed Kara's arms. "I love you. But I gotta go." I swiped my duffel bag off the floor and hooked it over my shoulder. "Are you coming to watch us rehearse?"

"No. You go." Kara smoothed her hands over her pencil skirt. "I'll finish up here and schedule in your fittings. Call me when you get home, and I'll come over for dinner."

"Sounds good."

I thanked Nina and rushed out of the bridal shop. A blast of hot, early September air swept through the narrow SoHo street as I ducked into my waiting town car. I texted the guys to let them know I was on my way.

Me: Leaving now. C U soon. xG

Slumping against the cool leather seat, I wiped my weary eyes.

Stupid wedding. I was over it before it had even happened.

As my driver weaved through the traffic and headed toward my band's rehearsal space in Brooklyn, I swiveled my engagement ring around my finger. It was stunning—teardrop shaped, just like a guitar pick.

In six weeks, I'd be Mrs. Kyle McIntyre.

If I survived that long.

At least I could tick off one item on my to-do list.

I got a dress.

A beautiful, simple gown. It was gorgeous.

A vision of Kyle's face when he saw me in that dress filled my mind. His espresso eyes would darken and smolder, take on that glint of possessiveness. His hands would tense, as if it took every ounce of self-control to restrain himself. Heat filled my cheeks, and a sly smile slipped across my lips. I couldn't wait to see his reaction. I couldn't wait to be his wife.

I wasn't someone who gave in easily and wasn't about to turn my wedding into some huge affair. But if Kyle's changes were minimal, like what to have for dinner, or what type of champagne to drink, I'd be okay with that. Anything to keep the peace. But there was no way I'd get hitched under an archway filled with twinkle lights with hundreds of guests present or walk down the aisle to Wagner's "Here Comes the Bride." *Hell no.* With shows, parties, and performances to knock off our agenda before our big day, I didn't want to worry anymore. As long as the gathering stayed small and I could go barefoot in the sand and got to say "I do" to Kyle, *I'd* be happy.

Because nothing and nobody would stop me from marrying the man of my dreams.

Chapter 2

KYLE

The old rehearsal studio in Brooklyn, with its velvet gray drapes surrounding the mock-up stage, smelled of stale cigarettes. I sat on a large amp, tapping my toes in time to the quick beat I plucked on my bass. *Da dada da, da da. Da dada da, da da.* I glanced at my watch. *1:23 p.m.* Gemma was late.

She'd texted saying she was on her way thirty minutes ago. It shouldn't have taken her this long to get here. *Where is she?* I didn't want rehearsal to run overtime. Tonight, when we got home, we had to discuss our wedding. She couldn't evade the subject anymore. I'd let her get away with her tactics for long enough. I half-smiled, chuckling low. I wouldn't let her run off to jam out a riff that had popped into her head, or disappear to write lyrics, or to distract me with sex. Although that would be hard. I loved Gemma's sense of humor and her feistiness, her courage, and confidence. I understood her fears and anxiety. She was my soulmate, a true angel. But damn, she could be stubborn. Especially when it came to something she'd wanted to avoid.

I knew why she didn't want a ceremony. The run-ins and scandals we'd faced over the years with the paparazzi, and the issues with her mother and father, had put her off public displays of affection. But I wanted a wedding more than anything. I wanted the day to be perfect. And to make our day even more special, I wanted to make a few changes. The challenge would be getting Gemma to agree.

Hunter, my best friend, stretched out on the wooden floor a couple of feet away, humming warm-up scales. Sophie, our manager, and our backup band, crew, and technicians hovered nearby, running through schedules before we jumped into this afternoon's rehearsal. A few impatient glances darted my way.

Hunter groaned, rubbing his palms against his eyes. "Where the hell is Gem?"

My fingers slipped down the neck of my bass, and I quickened my tempo. "She was with your girlfriend, dress shopping. That's why she's late."

"Kara and shopping, not a good mix." Hunter sighed, slouching his shoulders. "So should we start without Gem?"

"Nah. Give her a few more minutes."

Gemma never wanted to miss a rehearsal, or anything to do with our music. She'd be tearing her hair out and cursing at whatever was holding her up. *Come on Gem, where are you?*

"Kara probably made her try on every damn dress in the shop." Hunter leaned back on his hands and crossed his ankles. "Gem won't be happy when she gets here."

"Maybe she's late because she's found a dress." That would be awesome if she had. It was the only thing she had to do for our wedding . . . plus turn up on the day.

I lowered my chin and pictured her in a wedding dress, something plain and simple. Her dazzling smile. Her dark brown hair flowing down her back. Her gorgeous lips I couldn't wait to kiss. She'd be a beautiful bride. My heart thudded harder. I couldn't wait to marry her.

It'd taken just over twelve years for our friendship to evolve into love. A love that was intense. Profound. Wicked. I'd adored her for longer than I cared to remember. We'd connected through music from the day we'd met. We'd nearly destroyed each other through too much heartache and had even risked our careers. But two years ago, on her twenty-fourth birthday, the stars and planets aligned. We'd confessed our feelings for each other and hadn't looked back.

Now, the moment I'd thought would never happen was six weeks away. I'd marry her. I'd love her, protect her, and treat her right until I took my last breath. I'd be a great husband and partner for life, unlike my father was to my mom.

Hunter stretched and rubbed the back of his neck. "Bud? Are you okay? You're zoning out."

"Yeah. Just got a heap on my mind. Mainly wedding stuff." But thoughts of my parents had triggered too many haunting memories. Staring at my fingers, tension tightened my brow. I plucked my strings harder. Dad's violent outbursts, his drunken rampages, cutting backhands, and constant belittling always lingered in the far recesses of my mind. So did the vision of the always-present fear in Mom's eyes, her bruised and battered body . . . and the horrific night four years ago when my parents were killed in a tragic car accident. Nightmares still plagued me. Losing my sister, Emily, to leukemia, when I was fifteen, was just as brutal.

"Are you getting cold feet?" Hunter asked.

I chuckled. "Never."

Hunter had been my best friend since elementary school and had been by my side through every good and bad time. But Gemma had become my true strength since the start of high school. She'd witnessed my every wound, heartbreak, and downfall. We'd ridden every high and low together. And thanks to some miracle, she loved me. Every moment with her was a blessing. No matter how much she drove me crazy—or was frustratingly late—I loved her with every element of my soul.

Life with her was fucking awesome.

Somehow, I'd survived for years—the travel, the touring, the partying, the girls—thanks to Hunter, Gemma, and my band's entourage. I'd always been surrounded by people I cared about. I'd shared every high with Gemma and Hunter, but . . . I'd always been lonely. I wasn't anymore. Now, when everyone went home and the music stopped and I fell into bed each night, I wasn't by myself. No more emptiness loomed in my chest. No more pain crippled my heart. Gemma filled every void. I couldn't wait to call her my wife. To be hers, forever.

"Guys," Sophie called to us and jammed her hands onto her hips. "What's happening? Where the hell is Gemma? Has she texted again?"

"Nah. She can't be far." I tapped my fingers against my bass and glanced at my watch again. "Give her five more minutes or we'll start without her."

"Fine." Sophie rolled her eyes, smoothed her hand over her Chanel headband scarf, and returned to talking with our band. Not too much fazed Sophie, but like me, not being on time did.

Hunter grabbed his cell phone from the floor. "I'll fucking text her."

"No. Don't." A nerve pinched in the back of my neck. I sighed and slumped my shoulders. "That'll stress her out, and I need her to be in a good mood."

I hoped she'd cheered up since this morning. Conversations around the wedding hadn't gone to plan. I hated I'd stressed her out, but time was running out to get things organized. We needed to talk. Tonight.

"Why?" Hunter's fingers hovered over his cell phone, but he didn't type. "What's got your ball sacks in a knot?"

I grimaced and stretched my neck from side to side. "I need to talk to her about the wedding tonight. And . . . I want to make some changes."

Hunter let out a high-pitched chuckle and shook his head. "Oh shit. You're game."

"I know." Resting my arm on top of my bass, my leg jiggled. "But it'll be worth it." *I hope.*

Hunter put down his phone. "Is she still stressing over the details being leaked to the media?"

"Yep. I think that's got her freaking out the most. I've done everything to ensure that won't happen." I'd taken on the organizing so no wedding planner could accidentally slip information to the press and Gemma could remain stress free. "But I want to invite more people."

Hunter's eyes widened. "Are you insane? You do want to get married, right? Gem's not going to like that."

Over the years, certain people had become an integral part of our lives. Our band's entourage, backup band, crew, security, a few close relatives, and friends, should be at the wedding. These people were family. Family that went beyond DNA. I wanted them to be part of our celebration. I wanted to stand in front of everyone I cared about and vow to love Gemma for the rest of my days. Upping the number of guests wasn't unreasonable, was it? Going from six people to fifty might be a stretch, though.

"That's why I need her in the best possible mood." Grinning, I flicked my hair back off my forehead. How could I convince her it was right to invite extras? That it meant a great deal to me? I was confident we could work something out.

The door to our upstairs rehearsal room slammed open and in strode Gemma. My heartbeat jumped from moderato to allegro. My shoulders lifted. The unease in my stomach disappeared. Everything was right in the world when she was near. Her cheeks were flushed red, no doubt from rushing to get here. Her long hair was tied back into a disheveled ponytail like she'd just gotten out of bed. Her frayed denim skirt, old Bon Jovi shirt and Vans screamed bad ass rock chick. And just like every time she walked into the room, her smile stole my breath.

She dashed across the room, past Sophie, and our back-up band. They clapped as she passed. She threw them the bird.

Damn, I love her.

"About time you showed," Sophie called out to her.

"Not my fault. Give me two minutes and I'll be ready." She threw her duffel bag onto the floor. It skidded to a halt by the amp. I swung my bass out of the way just in time for her to slip into my lap and kiss me.

"Hi there." Her breath panted like she'd run a mile. "Sorry I'm late. Kara held me up. Traffic was a bitch. And have you seen the crowd outside?" She hitched her thumb toward the studio's large box windows that ran the length of the far wall. "There's about thirty fans outside. How'd they know we were here?"

I kicked Hunter's foot. "Hunt posted on Instagram."

He shrugged his shoulder and clambered to his feet, dusting his hands off on his jeans. "We got here early. I was bored."

"Nice one, goofball." She leaped from my lap, grabbed her transmitter off the nearby table, and clipped it onto the back of her skirt. "Without Chester, it took me ages to get inside. Dylan had to get out of the car and play bodyguard."

"Where's Chester?" I grimaced. She shouldn't go anywhere without security. Good thing her driver could step in when needed.

"He had to take his mom to the doctor." Gemma threaded her ear monitors underneath her hair and hooked them over her shoulders. "He'll be here soon."

"You should've called. Sam and Mick could've gone down to help." I glared at our bodyguards drinking coffee by the far wall. Just because our tour was over, it was no time to slack off. We were still busy attending events, performing, and attracting fans wherever we went. "We didn't know there was a crowd outside."

She waved her hand. "It wasn't too bad. Dylan didn't mind."

I set my bass aside, stood and searched her face and limbs for cuts or bruises. "Are you okay? Did you get hurt?"

"Nope. I'm fine. But . . . um . . ." Her brow furrowed as she snapped her fingers, over and over again. "I got held up outside by . . . what's that girl's name who runs one of our fan clubs? The Ringers chick?"

I grabbed my in-ears and transmitter and put them on. "You mean Taylah?"

Gemma clicked and pointed. "Yeah. That's her."

Hunter stepped over to join us, pulled a hairband from his jeans pocket and tied up his shoulder-length wavy brown hair. "Really? I didn't know she lived in Brooklyn. I only posted on Insta like . . . twenty minutes ago. News travels fast." His tone held an undercurrent of cockiness. His smirk hinted at being impressed by attracting a crowd so fast.

I leaned forward and kissed Gemma on the forehead. "We're just glad you're here. And safe."

"Always." Gemma tickled me in the ribs.

I flinched, ticklish as hell. "So? How did this morning go?"

Gemma's head fell back, and she groaned. "I hated wedding dress shopping with a passion." She swiped the print-out of our set list off the table, scrunched it into a ball, and pegged it at Hunter's face. It struck him on the forehead. "That's for your girlfriend being out of control. She doesn't listen. She thinks this is her wedding. And is driving me fucking crazy."

Hunter caught and juggled the ball, laughing a that-so-didn't-hurt-me laugh. At six-foot two, he towered over Gemma. "Why are you taking this out on me? She's your bestie." He flicked the paper ball back at her.

Gemma caught it one-handed. "Ha . . . too slow."

Before these two broke out into a wrestle on the floor, I wrapped my arms around Gemma and held her close. Normally, I'd join in with their play-fighting antics, but we needed to rehearse. We had a long afternoon ahead. "I take it dress shopping didn't go well."

She slumped and rested her head against my chest. "Kara made me try on all these dresses I didn't like. Such a waste of time."

"But did you get a dress?" I asked, rubbing her back.

Lifting her chin, she met my gaze. Flecks of silver glittered in her green eyes. She scraped her teeth across her lower lip and slid her hands down my chest, tugging on the center of my T-shirt. "Yeah, I got a dress."

My heart strummed like a symphony. "Well then, it was worth it." I dipped my head and kissed her, savoring the taste of her cherry-flavored lip gloss. "I can't wait to see you in it." Just thinking about it made my dick throb.

Hunter grabbed his rhythm guitar off the rack and hooked the strap over his head. "Before you two make me sick, let's get this over with so I can go home to my girl. Hopefully, she'll be in the mood to play dress-ups for me."

"Too much information." I grabbed Gemma's guitar off the rack and handed it to her. "But whatever does it for you, bud."

A smug grin inched across his face. He filled the air with a strum of his guitar. "Kara certainly does."

"Hey!" Sophie ambled toward us. "Two minutes is up. Y'all set?"

"Yep." Gemma plugged in her guitar and flicked the cord out of her way.

I swooped in to steal one more kiss from her. A decent kiss, not some lame-assed tease. One that would get rid of her fluster, make her feel good about getting a dress, be excited for rehearsal . . . and to show her how much I loved her. A flick of my tongue, a rush of hot breath, a gentle suck on her bottom lip. *Hmm.* Her body melted into mine and a soft moan murmured low in her throat. *Fuck.* I had to stop before I got a hard-on.

"Mmm." Her eyes glinted as she licked her lips. "What was that for?"

"I love you and I'm ready to play." I winked, picked up my bass, and placed the strap over my head. "Let's do this."

Not a day went by when I didn't count my blessings. I had Gemma and Hunter, my brother from another mother. These two were my family. We'd grown up together, experienced life together, achieved our dreams together. Love had taken us down some crazy, heartbreaking pathways. But the connection between the three of us could never be severed. It ran deeper and stronger than any bloodline. Nothing would ever tear us apart. I'd do anything for these two. Yep, I'd literally die for them. *So Bryan Adams.*

"Right, you lot." Sophie ambled toward us, batting her copy of our set list against her palm. "We've got less than one week until the benefit concert in Central Park, two weeks to Vegas; and a week after that, you're in New Jersey."

"Oh shit, really?" Hunter splayed his hand over his chest, his tone full of faux shock. "Guys, did you know we have some gigs coming up?"

"Enough of your smart-assing around." Sophie whacked him on the arm with the set list. "I'm just reminding y'all we've a shitload to do before time off, so let's get to it."

"Hey, before we start." Gemma snatched the set list from Sophie. "On the way over, I thought we should change out the song

'Only You' and replace it with 'Escape'. It's a better fit for the tone of the first section. We open with party songs, then do a mash-up of old hits, and close with a couple classics and our latest single. What do you think?"

Hunter stretched, arms reaching above his head. "Whatever. Doesn't bother me."

I adjusted the height of my mic stand. "Gem, that's an awesome idea. We love that song. It's the perfect fit. Done."

Why could we agree on everything for our music, but not for our wedding?

Our pending ceremony had shone a light on our differences. But I wouldn't let anything ruin our day. I'd move heaven and earth to make sure it went off without a hitch.

"If you want to change the set list, it's your call." Sophie gave a shrug. "I'll update it and get someone in the office to print off the sheet music." She bent down and picked up Gemma's duffel bag. "So you don't trip over this, I'll put it in with ours in the meeting room next door."

"Okay, thanks." Gemma tightened her ponytail and stepped in front of her mic, center stage.

I stuffed in my in-ear monitors and signaled to Slade on drums to set the beat. "From the top. Let's go."

After hours of smashing out a full rehearsal, twice, and a couple of reworked transitions, the reverberations from the killer session coursed through my veins. On a high, I followed Hunter and Gemma into the meeting room next door to grab our gear. It was time to go home. Time to sort out those wedding plans with Gemma.

I wiped my sweaty face on my T-shirt sleeve. Maybe after a nice hot shower with Gemma and a relaxing massage, I'd be able to negotiate the guest list. Would some seduction and spicy sex work? Possibly not with Gemma. But at least I'd enjoy the process.

No. No sex. No excuses. No distractions.

"What are the plans for tonight? Kar suggested coming over for dinner." Gemma fanned her face and tilted her head toward the air-conditioning.

Sweat saturated her shirt, clinging it to her slender curves. Damp strands of hair stuck to her neck and her cheeks blazed red. I couldn't wait to get home and peel off her clothes and feel her hot flesh against mine. *Yep. Shower, then talk.* "We'll take a rain check. We have plans."

She narrowed her eyes. "What plans?"

"Yeah, what plans?" Hunter ripped on a fresh T-shirt. "And why am I not included?"

I glared at Hunter, just to jolt his memory. "Umm . . . don't you have to play dress-ups with Kara?"

"Oh, yeah." A goofy grin lit his face.

Gemma held my gaze. My skin prickled. There was no way of keeping secrets from her; she was too perceptive.

Her shoulders slumped. "We've gotta talk about the wedding, right? Is that the plan?"

"Yep." *And you're not getting out of it this time.*

She bent down to pick up her bag, but left it at her feet. She straightened and held out a pale pink envelope. "What's this?"

I shrugged. So did Hunter.

She slid the envelope through her fingertips, a sexy smile curling across her lips. "Kyle, did you write me another love letter?"

"Umm . . . no," I jerked my chin back and shook my head. I'd written her several notes and a gazillion songs, but I'd never use pink stationery.

She ripped the letter open and unfolded the paper.

Her eyes widened.

The color drained from her face.

The paper trembled in her hand.

A chill shot down my spine. My heart lurched as I rushed to her side. "What is it?"

I scanned the page covered in big, black-typed font:

GEMMA, YOU FUCKING SLUT.
IF YOU MARRY KYLE, I'LL KILL YOU.
KYLE'S MINE. MINE. *MINE!*
ALWAYS HAS BEEN. ALWAYS WILL BE.

CALL OFF THE WEDDING. NOW.
OR YOU'RE DEAD.

Chapter 3

GEMMA

This was a sick joke. Clutching the letter, I stormed into the rehearsal room with Kyle and Hunter on my tail. Waving the pink page at our backup band, crew, and entourage, my voice sliced through my teeth. "Which one of you assholes did this?"

No one confessed.

That pissed me off.

I strode over to the bench seats by the window to question Sophie and our security team. But when Sophie read the letter, she turned white. Sam, our head of security, jumped to his feet and phoned the police. Sophie called Bec, our personal assistant, to come to the studio urgently.

What the hell? My head spun, trying to keep up.

"Is this necessary? For one stupid letter?" I shook the piece of paper at them.

"Um ... yes." Sophie's tone was firm but clipped. "There's more to it. We'll explain everything when the police get here."

"More to it?" Kyle stepped in beside me. "Like what?"

Sophie pointed toward the meeting room. "Please, go wait in there. I need to talk to Sam first."

Fire splintered through my veins. I was about to protest, and say 'don't tell me what to do', but the steely gaze in Sophie's eyes pulled me up short. My grip tightened on the letter, resisting the urge to crumble it and toss it in the trash. The guys and I had received thousands of fan letters over the years, some bordered on being obsessive. But as far as I knew, this was the first threat to one of our lives. *My life.* Whoever did this had hand-delivered the letter and gotten close. Too close. That wouldn't happen again.

Shit. I didn't need added stress before the wedding. So much for going home with Kyle and finalizing our plans.

I charged into the meeting room with the guys and slammed the door shut. I tossed the letter onto the table and stared at the pale pink note. "If no one here did this, who did?"

"I don't know." Kyle paced the length of the room, wringing his hands. "Maybe someone in the crowd outside slipped it into your bag when you passed?"

"I'm sure it's just another jealous fan, Gem." Hunter ruffled the top of my head. "Don't worry about it."

I slumped my shoulders and sighed. Hunter was right. It's just a stupid note. It's nothing to be concerned about. "I won't. I'm not."

"Well, I am." Kyle quickened his stride. His sharp tone cut the air. His jaw tensed as he mumbled under his breath. "Who did this? Who'd want to hurt you? What the fuck?"

Shit. I didn't want him to react like this. I'd seen his jealous side, and while it's amazing he cared so much, his overprotective nature was a beaver I didn't want to badger. "Kyle. Chill."

His face turned red. His volume dialed up. "How can I? Someone wants to hurt you."

I stepped in front of him and grasped his arms. I threw him a cold, hard glare. "We don't know that for sure. Please, just stop."

He took a few deep breaths—in and out, in and out. The wildness in his eyes cooled, and he shook his head. He sighed and drew me into his embrace. "Fuck, Gem. I won't let anyone hurt you."

His heartbeat thundered against my ear. Tension still quaked in his muscles. That didn't help me.

"I know." I slid my hands up his back and closed my eyes. I inhaled the scent of his freshly laundered shirt and deodorant mixed with the sweat from rehearsal, hoping to find release from my frustrations and fears, but failed. I clutched at his shirt. "It's okay. Everything will be fine."

I had to believe that.

Within an hour, the guys and I sat opposite two detectives, Jones, and Morris. Jones, with his cheap suit and skinny tie, had a permanent sneer stitched into the corner of his mouth. Morris was a spitting image of Chandler in the TV sitcom, *Friends*, and going by his attire, he lived for the nineties. I puffed at a loose strand of hair hanging over my face. It was nearly eight o'clock. I wanted to go home, eat and shower, not be stuck here at the studio. This meeting better not take long.

Sophie, Bec, and our security team filled every other chair around the oval table. Worry had etched deep furrows into everyone's face. My gaze continually returned to the letter. The police had sealed it in a plastic evidence bag. It now rested on top of folders in front of Jones. I'd read that letter more than a hundred times since finding it. The words had branded my brain. *If you marry Kyle, I'll kill you.*

What if someone wanted to hurt me?

Ugh. Don't think about it.

I didn't want management and security to be concerned. I didn't want to cancel any shows. And most of all, I didn't want Kyle to get overbearing. He'd been tight as a tension cable since he'd first read the letter. He'd want to take matters into his own hands, but dealing with a messed-up note was out of his control. And when it came to my safety, I knew how to take care of myself.

Bec tucked her bobbed hairdo behind her ear. Once. Twice. Three times. "I'm so sorry, Gem. We hadn't told you and the guys about the other letters because we hadn't heard from the police. We didn't know if the letters were serious."

Wait. What?

My head throbbed, tightening every tendon in my neck. "What other letters?"

Kyle, sitting to my right, clenched his hands on the table. The corded veins in his arms bulged. "You mean there are more notes?"

Sophie nodded slowly. "Tonight, was the fourth one we've received."

Four letters!

What the fuck?

Detective Jones waved his pen toward Bec. "You're lucky to have a good assistant who noticed the unusual."

I stole a sideways glance at Bec. She was a treasure. She'd been our PA for eight years. She knew every detail about us and ran our lives. Nothing happened without Bec knowing about it. She was a crucial employee, as well as a great friend. But keeping something like this from us wasn't acceptable.

"Bec? The fourth?" My voice caught in my throat. "Why didn't you tell us?"

Bec's eyes glassed over. She rounded her shoulders. "I'm sorry. I was following procedures. Until there was a pattern, an actual threat, or a breach in security, there was nothing to be concerned about."

Kyle jolted forward, redness creeping up his neck. His voice slid through his clenched teeth. "We should've been told about any threat."

I winced. He'd hate not being made aware sooner, hate being kept out of the loop. He liked to be on top of everything. So did I.

Bec's gaze hardened. She leaned forward on folded arms. "I told Sam and Sophie. Sam took the notes to the police. You guys have been so busy. With shows. And Promo. And travel. And Hunter and Kara's issues . . ."

Hunter, sitting at the far end of the table, froze, then lowered his chin. My heart ached. The loss of his preemie son five months ago had affected all of us. Now we had new threats to deal with.

Bec softened her tone. "We just thought . . . after everything that has happened lately . . . we didn't want to worry you until we knew it was a problem."

Sam folded his arms, his black T-shirt stretched tight across his bulky biceps. "You guys aren't naïve. You know you have some extreme fans. We were going through the processes, investigating the issue, before bringing it to your attention. Your safety and security is paramount."

The fiery vibe coming off Kyle prickled the air. Before he did something irrational, like fire Sam and our security team for doing their job, I placed my hand on his leg and gave it a firm squeeze. Getting the message to calm down, he flinched and sank back into his chair.

I drew in a deep breath and threw Sam a please-ignore-Kyle smile. Sam took our security to heart. He would've told us about any issue when necessary. I didn't doubt him or our team, not ever. I wouldn't let some stupid letters get to me.

But steam still vented off Kyle. His head turned sharply toward Bec. "When did the other letters arrive?"

Bec counted on her fingers. "The first one arrived after your engagement." *Eleven months ago.* "The second arrived after New Year's." *Almost nine months ago.* "The third, last week when we got home from the promo tour."

"We had a pattern, but no real threat." Sam splayed his hands and placed them on the table. "But the contents of this letter and it being put directly into your bag, changes everything."

Ya think?

Bec flicked her finger toward the letter on top of Jones's folders. "You know we keep any letters the admin team and I find and call 'the crazies' separate." Her tone was serious, but light, as if this was an everyday occurrence. "Letters that seem to go beyond the weird and normal fan love letters. You know . . . like . . . '*Oh my God, I'm gonna kill myself,*' '*I can't go on living without you,*' or '*I stood outside your apartment for four hours today, hoping to catch a glimpse of you.*' That kind of thing. We have a dozen archive boxes full."

I mouth fell open. My eyes nearly popped out of my head. "Holy shit. I didn't think we'd gotten that many psycho letters." I'd read a lot of fan mail. Most of it was sweet.

Hunter jutted his chin toward the detectives. "What's in the other letters?"

Detective Morris straightened his thick-rimmed glasses. He grabbed one of the folders from in front of Jones and slid more letters printed on pale pink paper sealed in plastic toward Hunter, but Kyle grabbed them first.

Damn, he was quick. I leaned against his arm and scanned them, too. The first read:

KYLE, HOW DARE YOU GET ENGAGED TO THAT WHORE?
YOU LOVE ME. NOT GEMMA.
I'M YOUR TRUE LOVE.
MARRY ME, NOT GEMMA.
YOU'RE MINE. MINE. MINE!

Kyle's hands trembled. He shuffled the pages around. The second said:

KYLE, DON'T DO THIS.
YOU'RE THE LOVE OF MY LIFE AND I'M YOURS.
DON'T MARRY GEMMA.
WE'RE MEANT TO BE TOGETHER.
END IT WITH GEMMA. END IT NOW.
YOU'RE MINE. MINE. MINE!

My heart stampeded like fans breaking through crowd control barriers at a concert. I sat on my hand to hide the shakes. The third read:

GEMMA, YOU HO. YOU'RE NOTHING BUT A FUCKING SLUT.
BREAK OFF THE ENGAGEMENT NOW.
KYLE AND I WILL BE TOGETHER.
I LOVE HIM MORE THAN YOU EVER WILL.
LEAVE HIM NOW, BITCH.
KYLE'S MINE. MINE. MINE!

Nausea pooled in the pit of my stomach. My throat, tight and dry, hurt when I swallowed. Each letter had gotten more violent. Aggressive. The one tonight . . . threatening. Someone wanted to kill me. Someone wanted Kyle. *Shit.* He had the kindest heart and the sweetest soul. He was a gentleman, passionately loyal and sincerely devoted. A true catch. And he was mine. We had millions of fans and followers. How would the police find who'd sent the letters?

I glanced at our security team to gauge their take on the situation. Sam had his game face on. Chester, my bodyguard, sat meek and quiet, but his eyes were alert, like a viper ready to strike. Mick, Hunter's bodyguard, slowly rubbed and rolled his hands together, his eyes on the detectives, taking in every word.

Their intensity added a new level of concern.

Shit. This was real.

My pulse thrummed hard and fast. There'd been more than one letter. A threat to my life. *Fuck!* No matter how hard I tried, I couldn't stop a sliver of fear from creeping across my skin. But I'd be okay. *Right?*

Hunter reached over and grabbed the pages. He read them, smirked, and let out a short laugh. "I can't believe someone is obsessed with Kyle. Are you kidding me? I'm the hot one. Where's my psycho fan letters?"

Bec glared at him and sniggered. "You want to read some? Next time you come into the office, I can grab the boxes if you'd like?"

"Maybe I will. Just for some kicks." Hunter returned the sarcasm.

Detective Jones tapped and spun his pen on the table. *Tap. Spin. Tap. Spin. Tap. Spin.* "I wouldn't joke about this, Mr. Collins." His sharp tone was loaded with *I-won't-tolerate-any-nonsense, you-listen-to-me, and let's-follow-the-rules* attitude.

"Good luck with that." I puffed air through my nose and shook my head. Did this guy know who he was dealing with? Hunter rarely did serious.

"This is a serious matter." Jones gathered the letters and piled them with the latest one. "We've had the first three letters analyzed by forensics. The report came back yesterday. We know they're printed off the same printer, with the same ink, on the same paper, and have been sent in envelopes from the same batch. But there are no fingerprints, no saliva, nothing. It makes it nearly impossible to track. The postmark on the letters is Manhattan-based. The letter you got today is addressed to your manager's office, exactly like the others, but not mailed. The person behind this knows what they're doing and knew where to find you."

A chill slithered up my spine and settled into the base of my neck. *Speculation* rattled my brain. Who could've done this? I glanced at Sophie; it couldn't be her. She was gay. It wasn't Bec; she ran our lives and was in love with Matty, her boyfriend of four years. Maybe it was someone here at the rehearsal studio who had lied. This wasn't funny. I was paranoid enough without suspecting everyone I knew. *God!* If this kept up, I'd turn into a recluse.

Jones leaned forward, pen poised over his notepad. "Gemma, is there anything unusual that happened in your whereabouts today?"

Taking a steady breath, I curled my hand around Kyle's thigh. Touching him grounded me, helped me clear my mind. "I went to Nina's in SOHO, dress shopping with my best friend, Kara. My bag was with me, in the same room, the whole time. When I came to rehearsal, Sophie put my bag in here. The only crazy thing that happened was when I arrived here, I had to wade through a group of fans. Maybe one of them slipped it into my bag without my knowing."

"It's possible." Jones dipped his head from side to side. "Sam talked to the owner of the studio and debriefed me. Unfortunately, the building has no daytime surveillance. The cameras are only active outside of business hours. We'll review the CCTV footage in the area, but it's going to take time. If we find something or someone acting unusual, we'll let you know as soon as possible. Bec is helping us; she has posted a teaser to your social media accounts to see if anyone will confirm they were outside the studio. We'll start with them."

"Wait." I sat ramrod straight. "What about Taylah? The girl who runs the Ringers Fan Club. She was here. She's obsessed with us. And she might know the names of some of the other people who were outside, too."

"Excellent." Jones penned notes on his pad. "We'll track her down."

My mind rattled. Could it be Taylah who'd sent the letters? She was one of our first truly dedicated fans. Years ago, she'd voted for us a gazillion times during the Discovered-On-YouTube contest we'd won. She'd attended our gigs and had social media pages dedicated to us. Had she grown obsessed with Kyle over the past eight years?

Bitch.

I pressed my hand against my stomach to settle the unease. It didn't help. I turned to Kyle and my heart ached. His espresso eyes, dark and glassy, loomed with worry. It would kill him if something ever happened to me, and vice versa. "Should we postpone the wedding? Until this blows over?"

"No." He slowly shook his head. "We'll be fine. Only our team here knows about our plans, and I trust them with my life. No one else knows when or where we are going."

"That's because you're a control freak." Hunter chuckled, low and soft.

Kyle flipped him the bird. "Fuck off. I just want to keep the day as private as possible."

"And some of us are feeling totally unloved about the no-invite rule." Bec pouted. No humor touched her eyes.

"Bec, you are truly loved and appreciated." I clutched her hand on the table and gave it a gentle shake. "I promise we'll celebrate at my bachelorette party in Vegas. But you know we don't want a big wedding."

Kyle nudged his elbow against my arm and leaned over to whisper in my ear, "*You* don't want a big wedding."

He raised his hand and held his index finger and thumb an inch apart. "I'd like it to be a bit bigger."

Crap. Was that what he wanted to talk about tonight? Inviting more guests? *Shit.* I really wanted the wedding to remain small. Having a threat on my life was exactly why we shouldn't have an extravagant event. I narrowed my eyes and waggled my finger at him. "Haven't we got enough to deal with?"

He grabbed my hand, kissed the back of it, then entwined our fingers and rested them in his lap. "Yes, but we'll talk later."

"Okay." *Maybe . . .*

Jones cleared his throat. "Kyle, I want you to think about people you know, friends or colleagues. Is there an ex-girlfriend upset by your relationship with Gemma?"

"Pfft." Air shot from my lungs. I knew every one of Kyle's past girlfriends. I'd take any of those bitches down if it was one of them.

Kyle ruffled his hand through his short dirty blond hair, rubbed his undercut. "This is insane. Gem and I have been together for two years."

"Clearly, someone isn't happy since you've gotten engaged." Jones arched one thick eyebrow, poised his pen to write.

Kyle sighed, leaned forward, and stared at the pile of letters. "Are we talking actual girlfriends? I've had a couple since senior year in high school. But if it's someone I've slept with"—his eyes flashed toward Bec—"shit, there could be hundreds."

I bit the inside of my cheek to stop myself from laughing. I'd forgotten Kyle had banged Bec for about a week when we'd first hired her as our personal assistant. Bec had also nailed Hunter, most of the guys in our backup band, and half our technicians, sound engineers, and road crew. She'd had a lot of fun. But then she met Matty and everything changed. He was it for her. There was no way the letters had come from Bec. I wouldn't believe it. Not for one second.

Hunter's azure eyes glinted as he chuckled. "Bud, aren't you being a little conservative? Only hundreds of girls? Wouldn't you be in the thousands?"

Kyle grinned, shaking his head. "I wasn't as much of a man-whore as you."

Closing my eyes, thousands of memories strobed through my mind like a slideshow at high speed. We'd had many escapades and wild times since making it big. We'd had more than our fair share of drugs, alcohol-fueled parties, and hook-ups. *Ah . . . the good old days.* But after too many incidents during our first world tour, we gave up the drugs. Sleeping around slowed down on tour three. For me, it stopped all together once I hooked up with Kyle, or even before that, if I included my short and very temporary stint with Hunter. *Wow. That felt like a lifetime ago.*

Jones's jaw tensed as if his tolerance had thinned as much as his sidekick's receding hairline. Morris at least smiled at our jokes. Jones could do with a good hit of happy gas.

His focus remained set on Kyle. "I'd like the contact details of your girlfriends before Gemma. Anyone that gives you a thread of suspicion."

A list of Kyle's exes swirled through my head. Laura, Trina, Vicki, and Debbie. We kept in touch with half of them.

"Gemma." Jones angled his head toward me. "Is there anyone who has been upset or has acted suspiciously since your engagement? Anything that may help?"

"No." I shook my head. "Could this be a hoax?"

"It could be." Jones interlaced his fingers and rested his hands on the table. "But in my experience, I don't think so. It's our job to take every threat seriously. Especially since you are . . . celebrities."

Did I detect acid in his tone? *Great.* I didn't want or expect special treatment, but I wanted this threat to go away.

Hunter pointed to Jones's cell phone. "You want to find the crazy, watch YouTube. There have been hundreds, if not thousands, of fanatical videos dedicated to us. We've watched a few for entertainment. Sorry . . . some of them are funny. But none stood out as threatening."

Jones nodded. "We'll have our cyber expert, Detective Marshall, back at the precinct, scan your social media accounts. Morris and I will follow up on any CCTV footage we can get our hands on, and work on your leads. Inform a select few of your trusted family and friends about the situation. And please, let me know if you think of anything that might help." He handed everyone a business card. "Be assured we will do our best to find who's responsible. We'll keep in touch." After shaking everyone's hand, Sam led Jones and Morris out of the studio.

I slumped in my seat. "Thank God that is over."

The moment Sam returned to his chair, Kyle slapped his hands on the table. "We need to up security. We need to ensure Gem's safety."

"What?" I grimaced. "No. We don't need more security." Wasn't twenty-four/seven enough?

Sam bobbed his head. "Sorry, Gemma. Kyle's right. A few extra precautionary measures won't hurt. We'll check and install extra cameras at your apartment buildings. We can already track you via your cell phones, in case of the unlikely event you are kidnapped, injured, or taken hostage."

The breath shot from my lungs. My pulse pounded in my ears. "Oh, for fuck's sake. Surely it won't come to that. It's just a couple stupid letters." *Wasn't it?*

But the steely looks on their faces stalled my false sense of security. Despite their military training, surveillance, and operations expertise, our bodyguards had only ever had to execute crowd control, protecting me and the guys from being swamped by fans. I prayed they never had to go into full-on save-our-life mode. I prayed they never got hurt, stabbed, hit, or even worse, shot in the line of duty.

Kyle eased his arm around my shoulders and jutted his chin toward Hunter's bodyguard. "I think Mick should give us, especially you, Gem, a refresher on self-defense."

I play-punched Kyle in the thigh. "I don't need a refresher."

"Ow!" He flinched, faking being hurt. His eyes glinted with humor. "You're evil, woman."

"Yeah. But you love me."

"True." He kissed me on the cheek.

"Sorry, Gem." Mick splayed his hands. "I agree with Kyle. Some new training would be good."

Mick, with his buzzcut, slender build, zero body fat, and five-feet-eight-inch height, didn't look very strong, but he could break every bone in someone's body. With a black belt in just about every code of martial art, the man was as lethal as a gun.

I sighed and rolled my eyes. More workouts. Fitness training for our tours and shows was hard, but Mick's defense classes were like military bootcamp. I'd have to whisper in Mick's ear to give Kyle an extra-hard workout for insisting we do this. Payback would be sweet.

But the jokes turned cold. The threats took hold. Scenarios skipped through my brain. What if a wild fan lunging at me with a knife? A crazed loon pulling out a gun? A mad maniac beat me with a bat? *Fuck.* What if someone really wanted to hurt me beyond words on a piece of paper? Kyle was right. It wouldn't hurt to take a few precautionary steps. Anything to keep us safe.

Sam rubbed the stubble on his chin. "I don't want you guys to worry. We'll be working with your management team to ensure your safety at events and shows, and we'll coordinate our efforts with event organizers. Every aspect of security will be under control."

Kyle rubbed my back and toyed with my hair. "And Gem, I don't think you should leave home without having someone with you—me, Hunt, one of your girlfriends, or security."

"Are you kidding me?" My voice pitched high.

Sam, Chester, and Mick shook their heads.

Fuck.

I slumped in my chair. *This is ridiculous.* The tension in my temples twisted tighter. "We don't need to get that extreme, do we? Surely I can go across the street to the drugstore without a bodyguard?"

Concern flooded Sam's dark eyes. "Sorry. No. Not at present. Someone could be stalking you. We need to stay close."

Damn it. My limited freedom was gone. What they'd suggested was an overkill. I didn't want to be babysat everywhere I went. I couldn't deny the letters had unnerved me. Everyone's concerns didn't help. But I had a life to live.

Hopefully the letters were nothing. A sick joke. Someone playing games. Or was it a cry for help? A mental health issue?

Ugh! Just what I needed. More things to worry about. *Not!*

Living in the spotlight for eight years had ground a solid amount of paranoia into my system. It had held fast ever since my mother and my ex, Ben, sold me out to the paparazzi, and naked pictures of me went viral. Being a public figure, risk was my daily reality. But I was strong. Careful. Street-smart. I wasn't about to do anything stupid.

Digging deep, I cemented determination into my veins. I wouldn't let this scare interrupt my everyday life.

Kyle glanced at our security, then gave me a reassuring smile. "We've got this. If someone wants you, they'll have to get through me first. And that's not going to happen." He kissed me on the side of the head.

I didn't need him playing superhero. But until the culprit was found he wouldn't let this go.

I was fortunate and grateful I had so many people care about me. Kyle and our security team could put whatever measures they wanted to into place, but it didn't mean I'd comply or follow all their rules. I'd worked too damn hard to get where I was and knew how to live within the constraints of fame. "I won't stop going out because of some crazed fan. If I did, the person behind the letters wins. And I won't let them do that. No one is going to fuck with me, my guys, or our lives. Not ever."

I've got this. I'm always careful.

No one will hurt me. Or Kyle.

Everything's under control. Everything will be fine.

No one fucks with this bitch.

Chapter 4

KYLE

Gem, where the fuck are you? Panic seized my chest as I ran up the stairwell and flung open the door to the rooftop common area of our apartment building. It hit the wall with a bang. The night's sultry breeze hit me, hauling me to a halt. *Gem's here. Thank goodness.* Relief washed over me in a rush. Dressed in my old Nirvana T-shirt she wore to bed, she stood on the far side, resting her arms on top of the wall. Her hair danced in the gentle wind, but her gaze seemed vacant as she stared across the city skyline. My heart ached. After the long afternoon at rehearsal and evening with the detectives, security, and our management team, my mind hadn't stopped racing, unable to erase the words written in the threatening letters. Once we'd gotten home and I'd showered, fear had gripped every inch of my body when I couldn't find Gemma.

Was I going to worry about her every second of the day? *Probably.*

Yep. Most definitely.

"Hey." I jogged over to her and wrapped my arms around her from behind. I nuzzled into her neck and inhaled the sweet smell of her rosy shampoo. *She's safe.* "I was looking for you."

She turned in my arms. The city lights shimmered in her emerald eyes. "I just needed some fresh air."

Rubbing her arms, I kissed the top of her head. Just touching her and holding her close calmed my mind. "Can you please not leave our apartment without telling me where you're going? You left your cell phone on the counter. I ran around like a madman trying to find you. I went to the pool, the gym, and the courtyard before coming here."

She groaned and rolled her eyes. "Fine. I'm sorry."

"This sucks. I know." I softened my tone as I swept her hair over her shoulder and tucked the loose strands behind her ear. "Do you want to talk about the letters?"

"Nope. I'm good."

I didn't expect anything less. She'd put on a brave front, but I saw through her façade. Today had gotten to her. The threats had everyone on edge. But when something upset Gemma, she put her guard up, over-analyzed everything, and usually took her frustrations out on her guitar, jamming for hours or writing some killer lyrics. It was just the way she handled things. She always kept a protective shield around her heart. But I'd penetrated it and knew her better than anyone else.

I widened my stance and met her eye to eye. "Well, I'm worried. Are you sure you're okay?"

She slid her hands underneath my T-shirt and rubbed my sides. My stomach tensed, tolerating her ticklish strokes, but her touch was a pleasurable torture. "Yeah. The letters freaked me out, but what else can I do? It's up to the detectives to find who sent them. I won't live in a bubble because of some nutcase."

I caught her hands and held them in mine. No more tickling. "I won't let anything happen to you. Whoever's behind them is sick. I just want the detectives to resolve this quickly." But I held reservations about Jones. He reminded me of my father. Another cop that preached the law, thought themselves above the rules, and pissed off people in the process. I hoped Jones proved me wrong.

Wrapping my arms around Gemma, I held her close.

She rested her head against my chest. "It wasn't fun dredging up the names of your ex-girlfriends."

Most of them I'd like to forget. Before Gemma, I hadn't had a girlfriend in years.

"No. It wasn't." The list of my past relationships flicked through my mind, but no one stood out as a threat. It frustrated me that no one seemed suspect. Were the letters just a cruel joke? The detectives didn't think so. Neither did our management and security teams. Tightening my arms around Gemma, determination gripped my heart. I'd do whatever was necessary to find who was behind the letters. Do whatever it took to stop them. I'd do anything to protect Gemma. "You even remembered some girlfriends I'd forgotten."

"I was there for every one." She patted her hand over my heart. "For every breakup, I was your shoulder to cry on."

"I didn't cry." *Okay, maybe. One or two times.*

"There were definitely tears and a lot of moping around for days."

Smiling, I kissed her hair. I didn't do heartbreak well. Solace was often found in the bottom of a Jack Daniels bottle, thrashing out my pain on my bass, guitar, or drums, or spilling my guts to Gemma. "I'm glad I never have to go through a breakup again. I have you for the rest of my days." I was content, happy, totally satisfied. My forever was with Gemma.

She played with the bottom of my pajama shirt. "Do you think the letters could be one of them? Someone we know?"

It terrified me to think it could be one of our past or present friends. "Geez, I hope not. I was never with anyone long enough to warrant a state of obsession."

"I don't know." She twisted and tugged on my shirt. "Now you're mine, I don't want anyone else to have you. So maybe I've gone a bit Ava Max."

"You're all sweet but psycho? I like that. Because I feel the same way about you."

A smile curled across her lips, but then seriousness washed over her face. "Umm ... can we change the subject?"

"Sure." I rubbed her back. "Can we talk about the wedding?"

"Hmm. I suddenly feel *very* tired." Humor glinted in her eyes.

There was no exhaustion in her tone.

Taking her face between my hands, I kissed her, then smiled against her lips. "No you're not."

"Have you changed you mind and you're happy to go to the clerk's office and get married there?" Hope skipped through her soft voice.

"No. You're not getting out of this. I want to have a ceremony. See you in a beautiful dress. Declare my love to you in front of our friends."

"I know you love me." She gripped onto my forearms. "I don't need anything else."

I held her gaze. "But I do. I want our day to be special. Memorable. About us. Not some quick fix."

"Most guys would jump at the chance to get out of a wedding."

"I'm not most guys."

"No." She cupped my cheek and ran her thumb over my stubble. "I'm glad you're not."

"So . . ." I jutted my head toward the stairwell. "Can we go sort out a few things?"

Gemma wrinkled her nose, like she'd smelled my sweaty sports socks.

I nuzzled her ear and whispered, "I promise to make it worth your while."

"You better." Her cheeks blushed. I loved the way her body reacted whenever I was suggestive. It made me love her even more, knowing I had a profound effect on her.

She gave me a quick kiss. "I'll need a drink."

After the harrowing day we'd had, that sounded perfect. "Deal."

We headed downstairs to our two-story condo. I grabbed the JD, tumblers, and ice from the kitchen and met Gemma in the living room. She curled her feet underneath herself on the sofa. Her shirt rode upwards, showing off her gorgeous legs and the edge of her black panties. God, I wanted to tear them off with my teeth. But we had to talk about the wedding.

I poured a shot into each glass. She snatched one drink and

knocked it back.

Grinning, I sat beside her. She didn't need to stress. But she stared at the wedding folder I'd left on the coffee table like it was Pandora's box and she was terrified of what horrors lay within. She swallowed hard. "So, what do you want to discuss?"

I opened my folder to several pictures of cakes I'd printed off the Internet. "Let's pick a wedding cake so I can sort it out with catering."

Gemma sank back onto the sofa. "Do we need one? There are only six of us."

"We're having a cake. No argument." I spaced out half a dozen images on the glass tabletop. "I've narrowed it down to make it easy. Let's pick one and it's done."

I gazed over the tiered masterpieces covered in flowers, satin ribbons, glittery trim, and golden beads.

Gemma winced and rubbed her eyebrow. "We don't need anything this big. These cakes would feed over one hundred people."

"I know." My grin broadened. "I'll order a smaller one."

The color drained from her face. I didn't understand why she stressed over such trivial matters.

"You pick," she pleaded. "I don't care."

"Gem, it's a cake." I clutched and rubbed her knee. "On the count of three, we'll both point to one, okay?"

She nodded and glanced at the images.

Looking at the pictures, I re-evaluated my selection. What was I thinking when I printed these? Gemma wouldn't like the one with cascading pink flowers; she hated pink. The three white monstrosities with swirls of white icing and silver beads . . . nope, too girly, definitely not. It was between the tiered round cake with red ribbons, or the square dark chocolate cake.

"Ready?" I shuffled forward on the sofa. "On the count of three. One. Two. Three."

Our hands slapped onto the picture of the chocolate cake. The beaming smile that shot across her face made my heart thump harder. God, I loved her. We were so in tune . . . most of the time.

"What's next?" She refilled her glass and took a sip.

The change I wanted most had me breaking out in a cold sweat. I took a steady breath, then let it out slowly. "I know we originally agreed to keep our wedding small, but . . . I'd really like to invite a few more people. Actually . . . quite a lot more."

Gemma shook her head and chugged down another mouthful of whiskey. "No. I don't want this to turn into a monstrosity."

"Just hear me out. I've got a plan. I think you'll like it." I grabbed a piece of paper full of names from my folder and read from the top. "I'd like to invite my cousin Kade, Sophie, Bec, Kate, our security team, backup band, and our regular crew. And—"

Gemma closed her eyes, tension tightening every muscle in her face. "Please don't do this." Anguish swirled like an undercurrent in her voice. "They'll be with us in Vegas at our bachelor and bachelorette parties. They don't need to be at the wedding."

Her soulful tone hit me hard in the chest, but I didn't want to back down.

I stared at my list, lead pooling in the pit of my gut. Kade and all my relatives lived in Seattle. We didn't see each other often. Bec and Kate had been through everything with Hunter, Gemma and me. They'd joined our band's team when we first signed with SureHaven and had followed us when we left. Bec was the best PA we could ever ask for. She organized our lives meticulously. Kate, our publicist, dealt with everything from our dramas, misadventures, and scandals to our accolades, awards, and celebrations. Sophie, our manager, had slipped seamlessly into taking over from Amie when we signed with Sony. Everyone had become a significant part of our Everhide empire. They'd become our friends . . . family. "Gem, they're part of our lives. They should be there to celebrate."

Her hand shook as she placed her glass on the coffee table. "Once you invite a few guests, more will need to be included. We know too many people. The list will blow out with colleagues and associates, partners, distant friends, and family members."

"I don't want to invite that many people." My voice jumped, but I reined it back in. I didn't want this conversation to turn into a heated argument. I rattled off the other names on my list.

"That's a lot of people. You want to go from six guests to fifty? No fucking way."

"Yes way. The more the merrier. We'd fly everyone to Belize, have them stay on the mainland, and charter a boat to get everyone to and from the island for the ceremony."

"It's too many people. It's too much."

My heart lurched. Why was she so stressed? What was she grappling with? "Gem? What's wrong? Are you afraid the paparazzi might find us? I can assure you, I'm doing everything I can to prevent that from happening. Are you afraid your mother will want to come? She can't. Janine isn't invited. I'll relocate the wedding if she turns up."

"I won't go if she's there. But with that many guests, information is bound to leak. I don't want helicopters, speed boats, and paparazzi ruining our day. This is the one day I want to be out of the spotlight. Why change things?" Her glassy eyes searched my face for the answer.

I placed my hand over my heart. "Because these people are our family and it would mean so much to me to have them there."

She closed her eyes. Her nostrils flared as she took a long, deep breath. "God, you can be *so* infuriating."

I gave her a quirky grin. I wasn't one to flash around my money, but our wedding was an exception. "Just think—it will be one hell of a party."

Her skin turned grayish. Her pulse throbbed in the veins on the side of her neck. "This is supposed to be about us. Not them."

"It will be." I softened my tone. "We have the whole island for three weeks. Lexi, Hayden, Kara, and Hunter are only staying with us for three days. We can skip having a rehearsal dinner. Everyone else can just come for the ceremony and reception, that's it. I'll organize everything . . . with a bit of Bec's help."

Gemma's hands trembled as she fidgeted with the necklace I'd given her for her birthday and twisted it around her finger, then she chewed on the gold pendant and tapped it against her lips.

Silence.

Her shoulders slumped and her hands dropped into her lap. "If this is important to you, can we compromise?"

My heart skipped a beat. Whatever she'd give me, I'd take . . . within reason. "We can do that. What did you have in mind?"

"Half the number. Make it less than twenty-five people. Is that okay?" She lifted her chin and jabbed her finger against my leg. "And Lexi wants to handle the photography. I know she's part of our bridal party, but she does incredible work. She can set everything up with timers and tripods. If Kate's coming, she can help with some photos. Deal?"

No professional photographer? Lexi was a hobbyist photographer, but she was incredibly talented. Since Gemma was compromising, I guessed I had to give a little as well. Entwining our fingers, I kissed the back of her hand and warmth flooded my heart. "I can work with that. Thank you."

She pulled her hand free and pointed at me. "But promise me, no more changes. No more guests. I won't go through with this if you suddenly want to book out the Waldorf and sign up for a magazine deal or reality TV show. Got it?"

My laugh reverberated deep in my chest. "There's no chance of that happening. I promise." I planted a big kiss on her lips. Over another drink, we culled names from my guest list until we reached the final number. *Done.* The negotiations hadn't been too painful. "Awesome. I'll send everyone an email to save-the-date. We'll have the best day. No regrets."

"We'll see about that." Smiling, she nudged me in the ribs. "Is that it? Are we done?"

"Yeah. For now." Food and other minor details could wait. I was on a win, so best to end on a high.

She downed her drink and slapped me on the thigh. "Good. If that is everything, I'll clean up. We have rehearsal all day tomorrow."

She went to stand, but I grabbed the back of her T-shirt and pulled her down onto the sofa. I leaped to my feet and grabbed our empty glasses. "Nah, I'll do it."

A wicked smile curled across her perfect lips. "I love my man in the kitchen."

"That's because I can cook and clean better than you," I teased, walking toward the counter.

She threw a cushion, hitting me in the back. "You're my slave to love."

"*I'm a slave for you.*" Singing in a sultry Britney Spears-like voice, I spun around and did my best attempt at a sexy body roll.

I scored another cushion, this time in the head. Gemma's laugh was worth acting like a goof.

As I put the last of the dishes away and turned the dishwasher on, Gemma stood by the kitchen island, skimming through her phone. The hem of her T-shirt barely reached past the bottom of her ass. I raked my gaze over her shapely legs. *So sexy.* I slid behind her, wrapped my arms around her waist, and rested my chin on her shoulder.

She stopped scrolling and tapped the screen.

"Everything okay?" I asked.

"Yea-p." She spun to face me. The scent of whiskey on her breath teased me, sending a buzz through my veins. "Just an email from Kara confirming a dress fitting. Nothing urgent."

I braced my hands on either side of her on the countertop, trapping her. "I can't wait to see you in your wedding dress."

"Are you sure?" She slipped her hands around my neck. "Don't you miss being single?"

The inquisitive tone in her voice caught me off-guard. Was she having doubts about marrying me, or just tripping down Memory Lane?

I clasped her hips, lifted her onto the countertop, and edged between her legs. Her T-shirt rode higher, revealing black lace panties. My favorite. A grin tugged the corner of my mouth. There would never be another woman for me. Only Gemma.

I cupped the side of her neck. Her pulse strummed steadily beneath my touch. "No, I don't. You're the one I love and want to spend the rest of my life with."

Her eyes sparkled. What was she playing at? "Remember our

first world tour? And we had that huge after-party in our suite in Miami? The one where the three of us were high as kites and we had one of the wildest nights ever?"

I'd never forget that night. We were nineteen years old. We'd done a few lines of cocaine and had drunk an excessive amount of alcohol. Music blared throughout the suite and people partied in every room. Hunter, Gemma, and I had dragged our evening hook-ups into the master bedroom. Hunter had banged some girl on the desk. I'd nailed some girl on the bed. Gemma had ridden some guy on the sofa. Damn, we'd done some crazy shit together. But I wouldn't change any of it. Everything led to her being mine. "What's that got to do with anything?"

She shrugged. "I was just wondering if you miss those days— the women, the partying, the wild sex. After everything we've been through, I can't believe you want me."

I buried my fingers in her hair and massaged the base of her neck. Worry spiked through my pulse. "Are you having doubts about marrying me?"

"God no." *Phew!* "We still party hard. Just without the drugs, sex fests, or hook-ups." She wrinkled her nose. "Are we getting old and boring?"

"You . . . could never be boring." I kissed a trail up the side of her neck and nibbled on her earlobe. I slid my hands up her thighs and slipped them underneath the hemline of her T-shirt.

She hooked her legs around my waist and stroked her thumb across my lips. Her touch ignited my skin. Sent my blood rushing south. "If this, being here with you, making music, and sleeping with you all the time, is boring, I'll take it any day. I love you. So much."

My heart swelled every time she said those three words. I eased my hands higher underneath her shirt and caught the edge of her panties. I curled my fingers around the edge of the lace. "Good." I nipped at her bottom lip. "Wanna be boring?"

"Always." She smoothed her hand over my freshly shaven cheek. "What did you have in mind?" Her voice, breathless and heavy, made my cock twitch and harden.

I slipped my fingers into her panties and met her arousal. Wet, warm, and slick. I circled my thumb over her clit, stroked her up and down. "Hmm. I know what I'd like to do." Smiling against her lips, I dipped my finger inside her. Drove it in slowly and deep. Teased her tenderly.

Her insides clenched around me. Her eyes fluttered shut. "Does it involve you, me, naked?"

"Oh, yeah." Hooking my fingers around the crotch of her panties, I tugged them lower. They caught on her ass. She wriggled. I pulled harder. *Shit.* My fingernails tore the lace.

Gemma giggled and clutched my shoulders. "Did you just tear my panties?"

I eased them down her legs, not caring about the flimsy bit of material. "I'll buy you new ones. Just so I can do that again."

As I lowered her panties, they snagged on her knees, then caught on her ankles, and hooked on her toes. I finally yanked them free.

"So graceful." Her smile was the sexiest I'd ever seen.

"Next time, I'll just tear them off."

"Promise?"

"Yeah." Snaking my hands around her, I lifted her off the counter and headed for the table. Her soft giggle was the sweetest sound. Her kisses sent shockwaves through my heart. She was so perfect.

I placed her on the surface, and we peeled off our pajamas. As Gemma's eyes skimmed over my body, heat burned in her gaze like she wanted to devour me. I wouldn't stop her. She was naked. I was rock hard and aching to be inside her. After our crazy day, I just wanted to love her. Take her mind off her worries. Make her come. Stepping in close, I drew her lips to mine. As I kissed her, I flicked my tongue against hers. Tasting her. Treasuring her. I took hold of my cock, teased her opening, then plunged into her hot depths. Her needy moan reverberated through my entire body. Set my soul on fire. She clawed my back as I drove into her again and again. I couldn't love her more than I did.

The threatening letters flashed through my mind. *Fuck.* I tried to block them by deepening my kiss, breathing in Gemma's floral scent, and savoring her warm touch. I clutched her tighter. Drove into her harder. I had to keep her safe. No one would ever take her away from me. If the psycho ever showed up, I'd never hesitate. I loved Gemma so much, I'd put my life on the line. I'd die to protect her.

I prayed it would never come to that.

Chapter 5

KYLE

Six days later, the detectives still had no solid leads into the death threats. My paranoia and concern hadn't subsided. It stalked me as I entered the foyer of the air-conditioned private after-party room beside SummerStage in Central Park. I peered through the single doorway into the function area full of ticket-winning fans and VIP guests. Worry gnawed at the base of my neck.

Was the letter-writer here?

The mid-summer benefit to raise money for the City Parks Foundation seemed innocent enough. The fundraising crowd occupied one side of the room, hovering around the bar or swiping food and drinks from waiters' trays; on the other side, behind a roped-off section, fans crammed into a fraction of the space, waiting to meet us. Hunter and Gemma huddled beside me and scanned the group like I did, no doubt looking for anyone acting suspicious. The threats had them on edge—at rehearsals, during our concert, and now.

Kate hugged her ever-present tablet against her chest. "You three ready? You've got fifteen minutes before we start the meet and greet. Grab a drink. Wait by the bar. I'll come and get you."

"Okay. We'll be ready." Gemma projected confidence, but her hand sweated in mine. She fidgeted and fussed with the neckline of her sparkly halter top. Her gaze remained focused on the crowd.

This was our first outing since we'd found out about the letters. I gave her hand a reassuring squeeze and kissed the side of her head. I wouldn't let her out of my sight. She was right about one thing; no crazed fan would stop us from living our lives. Security measures were in place. Event organizers had been briefed. Everyone was alert.

Kate nodded and ushered us into the VIP area. From across the room, the fans caught sight of me and my friends. With a flurry of flapping arms, they filled the air with shrieking screams and cheers. I waved and flashed them my friendliest smile, but my guts wouldn't unravel. I needed a stiff drink or two before signing merchandise and meeting the fans.

"Gemma. Kyle." A familiar voice hollered over the noisy benefit-goers.

I tugged on the belt loop of Gemma's dress pants. "Hey, the girls are here." I pointed to Vicki and Laura, our old high school friends, waving and drinking at the bar.

"Awesome." Gemma rushed over to them. "It's so good to see you. Thanks for coming. Did you enjoy the concert?"

Hunter and I stepped in beside her. With Kara and Lexi at a pre-New York Fashion Week dinner, Gemma had invited other girlfriends to our show. She didn't get to see them very often. Since high school, our lives had taken different paths. The moment she'd contacted them and mentioned *free party,* Laura and Vicki had come running.

Laura knocked back her flute of champagne like it was a shot of whiskey. Her cheeks were flushed, no doubt from too many drinks. Her chignon looked more like a tattered bird's nest than an updo and the thin straps of her short sequined party dress kept falling off her shoulders. She grabbed another drink from the waiter walking by. "The concert was a-ma-zing. You guys rocked."

"Glad you could make it." I greeted each girl with a quick kiss on the cheek.

"Good to see you, Garage Goose." Vicki's smug tone grated on my nerves. Her lame attempt at humor and my old pet name irked me. She'd given me the stupid name after we'd broken up and had never let it go. I hadn't been that socially awkward garage band guy since high school. I'd made something of myself. Hunter, Gemma, and I now sell out stadiums across the globe. Endless hours of media training and being thrust in front of cameras, journalists, and thousands of fans over the years had cured my awkwardness.

"Vicki, please stop calling me that," I groaned. "It's so old."

"Yep." Gemma murmured. "We're over it."

Yet another thing we had in common.

Vicki shook her head, her short blonde bob flicking against her cheeks. "No can do." A playful, no-chance-in-hell stubbornness flashed through her wide-set blue eyes. "Because some things never die."

"Girls." Hunter jimmied his way between Vicki and Laura and hooked his arms around their shoulders. "Did you miss me while we were away?"

"God, no." Vicki peeled Hunter's arm off her shoulder like it was a rotten banana skin and grabbed her drink off the bar. "The city's so much nicer when you're not in it."

Laura's eyes sparkled as she finished her mouthful of champagne-soaked strawberry and shrugged a shoulder. "Didn't even know you'd been gone."

"Oh. Don't say that." Hunter splayed his hand over his heart. "You hurt my feelings."

Chuckling, I puffed air through my nose. Sarcasm never ruffled Hunter; he usually fed on it. Before it turned into a game of wit and banter, I jerked my head toward the bar. "You'll get over it, Hunt. Let's have a drink before duty calls." I stole a quick kiss from Gemma. "You stay with the girls; I'll grab you a JD."

"No." Her fingers trembled as she touched her forehead. No one would've noticed that, but I did. "I mean . . . no thanks. I'm fine."

I painted on a smile, one that said *I know you're lying, but I understand*. My senses were in overdrive, taking in the surroundings—the guests drinking at nearby bar tables, the waiters walking by, the glances coming our way. I searched for anything unusual but found nothing. "Okay. Let me know if you want anything."

"Hey." Vicki caught my arm. "We're going soon. Laura's had too much to drink."

"Okay. See ya." I half-heartedly waved. Reluctant to leave Gemma's side, I headed to the bar with Hunter and ordered our drinks. As I waited, prickles skipped across my skin. A shudder ran up my spine. I felt eyes boring into my back. I spun around. Gemma stood nearby, laughing with her friends. *Nope—nothing unusual.* I scanned the crowd and the fans queuing to see us. *Nothing.* Where was the unease coming from?

Rubbing my eyes, I wished this night would end so I could get Gemma out of here. Home to safety.

The threatening letters flashed through my mind. *Shit!* What if Laura or Vicki had sent them? The very thought made me sick. We had so few trusted friends in our lives, it would be a devastating blow.

The barman placed our drinks on the counter. Hunter and I grabbed a glass each and clinked them together.

"Cheers, bud." Hunter shot down his whiskey and ordered another one. He jerked his chin in Gemma's direction. His tone took on a serious note. "Gem's worried, isn't she? I hate seeing her like this."

"Me too. But you know Gem. She's trying to be tough. Good thing we see through it." The three of us were so in tune sometimes it was scary. I slid my empty glass onto the counter and waved to the barman for a refill. "But what can we do? After getting those damn letters, I suspect everyone. Do you think it could be Laura or Vicki?"

"They're your exes. You tell me?" Hunter rested his elbow on the bar and leaned closer so only I could hear. "But to be honest, no. Between the two of them, they don't have enough brainpower to come up with such a scheme. Half the time, I don't know why Gemma remains friends with them. I know it's hard to make new ones and trust anyone, but I'm sure they only stick around because we're famous."

Laura and Vicki had been just average nice girls at high school. They didn't bully us or ridicule our music. We'd socialized occasionally. They'd basically ignored us until we grew popular in senior year.

I rested my butt on the bar stool and smirked. "Yeah. They only come to our big parties to drink our booze and pick up guys." We didn't have many close friends, but we treasured the few we had. "They're not close BFFs like Kara and Lexi."

"Nope. Far from it." Hunter grabbed the fresh drinks from the bartender and handed me a glass. He knitted his brows together. "Has something happened to make you suspect one of them?"

"No." I glanced at the girls. Gemma jabbered away as she fidgeted with her necklace. Then, the girl's mouths fell open, wider, and wider. They shrieked and laughed. They clutched Gemma's arms and jumped up and down. I smiled and shook my head. She would've just invited them to her all-expenses-paid bachelorette party in Las Vegas. "I'm questioning everyone I've ever been with. I'd like to forget I was ever with Laura and Vicki."

"Understandable." Hunter threw a filthy look in Vicki's direction, his voice dripping with spite. "Vicki cheated on you. In the locker room with some jock."

Yeah. Skank.

Old wounds flared in my chest. Vicki was my first heartbreak. She'd apologized, said it was a mistake, cried a ton of tears. But Gemma didn't let me fall for her excuses. *Thank God.*

"And Laura." Hunter raised his glass toward her. "She only ever blew you, didn't she?"

"She did everything." I half-grinned, but nightmares bombarded my head. Laura had tutored me in math. She wasn't an A-grade student, but I didn't care. She'd spent more time on her knees than teaching me algebra. My tone nosedived. "But dad scared the shit out of her." The day my father had walked in on us and backhanded me across the face was the last time I'd been with Laura. If she had some reason to hate Gemma and still pined for me, she really was sick.

I knocked back my JD. The whiskey burned like fire in my throat.

I didn't need this stress before my wedding. This was supposed to be one of the most exciting times in my life. It shouldn't be tainted by watching over my shoulder, worrying every time I couldn't lay eyes on Gemma, or suspecting everyone I knew. God, I'd turned into Gemma. I'd turned paranoid over everything.

Kate broke through the crowd and waved at us. "Guys, you ready?"

We nodded, grabbed Gemma, said goodbye to the girls, and followed Kate to the other side of the room.

Straightening the collar on my leather jacket, I scanned the queue. For the first time, I didn't look forward to meeting fans. What if the person behind the letters was here? Would they make a move? This was a private function. Our security team stood on guard, but would they stop anyone determined to hurt us?

My knees wobbled as I took a seat beside Gemma at the table. Hunter slid into a chair on the other side of her. With marker in hand, I was set to sign autographs and merchandise. But no matter how many times I chanted to myself that everything would be fine, my leg wouldn't stop jiggling. My pulse quaked in my veins. I rubbed Gemma on the back and gave her a kiss. "Love you. Are you sure you want to do this?"

"Yes." She spoke through thin lips. "We don't really have a choice. So stop pestering."

I wasn't pestering; I was fucking worried.

"Gem, he's not," Hunter butted in. "Now, play nice. It's fan time." Hunter pulled his shoulder-length hair back into a ponytail and put on his it's-showtime smile, but it didn't mask the worry flitting through his eyes.

For the next hour, we smiled, posed for photos, and signed hundreds of items. As the line dwindled, I glanced at the remaining fans. My heart jolted against my ribs. Taylah, dressed in skinny black jeans, Doc Martens boots, and an oversized, long-sleeved Everhide concert T-shirt, joined the end of the queue. I leaned over and whispered in Gemma's ear, "Look who's at the end of the line."

She scanned the row, and her eyes widened. "Oh, shit."

Our number one suspect, who the police hadn't talked face-to-face with yet, shuffled closer.

Crap.

I waved Sam over and spoke into his ear. "Taylah's here. Why didn't anyone tell us? Watch her like a hawk."

"I'm on it." Sam spoke into his headset and remained close behind us. Chester and Mick drew to attention and stepped over to cover both ends of the table.

Having security around did nothing to put me at ease.

Taylah's turn. She bounced past security and up to the table. "Hey Hunter." A nervous titter skipped in her tone. "So good to see you again."

"Heyyyy!" Hunter stole a quick sideways glance at us, then turned back to Taylah.

"I'm Taylah." She placed two Everhide shirts on the table. "From the Ringers Fan Club."

"I know who you are." Caution slithered in his tone. "How are you?"

"I'm excellent, thank you." Taylah dipped her chin. Her eyes sparkled as she gazed at him from behind her long black bangs and rocked back and forth on her feet.

I wiped my palms on my thighs, watched her every move, impatient for her to be gone.

Taylah thumbed toward security. "What's with them being so close tonight?"

"Umm . . . just procedure." Hunter scribbled his signature on the shirts as fast as he could. "Hope you enjoyed the show. Thanks for coming." With a quick flick of his hand, he pushed the shirts along the table.

I'd never seen Hunter get rid of a fan so fast. No photos. No boob signing. Nothing.

It didn't deter Taylah. With a bop in her step, she slid in front of Gemma. I draped a protective arm around her shoulders. A beaming smile charged across Taylah's face. "Hi Gemma. You rocked this afternoon."

Gemma sucked in a deep breath, straightened, and sat rigid in her chair. "Hi . . . um . . . thanks. The crowd was awesome today.

Thanks for being a part of it."

Taylah swept her bangs off her face. Her charcoal eyeliner, smoky shadow, and thick mascara made her eyes look as black as onyx. "I'd do anything to see you guys play. Today was the thirty-seventh time I've seen you perform."

I gaped; my breath got stuck in my lungs. *Thirty-seven!* Was this girl obsessed or what?

"Really?" Gemma pulled off her marker's cap and signed the shirts. "That's . . . fantastic."

She slid the merchandise to me. The quicker we got rid of her, the better.

Taylah's face lit up like an auditorium full of cell phone lights when she stood in front of me. "Hey Kyle. You. Were. Amazing. I looove your voice so much. In fact, I love everything about you." She placed her hand over her heart. "You're incredible. When you sing the chorus in 'Broken Hearts' and hit those high notes, I just melt."

I grinned and nodded. A mix of humbled appreciation and shaky apprehension pummeled my chest. Had she turned from a fan into a sick freak? Was there any way to tell? I didn't want to find out. I'd just play it cool and get her to move on, quick. "Ah—thank you. I'm glad you enjoy our music."

"Enjoy it? I *love* it. I connect with every song. I feel every line. Your music has saved my life on more than one occasion. I love you so much." She spoke faster and faster. I loved the fact people connected with our songs. That touched my soul. But Taylah didn't draw a breath. "I'm going to Vegas in two weeks to see you perform at the iHeartRadio Music Festival. I've never been to Vegas. I'm so excited. I like to claim I was your very first fan, therefore the oldest and longest. Do you think that's true?"

"Wow. Yeah . . . maybe." I wasn't keeping stats. But I smiled politely, signed her shirts, and held them out for her to take. She crushed them against her chest, but didn't budge.

"So . . . when's the wedding?" She swung her finger at Gemma and me. "Rumors online say it's soon."

My blood pressure spiked. I gripped my pen tight, surprised it didn't snap. Placing my free hand on Gemma's thigh, I gave her a gentle squeeze. "Ah . . . we're not releasing that information." What was it going to take for Taylah to leave? Should I give the signal to security to haul her ass out of here? "I'm sure you can appreciate all aspects of our wedding are private."

"Oh, I'm sorry." She nodded. "I understand. I'm just so excited for you guys."

Kate, standing at the edge of the roped area with Bec, stepped toward us. *Yep.* Taylah's time was up.

"Oh." Taylah caught sight of Kate. "Before I go, Kyle, I have to show you this." She pulled up one sleeve of her long T-shirt. Before I could blink, security rushed forward. My breath hitched, and my arm shot across Gemma's chest. Half standing, I leaned over to protect her.

Taylah grimaced and glanced from Mick to Chester to Sam and back again. "Hey. Chill guys." Security stood their ground. "I just wanted to show Kyle my tatts."

Oh shit! I was certain we'd all thought she had a knife.

Chester grabbed her arm, inspected her skin, and nodded.

I let out the breath I'd been holding and fell back into my chair. I focused on Taylah's forearm. The Everhide logo tattooed her flesh. It wasn't the first time I'd seen our logo emblazoned on someone's skin, but it was the first time it had creeped me out.

Taylah twisted and turned her wrist. "I got this done last year." Pride boomed in her voice.

I blinked, jerking my head back. "That's . . . true dedication."

Gemma draped her arm across my back and clutched my jacket. Hunter had his hands on the table like he was ready to launch himself across it and take the bitch down if she put a hair out of place.

Taylah changed arms and pulled up her other sleeve. "And this one . . ."

Oh. My. God!

The hair on the back of my neck stood on end. My pulse whooshed in my ears. "You got my face inked on your arm?" *Why?* "Wow. That's wicked." I kept my tone lighthearted, but my insides shuddered.

What the fuck? My face? On her arm? That was extreme.

Gemma's hand stilled on my back as she stared at the tattoo.

Taylah gloated. "Shows how much I love you, Kyle. Now, I can look at you all day long."

I gawked at the outlined caricature. "That . . . is . . . full-on."

Taylah straightened her shirtsleeves over her wrists. "You guys mean the world to me."

To the point of obsession? *Not cool.* My jaw locked. I had no words.

Chester shuffled half a step toward Taylah. "Come on, miss. Time's up."

"Wait." Taylah held up her hand and glanced at me and my friends. "Does this extra security have something to do with your rehearsal in Brooklyn? I've been away, but I've gotta meet with some detective dude tomorrow. Is everything okay?"

I bobbed my head. "It will be."

"Cool." Taylah smiled a fan-struck smile. "I'll do anything to help."

Gemma cut in, her face pale. "Taylah. I'm sorry. We have to go."

"Oh." Taylah straightened. "Okay. Thanks for the chat." Chester steered Taylah off the stage and toward the door. She glanced over her shoulder; her eyes set on me. She waved and blew me a kiss. "Love you, Kyle. Bye. See you in Vegas."

The three of us slouched in our chairs. Thank God, that was over.

"Fuck me," Hunter groaned and rubbed his palms against his eyes. "She's one crazy fruit loop."

"That's an understatement." I rolled my shoulders and stretched my neck from side to side, releasing the tension in my nape.

Gemma slapped our legs. "Guys, let's get the fuck out of here. I'm done."

I stood and held out my hand for Gemma. Her hand shook as she slid her clammy fingers into mine. Drawing her into my arms, I hugged her. "I got you. Always."

Kate came over to the table, her eyes wide. "That was one of the more eventful signings, wasn't it? Chester is escorting Taylah from the venue. Once he gets back, security will take you to your trailer so you can grab your things and head home."

"Thanks." I said, but couldn't relax. Was every function going to be like this until the perpetrator was caught? I didn't want to live in fear. I'd done that, living under the same roof as my father. Back then, I didn't have the physical strength or skills to defend myself. Now, I did. Would that be enough to deter or stop someone who was out to hurt Gemma? Would security and technology help? I'd never live with myself . . . no, I wouldn't want to live . . . if something happened to Gemma.

Chester returned and ambled over to us. "You have some overzealous fans. We hope that's all she is. Until the detectives interview her, there's nothing more we can do."

"Thanks, man." I slapped Chester on the back. "Having you guys around takes a load off."

I hooked my arm around Gemma's shoulders, and we headed outside. Hunter and security followed close behind. As we made our way toward our dressing room trailer at the back of the SummerStage setup, my skin prickled. Walking along the darkened path lit by the odd streetlamp, I watched the shadows, strained my eyes between the buildings, and constantly glanced over my shoulder. Everyone else did the same.

Approaching our trailer, my steps faltered. My heart hammered, hard and fast. I yanked Gemma to a halt. I shot up my free hand to stop everyone in their tracks. "Guys. Wait."

"What is it?" Gemma's gaze darted from the dark park to the fence line, to the stage.

"Look." I pointed to the trailer and turned to Sam. "The trailer door. It's open. Someone's fucking broken in."

Chapter 6

KYLE

I took hold of Gemma's trembling hand and took cautious steps toward the trailer. The door creaked in the warm breeze and slapped against the metal frame. The chrome handle hung at an awkward angle, snapped, jimmied open with something. *Who did this?* I glanced into the darkness beyond the edges of the park lights, searching for any sign of movement. Was the intruder still around?

Sam grumbled behind me. "Did one of you forget to lock up?" He pulled me out of the way and glanced at the handle. "Shit."

"I was the last to leave. I locked it." Hunter jiggled the keys in his jacket. He'd tussled with Bec over keeping them in his pocket. Hunter had won. Fat lot of good the keys were now.

"Stay here with Mick." Sam pointed at the ground, ordering us to obey. "We'll check it out." He climbed the steps and led Chester into the trailer.

Seconds later, the door flung open. Sam held his cell phone to his ear and came down the stairs. "Jones. Better get to SummerStage. We've had another incident."

My heart barreled up toward my throat. "What is it?"

Sam blocked the entrance with his arm. "Are you sure you want to see this?"

"Yes. I do." Gemma's voice shook with fear, anxiety, and a morbid curiosity.

She released my hand, but I caught her arm. Terrified, not knowing what to expect, I yanked her away from the steps. "Gem. Wait."

Flames flared in her eyes, but she gave me no time to argue. She jerked her arm free and dashed up the two steps into our trailer. I rushed after her. Hunter and Mick were quick to follow.

As I stepped inside, I scanned the black leather bench seat, table, and kitchenette; nothing looked out of place. But when I reached the middle of the trailer, I froze. My mouth ran dry. "What the fuck?"

There. On the floor. By the bed.

Gemma's duffel bag was slashed to pieces.

Her clothes. Her journal. Everything was torn to shreds.

My jeans and toiletries from my backpack were flung across the mattress. Hunter's bag and our guitars lay stacked on the table … untouched.

"No. No. No. No. *NO*." Gemma fell to her knees and swept up the torn pages. "Not my journal. God. Damn. Motherfuckers."

I rushed forward, kneeled beside her, and rubbed her back. "Oh shit, Gem."

Sam shot forward, holding out his hand. "Gemma. Don't touch anything. Jones is on his way."

"It's my journal. You don't understand. These are my lyrics, my work, notes, melodies." She scratched and scraped the shreds together.

I placed my hand over hers and pulled her to her feet. I wrapped my arms around her and crushed her against my chest. She trembled from head to toe. "Shh. It's okay. We'll piece them back together like a puzzle later."

Seeing her massacred journal tore my heart. I wasn't sure it could be salvaged. That was the least of our worries. A million horrible images flashed through my mind—of blood and cuts and bruises covering every inch of Gemma's skin like those that had covered my parents' bodies after their accident. Did the person who destroyed Gemma's gear want to hurt her? Slash her with a knife?

I couldn't lose her. No matter what the cost. The death threats were no longer about an obsessed fan; this was a psychopath who had to be stopped. I wouldn't rest until whoever did this was caught.

"Wait." Gemma pointed underneath her bag. "There's an envelope."

Oh, crap. I dashed forward and retrieved it. Short, sharp breaths ripped my lungs as I tore it open and unfolded the pink page. *Fuck . . .* It was just like the others. I read out loud, my voice scraping my dry throat.

BITCH, WHAT'S IT GOING TO TAKE FOR YOU TO
LISTEN?
I'VE WARNED YOU.
I WILL KILL YOU.
KYLE IS MINE. MINE. MINE!
CALL OFF THE WEDDING NOW.
OR YOUR DAYS ARE NUMBERED.

"Who'd do this?" Gemma slipped into my arms and buried her face into my shirt. I dropped the letter onto the table and held her tight, praying for this nightmare to end.

Hunter stepped over and joined our hug. "Fuck, guys. This is shit."

Huddled together, we didn't move. Just held each other like stone statues.

"What are we going to do?" Gemma whispered, clutching onto me harder, her fingers digging into my back.

I hated she was scared. No one should've gotten this close to our trailer. Event security should've been tighter.

"We'll find them, Gem." Hunter eased back. A daunted yet determined look had chiseled into his face.

Chester stepped toward us, his eyes dark, and resolute. "Gem, I won't let this bitch get to you. You hear me?"

Chester was just as hell-bent as I was on keeping Gemma safe.

She nodded, her gaze falling to her gear on the ground. "I loved those shirts. Damn it."

I smiled a sad smile. She latched onto random old clothes and wore them to death, just like my worn-out T-shirts—her favorite things to wear to bed. I stroked her hair and kissed her head, but stopped at the sight of our cell phones smashed on the floor beside her bag. An ache in my chest flared. The selfie of us, cheek to cheek, lying on our sofa at home, was frozen on Gemma's shattered screen.

Taking a lung-filling breath, I closed my eyes. *Who the hell did this?*

Sam made another call. "Jones? We have another letter . . . Yep . . . A-ha . . . Do you need them to stay? . . . Okay . . . See you soon." Sam hung up and stuffed his phone back inside his jacket. "You need to stick around so Jones can ask you some questions. Better make yourselves comfortable; it's going to be a long night. Let's wait outside."

Gemma nodded and slipped out of my embrace. The sparkle in her emerald eyes had disappeared. It cut me to the bone to see her feisty spirit had taken a harrowing blow. She held out her hand toward Hunter. "Can I borrow your phone, please?" Her voice had lost all trace of its vibrant sass, only to be replaced with weariness. "Bec and Sophie should've finished at the function by now. I'll call them. Get them to bring us coffees."

"Gem, I'll do it." He grabbed his backpack off the table and dug his cell phone out of the front pocket. His gear had been ignored.

That was worrisome. Whoever did this had known our belongings. *Fuck.*

So much for heading home.

There was no chance of that happening anytime soon.

We headed out of the trailer. Everyone stood around with shock paling their faces. Adrenaline, spiked with fear and fatigue, coiled through my veins. I searched the corners of my mind for who could've done this. *Who hated Gem?* Who wanted her out of the way? *No clue.* Had I missed something? *God only knows.* Every unanswered question gnawed at my insides like a rat chewing an electric cord. How long until it went zap?

Jones arrived with his team. The two people with him, bright and fresh in their sharp uniforms, must have been on night shift. My father used to work a lot of night shifts. Those were the good nights—when he wasn't home drinking and being a fucking prick.

Jones, on the other hand, looked like he could use a stiff shot of hard liquor. His hair was unkempt, his face unshaven, and his clothes crumpled. Excusable, since Sam had dragged him out of bed.

Bec and Sophie rushed down the pathway, balancing cardboard trays loaded with steaming takeaway coffees in their hands. After handing them out, their faces paled as Sam relayed what had happened.

"Holy shit." Bec drew Gemma into a hug, stepped back, and clutched her hand. "As scary as this is, thank God it's only your gear, not you."

A shiver ran up my spine. I clutched my coffee tighter. I couldn't unsee the horrific images my mind had concocted before.

Sophie rubbed and squeezed Gemma's arm. "You're all safe. That's what matters."

"Yeah. We are." Gemma nodded. Worry still loomed in her eyes. I wished I could take it away.

As I sipped my coffee, the detective, and his team, Gavin and Serena, went to work. After blocking off the area with crime-scene tape, Serena snapped on blue latex gloves and dusted the trailer door for fingerprints. Jones and Gavin had gone inside the trailer with a large camera and work bag.

Every muscle in my neck and jaw ached. I hoped Jones would find something, anything, to nail who did this. That security footage would identify the culprit. Whether it was someone from our concert, the benefit, or a crazed stalker, what unnerved me the most was that tonight's move had seemed calculated and timed. They'd only ransacked Gemma's gear and had rummaged through mine. They knew our movements, our whereabouts. Who the fuck was it? Was it Taylah?

At two a.m., when tiredness had taken its toll, and everyone yawned and stretched, Jones emerged from the trailer. "Okay." He jerked his thumb over his shoulder. "In here, please."

We headed inside. Gemma sank between Hunter and me on the seat by the door. Security, Sophie, and Bec shuffled past us and sat around the booth-styled table.

"Shit," Jones leaned against the kitchenette counter and mumbled, "I didn't need all of you; just Kyle and Gemma."

"Too bad." Bec wriggled in her seat next to Sophie and placed her folded hands on the table. "You want them, you get us. That's the deal."

I swiped my hand over my mouth to hide my grin. With eight people mushed into the seats, and with Jones and Gavin standing in the middle of the trailer, it was fucking cramped.

"Aren't I lucky!" Jones feigned a pathetic smile. "Right." He waved at Gemma's gear on the floor, then at my backpack on the bed. Little yellow markers with numbers stood beside our bags, our cell phones, and our clothes. It looked like a murder scene on *CSI*. "Gemma and Kyle, before we wrap this up, can you see if anything is missing, please?"

Gemma went first. She kneeled on the floor, sifted through her clothes, and peered inside her duffel bag—well, the shreds of what was left of it. Tears swelled in her eyes as she flipped through her torn journal. My chest ached at the loss. After rummaging around in her purse, she shook her head. "No. Nothing's missing. Even my wallet is here." She opened it up and scanned her credit cards and cash. "They took nothing."

Jones gave a curt nod. "What about your house keys? Car keys? Medication?"

"Damn." Gemma flopped her hands into her lap. "I took all my drugs before I went onstage."

I flashed her a stern look. I loved her quick comebacks, but now wasn't the time.

She caught my gaze, sighed and turned to Jones. "I *am* joking."

Jones's eyes narrowed into thin slits. "This is no laughing matter, Ms. Lonsdale."

Yep. Jones's sense of humor was as dry as the summer heat. Best not to piss him off.

"I know it's not." She wiped a stray tear from her cheek, straightened and put her strong front back into place. "But I have to make light of this or it will send me crazy."

"I understand." Jones's tone softened with the first element of compassion I'd witnessed since we'd met him. "The offender may be a drug addict looking for cash or their next hit. Or they may have gotten your home address off your ID, taken your keys and be heading in that direction. We'll get security to thoroughly check your home."

Nausea pooled in my gut. Was our home no longer safe? I'd get Sam to change our security access cards, codes, and locks first thing tomorrow.

Gemma dug through her purse again and held out her keys. "They're here." She dropped them back in her purse along with her wallet and scanned the floor. "Can my journal be saved? Can I get the torn pages back?"

Jones dipped his chin. "Yes. After we've finished, you can have them."

The nausea in my gut eased. Not all was lost.

In a daze, Gemma slid back onto the seat.

I leaned in and kissed her temple. "You okay?"

She nodded, but I could tell she wasn't. She nudged my arm. "Your turn."

I lurched from the seat and headed for the bed. Searching through my backpack, my blood ran cold. Shards of ice lodged in my lungs. "My T-shirt is missing. The one I wore onstage." I hated the idea of someone smelling it or sleeping with it under their pillow, or worse . . . getting off on it. *Ugh.* It would stink after I'd sweated in it for hours.

"You think Psycho Fan took it?" A twisted smile drew across Gemma's mouth. "Detective, you may find out who's done this sooner than you think. If someone turns up mysteriously dead, Kyle's sweaty T-shirt might be the cause. It will reek. Death by body odor is highly possible."

"Hey." I sniffed my armpit. I'd showered and changed after the show. "I smell great." That missing shirt . . . not so much.

"Most of the time." She winked at me.

I threw her a mischievous behave-yourself glare.

Jones shook his head and scratched his dark stubble. "Gemma, I wish it was that easy. Kyle, anything else missing?"

"Nope." I sifted through my bag again. "The rest of my clothes are here. Just my cell phone was taken out and broken, like Gemma's." I pointed to it smashed on the floor next to Gemma's.

That was a bitch. I'd just gotten used to that Samsung. It wasn't my first lost or damaged cell phone. But Gemma held the highest tally for that. She was notorious for leaving her cell phone in hotel rooms, dropping them, or sitting on them.

"Yep. We've got that." Jones ran his hand over his messy hair, then jutted his chin toward our bags. "You can take your keys and wallets. We'll keep everything else for evidence. Thank you. You can head home. My team and I will finish up."

I threw my backpack onto the bed. "Why haven't you gone after Taylah? She's our number-one suspect. She was here tonight."

Jones's eyes flared with don't-tell-me-how-to-do-my-job attitude. Of all the detectives on the planet, we'd gotten Mr. Textbook. "We haven't been able to interview her yet. She's been in Boston, attending a family funeral. We're scheduled to meet her tomorrow afternoon unless a positive ID from security footage or forensics comes back sooner. Without further evidence, we must follow procedures."

I took a step toward him and stabbed my finger at his face. "Fuck your procedures. Haul Taylah's ass in and question her."

I didn't like Jones. There was no sense of urgency in his actions. Everything was by the rule book. Didn't Jones think our case was critical? Gemma's life could be in danger. Jones gave me little to no faith in the system. It riled me to boiling point. Did something more serious have to happen before Jones took notice?

I couldn't handle that.

"Kyle." Gemma shook her head. "Chill. This is just some sick fan wanting attention. It's someone playing games. We're fine. Let

Jones do his job."

No. I wouldn't let her play this down. She hid behind her smart comments and acted like everything was okay, but her eyes could never lie. Not to me. "Gem, this is serious."

"I know—"

The trailer door swung open and hit the wall. *Bang.* I nearly launched through the roof, as did everyone else. My hand shot over my racing heart. I hated being on edge. "Geez. You think you could knock next time instead of giving us all a heart attack?"

"Sorry." Serena smirked, then turned to Jones. "Just letting you know I've finished up out here."

Jones nodded. "Excellent. We're done in here, too." He tilted his head toward the door. "Everyone can go. I'll call you if we find anything. Someone's got a grudge, and we need to find them as quickly as possible."

Finally, Jones agreed with me.

Ten minutes later, Gemma, Hunter and I climbed into the back of the Suburban summoned by Chester.

My head fell back against the leather seat. Exhaustion seeped into the marrow of my bones. As we headed down the West Side Highway, past the piers and the Intrepid Museum, Gemma curled into my side. I kissed the top of her head. I wanted to go home, pack our bags, and take off. Disappear. Get away from the city. Protect Gemma. But running away wouldn't eliminate the threat. Whoever had written those letters was still out there.

Hunter flanked the other side of Gemma like a protective shield. Concern loomed in his eyes. He loved and would do anything for Gemma, too. No hesitation.

Resting my cheek against Gemma's head, I closed my eyes. What could we do to find this person without endangering anyone? Could Kate send out a fake press release stating that Gemma and I had broken up? *No, Gemma would never go for that.* Should I put myself up as bait? *How?* Would something like that work?

This was one of the worst things we'd experienced since becoming famous. Definitely the most frightening. But we were fighters. We'd made our way out of the gutters of New Jersey and had climbed to the top of the music world. We'd put up with scandals, scathing reviews, and people out to sabotage our career. Together, the three of us had overcome everything and every odd. But no matter what happened, nothing would taint my relationship with Gemma. Our love was as solid as a rock. We could survive anything.

Anything.

No crazed fan would break us.

We wouldn't let them win.

Not ever.

No fucking way.

Chapter 7

GEMMA

The security intercom on my nightstand buzzed. Twice. I groaned and rolled onto my back. *Who the hell would be here at this hour?*

It buzzed again.

You've gotta be kidding me?

"Who's that?" Kyle mumbled into his pillow. "Tell them to fuck off."

I glanced at the digital display. *9:30 a.m.* Surely I was dreaming. Our friends knew not to call or visit before midday after a show. Rolling onto my side, I cuddled Kyle from behind and realigned the sheet over us. I pressed my lips against his bare shoulder and settled in to go back to sleep. I needed it.

After getting home just after three thirty this morning, I hadn't slept well. Every time I closed my eyes, the image of my slashed gear flickered through my mind. The words of the letter flitted behind my eyelids. *I've warned you. I'll kill you.* Each letter had gotten more and more threatening. More desperate. Despite the fear crawling through my veins, I had to stay strong. If I didn't, Kyle would get even more overprotective, take matters into his own hands. He'd already upped our security; I didn't need any more restrictions. I didn't need him to do something reckless. The detectives were on the case. They'd handle it.

I took a deep breath, pushed my concerns aside and snuggled into Kyle. I nuzzled the back of his neck and inhaled the fresh woodsy scent of his skin. *So good.* His short hair tickled the tip of my nose. His warm, sun-kissed skin was soothing to touch. A whole day in bed together might be on the agenda. It'd help me forget last night ever happened.

But the downstairs door to my apartment clicked open.

Fuck! My eyes shot open. *Someone's here.*

"Gem? Kyle? It's me."

Bec? Shit. I let out the breath I'd been holding. My heart beat again. What the hell was she doing here?

"I'm here too," Sophie hollered. "You two in bed? Make yourselves decent. We're coming up."

What? Why? Maybe the detective had caught our stalker, and they'd come with urgent news. But even that could've waited until after lunch.

Footsteps thudded up the wooden staircase. Kyle moaned. "Nooo. I need more sleep."

I draped my arm over his waist and whispered, "Maybe if we're quiet, they'll leave."

There was a loud knock on the wall in the hallway.

"We're coming in." Warning rolled through Bec's tone. It would be the first time she walked in on us in bed . . . and probably not the last. But at least we weren't doing anything that would scar her eyeballs for life.

"Go away," Kyle groaned and covered his head with his arm.

I rolled onto my back and adjusted the pillow beneath my head. "What are you doing here, Bec?"

Bec and Sophie hovered in the bedroom doorway. Bec, dressed in workout gear, leggings, sports bra and loose-hanging tank top, didn't look like she'd been to the gym. There was no perspiration or mangled hairdo. No flushed cheeks. Sophie lacked her normal business attire, dressed down in a pair of three-quarter-length cargo shorts and an Armani Exchange logoed T-shirt. Fresh concern etched their faces.

The hair on my arms stood on end. "Bec? Sophie? What's

wrong?"

Kyle rolled over and peered at them. "Ladies?"

"Um." Bec took a couple of steps toward the king-sized bed. She wrung her hands and cracked her knuckles. "I'm sorry to barge in here like this, but I didn't know what else to do."

I blinked to clear my bleary eyes. "Is it the detective? Have they found who sent the letters?"

Sophie shook her head and eased in beside Bec. "It's not about last night."

Bec's face paled further. She twisted and turned the dress ring on her middle finger, around and around. Never a sign of good news.

"Bec?" I pinned her with my gaze. "What is it?"

"Um . . ." She winced and turned to Sophie.

Sophie drew in a deep breath and smoothed her hands over her cargo shorts. "Gem . . . Richard called."

"Our lawyer?" I scrunched my nose. "What does he want?"

"You need to see him as soon as possible," Sophie added.

I raked my brain, searching for a reason. What had I done now? Had I said something to upset someone? Was I being sued? What fresh scandal had hit the headlines? Nothing prominent came to mind. Without a new cell phone, I couldn't quickly check the Internet.

Kyle propped himself up on one elbow and rubbed his tousled hair. "Why? What's up?"

Sophie sighed and slumped her shoulders. "Gem . . . it's about . . . your father."

I shot up, wide awake, as if someone had thrown a bucket of ice over me. Kyle did the same. Had I heard correctly? "My father?" My voice pitched high. "Did . . . did Richard find him?"

The remnants of color drained from Sophie's face. She swallowed hard and licked her lips. "Um . . . no . . . well . . . yes. Richard received a copy of his will."

I couldn't draw air into my lungs. Couldn't focus. White noise filled my ears. "He . . . what? My dad . . . he's dead?"

***

Downtown at Richard's office, I waited with Kyle and Hunter in a small meeting room decked out with funky blue office chairs and a round mahogany table. It'd been an hour since Bec and Sophie told me the news about my father. I'd been in a daze ever since, unable to process how or what to feel.

My dad?

Dead.

After years of trying to find him, and hiring private investigators, I'd never found a trace. I'd drilled my mother for information, never believing she didn't know where he was. He obviously hadn't wanted to be located and didn't want anything to do with me.

I'd hoped one parent cared about me, but nope . . . neither of them did.

Kyle entwined his fingers with mine and kissed the back of my hand. "We're here for you."

Hunter, on my other side, nudged my arm. "Always, Gem."

I nodded, warding off the sting in my eyes. "Thanks. I couldn't do this without you guys."

The door to the meeting room flew open and Richard entered, carrying some folders and a shoe-sized box, and placed them on the desk.

Bile rose in my throat. *Shit . . . please don't be an urn of ashes.*

"Hey guys." Richard gave us a warm smile, his teeth luminous against his black skin. He straightened his tie and lowered into his chair. "Haven't seen you for a while. If you haven't got me working on recording contracts and label negotiations, severing, and signing managers, or documenting paternity and parental agreements, it's handling wills and estates. I have to say, you're one of my more interesting clients."

I didn't share his levity. The past three years had been some of the best and worst in my band's lives.

"Let's cut to it," Kyle said. "What's this about Gemma's dad?"

Richard grabbed a letter from his folder and put on his

reading glasses. "Gemma, I received notice from your father's lawyer in Kingfisher, Oklahoma, along with a box of his personal belongings. As we're aware of your recent issues, we've had the items opened and scanned to ensure there was nothing sinister. All were cleared."

"Good. Thanks." My voice deadpanned.

Richard skimmed his notes. "Your father's lawyer stated that Henry Lonsdale died on August sixteenth from a heart attack, aged fifty-six, at his place of employment, Jimmy's Car Repairs. It seemed he liked to live off-grid—he got paid in cash, paid rent in cash—under the false name of Kevin Reid."

"Kevin? What kind of dipshit name is Kevin?" My lip twitched on its own accord. No wonder it had been impossible to find him.

Richard handed me an envelope. "This was in the package. I hope this has some answers."

My hand shook as I took the envelope. Envelopes hadn't been my friend lately. But this was from my dad. Would it offer closure? Was it some sob story, the truth, some trash to make me feel better? He'd never had the guts to contact me, so why bother to leave me with this?

I glanced from Kyle to Hunter. The two people I cared for most in the world sat beside me, but right now, I'd never felt more alone. I'd always hoped my dad would come home, and we'd reconnect. Have some semblance of being a family. But there was no chance of that happening now.

I stared at the envelope. My heart jolted against my ribs.

The sooner I got this over with, the better. There was no point in delaying the inevitable.

I let out a shaky breath and ripped the envelope open. Two handwritten pages of thin white paper with pale blue lines fell into my hands. Scraggly, large cursive writing filled the front and back of each page. Each side contained lines and words crossed out, coffee stains and smudges at the bottom of each corner.

I read the first page. *Dear Gemma.* My hands shot to my mouth to muffle my sob. A shudder ripped through my chest and splintered my bones.

"Gem?" Worry licked Kyle's voice. He wrapped his arm around my shoulders and drew me against his side. As I rested my head against his arm, tears stung the back of my eyes.

But no . . . I wouldn't let my tornado of emotions get to me.

I needed to read this.

I needed answers.

Clenching my teeth, I straightened. I wouldn't cry over someone who'd walked out on me. Who'd left me alone. Abandoned me.

Richard cleared his throat and stood. "I'll give you some privacy. Call me if you need anything. I'll be in my office."

The door clicked closed behind him, leaving me with the guys. They were as edgy as I was. They knew the hell I'd been through growing up without my father and how I'd had to live with my pathetic excuse of a mother. I needed Kyle and Hunter's strength. Their support. Sucking in a deep breath, I blinked the welling tears from my eyes and read.

> *Dear Gemma,*
>
> *Where do I start? Maybe with the reason I left. I'm sure this comes as no surprise, but your mother's affairs caused an irreparable rift between us. She lied continually, even when I caught her in the act. Her disregard of our marriage became unbearable. She hurt me. Broke my heart. I could no longer tolerate her behavior.*
>
> *When I walked out the door, I knew you'd be upset. You'd hate me, even try to find me, but I had to make sure you never did. Your PI got close about three years ago when I was in South Dakota. I left town quickly, without a trace.*
>
> *I've made many poor choices in life—your mother, becoming a father, and my job. Getting involved in stealing cars, stripping them down and selling the parts became an addiction. Each deal got bigger and more dangerous. One night, things went wrong. The men I worked for wanted*

their lost money in blood. Afraid of being caught, doing jail-time, or being killed, I took the easy way out and fled. The only thing I could do to protect you was to stay away.

I couldn't give up the cars. The deals. The cash. I kept moving and changing names. I could never settle down. I could never come back. You were better off without me.

Your band has done well. I've kept an eye on your success. I'm glad you got out of the hellhole we lived in. That you made something of your life.

I'm sorry I wasn't a good father, or a decent man. I hope one day you find someone who treats you right and makes you happy. I read online you're engaged to Kyle. Hope he's good to you. I wish you all the best.

Six months ago, my heart condition worsened. I couldn't afford surgery. No such thing as insurance. Doctors warned me to take it easy. Guess if you're reading this, I didn't.

Maybe this is penance.

I'm leaving you this letter, so you stop looking for me. Stop wasting your time, money, and effort on a man who never wanted to be found.

Live your life. Be happy. Good luck, kiddo.

Henry.

I wiped a tear from my eye. Hurt and anger and hate blistered my veins. "He was a criminal. A coward. A selfish prick. Nothing but an asshole."

"Hey." Kyle rubbed my back. "Of course he was. He left."

Hunter stared at the letter and shook his head. "Fuck. He's as pathetic as our dads. He didn't care how shitty he made you feel."

My heart hurt, and an ache shuddered through my chest. Hunter's dad had chiseled away at Hunter's self-esteem for years. Drummed into him he was wasting his life pursuing music and would never make it. His parents' time had been consumed by caring for Jenny, his autistic sister. They'd rarely given Hunter the time of day. He'd been left to his own devices and spent most of his time with Kyle and me.

I nudged his arm. "We had each other."

Hunter nodded, but sadness swallowed the shimmer in his eyes. "Like you, Gem, I wouldn't have survived without you and Kyle."

The three of us connected the moment we met. We'd shared a dream. Music was it. We'd believed in each other. Supported and cared for one another. Failure wasn't an option. We'd worked hard, made sacrifices, and had made it in a ruthless industry. We'd found where we shone and belonged. But in the process, Hunter had grown an ego the size of North America to hide his pain. Kyle and I knew it was a mask. We knew the truth that others never saw.

"So true." Kyle kissed the side of my head. "Fuck our dads."

Kyle's dad had been great until he'd hit the booze. What had started out as Friday drinks became a daily occurrence. I'd hated it when Kyle turned up to school with bruises from being hit. His mom, Claire, had turned a blind eye, fearing being pushed and shoved. She was the sweetest, most talented music teacher. Kyle could play so many instruments proficiently thanks to her—the drums, guitar, bass, and piano. Claire had taught me to play and sing, never asking me for a cent because she knew I couldn't afford it.

I'd never forget the night when the guys and I were sixteen years old. Kyle's dad, William, had scared the shit out of us when we were jamming in the garage, making too much noise. He'd charged in, red-faced and loaded with booze. He'd grabbed Kyle by the scruff of the shirt, hit him, and had slammed him into the keyboard and drums. Hunter had yanked William off Kyle, thrown him onto the ground, and the three of us fled for our lives. We'd run the two streets back to my house and had hidden in my room. My mom, as usual, wasn't home, so we were safe. That night, as we'd trembled and cried, bled, and held each other on the floor, had bound us together forever.

Our dads were assholes.

But Kyle and Hunter had one thing over me. They'd known their dads. Known where they were. I hadn't. "I wish he'd been rotting in prison for his crimes or was killed by his thugs. At least I would've known where he was. Not a word for fourteen years and I get this." I flicked the paper with my fingertips. "What bullshit. He's as bad as my mother."

When I was a kid, I'd been nothing but an inconvenience to my mother. I was often dumped at the neighbor's house, or left alone and hungry, or told to stay in my room until she'd finished fucking her men. This letter said I was nothing but a problem for my father, too. The longing for my father disintegrated. Loss spread—ate my insides like rust corroding metal.

Kyle's brow furrowed as he reread the letter.

I stared at the pages, my gaze unfocused. "You know what's the worst? Not once, in this entire piece of crap, did he say he loved me. Not once. He didn't want to protect me, only himself. My mother always said I was a mistake. This proves it. My parents never wanted me. They're selfish shitheads. Left me alone to fend for myself, to deal with everything on my own. I was a child, for God's sake."

Some people on this planet should never have children. My chest tightened, threatening to crush me. My parents, who were supposed to love me, didn't. To them, I was worthless. Unloved. Unwanted. When things had gotten tough, they'd taken off. They'd only looked after themselves, no one else.

But something good had come out of this. My father's letter had given me closure. The curtain had closed. No more searching. No more worrying. It made me sick knowing I'd wasted years of my life wondering where he was. To hell with him. I'd never give him another thought.

Hunter play-punched me in the arm. "It's made you tough, Gem. Resilient. You're one of the strongest, most ambitious people I know. And I fucking love you."

His friendship meant the world to me. Always would.

"Your parents missed out on seeing how amazing and talented you are. It's their loss, our gain." Kyle squeezed and rubbed my hand. "I love you, with everything in my soul."

"I love you, too." I kissed him on the cheek, then fell back into my chair. A bewildered laugh escaped me. "Karma got my father good."

Kyle winced and nodded. "Yeah. It got mine too."

Maybe karma played a part in that truck running a red light, ending his life. But Claire hadn't deserved the same fate. Everything had a price.

Kyle swiveled toward me. Warm soulfulness darkened his gaze. "Gem, you found your dad. It wasn't the resolution you wanted, but it is one. You can move on. Like you always do. You're a fighter. *Our* love is stronger than any bloodline. We're family. Remember that. We have an amazing future to look forward to."

With a flick of my fingertips, I wiped tears from my cheek. Kyle was right. I had my answers. My dad drama had finally concluded. I could move on. I hooked my arms around Kyle's and Hunter's shoulders and drew them into a tight embrace. "I love you guys so much. Thank you for being here. I don't know what I'd do without you."

Hunter drew out of our embrace and ruffled the top of my head. "I never want to find out."

Kyle nudged my side. "Me either."

But the ache inside my chest still lingered. Maybe I needed time to grieve, to process the news and shock that the search for my father was finally over. I'd never been a priority in my father's or mother's life, but I was to these guys. And they knew exactly what to do to cheer me up. I slapped my hands on their thighs. "What's the one thing we do when shit happens?"

An understanding smile slid across Kyle's face. "Go jam and get wasted?"

"Abso-fucking-lutely." I nodded. Music always hammered out the dents in my soul. "You know me so well. Let's smash out our set for Vegas and do some damage to a bottle of JD."

Whiskey would drown my sorrows. My father was gone. For good. Maybe I'd finally find some peace. Wouldn't that be nice? But the unresolved death threats and wedding plan stresses still played on my mind. I wanted to put these lingering issues behind me. To feel normal again. I wanted to be excited about my future. To live for our music and be happy. Was it possible to start a married life with Kyle with a clean slate? To have no complications? The only things I was certain about were I loved him . . . and I swore I'd be nothing like my parents.

Chapter 8

GEMMA

I drowned the news of my father's death with copious quantities of Jack Daniels. The place in my heart that had been reserved for him had been replaced by anger. Anger at myself—for wasting time, effort, and money searching for someone who didn't want me. Anger that I'd held onto hope only to have it crushed. And anger at Detective Jones—for not finding the suspect behind the death threats, for treating the case with no urgency.

It had been almost two weeks since I'd received the news about my father. It had been two days since the latest death threat.

KYLE AND I WILL BE TOGETHER
GET USED TO IT
OR YOU'RE DEAD
HE'S MINE. MINE. MINE!
SEE YOU IN VEGAS, BITCH!

The letters annoyed me, unnerved me, tainted everything I did. Was this person a coward? Were they waiting to make their move? The detectives had talked to Taylah, but no concrete evidence or solid intelligence convicted her of the crime. I had to trust the authorities to do their job. But it chilled my bones, knowing Taylah planned to be in Las Vegas for our show. Until the stalker was found, Taylah would remain our top suspect.

Sam had briefed me and the guys during our flight. "Security will be at a maximum at the festival, at your hotel and at your parties. There are no guarantees these days, but I can assure you we've done everything we can to ensure you're safe."

"So there's no reason to cancel?" I questioned. "No imminent danger?"

"No more than usual." The calmness in Sam's response should've eased my worries, but it didn't. Uncertainty still lingered.

The jet's wheels hit the tarmac. Rubber screeched, and the cabin lurched on touchdown. The combination of a few JDs and heightened nerves swirled around in my stomach like leaves caught in a jet stream. As we taxied toward the private plane terminal, I closed my eyes and tightened my grip on Kyle's thigh. He placed his hand over mine and threaded our fingers together. He brushed his thumb against my skin, relaxing me with his touch. *Everything will be fine.*

With a deep breath, I packed my frustrations, fears, and wedding frets into a ball of hardened resilience. For the next five days in Vegas, I'd forget about my father, forget about the threats, and focus on having fun. Rehearsals, the iHeartRadio Music Festival, and a weekend celebrating my bachelorette and Kyle's bachelor party would take my mind off my problems.

The plane jerked to a halt. As we stood, Kyle grabbed my purse off the floor and handed it to me. "Ready to go?"

I caught the top of his jeans, pulled him forward, and kissed his lips. "Always."

"Cool." He waved me down the aisle and followed close behind. He'd been so supportive the past two weeks. He'd sat by my side when I'd gone through the box of faded photos and trinkets from my dad. Nothing in it had been of value or had meant anything to me, so I'd thrown the box in the back of the hall cupboard to be forgotten. Kyle had cooked, cleaned, and made breakfast every day. We'd spent long hours rehearsing for the show and mucking around in our studio. But the moment I wanted to leave the house by myself, to catch up with my friends, go to dress fittings or get my hair done, he'd turned into a protective overlord. He wouldn't let me leave home without him or security. *As if I would with a psycho after me.* He'd messaged me during my appointments. *Sweet, but too often. Except sexting . . . that was cool.* He'd call me if I wasn't home on time. *Fifteen minutes was* not *late. For rehearsal, yes. Home, no.* I understood his concerns, loved that he cared, but I didn't want to be suffocated.

Stepping off the private jet, the dry desert wind blasted my face. Las Vegas in mid-September burned with a cruel heat. A heat that stung my skin. Cooked me inside and out. Security ushered our group, through the terminal and into the waiting cars. We headed for The Strip.

After checking into our suites in the Encore Tower at Wynn, we headed to dress rehearsals. We ran through our five-song set for the iHeartRadio Music Festival, caught up with the other artists, then headed back to the hotel for an early night.

Friday hit.

Backstage at the T-Mobile Arena, the electric vibe surrounding tonight's festival set me on a high. In the large dressing room we shared with two other artists, adrenaline pumped through my veins like wattage in an amp. In our semi-cordoned off section surrounded by racks of clothes, mirrors, and makeup tables, the guys and I couldn't sit still. We lived to perform. Our backup band lazed on black leather sofas, talking to other musicians in the common area. Interviewers, production crew, and managers talked in groups around the room.

As I held up my hair, Kara zipped me into a shimmery sleeveless top. Carla stood next to us, styling and making the final touches to Hunter's and Kyle's hair.

"You look amazing." Kara turned me to face the full-length mirror.

My long hair had been straightened. Heavy black eyeliner, gold glitter, and thick mascara highlighted my eyes. Dark red lipstick coated my lips. I ran my hands over my black leather pants. They fit like a glove and felt smooth and sexy against my skin. There'd be no costume malfunctions in this outfit. "You've outdone yourself,

Kar. I love these clothes."

I'd wear this gear out on the town, not just onstage.

"What can I say?" Kara's eyes glinted. "I've found my calling as a rock star stylist."

I loved that she'd left Conrad's Fashion House as a designer to come and work for Everhide. Having my best friend around all the time had brought us closer together. Except for wedding dress shopping, she'd made choosing outfits for events and selecting costumes for performances so much fun. She knew our style, our tastes, and had every fashion house begging her to get me and the guys to wear their gear. It was one perk I didn't mind in this business.

I gave Kara a quick hug. "You're the best. And I love you."

"Same. But be careful tonight. Okay?" Kara's words stabbed my lungs. The threats had made everyone wary.

"Always." I pulled out of our embrace and glanced at the guys. They were jostling around, play-fighting, dueling with a pair of hairbrushes. They turned to me, and their faces lit with mischievous grins. I knew those looks. They were no doubt ready to grab me to join their playful battle. I giggled and gave them a don't-you-dare point of my finger. I'd just finished getting ready. Carla would kill me if my hair and makeup were ruined.

We hit the stage in twenty minutes.

It was time for warm-up vocals.

Just as the guys and I fell into a circle, Sam charged through the door. Mike and Chester followed.

No one looked happy.

Shit. What the hell has happened?

Chapter 9

GEMMA

A chill shivered up my spine. "Sam? What's up?"

Sam strode into the center of the room. If he had hair, I was sure it would be ruffled. "Jones just called. He sent images and CCTV footage from outside your rehearsal studio in Brooklyn and the concert in Central Park." Sam handed me his cell phone. Kyle and Hunter huddled around me and peered over my shoulder. I swiped the screen and zoomed in on the blurry images of someone dressed in a black hoodie, bulky jeans, a broad-brimmed bucket hat, scarf, and sunglasses. It was summer. They'd be melting in that gear. Sam leaned forward. "Do you recognize who it is?"

My hands trembled as I scrolled through the photos again. In the stills from Brooklyn, it was hard to get a clear view of the person in the crowd. The nighttime footage from Central Park was heavily pixelated. The person had worn similar disguises in both instances. Their build made it impossible to determine gender. As the video replayed, I thought of everyone I knew—who looked like this? No one came to mind.

Think. Think. Think. Who could it be?

"Sorry, I don't know who this is." I stared at the cell phone. "Sam, without a clear shot, it's impossible to tell. Is it Taylah? Dressed in disguise?"

"Maybe. But I watched her closely at the meet and greet." Sam drew his huge shoulders back. "I took note of her body language. Her walk. Her actions. They don't relay to the person in the video."

Kyle took hold of the cell phone and scanned the images. "Yeah, but anyone can change their walk, or stoop and slink along when they're trying to hide."

What lengths would someone desperate go to?

Sam shrugged his shoulder. "True. Anything's possible." He wouldn't rule out any option.

Hunter grimaced at the images. "If it's not her, who the hell is it?"

My chest ached. I hated seeing him worried. He'd had enough trauma over the past year, losing his child. He didn't need another issue to deal with. None of us did.

Sam took his cell phone back from Kyle and slipped it into the inside pocket of his black security jacket. "Trust me. We're working on it."

"Why show us this now when we're about to go onstage?" Kyle's tone shook with a nervous edge. "You trying to freak us out?"

Too late for that. The images on Sam's cell phone flashed through my mind. I wrapped my arms around myself and shuddered. Was it Taylah? Was she that smart she had evaded being caught? But if it wasn't her . . . *shit* . . . it could be anyone. It had been three weeks since we'd gotten the letter in Brooklyn and were told about the other threats. Still, no culprit had been found.

Sam held up his palms. "No, I'm not trying to scare you. God no. I thought you might recognize who it was so we could see if they were in the audience."

My pulse spiked and whooshed in my ears. *Shit.* The threat could be here. "Is . . . is Taylah in the audience?"

"Yes," Sam dipped his chin. "She's in row eight, seat thirty-seven. On Hunter's side of the stage. We're watching her."

My knees wobbled, and my blood pressure kicked up another notch. That didn't help.

Deep furrows filled Bec's brow. She fidgeted with the neckline of her blouse. "Isn't speculation enough to haul Taylah's ass out of the crowd?"

"Unfortunately not." Sam smoothed his hand over his bald head. "Jones has questioned her, but can't link her to the letters or the trailer incident. If it is her, let's hope she doesn't do anything stupid."

"Like what? Kill me?" My head spun. My mouth ran dry. So not good before performing.

Kyle tensed. Worry flooded his eyes. "Please don't make jokes like that."

I gave him an *I'm-sorry* smile and hoped he bought it. He'd cancel our set if he knew I was scared and my nerves shook like a tambourine on crack.

"Gemma. Guys." Sam's calm tone never faltered as he wriggled the security wire and bug stuffed into his ear. "Every person here has gone through a security check. The entire team is watching her. We've got you covered."

Was that enough? Sam's reassurance didn't erase my dread or stop the fevered perspiration from breaking out on my temples. I swayed on my feet. *Shit.* Should we go onstage?

Sophie took a step toward me and the guys. "If you don't want to do this show, just say the word. We'll cancel. I don't care that it's five minutes until you go on."

Cancel?

I looked from Kyle to Hunter and back again. I read them like a book. Uncertainty darkened their eyes. Tension ticked in their jawlines. Worry had embedded in their brows. They'd let me decide. Did I want to cancel? Could I do that? Was there any more risk than normal?

Kyle snaked his arm around my waist and kissed me on the forehead. "Maybe we should, if you don't feel safe."

"It's your call, Gem." Hunter scuffed his boot and stared at the navy carpet. He'd hate not going on stage. And so would I.

"No. We're not canceling." My voice came out steady and strong, but my insides flipped like pancakes. Taylah was here. Security was in place. I was a goddamn professional. There were thousands of fans in the auditorium. I didn't want to disappoint any of them. I hadn't flown all this way to be a no-show. "We're going on."

On shaky legs, I shuffled over to the nearby drinks table. Closing my eyes for the briefest second, I drew a deep breath into the base of my lungs. *I'm okay. I'm good. The guys and I will be fine.* After fumbling with the lid on the bottle of JD, I poured three shots. I turned and handed Kyle and Hunter a glass each. "Let's rock the fuck out of this place."

"Hell yeah." Hunter hollered as we clinked glasses.

"Alright." Kyle half-grinned, then knocked back the whiskey.

I downed my JD. It burned and soothed my throat.

Yep. I'm ready.

I high-fived the guys. We grabbed our transmitters and in-ear monitors, and put them on. Then Sophie led us out to the stage. Security surrounded us every step of the way.

We stood offstage, waiting for Khalid to finish his set. There'd be a quick equipment change, and our backup band would get into position. As I fidgeted with my necklace, I scanned the monitors displaying the front-of-house control panel, camera stations, and stage areas. There was no feed of the crowd. *Shit.* Security monitors would be elsewhere. *Was the stalker here? Would they try to hurt me?*

"Hey?" Kyle tugged the back of my top. "Are you sure you want to do this?"

For the hundredth time. Yes . . . maybe . . . no. Fuck!

I mustered up a warm smile even though the fluttering butterflies in my stomach had turned into a swarm. "Yep. It's only five songs. Easy." No one would take me down in that timeframe . . . *Right?*

Hunter flung his arms around our necks. "All right then. Time to par-tay!"

Sophie handed us our mics.

As we waited for our cue to run onstage, Ryan Seacrest, the emcee, revved up the crowd with antics and jokes and laughs. The muffled noise filtered through my in-ears.

I closed my eyes. My heart rate hit techno speed.

The mass shooting that had happened at Las Vegas's Harvest Music Festival speared my brain. *No. Don't go there.* Nothing like that could happen here. *Could it?* Everyone had been through security screening. The threats had targeted me. No one else. They wanted *me* out of the way. To get to Kyle.

Oh fuck. I'm going to be sick.

The lights in the auditorium dimmed. I swallowed hard and licked my lips. *Breathe. I've got this.* Pasting on a smile, I nudged my hip against Kyle, then Hunter, and mouthed, *"Love you guys."*

As our backup band hit the introduction to our first song, the screaming crowd hit a new frenzy. Music filled my ears. My sweaty hand cramped around my mic. I scanned the auditorium—people jumped, hollered, and waved their screen-lit cell phones in the air. Cameras flashed.

Was anything out of place? Anyone causing havoc? Was there anything unusual?

No . . . focus.

Wait. Taylah?

Where's Taylah?

I scanned the front seats and counted back eight rows. *Shit!* I couldn't see thanks to floodlights pointed at the stage. Lasers seesawed across the stage. Smoke billowed across the floor. The spotlights beamed brighter.

My heart pummeled my ribcage with hard, pounding jolts.

We were on.

Running to the center of the stage, we hit our first song, "Maybe We Should." The guys and I were not dancers, but every detail in our show was meticulously choreographed. Every step, every song, every word. Everything was timed to perfection. Walk stage left; swap position; head to stage right. We'd performed this song so many times, I could do it with my eyes shut.

Except they weren't. Not tonight.

I watched everything on high alert. The security on the floor guarding the barricades in front of the stage. The camera crew hiding behind lenses. The audience cheering and dancing.

I searched through the mass of people waving their arms for anything that wasn't a water bottle or a cell phone.

Damn it. Stop. Concentrate.

Leading into our second song, I struggled to regulate my breathing. I cut a high note short. I cursed myself for not holding it for as long as usual. Both the guys shot me worry-filled glares. I threw them an *I'm-okay* smile. But during the third song, dizziness spun through my head . *Shit!* I wiped my sweaty brow. I usually didn't perspire this much so soon into a performance. What was wrong with me?

We hit our final song, "Traveled," our latest chart-topping single.

Only one more song to sing.

But something didn't feel right. Unease swayed through my stomach.

The lights blinded me. I squinted and scanned the crowd.

Hunter hit the first verse, standing right on the edge of the stage, swooning at the girls.

> *I had so many dreams I wanted to chase*
> *Had so many demons I had to face*
> *Had to find something to call my own*
> *Worst thing was leaving you alone*
> *Took time to know you held my heart*
> *Now I know I never want to be apart*

The lyrics Kyle wrote for me warped with a new meaning. Some fan was obsessed with him. They didn't want to be apart from him. *Don't be stupid. Sing.* I struck my pose in the middle of the stage, gripping extra tight onto my mic.

> *I've traveled the world all over*
> *Each mile draws us closer and closer*
> *With your love I've found my home*
> *With you I'm no longer alone*
> *Can't breathe when you're not near me*
> *Together, forever, we're meant to be*

Everyone in the audience was out of their seats, singing and dancing.

But there . . . In the crowd . . . What was that? *Shit.*

A girl. Screaming. Angry. Clambering over the chairs. *Crap.*

My legs wobbled. My heartbeat raced. The spotlight spun and I lost sight of her. *Fuck.*

Kyle took to the mic.

> *I'd sit in my hotel room every night*
> *Lying awake with you on my mind*
> *I knew I had to make you mine*
> *Even if it took 'til the end of time*
> *Can't believe you're the dream I've been chasing*
> *You're the only one who gets my heart racing*

The lighting changed. Dimmed.

There. I caught sight of the girl again. Security rushed toward her,

Fuck. What was happening?

My lungs seized. My vision blurred.

I stepped back from the front of the stage. *One. Two. Three.*

A ringing in my ears took over the music in my in-ears. Piercing. Deafening. *Fuck!*

Kyle and Hunter kept performing, never missing a beat. But me . . . I couldn't breathe. Couldn't sing.

Security had the girl.

Couldn't the guys see what was happening?

What was she holding? What was in her hand?

I wanted to scream, drop to the floor, warn the guys, protect everyone.

But my throat seized. My whole body trembled—my hands, my knees, my stomach.

Security dragged the girl out of the third row.

Holy fucking shit!

Perspiration ran down my face. My head spun. Panic took

hold, and I rushed off stage.

I charged past the production crew. Sophie followed me. Chester caught my arm and stepped in front of me, shielding me with his back.

"Gem, what's wrong?" Chester handed Sophie my mic, scanned me up and down.

I ripped out my in-ears, bent over and clutched my knees. Panting, I sucked air into my lungs. With a flick of my hair, I straightened and flapped my hands in front of my face. "Someone. In the crowd. Security got them. Did anyone get hurt?"

Chester spoke into his headset, then shook his head. "No, Gemma. I'll get a full report once you and the guys are safe."

Somehow, Kyle and Hunter finished our set.

> *I've been to London and Rome*
> *To Tokyo and back home*
> *To LA and the stars*
> *I always wind up at the start*
> *Doesn't matter where I've traveled*
> *Or if we have time apart*
> *I know you're the one I love*
> *Yeah, you're the one I need*
> *You own my heart. You own my heart*

They blew quick kisses to the crowd, waved farewell and ran offstage. At speed, they rushed to my side.

"Gem, what's wrong? What happened?" Panicked, Kyle reached out to embrace me, but I held up my hand.

"I'm okay." I needed space. A moment to clear my head. To catch my breath. Tears stung my eyes. *I'm a fucking mess.*

Chester led us back to the dressing room. Concerns from other performers and crew drifted past my ears. *"Gemma, are you okay?" "Are you sick?" "Can we get you anything?"*

I ignored everyone.

Inside the dressing room, I threw my transmitter and in-ears onto the equipment table, grabbed a bottle of water, and paced the floor. Sam and Mick burst through the door.

"Gemma?" Sam dashed over to me. "Are you okay?"

"You tell me?" I waved toward the door. "What the fuck happened out there? Security jumped over some girl in the third row."

"Oh. Oh shit, Gem." Sam's shoulders sank three inches. He shook his head and rubbed the back of his neck. "It was just a drunken fan. She was pissed at the people in front for blocking her view."

"What?" I screeched. "Are you fucking kidding me? I thought she had a gun."

Sam pursed his big lips together and lowered his chin. "No. There was no gun. Just someone loaded with too much booze."

"Fuck." I sliced my fingers into my hair and pulled on it. "So it's just me going insane?"

"Hey, come on, Gem." Kyle stepped toward me, but I flinched and fell back a step. Hurt flickered through his eyes. I hated that. But I felt like an utter idiot. He held his arms wide. "It's okay. We've all had to leave the stage before . . . to throw up, rush to the toilet, or from not feeling well. Don't worry about it."

"Worry?" Fire flared in my veins. "I'm going out of my mind. You're all turning me into a fucking nutcase." I flicked my hand at Sam. "You should've never shown me those pictures before our set. I was fine before that." *Kinda . . . not really. Shit.*

Sam clutched his hand over heart. "I'm so sorry, Gemma."

I ground my teeth. "I looked like a fucking fool out there."

"No. You were great." Sam said.

My performance was far from great. I'd beat myself up for days over it. I had to make sure this mistake never happened again.

Hunter grabbed a towel off the table and wiped the sweat from his face. "You were fine, Gem. A bit off. We've all had days like that."

"I don't want to be off." Tension rippled through my tone. "I don't want this stress. I hate not feeling normal. I hate that I let you down."

"Oh, babe." Kyle eased forward and wrapped his arms around

me. This time, he didn't let go. He just tightened his hold on me and rubbed my back. "You could never let us down. We nailed the set."

Okay. It hadn't been a total clusterfuck. That was true.

But as security and our entourage surrounded us, the concern remained etched on their faces. The reality was the threat was still out there.

I closed my eyes and clutched Kyle's T-shirt. With my cheek pressed against his steamy chest, his warmth slowly enveloped me and lowered my blood pressure. I breathed easier. Relaxed a touch. I was safe. So was everyone I loved.

Thank goodness.

I'd come to Vegas with a purpose. To forget about my problems. But I'd failed. My paranoia had jumped into overdrive. I had issues, but music was my life. Being on stage, performing, was where I thrived. Tonight, I'd cracked under pressure. I wouldn't do that again. No way.

I had too much going for me. My music. My friends. Kyle. Getting married.

I wouldn't live in a cave.

Tomorrow, I'd rock up a storm for my bachelorette party. I was getting hitched in two weeks. After that, everything could reset. Be right. Be normal.

But first . . . I needed to get out of this venue.

I eased out of Kyle's hold and clutched his hands in mine. "Thank you. I needed that." His hugs were the best. They always had a calming effect on me. He was my Valium. "But I'm going to skip the after-party. You guys go. Chester can take me back to the hotel."

Kyle shook his head slowly. "I'm not leaving you by yourself."

"Me either." Hunter came over and hooked his arm around my shoulders. "So that means drinks are on you. In your room."

Maybe the night had rattled them, too.

Chilling out with the guys and Kara to regather my thoughts and forget about tonight's horrid performance would be perfect. "Now that, I can do."

But on the drive back to the hotel, too many what-ifs played through my mind. What if that girl had a gun? What if I'd been shot? What if the guys had been hurt? What if *I* was losing my mind? The psycho fan didn't make their move tonight, so when would they? The niggle in the back of my neck twisted tighter and tighter into a tangled knot.

Ugh! I had to stop overthinking everything. Live in the present. Enjoy and cherish every moment I had with my friends. I loved music and performing. I'd never give it up.

Tonight was a wake-up call . . . to treasure every second on this earth.

I'd be resilient. Strong. Undeterred.

I'd make Kyle promise to have wild fun at his bachelor party, and I'd make damn sure I'd celebrate in style with the girls.

It was time to say goodbye to the single life.

It was time to forget our issues.

It was time to fucking party.

Chapter 10

KYLE

"Go." Laughing, Gemma pushed against my chest, but I caught her hands and pulled her in for a kiss.

Standing in the open double doorway of our suite's master bedroom, I cradled her face and chuckled low and soft. My big smile made my cheeks ache. "Why are you so eager to get rid of me?"

I was torn about heading out. I wanted to catch up with the guys and have a wild night at my bachelor party. But I didn't want to leave Gemma. Not for one second. She hadn't bounced back to her normal self after last night's festival performance. Not even after several JDs. Worst of all, she'd pushed me away. Twice. She'd never done that before. That had hurt. All I wanted to do was hold her. Keep her safe. Love her till the end of time.

Was it wrong I'd much rather be with her than out getting drunk and being inundated with strippers?

Shit. I've become a homebody. I've gone all Chris Hemsworth.

As the late afternoon sun filtered through the enormous windows of our three-bedroom suite at Wynn, Kara, and Lexi flitted around the living room, lining the bar's marble countertop with plastic tiaras, silver sashes, shot glasses and liquor.

Gemma rose on her tippy-toes and touched her lips to mine.

"I love you. But go. The other girls will be here soon." Her voice slid with sultry seductiveness. "There'll be lots of drinking games, food, and fun before we head out to see buffed men get their gear off."

I'd gladly do a private strip show for Gemma. Any day.

With extra-tight security, only our entourage and only a few close friends from New York had flown to Vegas for our parties. I had to believe Gemma would be safe.

My body ached from lack of decent sleep. I hadn't slept well since the threatening letter had been planted in Gemma's bag in Brooklyn. Finding out there had been more than one hadn't helped. Potential suspects kept sifting through my mind. No one stood out as much as Taylah.

I took Gemma's hands in mine, tugged her closer. "Maybe I should stay because I'm very interested in seeing what you do with those." I jutted my chin toward the bowls of penis-shaped candy and squishy toys on the glass-topped coffee table. "I might get a complex. Although . . ." I led Gemma over to the goodies, grabbed a lollipop from the dish, and swiveled it between my fingertips. ". . . I don't think I have too much to worry about. My dick is much bigger than this."

Gemma snaked her hands around my waist and clutched my ass. She tilted her head back. God, she was beautiful, dressed in slim black dress pants and a leather vest, with only a hint of makeup. She warmed my blood and sent it rushing south.

Her eyes twinkled, and she smiled a saucy smile. The smile she always gave me when my body reacted to her touch, her kisses, and holding her close. She snatched the candy from my hand. "Yes. And you're much more satisfying. But you have to leave. It's time to party."

I expected nothing less than wild Gemma to be unleashed tonight. It would do her good to have fun with the girls. She needed it after everything that had happened.

I brushed the tip of her nose with my fingertip. "Are you going to behave?"

"Absolutely." Her voice may have been coated with sweet

innocence, but her eyes hinted at all kinds of mischievous trouble.

"Liar." Chuckling, I kissed her forehead.

She wrinkled her nose. "You know me too well."

Yes, I did.

Somehow, she'd glued her resilience back into place, but I knew it was paper thin.

"And what about you?" She raised an inquisitive eyebrow as she jabbed her finger against my chest.

I shook my head. "I have absolutely no idea what Hunter and Hayden have planned. As long as they don't shave off my eyebrows or ink me with more tattoos . . . well . . . not with something I'll regret. I'm down with anything."

Gemma slid her hands over my shoulders and linked her fingers behind my neck. "I'm sure they'll have a variety of lurid and fetish-oriented strippers lined up for you."

"Hunt's told me a few things." Kara eased in beside us. Playful bewilderment glinted in her dark blue eyes. "Kyle, you'll crave a quiet and boring life after tonight. Trust me."

What am I in for?

Nerves had one foot glued to the floor, excited anticipation had the other one dragging me toward the door. "Typical Vegas night out with the boys, then?"

Gemma tugged on the collar of my leather jacket and gave me a gentle shake. "Damn it. I hate missing out. We should've had a joint party." She pouted and sulked, then her lips morphed into a sexy smile. "But go. Enjoy your lap dances, your titty fests, your booze. Because the girls and I will be all over some hot men."

I drew her into a hug. "You are the most amazing woman. You know that?"

"Yep." She slapped my ass. "Now get out of here."

"I love you." I kissed her long and hard, savoring her minty breath. Showering with her an hour ago had already made my night. Satisfied me in every way. Gemma was all I'd ever need. But I better turn up to my party for the guys. "Have fun. I'll see you in the morning."

I picked up my overnight bag and headed out the door.

Hunter, here I come.
Bring on my bachelor party!
Gem, please stay safe.

***

My head spun. My vision blurred. The grin on my mouth was as wide as the Las Vegas Strip was long. The buzz coursing through my veins was from alcohol, not the topless stripper writhing on my lap. She gyrated her sequined-G-string against my crotch. Thrust her tits into my face.

Beers, JD, and pizza around the pool at sunset led to dropping a ridiculous amount of cash across a high-rollers blackjack table in the casino. Then, we'd ventured to a private function room at a strip club. The JD was constant. The lingerie waitresses were easy on the eye. Candy was stripper number two.

Thank God no phones were allowed in here. I didn't need photos of this hitting the Internet.

"Don't Cha" by the Pussycat Dolls boomed through the room's speakers. I sat on the chair in the middle of the gold velvet-draped room, surrounded by my friends. With drinks in hand, they hovered by the bar, sat on stools, or lingered near the billiard table, cheering me on.

"Sucks to be you, Kyle!" Hayden hollered.

"Get a load of those babies." Slade, our backup band's drummer, hooted.

Candy grabbed my hands and placed them over her breasts. A sly grin inched across my mouth. *Her tits?* Way more than a handful. Fake. Hard nipples. Pert. But they weren't Gemma's. Gemma's were small, real . . . and perfect.

Fuck! Would Gemma be groping some male stripper? Have her hands writhing over his body? Crushed against his cock? *Ugh!* I didn't want to think about her touching someone other than me. But I hoped she was having a good time. My lap dancer pressed my hands harder against her breasts and rolled them around in circles. I chuckled and shook my head. *Yep. This is ridiculous, but fun.*

Grinning, Hunter held up his hands and shimmied them in the air. "How do they feel?"

Kade laughed a raucous laugh. "Gem needs to get a set of those puppies."

No, she didn't.

Candy arched her chest toward me and pulled my face into her cleavage. *Shit.* I couldn't breathe. I ripped my head back and gasped for air. She ignored me and continued her routine.

Luckily, it didn't go on for too long.

Once she finished, and I downed another two shots of JD, there was more entertainment. Two strippers, whipped cream, and some girl-on-girl action. I couldn't deny it was wicked to watch. Totally hot. But time disappeared. I lost track of how much I'd drunk. I covered my mouth and belched. *Yep.* I was drunk. But I still needed to keep some wits about me.

Hunter handed me another shot. "Drink up, bud. The night is still young."

How could I refuse?

I took the JD and swallowed it down. The whiskey burned the back of my throat and pooled heavy in my gut. *Fuck.* I'd have one mother of a headache tomorrow. But it'd be worth it.

Sometime after midnight, Hayden, and Hunter hooked their arms around me and dragged me back to the nightclub at Wynn. Our friends and security followed us as we entered the cordoned off VIP section. The club's atmosphere was electric, full of partygoers and a DJ pumping out deafening tunes. Lights bathed the area, blue, then red, then green. Patterned projections swirled across the floor—snowflakes, squiggles, and squares. In the center of the room, the dance floor overflowed with guys and girls, gyrating to the beat. I blinked to focus. *What the hell?* The girls were here? *Shit.* But where was Gemma?

So much for keeping our parties separate. But I wouldn't complain about hooking up with my fiancée.

"Guys." Hollering above the noise, Laura jumped up and down and waved us over. Then she gave me the sexy eye, fucked the air with thrusts of her hips and pumped her fists. "Come dance with us. You know you want to."

Nope. Dirty dancing with her wouldn't be on my agenda.

Vicki rushed over, flashed security her VIP pass, and jumped to a halt in front of me and Hunter. "Hello boys."

Hunter slung an arm around my shoulders and slapped me on the chest. "Kyle, you go with the Hayds and get drinks. I'll sort Vicki and the girls out. They shouldn't be here."

"Oh, come on, Hunter." Vicki wound her arm around his waist. "If you guys are just hanging, why can't we join you? We're just there." She pointed to the booth two away from ours. The table was covered in colorful cocktails, crystal glasses, and champagne on ice.

I swayed and stumbled half a step sideways. *Whoa.* "We're not supposed to meet up. This club is on our schedule, not yours." I searched the dance floor, the bar, and the patio overlooking the waterfall and pool area, but still couldn't see Gemma. "Where's Gem?"

Vicki shrugged her shoulder. "Not here. She passed out ages ago."

"She what?" I whipped my head around so fast I nearly gave myself whiplash. "Passed out?" That wasn't like Gemma.

A deep groove formed between Hunter's eyebrows as he shook his head. "Gemma doesn't pass out."

Vicki jerked her chin back and splayed her palms. "Well, she did tonight. Stone cold. She had a lot to drink at the revue. She wanted to come back to her suite before heading out again. But bang. Gone. Out cold." With a flick of her hand, Vicki brushed off any concern and softened her tone. "She'll be fine. She just needs to sleep it off. Kara and Lexi are with her. Sophie, her girlfriend Gayle, Kate, and Bec went to bed. Carla, Laura, and I wanted to keep partying."

I rubbed the ache in my forehead. I couldn't comprehend Gemma had gotten so wasted. She could drink most people under the table. Something wasn't right. "You can stay; I don't care. I'm gonna check on Gem."

"Whoa. Whoa. Whoa." Hunter blocked my path. He had that are-you-insane look in his eyes. "No. You're not. It's your party. You can't leave. There are a heap of girls out there on that floor we need to dance with. More drinks to drink. You're not going anywhere. Gem will be fine."

The DJ spun a new track. Partygoers hanging around the tables and the bar abandoned conversations and drinks and rushed to join the thick crowd on the dance floor. Arms waved in the air and everyone jumped to the heavy beat.

Hunter was right. Relaxing my shoulders, I held up my hands. "Okay. Okay. Just let me send her a quick text."

"Awesome. You do that and I'll get those drinks." Hunter slapped me on the back and headed toward the bar.

I grabbed my cell phone out of my jacket and texted Gemma.

> ME: HEARD YOU PASSED OUT. EVERYTHING OKAY?
> TEXT ME IF YOU'RE UP.

Resisting the urge to run back to my room and check on her, I turned to head over to the booth and join the guys, but Vicki stepped in front of me. She jerked her head toward the dance floor. "Hey, are you sure you don't wanna dance? Get your groove on? Because if you do, and wanna ramp up the fun a notch ..." She edged forward, caught the neckline of her blouse, lowered it two inches, and flashed me a small packet of pills stuck underneath her bra strap. "... I've got a little something that'll help."

Shit. "Are you insane? *No.* I don't do that shit anymore. Haven't for years."

She realigned her top and rolled her shoulders. "Don't you want a hit for old times' sake? Or are you turning into a bore like you were in high school?"

Maybe I was back then. She'd never understood that music was everything. I didn't screw around like she had.

"I think we both know that's not the case." I'd grown up and changed. If she didn't see that, it wasn't my problem. I may not be as loud and vibrant as Hunter or Gemma, but I lived for fun. Vicki hadn't gone on tour with us, didn't go to every party, was never around when we hit some adrenaline-fueled adventure when we were somewhere in the world with a day off. If black run snowboarding in Japan was boring and so was bungee jumping in Queenstown, New Zealand, and so was zip lining in Hawaii, so be it. If tonight, hanging out with my friends, going to a strip club, and drinking a shitload of booze was dull, I'd own it. "Call me boring. I don't care, Vick. I'm getting married. In two freaking weeks." *Oh shit.* An invisible punch landed in my guts. Vicki wasn't invited to the wedding; I shouldn't have let the timeframe slip. Alcohol had loosened my tongue.

Her mouth fell open like a clown at a county fair. "Two weeks?"

"Yeah." My pulse strummed in my ears. I had to backpedal somehow. "You had to assume it was close since you're here for Gem's bachelorette party, right? Please don't tell anyone."

"Who am I gonna tell?" Vicki quirked a smile, turning her head from side to side, and glanced around the club. "I think your secret's safe with me."

"Good. Thanks." *Phew!* I hooked my arm around her shoulders, and drew her toward our table. "Let's have a drink. But first . . ." I thumbed toward the restrooms. "I need to piss. Slade will look after you. Back in a sec."

I left them be. They'd hook-up for sure.

As I weaved through the crowd, ignoring the *OMG-it's-Kyle* whispers, I quickly checked my cell phone. *Fuck.* Still no reply from Gemma. I didn't want to cross any line. Be over protective. But I had to make sure she was okay. I quickly shot off another message to her, then one to Lexi, Kara, and Chester. Surely one of them would text with an update or call if something was wrong.

After doing my business, I staggered out of the restroom. I checked my cell phone again. *Fuck. Still no texts.*

"Kyle? Oh my God. It's you!"

I looked up, blinked, and focused.

Fuck!

It was like I'd jumped into a frigid plunge pool. I sobered within a split second. "Taylah?" I searched for Sam. He stood vigilant a few feet away, eyes set on Taylah like a jaguar about to pounce. I turned back to Taylah. "What the hell are you doing here?"

Taylah fidgeted—with her phone, her hair, her earring. "I told you I was coming to Vegas to see you at iHearts. Is Gemma feeling better?"

"Yeah. She is." *Hopefully. If someone would just fucking text me.*

"There were posts saying you were here at Wynn." She waved her phone at me, then hugged it to her chest. "I had to come and scope the place out. The likelihood of running into you was slim. But this . . . this is just . . . just wow. It's made my trip even better."

I held up my hand and took a step back. "Taylah, you need to leave." I could hear Sam murmuring into his headset.

"Why?" Her smile turned upside down. "I just wanted to say hi."

"Great. Hi. I'm sorry, but I've gotta go." I went to step around her, but I halted in my tracks. I clenched my hands into tight fists by my side. Detective Jones had said they couldn't link Taylah to the death threats. That hadn't gelled with me, especially when there'd been no other suspects. Jones had said don't do anything, don't get involved, leave the investigation to the police. But having Taylah in front of me set a fire blazing through my blood. I wanted to find out why she wanted to hurt Gemma, why she was obsessed with me, and tell her to stop. I threw her an icy glare. "Just one thing. Why do you hate Gemma?"

"What?" Her eyes widened, the white eerily vivid against her dark markup. "I . . . I don't. She's amazing."

Sam stepped closer, but I held up my hand to stop him.

"Come on, Taylah." I couldn't hide the frustration in my voice. I flicked my hand at her. "Don't lie to me. We know what you've been doing. The letters have gone too far."

"What are you talking about?" She eased back, putting a clear three-foot gap between us. The bar blocked her retreat. "What letters? You mean the card I sent to congratulate you and Gemma on your engagement? You got that?"

I inched closer. Alcohol had boosted my confidence. "We've got *all* your letters. Understand this—I love Gemma. I'm marrying her. I don't know what game you're playing, but it stops now."

"Stop what?" Vicki slipped out from behind a group of guys ordering drinks at the bar and edged in beside me. "Do you need saving?"

Ugh. No.

Taylah held out her hand for Vicki to shake. "Hi. I'm Taylah. I run Everhide's Ringers Fan Club."

Vicki raised one thin eyebrow, scanned Taylah from the ground up, then shook her hand. "Hiiii," she drawled. "I'm Vicki. I'm one of Kyle and Gemma's friends. We go waaaay back." She nudged her hip against mine. Threw me a wink. Turning back to Taylah, she lifted her chin. "I've heard of the Ringers. Isn't it just TikTok, Insta and Facebook posts dedicated to Kyle?"

Taylah blushed, tucked her hair behind her ear, and lowered her gaze. "No. We have a website, a newsletter, we run giveaways, sell merch, and write some fan fiction. I try to keep the social posts even, but Kyle's my favorite. Even when he's drunk and weirding me out."

"Sorry, not sorry." Meeting fans usually humbled me, but Taylah made my skin crawl.

A group of girls at the nearby bar table snapped pictures of me. Perfect timing and an excuse to get back to the guys.

But Taylah tilted her head and waggled her finger at Vicki. "I know you from somewhere. Have we met?"

Vicki shook her head. "Don't think so. Maybe at a concert or something." She plastered on a smile and hooked her arm around mine. "Taylah, it's nice to meet you, but you're keeping Kyle from his bachelor party. Only two weeks until the big day."

Taylah's hands splayed across her chest. "It's your bachelor party? Why are you standing here? Go. Go party."

I groaned and jerked free of Vicki's clasp. "Gee, thanks Vick." I waved toward the DJ. "Do you just want to go up there and announce to everyone what's going on?"

"Oops, sorry. My bad." Vicki fluttered her eyelashes, playing the innocent.

I clenched my jaw, closed my eyes, and took a deep breath. *Fuck.* I wanted to kick myself for slipping up and telling Vicki the wedding timeframe. She'd blabbed it to someone else within minutes. Who else could've overheard? *Gemma will kill me when she finds out I'd stuffed up.*

Swaying, I glanced at my watch. 2:49 a.m. "Shit. I gotta go. I need to make sure Gem's okay."

Vicki threw her head back and sighed. "I told you … she's fine."

It wasn't that I didn't believe her, I just wanted to check for myself. Another text wouldn't hurt. I grabbed my cell phone. Still no messages. I tightened my hold on my phone, gripped it tighter and tighter. The pressure in my temples mounted. Pounding. And throbbing. And aching.

"Kyle?" Taylah took half a step forward and held out her hand. "Are you okay?"

Stepping back, I nodded. I didn't want her to touch me. "I'm fine."

"Before you go." Something in her voice made me stop. "What were you saying about the card I sent?"

"Just don't send any more fucked up letters." My voice slid through my teeth as I threw her a cold glare. "No more."

"Letters?" Vicki's voice peaked and gave me a quizzical look. "What letters?"

"It's nothing." *Shit.* Vicki hadn't been part of the few people we'd briefed about the threats for security purposes. I straightened my shoulders and found a fragment of composure. "I'm sorry. I shouldn't have said anything. It's nothing the police can't handle."

"Police?" Vicki lifted her chin, her eyes narrowing with intrigue. "Kyle, what's going on?"

Taylah cut in. "Has this got something to do with Brooklyn? I met with the detectives. I answered a heap of questions, but there was no mention of other letters."

What the hell was Jones doing? Wasn't he doing his job?

I rubbed my blurry eyes. Fuck, I needed to keep my mouth shut. I'd already said too much. "I'm sorry ladies, I gotta go."

Taylah nodded. "Thanks for saying hello. If you need any more information, I'll do whatever I can to help. You know that?"

I dipped my chin and feigned a smile. "Yeah. Thanks. *Ciao.*" I turned and waved over my shoulder.

Walking back to the VIP area, I couldn't shake the slimy feeling of vines twisting and wrapping and tightening around my spine. Was it a coincidence Taylah was here? It was so hard to distinguish between the normal fandom we experienced wherever we went and if Taylah was a real problem. The threats, her being in Brooklyn, at Central Park, and how she'd traveled halfway across the country to see us again set alarms off in my head. I staggered on my feet. I just wanted to see Gemma. Help the girls look after her. Be there when she woke up.

At the booth, I leaned down and spoke into Hunter's ear. "Gem hasn't replied to my texts. Nor has anyone else. I've gotta check on her. I'll be quick. Back in ten minutes."

"Noooo." Hunter shot to his feet. "You can't leave."

"Please," I pleaded. "For my sanity. She passed out. I have to make sure she's okay."

"I'll call Kara." Hunter pulled out his phone and dialed.

No answer.

I flicker of concern shot through Hunter's eyes. "Her phone might be on silent if she's asleep."

"Another reason for me to check on Gem. She might be sick and need help." My anxiety crept a rung higher. "Keep everyone entertained. I'll be back."

Hunter didn't stop me. He cared for Gemma. With a nod, he let me go.

Sam guided me through the crowd, past Vicki and Taylah lingering by the bar, and aimed for the door. Gemma and I should've had joint parties. I hated not knowing if she was okay.

But as I neared the nightclub's entrance, ice crept up the back of my neck. My skin prickled and my bones shuddered. I didn't look over my shoulder, but with every step, I felt Taylah's eyes pinned to my back.

Chapter 11

GEMMA

My arms weighed a ton. As I drew the silky Egyptian cotton bed coverings over my waist my fatigued muscles ached. The air-conditioning chilled me to the bone. I cuddled into Kyle for warmth.

Wait.

What?

I loved waking up next to him every day. But not today. He shouldn't be here.

I peeled my heavy eyes open. With the bedroom's blackout blinds down, it was dark, not pitch black. Kyle lay beside me in the king-sized bed, wearing only his boxer-briefs. His chest rose and fell slowly with each breath. The hint of liquor lingered in the air. His messy hair, fair whiskers, and eyelashes highlighted his handsome face.

Damn, I'm lucky.

But pain erupted inside my head. I flopped onto my back and press my palms against my eyes. Why did I feel like death? So lethargic? I could barely move a muscle. I licked my lips; my mouth, dry. My stomach squished and squelched like boots in the thick mud. I couldn't remember Kyle coming in last night. When did he get here? In fact . . . I couldn't remember coming to bed at all.

My bachelorette party flashed through my mind—drinks and games with the girls, the male revue show, more champagne back here, then . . . nothing.

What the hell happened? I never blacked out. It must've been a wicked, wild night. Even for me.

Kyle stirred, blinked his eyes open, and smiled a sleepy smile. "Hey, beautiful."

"What are you doing here?" I whispered as I rolled toward him. The neckline of my T-shirt dug into my throat. Twisting and tugging, I released the stranglehold. Why wasn't I wearing his old Pearl Jam shirt? It was my favorite thing to wear to bed. This top was too short and didn't even cover my tummy.

Kyle scooped my hair back over my shoulder. Warmth lingered on my skin beneath his soft touch. "Vicki told me you passed out. You didn't return my texts, so I came to check on you."

I rubbed the confusion from my brow. "You saw the girls?"

"Yeah, Carla, Laura, and Vicki turned up at the club."

My head ached. I didn't remember them leaving. Or anyone else. I picked clumps of clogged mascara from my eyelashes. I must look like a hungover panda. "What time was that?"

"I came in at three. You were totally out of it. Didn't wake when I shook you. I wanted to call the doctor. But Lexi and Kara insisted you were just wasted. I woke them up when I ran into the table and knocked over a champagne bottle."

And I hadn't heard him? I was a light sleeper.

I couldn't remember drinking that much. I'd knocked back quite a few drinks, but nothing earth-shattering. My head spun like a centrifuge. Every bone in my body grew heavier. Soon, I'd sink through the mattress. But none of this changed the fact he shouldn't be here. I hoisted myself upright, wriggled backward and leaned against the padded headboard. I crushed a pillow to my chest. "So, after checking on me, why didn't you go back to the guys?"

He propped his head on his hand and slid his other arm over my legs. His fingers trailed up toward my hip and circled my skin near the waistband of my panties. If nausea wasn't swirling around in the pit of my stomach, I'd love him to rip off my underwear with his teeth. Kiss every inch of my body. Fuck me senseless. But beads of sweat broke out on my brow, and I fought the urge to vomit. I drew my knees up. He just leaned forward, kissed and cuddled my legs. "I was worried."

"I know." But I was with my girlfriends; he didn't need to check on me every five minutes. "Can't you leave me for one night?"

He pinched his eyebrows together and jerked his chin back. "Don't be mad."

"I am mad." I dug my fingernails into the pillow, struggling to keep my breath steady and my blood pressure normal. I loved him so much, but he didn't need to be overprotective. "It was my night with the girls. They would've called you if there was a problem. You didn't have to check on me."

A muscle ticked in his jaw, and his gaze turned steely. "Yeah...I did. It's not like you to pass out. After running into Taylah, and no one texted me back, I got worried. I had to make sure you were okay."

"Oh, shit." I tossed my pillow aside and shot my legs out straight. "You saw Taylah?" Well, now I felt like shit. I would've been worried, too. *Fuck.* She had popped up in too many weird places lately, constantly ramping up our suspicions.

Kyle's hand draped across my thighs again. "She tracked us down in the nightclub. I confronted her about the letters, but my interrogation skills under the influence of alcohol failed dismally. I got nothing. Then I panicked, thinking something bad might've happened to you. Once I got here, I didn't want to leave. Gem, I'm sorry . . . I didn't think staying here would ruin your night."

I stared at the cabinet at the foot of the bed that held the hidden flat-screen. I loved him being here and hated it at the same time. He should be with the guys, partying, not here playing nurse. But I didn't have the strength or energy to argue. I sighed and threaded my fingers through his tousled hair. "You didn't ruin my night. I did a fine job of that myself. You don't need to apologize. I'm sorry." I loved how much he cared for me. I had to remember with the threats looming over our heads, life wasn't normal. But I could take care of myself.

He traced my small tattoo of a treble clef centered in a tilted heart, peeking out from the top of my panties. His soft strokes were cool against my hot skin. Then he stopped. His gaze turned dark and distant. "Vicki had E. Did you take one?"

My head jerked back, hitting the headboard. "No. God no." *Shit.* Vicki had never done drugs of any kind at the wild parties we'd thrown back in our early days. As far as I knew, she was straight as a line. I guessed people changed. What kind of friend was I if I hadn't noticed? "I didn't take anything. I didn't even drink that much. That's why this is so weird. I feel *weird.*" The life-sucking aftermath draining my body felt like no party drug or crippling hangover I'd experienced before.

I closed my eyes, unable to recall all the details from last night. That spread another layer of fear into my system. It shuddered from my head down to my toes. Did Vicki slip something into my drink? *I'll talk to her; kill her if she did.*

"Maybe you should go to the doctor and get checked out?" Concern quaked in Kyle's voice.

"No."

"Please?"

"No." I slumped my shoulders. "I'm fine. With everything going on, and everyone telling me what to do and how to do it, I guess I got carried away and lost track of how much I drank." Surely that was it. The long days leading up to the show, the threats, the wedding pressure, and my anxiety had gotten to me. My life wasn't my own. "Everything just sucks at the moment."

He hooked his hands underneath my hips and pulled me down onto the mattress. He leaned over and kissed my lips. "Not everything." A warm glint shimmered through his eyes. "Our life outside our doors may be crazy, but no one will ever take moments like this away from us. You. Me. Together forever. I know spending time with the girls is important to you, so I'm sorry I intruded, and your night didn't go to plan." A seductive smile promising all kinds of pleasure inched across his mouth. "Can I make it up to you?"

Hmmm. I knew that tone, playful and suggestive. That look, seductive and ready to ravish.

He dipped his head and nipped along the inside of my arm. He scraped his teeth over the *'Live life to the fullest'* cursive tattoo on my inner bicep. *Damn it!* My weak spot. Okay . . . if he kept doing that . . . *Nope. Not even.*

I shoved my hands against his shoulders. "I love you. But later." I didn't feel well. This was the weirdest hangover ever. *"I'll* make it up to you when I don't feel like crap."

He rolled off me, grabbed his straining erection through his boxer-briefs and clasped it. "Cruel, Gem. Cruel. You gonna leave me with aching balls?"

"Yep. Sorry, not sorry."

"Gotta say I'm not feeling the best either." He covered his eyes with his arm. "I had way too much JD last night. Later definitely sounds good."

"Yeah. Absolutely."

Resisting the urge to run to the bathroom and throw up, I took a calming breath and rubbed my queasy tummy. Last night had turned into a huge clusterfuck and my performance at the iHeartRadio Music Festival the night before had been a train wreck. What was supposed to be a weekend of fun had ended in a blackout and a hangover from hell. Was everything affecting me more than I'd thought? *Maybe.*

Nothing about our life was simple or normal. The little things, like him winding up in my bed after a crazy night, weren't even worth causing a fuss over. But I'd have to establish new boundaries and rules so I could spend time with my friends without him freaking out. He didn't need to hold my hand every second of the day. I'd break it if he did. I wanted our future together to work.

I didn't want the honeymoon to be over before it began.

Chapter 12

GEMMA

At brunch by the poolside bar, I sat under an umbrella-covered table with Kyle, waiting for our friends. I skimmed through my social feeds. They'd gone into meltdown with fans posting pictures of us entering and leaving our party venues, and Kyle and the guys at the club. Speculation about a wedding in Vegas ran hotter than a steaming pipe. But as I scrolled past each image, the fog in my brain remained thick. I still couldn't recall everything I did last night.

Why not?

I slipped on my dark sunglasses and sipped a fruit smoothie. The guests at nearby tables whispered, took photos of us, and watched our every move. Most days, the guys and I dined in private areas, were cautious about where we went out, and avoided open public spaces. But I was under the weather. Needed sunshine. Security stood nearby. Everything would be fine.

Hunter and Hayden stumbled out of the hotel, laughing and holding each other upright. They veered around the garden, tables, and chairs to join us.

"What happened to you, Kyle? You big pussy?" Totally tanked, Hunter swayed on his feet beside me. With going-out clothes still on, Ray-Bans covering his eyes and his long hair loose, it didn't look like he'd been to bed. Same with Hayden.

"Knew you'd pike once you left," Hayden slurred and staggered. "Got your text, you slackass."

Kyle took a sip of his coffee, then placed the cup back on the saucer. His grin held no shame or regret. "Sorry. Gem was still passed out. I had to stay with her."

Hunter bent down and kissed the top of my head. "You okay?"

"Yeah." I nudged my arm against his legs. "But still not feeling the best."

"Kyle, you're so whipped." Hunter clipped Kyle on the head, then pointed at him. "I'll let you get away with it, just this once."

More friends arrived, filling tables and nursing hangovers as they devoured greasy food for brunch. I picked at an omelet, unable to eat much. My stomach was still on a bender.

Kara and Lexi begged me to go shopping, but I declined. At midday, I said a quick farewell to Laura and Vicki. They'd slept in and had to rush to the airport for their flight home to New York.

At one o'clock, I crawled back into bed to sleep the afternoon away. Were my hard-partying days over at the tender age of twenty-six? Were all-day hangovers my new thing? *Better not be.*

In the early evening, I woke to the sound of the bathtub running. Facing the windows, the glittering lights of Las Vegas spread like a blanket of colored stars toward the horizon. I hadn't heard Kyle open the blinds. *Damn.* I must've been beyond exhausted.

Fuck, I needed a decent vacation.

My honeymoon couldn't come soon enough.

I'd just put last night down to a bad night.

I stretched my arms over my head, finally moving without each limb weighing as much as an elephant. I rolled over to face the master bathroom. Kyle sat on the side of the tub, naked, swirling his fingers through the bubble bath. *Hmm. Nice view.* His tanned body was toned to athletic perfection. Several tattoos decorated his arms and chest—an armband of intricate swirls on his right bicep, our initials on his inner left wrist, and his latest addition, the small tulip with my name on a ribbon over his heart, permanently branding me as his. He turned off the faucet and stood.

Oh yeah! I'm better.

Time to make up for earlier.

I wriggled out of my clothes. Once he'd submerged into the huge white marble bath and rested his head against the bolster pillow, I tiptoed into the steam-filled room. I stepped into the hot tub. A lazy smile curled across his mouth. His hands snaked around my calf muscles. I eased into the water, turned and nestled between his legs, resting my back against his chest. The perfume from the jasmine-and-vanilla-infused bubbles filled the air. Hot steamy water and bath foam enveloped our bodies. If it wasn't for Kyle's arms wrapped around me, I would've sunk like a rock to the bottom.

"I hoped you'd join me." He kissed the side of my neck, his wet hair tickling my cheek. "Feeling better? You've slept all afternoon."

"I must've needed it." I curled my hands around his forearms. "What did you get up to?"

"Had a nap, worked on some wedding stuff, and watched you sleep."

"You being creepy again?"

"No. Never." His warm breath on my neck sent goose bumps skipping across my skin. "Just love that you are mine."

I hugged his arms across my chest. With the craziness of the past few weeks, he'd taken care of the wedding plans, made my life easier, and put up with all my issues. Sometimes, the depth of his unwavering love scared me. I often didn't feel worthy of such adoration. I loved Kyle with all my soul, but was that enough? Was there more that I could give? My family had never shown me any care or affection, so his often felt surreal. Like a dream. Too good to be true. Our love was so intense and uncanny, I worried it would blow up in a puff of smoke. I couldn't let that happen. I couldn't exist without him.

I turned in his embrace. Bubbles and water swirled like silk around our bodies as I straddled his lap. "About this morning . . ." I skimmed my hands across his smooth shoulders, kissed a trail across his collarbone, and licked the droplets of water from the side of his neck. I touched my lips to his. "I'm sorry for getting mad."

"Hmm. I've seen you mad. You weren't even close. There was no yelling or screaming. We were both tired, frustrated, and worried. That's all." The deep rumble in his throat reverberated through my veins, hummed across my skin, and hardened my nipples into aching peaks. His hands glided over my back, my shoulders, then caressed my face. "I'm sorry for coming to check on you. But I'll never be sorry for worrying and caring about you."

"Me either. So . . ." I caught my lip between my teeth, arched my eyebrow. "What are we going to do about that?"

His cock hardened beneath me. His dark eyes glinted as a wicked smile curled across his lips.

I took my weight onto my knees and rubbed the tip of his dick against my pussy. Teasing him. Taunting him. But not taking him in. As I hovered my lips an inch from his mouth, my breath quickened. My heartrate doubled.

He buried his fingers in my wet hair. He clutched the back of my head and drew my lips to his. Languid, tender kisses quickly turned hungry and hot. Every rush of his breath sent goose bumps charging across my skin. "I have an idea, but first, stop teasing and let me inside you."

"Can't I torture you first? Just a little?"

"If this is my punishment for making you mad, please continue."

"Foreplay is overrated. Can I just fuck you?"

"Hell yeah."

I lowered onto his cock. Warmth coiled up my spine and settled in my chest. *So good.* Clutching onto his shoulders, I rocked my hips against his, taking him deeper and deeper. I rode him slowly. Water swirled around us. My core ached for more. More friction. More pace. More penetration.

Kyle cupped my face. Kissed me. Then his gaze locked onto mine.

The air sparked around us.

There it was. That fire.

Our connection.

That moment when nothing other than the two of us existed.

I'd been an idiot.

Last night he'd checked on me because he'd been scared for my safety. He truly loved me. I had to stop stressing about our wedding, the guest list, and the threats. When I was with him, I was afraid of nothing. I tilted my hips, rubbed against him. "Mmm. This is good."

"Any sex with you is good sex." He dipped his head and took my nipple into his mouth. He licked and flicked his warm, wet tongue over my hardened bud. His calloused fingertips tweaked and teased the other one, sending ripples of pleasure and pain charging toward my toes. He moaned, gravelly and low. I arched my back, craving more of his touch. The water and bubbles licked my ribs as he sucked and teased my boobs. *Oh yeah.* Every stroke tightened the tension in my core. I clenched around him, rocking harder and harder.

Clutching Kyle's hair, I drew his lips to mine. Our pants entwined, as did the fiery swipes and hot flicks of our tongues. Steam thickened the air and sizzled against our skin. He tightened his hold on my waist and tugged me closer. His cock filled me, driving in deep. Rushing his breath across my skin, he trailed kisses toward my ear. Every nerve in my body sparked with electricity. Tingled. Prickled.

"Marry me. Now. Here in Vegas," he whispered, hot and heavy.

What the fuck?

I lurched off him backward. Giant waves of water sloshed over the edge of the bath and flooded the floor. My heart thundered up to my throat. Leaning against the end of the bathtub, I panted. I blinked. "What did you just say?"

Get married. In Vegas.

"Can't talk." He groaned and winced, clutching his crotch beneath the water. "I think you broke my dick."

"Shit. Sorry." I hadn't meant to hurt him. But that wasn't the first time he'd pulled out of me in a hurry. We'd often been caught banging in awkward places and at awkward times. Especially during the tour. "But I'm in shock." My heartbeat still raced like an F1 car.

Kyle's mouth twisted into a smile, a mix of humor and sheer agony. "You wanted a no-fuss wedding. Our friends are here. Let's just get it over and done with. Just like you want."

Like I wanted? A Vegas wedding wasn't what I wanted. Why did he want to change the plans again? "No, it's not." I shook my head and softened my tone. "I want a beach wedding. With just our four best friends, not a crowd."

He shuffled around onto his knees and glided through the water toward me. He wriggled his eyebrows, then nuzzled my neck. "We can just go to Belize for our honeymoon."

To have the wedding over and done with had merits. But I didn't want a chapel-styled wedding. It wasn't us. "We could. But we wanted to get married there too."

"I just can't wait for you to be my wife." He grabbed my hand and kissed my engagement ring. "Marry me, Gem. Tonight."

Shit. Shit. Shit.

Dizziness swam through my head. My heart plummeted like a brick to the bottom of the bath. Did he think this would make me happy? He knew me better than that. As I searched his face for an answer to why the sudden urgency, my brain scrambled for logic. Why did he want to get married now? After all his planning? Did he hope it would put an end to the threats as much as I did? *Fuck the threats.* We wanted to get married on the beach. In Belize. That was our dream wedding. Not Vegas.

I couldn't believe what I was about to say.

I brushed my fingertips down his cheek and caught his chin. "No."

"What?" Confusion shot through his voice. "You're the one who likes to be spontaneous."

True. But I only wanted to get married once, and I wanted to do it the right way. Our way. "It's tempting, but no. I want our day to be special. Like we've planned. I want to marry you in Belize."

His gaze softened as golden shards shimmered in the depths of his espresso eyes. "Are you sure?"

"Yes. I am." *Fuck.* I'd opted out of a no-fuss wedding. What the hell was wrong with me?

But when Kyle smiled and his chest swelled, there was no doubt in my mind. I'd made the right decision.

Wrapping his arms around me, he crushed me against his pecs. "Do you know how happy you've made me?"

"Yeah, I do." I swept his wet hair off his forehead, then clutched a handful of his hair at the back of his head and gave it a gentle shake. "If you stop changing our wedding plans, I'll be happy."

"Deal." He hooked his hand underneath my knees and pulled me through the warm water onto his lap. As I straddled him, his voice took on a sexy you're-mine tone. "Our day will be perfect. I promise."

"We'll be together. That's all that matters."

"Always." He slid back to the other end of the bath, taking me with him. His voice was nothing but a breathy rasp against my lips. "Can we pick up where we left off? Practice what we can do on our honeymoon?"

Smiling, I touched my lips to his. "I'd like that." I slid my hand between our bodies, took hold of his hard cock, and guided him toward my opening.

"Mmm." He rocked his hips forward and thrust into me. Heat shot up my spine. He kissed me, hard and hot. "God, I love you."

"Love you, too."

Clasping onto the tub on either side of his shoulders, I rode and rocked against him. Taking him in deep, fucking him hard, I pulsed and clenched around him. Water slapped and swirled around our chests with each thrust and drive.

"I can't wait to marry you." His hands skimmed over my arms, my back, my ass. One hand slipped between my legs. His fingers circled and stroked my clit. *Oh yes.*

I rubbed against him. The need for release burned hotter and hotter. My pussy clenched tighter and tighter. "Same."

Opting out of a Vegas wedding was the right thing to do. Having a ceremony was more important to him than me. I didn't want him to have any regrets. We wanted a beach wedding . . . that was what we'd have.

He moaned; the low rumble meandered through my body. "I

love you fucking me." His fingernails scraping down my back set fire to my flesh.

My insides ignited. Every muscle begged more, more, *more*.

Tilting his hips, he closed his eyes. His jaw tensed. "Shit Gem, I can't hold on. Fuck." His head fell back. His body convulsed and jerked. His throbbing cock hit me deep inside as his hot release filled me. He dug his fingers into my hips and tugged me forward. A goofy smile curled across his lips. The friction, the rubbing, the heat, sent me over the edge. My orgasm ripped through me, coursing through my body in quaking waves. Electricity zapped every nerve ending, coiled up my spine and tingled the base of my neck. Goose bumps skipped across my skin.

Panting, I wrapped my arms around his shoulders and kissed him. His cock still throbbed inside me. "Mmm, that was good."

"I can't wait to marry you."

"Yeah? Only two weeks to go." I smiled, my lips lingering on his, savoring his delicious kisses and the taste of his tongue. But it was getting late. I eased back and waved my spongy fingers at him. "We'd better hop out before we dissolve. We have to meet everyone for dinner."

"Yes, we better." Grinning, he rested his head back on the tub. A blissed-out, *I-don't-want-to-move* contentment filled his gaze.

It was nearly eight. We had to move. I didn't want to be late.

I stood, grabbed his hand, and hauled him to his feet. He helped me out of the bath and wrapped me in a big fluffy white towel. After drying off, we dressed. I slipped on a black mini skirt, shirt and jacket. Kyle, jeans and a T-shirt. Grabbing my socks and my Jimmy Choo combat boots, I flopped onto the bed to put them on. Like a low blow, the threats returned to the forefront of my mind.

The last letter had said '*See you in Vegas*', but we'd had no security breach and no one had been hurt. We were having dinner in a private room tonight. We flew home early tomorrow. Surely we were safe. Hopefully, Jones would have news for us when we got home. That we could put an end to this scary mess.

I stuffed my feet into my boots and zipped them up.

For the first time, thoughts of my wedding set off a wave of light, fluttering butterflies in my tummy, not ones that swirled like a tornado.

I pictured the white sand beneath my feet. My beautiful dress. Kyle, all sexy and handsome in a suit. The gentle breeze teasing his hair. Good things lay ahead. I had to focus on them. Focus on my future with Kyle.

With just under two weeks until the wedding, surely nothing else could go wrong.

Chapter 13

KYLE

Hanging out at home with Gemma and our four best friends was exactly how I wanted to celebrate turning twenty-six. We'd been back from Vegas for two days, hitting rehearsals hard for our last show this coming Saturday. Then we had time off.

The countdown to the wedding was on.

Three days until our last show. Six days until we flew out. Nine days until Gemma and I tied the knot.

Lexi and Hayden sat on the floor next to the coffee table, which was covered in bottles of beer, wine, and spicy Chinese dishes they'd brought for dinner. Kara and Hunter lounged on the adjacent sofa with drinks in hand. Gemma sat next to me, strumming softly on her old guitar. The one her dad had given her. The fragrant aroma of ginger and sweet sauces lingered in the air. Everyone was chilling . . . except me.

I had so much to do for the wedding—finalize the charter plane, confirm catering, send the final wedding details to our guests. So far, all they'd been told was to be ready to fly somewhere in the world on a date in early October. It had blown my mind that Gemma had turned down a Vegas wedding. I'd thought a quick no-fuss service would've been what she wanted. But I'd gotten it wrong. Maybe it was bad timing after the festival and parties. I hated I couldn't read her like I normally could. Something wasn't right.

Since her bachelorette party, her headache had lingered along with her lethargy. At rehearsal today, she'd gone through the set list twice and called it quits. No matter how much I'd sensed it and how much I'd asked her what was wrong, she'd brushed me off. Her laughter was shallow. She kept gazing off into the distance. She'd lost her sassy spark. Was it wedding jitters or something else? At what point did I lose my shit? She could tell me anything. Nothing would change the way I felt about her.

I spiked a piece of chicken onto my fork and waved it in front of her mouth, but she pursed her lips and shook her head. She smiled, but her eyes remained dull and gloomy, like she was dead tired. Maybe she was. She'd woken me early to make love—the perfect way to wake up. The perfect birthday present. The new Range Rover in the garage—the perfect surprise. I tossed the fork down, then smoothed my hand over the back of her hair and massaged her head. "Hey. You haven't eaten much. Do you have another headache?"

She closed her eyes. Every muscle in her jaw tensed. "For the tenth time, I'm fine."

"Gem, you haven't been well since Vegas." I lowered my voice so only she could hear. "I think you should go to the doctor."

"No." She tilted her head back and groaned. "Can you please drop it?"

I held up my hands, defeated. "All right. All right. I'm just concerned."

Hayden chewed and swallowed his mouthful of fried rice. "Kyle, you guys have had a huge week—the festival, the parties, the travel. Hell, I'm still recovering from Vegas. Leave Gem alone." Sympathy warmed his tone. "You're allowed to be tired, babe. Ignore Kyle."

Hunter smirked and refilled Gemma's wine glass. "Gem's tired because she keeps fucking Kyle. I busted them at rehearsal today. I'm bad, but these two . . . damn."

Heat rose in my cheeks. Yeah, that had been the perfect

birthday bonus. Slipping into the back office during the break with Gemma was hot. She'd instigated it. But it was different, like she'd needed to be close, connected, to burn out her frustrations. Still, who was I to deny her an orgasm? As I curled my hand around her thigh, I jutted my chin toward Hunter. "Jealous it wasn't you and Kar?"

"Nope." Hunter took a large gulp of his wine. "We did it this morning. Twice." Cocky arrogance swayed through his tone. He twisted his wrist and glanced at his watch. "And before the day is out, might get another round or two in."

Kara blushed as red as the sweet chili sauce on the coffee table. But she arched one thin eyebrow and gave Hunter a saucy smile. "If you do what you did to me this morning, I'm so there."

Strumming a chord on her guitar, Gemma giggled. "What did he do?"

Hunter flicked his tongue like a python and took a quick sip of his beer. "I ate her out until she screamed my name."

I chuckled and shook my head. Hunter had no filter. Not ever.

Kara play-punched Hunter in the thigh. "Do you have to give them details?"

Stealing a sideways glance at Gemma, I gave her a *I-so-wanna-do-that-to-you* look. She scraped her teeth across her bottom lip with a yes-please glint in her eye. *Sweet.*

She put her guitar down and entwined her fingers with mine, resting our hands against her leg. "Kar, we have no secrets. You should know that by now."

No secrets? My chest cinched. Why was she keeping something from me? What couldn't she tell me?

Hunter dipped his head from side to side. "Gem's right. Get used to it, babe. But . . ." He clutched his crotch. Grimaced and wiggled as if in agony. "We better stop talking about fucking because it's making me hard."

"I'll change the subject." Lexi dished stir-fried chicken onto her plate, grabbed a spring roll, and licked her fingers. "I'm so looking forward to the wedding. My new cameras are set. Hayds has hated me taking photos of him, testing out the settings in different lighting."

Hayden stabbed his chopsticks at her. "It's weird being a fucking model. But, hey . . . what are awesome roommates for? I'm glad I could help."

Hayden was totally model worthy. Tall, tanned, striking platinum eyes, and with cheek bones even I was envious of. He was an incredible drummer, playing for his own band, The Saylors, a show on Broadway, and did part-time sessional work at an indie studio. Hunter, Gemma, and I had tried so hard to give Hayden's band a helping hand to find success in this ruthless music industry, but their lead singer, Kilt, was a dick. Kilt was convinced The Saylors would make it on their own. So be it. We could only do so much. I hated seeing talent like Hayden's go to waste. I hoped one day soon he'd get his break.

"Awesome," I sank deeper into the sofa. "Everything is booked for the big day. Only thing left is flowers. Tulips in Belize have been hard to track down."

Gemma swept her bangs off her face, tucked her hair behind her ear. "We don't need flowers. It's too hot. Tulips will just wilt."

Oh shit. I hadn't thought of that. "Don't care. They are your favorite flower. I'll fly them in if I have to."

Her eyes widened. "Don't be stupid."

"Gem, you'll have tulips." I typed a reminder into my phone to see if it was possible to fly tulips in.

"Do I get to have any say in our wedding?" Her playful tone rippled with a touch of bite.

I ignored it. "Nope. All you have to do is turn up."

She clambered onto her knees, caught me across the shoulders, and pushed me down onto the sofa. She straddled my hips and pinned my hands beside my head. "You're crazy. You know that?"

"For you? Yep." I wrapped my arms around her and drew her in for a kiss.

The intercom by the front door buzzed. I slapped Gemma on the ass so I could get up. I jumped from my seat and strode over to answer the call. On the screen, caller ID displayed 'Reception.' I pressed the talk button. "Hey, Marcus. S'up?"

"Sorry to disturb you, but I just missed a courier delivering an envelope for you. Would you like me to bring it up?"

"Umm…" I grimaced, glancing at the wall clock by the kitchen. 9:43 p.m. "It's a bit late, isn't it? We aren't expecting anything."

Was it another birthday surprise? I doubted it. Gemma had given me a car and custom-made cuff links in the shape of bass guitars from Leonard's Jewelers. *So cool.* Hunter and my friends had bought me expensive bottles of whiskey and dinner. Surely there was nothing else.

"It's from a courier company I don't recognize. There's no sender information on the back. It's just addressed to you."

My stomach twisted into a knot. What if it was another threat?

"Do you want me to notify your security or the detectives?" A hint of anxiousness wobbled in Marcus's tone. Sam and Jones had debriefed the staff working at the apartment complex about our situation. To be aware of anyone suspicious loitering around the place.

What if the letter contained anthrax or something similar? *No.* Psycho Letter Writer wanted me alive. The envelope was addressed to me, not Gemma. I swallowed the dry lump in my throat. My heart thudded too fast. *Crap.* "No, Marcus. Whatever it is, I'll deal with it. Send it up."

A few minutes later, I opened the door and took the delivery from Marcus. My hands trembled. The light and flimsy letter-sized courier envelope looked as if it was empty other than the outline of an envelope embossing the surface. A wave of bile swirled through my guts. "Thanks, Marcus."

I turned and met Gemma's gaze. Her eyes locked onto the envelope. Nausea flooded my gut. I knew it was another threat even before I opened it.

"Kyle?" Gemma rose like a ghost from the sofa and drifted over to my side. She hugged her arms around herself, and tears welled in her eyes. "You think that's from—"

Everyone gathered around the dining table. Silent. All eyes were on the packet in my hand. With fumbling fingers, I ripped it open. Out fell a pale pink envelope.

Gemma clasped her hand over her mouth, muffling her gasp.

My eyes glassed over, and I struggled to draw breath. "This was delivered to our home? What the fuck?"

I tore open the letter. With a shaky voice, I read out loud:

KYLE, YOU HAVEN'T LISTENED.
I'VE DONE NOTHING BUT LOVE YOU.
NOW IT'S TIME TO SHOW YOU HOW MUCH.
YOU ARE MINE. MINE. MINE!
I CAN'T LIVE WITHOUT YOU. I WON'T LIVE WITHOUT YOU.
GEMMA WILL PAY.
THAT WHORE DOESN'T LOVE YOU LIKE I DO.
SHE DOESN'T DESERVE TO LIVE.
WE WILL BE TOGETHER.
I PROMISE.
P.S. VEGAS WAS FUN!
P.P.S. HAPPY BIRTHDAY.

Gemma's breath sawed through the air like a lumberjack's blade. She clutched at her chest and grabbed onto a chair.

"Oh, shit." Kara's face turned from porcelain pink to pasty white. "Who the fuck is this bitch?"

I grabbed my cell phone off the sofa and called Jones. "We got another letter. It was delivered to our home."

"Okay. Okay." Jones's monotone drawl was back-loaded with *fuck-I-don't-need-this-crap* attitude. I may have woken him up, but I didn't give a shit. "Call your security team to meet at your apartment. I'll be there in thirty minutes."

After hanging up, I drew Gemma into a hug and held her tight against my chest. She trembled in my embrace and clutched my shirt. Her heartbeat hammered against mine. "Kyle, this has to stop."

"I know, baby. It will." I closed my eyes and rested my cheek on top of her head. I'd thought our home was safe, but the person threatening us knew where we lived. My pulse throbbed in my temples. Did we have enough security to stay safe? Had I done enough to protect Gemma?

I wanted to run. Run to the rooftop and scream for this to end. Run after whoever it was and take them down. Just get away from here. Run away with Gemma.

"Hey, guys?" Lexi came over and gave us a hug. "Not sure we can be much help. I have an early start. Do you want us to stay or are you okay if Hayds and I head home?"

"You go. We'll be alright." Gemma led them to the door. "We'll keep you updated."

Lexi and Hayden took off and left us to deal with the detectives. Sam, Chester, and Mick arrived within thirty minutes, and Jones and Morris, moments later. Everyone stood around the dining room table, taking turns to read the letter.

Jones stood with his feet shoulder-width apart, his arms folded, and nonchalance smeared across his face. I clenched and unclenched my fist. What would it take for this guy to treat our case with urgency? I hated using my celebrity status for priority treatment, but I'd play that card if I had to. Demanding a new head detective on the case would be my first move.

Jones stepped forward and slipped the letter into an evidence bag. "They're getting desperate. Delivering this to your home was a mistake. It should be easy to track. We'll contact the courier company and find out who sent it."

"They've avoided being traced so far." Gemma slumped against my arm. The dark circles under her eyes were more evident under the downlighting. "What makes you think this isn't beyond their expertise?"

Jones' lips curled into a cocky smirk. "I've dealt with many stalkers. Eventually, they stuff up. Let's hope this is the time."

Great. Jones's smug tone reminded me of my dad's—full of himself, arrogant asshole.

Thoughts of Taylah loomed to the forefront of my mind. She'd been in Brooklyn, Central Park, Vegas. Tracked me down at our hotel. A shudder slithered down my spine as I caught Jones's level stare. "Are you one hundred percent certain it isn't Taylah? She's been everywhere lately."

Morris cut in, scratching his well-groomed stubble. "Other than her being a nuisance and a fan, we don't have any evidence to link her to the letters. No fingerprints, no witnesses, or security footage."

I leaned forward and gripped the edge of the table. "It's not good enough." My voice sliced through my teeth. "She's a suspect. I don't want her near us."

My friends nodded, agreeing.

Jones sighed and rested his hip against a chair. "I'm not convinced it's her. But given the heightened circumstances and no other leads, we can issue her with a formal restraining order. Ban her from upcoming shows and events. Stop her from contacting you or coming near your home. If it's her, the legal warning should be enough to put an end to the letters."

"It fucking better." I drove my fingers through my hair, then waved toward the door. "What if she gets into our building, past the front door and foyer? What if the warning has the opposite effect?" My heart faltered at the thought.

Sam folded his burly arms. "Your place is like Fort Knox. No one unauthorized can get in. I know it's scary, but she wants to intimidate you. She thinks she's winning."

"She is." Gemma's voice quaked. "What about our show on Saturday night? How the hell are we supposed to perform in front of a crowd knowing she's desperate?"

Hunter lifted his chin. A dark storm, loaded with concern, swirled through his eyes. "Gem, you're more important than a fucking show. Do you want to cancel?"

I blinked. *Wow!* For Hunter to suggest canceling meant he was worried. He lived to be on stage.

I jammed my hands on my hips and bowed my head. Had it come to this? Canceling shows? I looked up at Gemma. A cocktail of fear, hate, fiery fight, and frustration swirled in their depths. "It's up to you, Gem. We could take off for a few days, go out to the mountains, somewhere where no one knows we exist. We could go to the beach house, but if the stalker knows we live here, they might know about our place out there, too."

"I recommend you stay put," Jones butted in. "You have better security here."

"So what?" I threw Jones a cold stare. "You want us to stay locked up in our home and do nothing?"

Jones jabbed his finger against the table. "My advice is the same as it was at our first meeting. Make sure your trusted network of friends and family know of the situation. Inform them to be on the lookout for anyone suspicious, and until we resolve this, be diligent with your security measures."

"We're doing that." Steam shot through my veins. I'd had enough of Jones's blasé approach. "We need to do more. This is code red. Do you need more resources? Should we hire private investigators?" I shoved the dining chair against the table. "You need to convince me you're doing everything to catch this psycho. Because from where I'm standing, not a lot seems to be happening."

I didn't want to lose my cool, but I didn't want Gemma to get hurt. It terrified me more than anything. I was desperate to protect her. Catch this stalker and lock them away for good.

Redness flushed Jones's neck. A muscle ticked in his jaw. His gaze darted toward our security team, then returned to me. Resting his hands on the table, Jones leaned forward. "While I feel that I have much more serious cases to work on, trust me, you and your A-list friends are a priority. Morris is working with forensics. Marshall is monitoring your social media. I'm investigating every lead, every bit of CCTV footage, and interviewing every hint of a suspect. We're not sitting around, twiddling our thumbs, drinking coffee, or eating doughnuts. Got it?" Jones picked up the evidence bag with the letter in it and headed for the door. He turned to Sam and flicked his hand toward me. "Keep this one under control. We don't need anyone to do anything stupid."

Sam huffed. "I'll do my best."

Morris scurried out the door after Jones. I couldn't close it behind them quickly enough.

"Kyle?" Gemma snapped the second the door clicked shut. "You shouldn't piss Jones off like that."

"Someone needed to light a fire under his ass." I stepped toward Sam, Mick, and Chester. "Can we hire a private investigator?"

Hunter grabbed bottles of water from the fridge and handed them out. "Is that really necessary? Jones said he was doing everything."

Sam cracked the lid off his water bottle. "I'm with Kyle on this. Jones seems to be dragging his feet. I'll make some calls. See if one of our guys can take this case on. But one thing I strongly recommend is to avoid being out in public over the next few days. Let's not take any chances this close to the wedding. I think you should also seriously consider canceling Saturday's show. Lie low until after your vacation."

"Cancel?" Gemma closed her eyes and pressed her lips together, hard. She took a few slow, deep breaths, then slumped her shoulders. "Can we think about it overnight?" Her voice was soft but strained. "Let's not freak Sophie and Kate out with a PR nightmare just yet."

I wrapped my arm around her and held her close. "Okay. We'll sleep on it. No rush."

The only thing I wanted to rush was the end of the threats. Gemma would mull over canceling, over-analyzing every pro and con. I just wanted to focus on the wedding and leave these stresses behind. After everyone left, I had to convince her the show didn't matter. Not to me. Nor Hunter. She was all we cared about. I might be in for an uphill battle, but it was one I had to win.

Gemma came first. Always would. No matter what.

Somehow I'd get my way.

No compromises. Not this time.

Chapter 14

GEMMA

My home had become a prison, a mental mind-fuck, one I desperately wanted to escape. I could perform in front of thousands of people, speak my mind, stand up for what I wanted, and inspire others. But a few threatening letters had derailed me.

Swiveling back and forth on an old chair in my music room, I strummed my acoustic guitar. The low, slow chords filled the room. It was two o'clock in the afternoon. Today's rehearsal had been canceled. Kyle was out running errands and getting a haircut. I was home alone, and the day had been nothing short of unhinged.

The letter delivered to our home last night had frayed my grip on sanity. Sophie's call around lunchtime had made it even more threadbare. Two more threats had arrived at her office, postmarked a day apart, but had been delivered on the same day. After Sophie read the letters out, each one more violent and horrific, I told her to send them straight to Jones. It sickened me to my stomach, but I didn't want Kyle to know. I didn't want him to worry and become more fanatical about my safety than he already had.

I was over it.

Walking out my front door without security was impossible. The mounting threats had rattled me. I just wanted the threats to end so I could get my life back.

My eyelids drifted shut. Usually, having the place to myself was bliss, but now the stillness and the silence hovered with an eerie edge. Every rattle in the air-conditioning vents, every gust of wind against a window, every creak of the floor made me halt. Wait. Listen. Check every corner of the room.

Fuck.

This is crap.

I couldn't wait for vacation. My honeymoon would be the perfect opportunity to put the threats behind me, wind down, and start afresh. A much-needed retreat to regather my strength. With Kyle.

Our wedding couldn't come soon enough.

As I glided my hand along the neck of my guitar and plucked at the strings, I hummed a tune. *Hmm mm mm m mm mmm mm.*

> *Not afraid to admit I'm scared of the dark*
> *Not afraid to admit I don't like being apart*

The front door's keypad beeped. The door opened.

Creeeak.

I froze, held my breath, and waited for footsteps.

Waited. Waited.

Waited.

"Gem, I'm home."

My breath rushed from my lungs. *Kyle. Thank goodness. I'm such an idiot.*

I rolled my shoulders and stretched my neck from side to side to release the twisting tension. Working my fingers over the frets, more lyrics came to mind.

> *All night I lie awake thinking of you*
> *When I'm alone there's nothing I'd rather do*

A riff jumped into my head. I worked the strings, the chords, and played different combinations until the tune took form. I repeated and tweaked it again until I loved the sound, the tone, the feel. I grabbed a sheet of music paper off the desk and scribbled the notes and lyrics onto it, then played the tune once more.

Am I foolish for feeling this way?
Am I foolish for loving you each day?

Warmth filled the air and wrapped around me. *Kyle.* I smiled and didn't look up. He stood in the doorway, leaning against the doorjamb, watching, listening.

I didn't want to stop. The music had taken over me. I didn't want to lose the melody flowing from my fingertips.

I slowed down the tune, dragging out each strum. Kyle slid into the room, picked up my electric Fender, plugged it in, and sat on the stool next to me. He focused on my hands. Read my notes. Got absorbed by the tune, just like I had.

He positioned his fingers over the strings and struck a couple of notes. Within a few minutes, he mimicked me perfectly. The long, drawn-out electric sound blended seamlessly with the acoustic. Soulful like the blues, sad like love lost, slow-burning, like longing for your soul mate. It matched my mindset perfectly. Sweet but twisted, like a romance novel entwined with a psychological thriller.

Lyrics rolled off my tongue.

We have a love, the crazy kind
We have a love that blows my mind
I don't want to scare you, but it's so intense
I'll always be with you until the end
'Til the end

I played harder. My heart constricted and ached. I had to get these words out. Words that had corrupted my thoughts. I pictured my stalker, how obsessed they were with Kyle. Was I just like them? Manic in some way? *Obsessed?* I loved Kyle so much. The thought of losing him was unbearable. Inconceivable.

I'd do anything for him. I played faster, strumming, striking, and shredding out notes. My breath heaved in time with the tune. The grooves in Kyle's brow grew deeper.

More words rolled off my tongue.

> *Those eyes on you, when you walk into a room*
> *That's me watching everything you do*
> *Have I gone crazy? Am I out of my mind?*
> *Can't go to sleep without you by my side*
> *All through the night, and throughout the day*
> *You're all I want, yeah I'm here to stay*
>
> *Am I foolish for feeling this way?*
> *Am I foolish for loving you each day?*

Every breath hurt. Kyle just let me play, following my lead.

> *Don't want to scare you*
> *Our love is so intense*
> *I'll always be with you*
> *'Til the end. The very end*

I stopped and stared at Kyle. A tear slipped down my cheek. The concern darkening his eyes tore at my heart. I didn't want him to worry. I just needed to vent via music. Let him know how crazy in love I was.

He brushed my tear away with the pad of his thumb, his touch warm and soothing. "Feel better?"

"Yeah. I needed some therapy. Churning out music and pouring out some stupid lyrics always does the trick."

"They're not stupid." He skimmed my pages. "They're a little dark, but we can turn them into something awesome."

"You don't like my words?"

"I do." He set the guitar out of the way and kissed my lips. "Because I feel the same way about you. We are beautifully intense; our love is off-the-charts scary, and I'm here for you no matter what. I love you. Always."

Tears burned at the back of my eyes and threatened to fall. He could be so wonderful and understanding one minute, overbearing and suffocating the next. I should tell him about the new threatening letters. It went against every grain in my soul to not do so, but I couldn't have any more shackles weighing me down. I didn't want him to worry even more. Nothing else could be done. So there was no point . . . *right?*

I just wanted to keep the peace. Keep him happy, and focus on our wedding.

He clutched my hand and entwined our fingers. "I know this isn't the best of times to bring this up, but we need to talk about the wedding. Something's come up."

"It's okay. You don't have to tiptoe around the subject anymore. As long as there are no more changes, I'm cool."

Before Kyle could say another word, my cell phone rang. My ringtone "Evil Woman" by Electric Light Orchestra sent it vibrating across the desk. *Great! My mother!*

Kyle glared at my cell phone as if it was pure poison. "Why's she calling? She's not supposed to do that."

My mom, desperate to feed off our lives, was a parasite. The lowest of the low creatures on earth. I could let the call go through to voicemail. But that would only make her try harder to contact me. *Ugh!* "We've been in Vegas. Photographed everywhere. There is gossip online about what we did at our parties. It'll be driving her insane, wanting to know the inside scoop."

Kyle puffed through his nose. "She's a piece of work."

"She certainly is." I sighed and swiped the screen, putting the call on speaker. Best to get this over and done with. "Mom, hi. How are you?"

"Gemma." Janine's shrill voice grated down my spine like metal teeth on steel. "That bitch of an assistant of yours hasn't put my calls through for two days."

God, I loved Bec. "She's doing her job. She's paid to keep people like you away." Ever since Mom had tried to sell me out to the tabloids *again*, I had severed all ties with her except for a fine thread of communication. She was lucky if I called once a month.

"You went to Vegas?" Mom's voice pitched higher. "For your bachelorette party? And I wasn't invited? I'm hurt, Gemma. Really hurt."

I coughed. "No, you're not." I couldn't keep the sting out of my voice. "You're pissed because you missed out on a free trip, expensive champagne, and 5-Star accommodation. Or was it the chance to have your photo with me splashed across the Internet?"

Every time we'd talked, I wished she'd apologize for the awful things she'd done over the years—from cruel neglect to callous betrayal—but it never happened. Our relationship had just gotten worse. During our last tour, when I'd made an effort to catch up in Florida, she'd hired a photographer to take photos of us in a restaurant and sold them for money . . . *again*. Her latest fiasco was an online betting game to see how long my relationship with Kyle would last.

I owed my mother nothing. Not even the time of day.

Kyle scratched the tip of his chin, his voice low so only I could hear. "I'd say she wanted both."

Janine's tone took on a prying, slithering edge. "So . . . that means the wedding is soon. I haven't received my invitation yet. When is it so I can clear my calendar? It must be in two or three weeks, right?"

I dug my fingers into my thigh. There it was—the truth. She'd called to find out the wedding details. So she could tip off the paparazzi? *No. Fucking. Way.* "I've told you. You're not invited."

"But I'm your mother." Janine's voice ricocheted through my ears and grated on my nerves like an out-of-tune violin.

Kyle leaned forward, his jaw tense. "Janine, can you honestly say you wouldn't sell pictures to the highest bidder, post the details online about the venue, and leak information about the date?"

Silence.

Then more silence.

"I thought not." Kyle sat back on the stool, rolled half a foot backward, and hit the wall. "Sorry, but that's why you're not, and will not, be invited to the wedding."

Warmth flooded my chest. He knew exactly how I felt. I'd

tried for years to have a civil relationship with my mother, partly at Kyle's insistence. After he lost his parents, he didn't want me to have any regrets about not having her in my life . . . now I wished she wasn't. Her continual narcissism, toxic belittling, and ruthless pursuit of selling anything personal about me and my friends to gossip magazines had become too hurtful. Too cruel. I could never trust her, not with anything. The less we had contact, the better.

A metallic *tink, tink, tink* came through the speaker. Mom, no doubt, tapped her latest gaudy dress rings against her phone. "I should be. And what I do with my personal photos is my business."

"No. It's not," I snapped.

"I'm devastated you don't want me there." Janine sulked. "It's disrespectful."

My mother didn't know the meaning of the word. How could someone be so spiteful and hate their child? Want to make money off them? The hole deep inside my chest ached—a reminder my parents had never wanted me or loved me. "Disrespectful? That's a joke. Be honest, Mom. How much will you make off our wedding photos? Some shitty gossip site or magazine will be tempting you with cold, hard cash."

"No, they're not." She was such a bad liar. Within a single breath, her voice turned sweet as honey. "I just want to come to my daughter's wedding."

"Bullshit." I balled my fist, cutting off the circulation to my fingers. "How much?"

"Oh . . . it's . . . it's just a few dollars. It's nothing."

"How much?" My words cut through my clenched teeth.

"Five hundred thousand."

"Are you fucking kidding me?" My mother's audacity spiked my blood pressure. "And that's why you won't be there. I can't trust you. You're not invited. That is final."

I hung up and threw my cell phone onto the desk. My shoulders sank to the floor. I'd gone from playing my heart out with Kyle to feeling less than worthless.

"Hey." Kyle held out his hand. "Come sit with me."

I placed my hand in his. He led me over to the small blue sofa on the far side of the room. He pulled me sideways onto his lap and wound his arms around me. I rested my head against his shoulder. He combed his fingers through my hair in long, slow strokes. "Don't let her get to you. She doesn't fall into the realm of human decency. She may be your blood, but she's not family. You and I are. Hunt is. Our connection is greater than any DNA. Remember that."

"Yeah. I do." I drew circles on his chest. We had an unfathomable bond. Life kept testing us, but we'd survived, grown closer, and had become inseparable. But with some stalker wanting me dead, security at a max, and letters arriving more frequently, I didn't know how long I could hold on before I fell apart.

Love caused nothing but problems and I was scared it would destroy us.

I nuzzled into the small of Kyle's neck and inhaled his woodsy scent. It soothed my twisted thoughts, buried them deep into the back of my mind. He was my antidote to any venom in my life. My happily ever after couldn't come fast enough.

"What did you need to speak to me about before we got rudely interrupted?"

"Two things." Stuffing his hand into the back pocket of my jeans, he cupped my ass. "One, it's about the show this weekend. And two, the wedding."

Both had kept me awake last night. I'd heard Kyle on the phone this morning, talking to Hunter. It twisted every sinewy tendon in my arms into knots, but I had to put our safety first. "You want to cancel this Saturday?"

"Yeah." The anguish in his voice reflected my sentiments. "Hunt agrees, so it's two against one."

"No, it's not." The nerves in my neck pinched. This wasn't a contest. "I hate having to cancel, but I agree with you. Let's just focus on getting married."

A sexy smile played across his lips. "I like the sound of that."

"We'd better call Kate and Sophie." Canceling two days before a show wasn't fun. The fallout and speculation why would create a media frenzy. But safety came first. I patted his arm for him to release me, but he didn't let go.

"There's one more thing."

Crap. This wouldn't be good news.

I sank into his embrace. I'd hidden the new threats from him, written a crazy song, my mother had rung, and I'd had to cancel a show. What else could go wrong? "What is it?"

He played with a strand of my hair, curling it around his fingertips. The gentle tugs tweaked my scalp. "We have a minor hiccup. Regarding the legalities of getting married."

I jerked my chin back and quizzed him. "Are you an illegal alien and I can't marry you?"

"No." His eyes glistened as he smiled.

"You're already married?"

"No." Chuckling, he shook his head, but then seriousness washed over his face. "I haven't received the documents from the Belize wedding officiant. So we either have to stay on the mainland for three days before we can apply for a marriage license . . . or . . . Richard can expedite a special application for us, but we would still need to sign documents in Belize . . . or . . . we head to the city clerk's office . . . or . . . one of the lawyers in Richard's office is an officiant and could legally marry us before we go."

I shot upright. Holy shit, that was a lot of options. "Marry? Before we go?" *Some small snag, alright!*

He rubbed his hand up and down my back, waiting for my reply. Daydreams of saying 'I do,' filled my head. Our wedding was so close. "If we have to stay on the mainland, we'll need extra security, risk getting seen. I just want to get out to the island as quickly as possible, undetected. Let's just sign the legal paperwork here and get it out of the way. Saying our vows on the beach will still be the moment we marry."

Damn it. We should've gotten married in Vegas.

His hands stopped. "So . . . here before we go?"

He'd be disappointed his plans had been messed up, but considering our options, this was the best choice. Less hassle.

This news about the wedding was good news.

I cupped his cheek and swiped my thumb over his fine stubble.

"Yes. I get to call you husband sooner rather than later."

His gaze softened, and he nodded slowly. "Name the day. I'll make it happen."

Butterflies swarmed in my stomach. To hell with threats, work, and worry. They'd muddied my thoughts for long enough. It would be a relief to forget about them for a while, hopefully for good. Kyle adored me and I adored him. With our show canceled, this would be perfect. It would give us a few more days to relax before we set off for Belize.

I slid my hands up his chest and linked them behind his neck. I pressed my lips to his. My heart thudded like rapid quick-fire. "Friday. At Richard's. Let's get married."

Chapter 15

GEMMA

I woke to the smell of coffee, pancakes, and bacon, the clatter of plates and cutlery, and the sizzle of frying food. *Mmm.* Kyle was in the kitchen downstairs, cooking up a storm. Stretching my arms over my head, I smiled and leaped out of bed. My belly rumbled with hunger and rippled with nerves. Good nerves. The kind where you wished time would fly by at sonic speed, but no matter how busy you kept yourself, the clock ticked by at a tortoise pace. I glanced at the blue digital clock on my nightstand. 8:03 a.m. Seven hours to go. Today, at three o'clock in Richard's office, I'd marry Kyle . . . legally, on paper.

I only had to go to Nina's Bridal at twelve-thirty.

Come home and change.

Head downtown.

Get married.

Easy.

I grabbed my cell phone off the nightstand and skipped down the stairs. I dashed across the floor to the kitchen and jumped into Kyle's wide-open arms. Wrapping my legs around his waist, I kissed him.

"Good morning." His eyes shimmered with saucy, sexy love. He slipped his hands underneath the hem of my T-shirt, his fingertips hot against my cool skin. "I have to admit; my Pearl Jam shirt looks much better on you than me."

Any shirt of his was comfortable to sleep in, but this one was my favorite.

He kissed my lips and placed me on my feet. He grabbed the flipper off the counter and rushed over to the cooktop to flip a pancake. His gorgeous smile brightened his entire face. "Today's the big day. You ready to sign your life away?"

"Yep." I put my cell phone down onto the counter, grabbed the cup of steaming coffee waiting for me, and took a sip. "Now we get two weddings—one with just our friends and one in Belize. It's a total win."

"Yeah, I know." He threw me a playful wink.

The wedding hadn't quite gone to plan, but we had a backup.

This was a good change. One I could handle.

I blew into my cup of hot coffee, taking in everything laid out on the granite countertop—berries, syrup, cutlery, napkins, pastries. Bacon and pancakes were on the stove. Kyle had prepared a feast. My cooking was nowhere near as sensational as his. "Can I do anything to help?"

"Nope." He placed a pancake onto the stack beside the cooktop. "Sit. Relax. Enjoy your coffee. These will be ready in a few minutes."

"If you insist." As I slid onto the kitchen stool, my cell phone vibrated. Kara's name lit the screen.

I tapped my phone to answer the call and put it on loudspeaker. "Hey Kar, what's up?"

"You wouldn't believe what's happened." The stress in Kara's voice jolted my pulse. I took a steady breath and found my calm. I wouldn't let anything get to me today.

"Tom Ford wants to meet this morning, not on Monday." Kara spoke so fast, I had to concentrate. "If I don't go, they're unavailable for another month. You know how long I've been trying to get them onboard to be a supplier for you guys. I have to go."

Is that all? I thought there'd been a catastrophe. I let out a relieved breath and smiled. "That's okay, Kar. I can go to Nina's by myself."

The several fittings I'd had at Nina's bridal shop over the past few weeks, slotted in around rehearsal times and travel, had been worth it. Deflecting Kyle's suspicions about why I had to have so many in-store visits was about to pay off. My wedding dress for Belize was ready . . . and so was my dress for today. The outfit I'd planned to wear to dinner on the night we arrived in Belize would be perfect for our nuptials at Richard's office.

"You sure?" Kara's voice swung with stress. "Call Lexi. See if she can go with you."

"She can't." I shook my head. "She's working until about one-thirty so she can finish her articles that are due. She'll meet us at Richard's office."

"Gem." Kyle waved a piece of crispy bacon at me. "I'll go with you."

"You can't. You have to pick up your suits with the guys."

He shrugged his shoulder. "I'll change our appointment to Monday."

"No, you can't do that." Kara blurted. Time was limited over the next few days before we flew to Belize. "Stacey at BOSS is swamped with fittings for awards season. You can't change the time. She'll kill me. The suits are done. Just try them on. Everything should be perfect. And didn't you want new ties for this afternoon?"

That pulled Kyle up. "Shit. Fine. We'll go." The corner of his mouth tweaked into a half smile. "But I'd sooner go with Gem."

I gripped my coffee cup tighter. The fine line between Kyle being loving and adorable and him being overbearing and obsessive about my safety blurred. With the threats hanging over our heads, I understood his concerns. Hell, I was always on edge constantly. But I'd have security with me. There was nothing to worry about.

I dug my nails into my palm but kept my voice switched onto sweet. "Don't be silly, Kyle." He didn't need to drop everything to be with me or see my dress before the wedding. Wasn't that bad luck? Good thing I wasn't superstitious. But to be on the safe side, Kara would mind my dress until Belize, so Kyle couldn't sneak a peek. "And Kar, don't stress. I'll be fine."

"Are you sure?" Kara asked.

I dragged my fingers down my face, then rubbed my eyes instead of tearing my hair out. I was over everyone's apprehensions. "Yes. Go." Kara had been working overtime with Tom Ford's team to finalize a supply contract, and they'd hinted at wanting to do an advertising campaign with us. That would be fun. There's no way I'd deny her this opportunity to meet them. "You go schmooze, girl. Have some fun."

"Okay." Relief flooded through Kara's tone. "The meeting's at eleven-thirty. It should only go for an hour. I'll call you when I've finished. I'll be back at your place by one to get ready."

"Sounds like a plan. Love you." I ended the call and put my cup down.

Kyle threw me a wary glance as he placed the bacon onto a paper towel-covered dish. "You need to go with someone."

My forehead ached. I could go pick up a fucking dress without being handheld. Everyone was busy at work. I didn't want anybody to see my dress before Belize. "I'm not calling anyone. Chester will be with me." Not having Kara with me would fizzle out the element of fun, but I wouldn't disrupt anyone else's plans. "My appointment won't even go for an hour. I'll go straight there and come home to get ready. I'll meet you at Richard's, as planned."

Kyle's brow furrowed; any deeper and there'd be a new Grand Canyon. The tendons on the side of his neck strained as he finished cooking and rinsed the skillet in the sink.

Less than a dozen people—our four closest friends, plus Bec, Sophie, and Kate, and our security team—knew we were getting married today. As long as our fans didn't catch wind of what we were doing, and the paparazzi didn't follow us, everything should go off without a hitch. Since we'd come home from Vegas, there'd been a swarm of gossip-mongering cameramen with long-range lenses loitering around our apartment building. The online entertainment news sites had been flooded with speculation about my health—was I ill? Pregnant? On the verge of a breakdown? *Hmm.* Breakdown might be close to the truth if I couldn't get my life back to normal.

Stupid threats. I'm over them.

The smell of sweet pancakes called to me like the Pied Piper had entranced me with his flute. My mouth watered as Kyle dished up warm plates of pancakes covered in a mix of blueberries, raspberries, and strawberries, laid out with a side of crunchy bacon, drizzled in golden maple syrup. *Yum!*

He grabbed our plates and cutlery and headed over to the table. Plonking them down onto the surface, he fell into his chair. He puffed at his hair, clearly not happy.

I rolled my eyes. *Men!* I grabbed the bottle of syrup and joined him.

He picked up his knife and fork and jabbed them against the table. "Is there no one else who can go with you? For moral support and extra security?"

"Stop worrying." I reached over and clutched his arm. "I'm not about to do anything stupid." I picked up my cutlery and gave him a cheeky smile. "Or are you stressed I won't turn up this afternoon? Maybe I'm the one who should be freaking out." I stabbed a piece of my pancake with my fork and waved it toward him. "Should I be worried about you? What if you suddenly get cold feet? Change your mind about marrying me? Are you going to leave me stranded, waiting at the altar, desk, table, or whatever it is we're going to sign our marriage certificate on today?"

I was joking, but the horrible notion flared in the back of my mind. A life without him was incomprehensible. I wanted to spend the rest of my days with Kyle. Be his for all time. The count to tying the knot was down to hours.

Kyle flashed his panty-dropping grin. He stole the piece of pancake off my fork and ate it, then leaned over and kissed me. "I'll be there. Nothing will change my mind. I swear." Worry flickered in his dark eyes. "But please be careful today. Promise?"

I stroked the side of his cheek and gave it a firm tap. "Yes. I promise."

***

"I'll see you at two forty-five sharp. Don't be late." Kyle dipped his head and brushed his lips against mine. Soft and gentle. Sweet, and tender.

"I won't be." I blushed under his *you're-so-mine* gaze. *Mmm,* making love for the first time, as his wife, couldn't come soon enough. But there were things to do before that happened. I slapped him on his ass. "Get going. I'll see you in a few hours."

"Love you." He kissed my forehead, grabbed his backpack and the suit he'd wear for our wedding today, and headed toward the door.

"Love you. Bye." I stole one last kiss before he left. I closed the door behind him and let out a long, slow breath. *Wow. In five hours, I'll be Mrs. McIntyre.* Time to kill.

I cruised around my apartment, putting the last of the breakfast dishes in the dishwasher and turned it on. Upstairs, I packed a bag for our getaway tonight—the second surprise I'd planned for Kyle. After conspiring with Bec and security over the phone and via email yesterday, I'd booked a night at the St Regis Hotel. I'd never stayed there before and looked forward to spending our first wedding night there. I sifted and sorted through my closet, my shelves, my dresser. I had no idea what to wear. Nothing seemed like a good option. My cell phone, lying on the bed next to my bag, buzzed. It was Chester.

"Hey, are you here?" I propped my cell phone between my shoulder and ear as I threw a couple of silky shifts Kara made me buy on our last shopping expedition into my overnight bag. "You're early."

"Gemma, I'm stuck in bloody traffic." Chester's voice hissed with fire. "There must be an accident. I've been sitting at the entrance to the tunnel for ten minutes and haven't moved a foot."

Shit. Not a good day for the roads from Brooklyn to be blocked. I glanced at the clock. 11:23 a.m. My appointment at Nina's Bridal was in an hour. I strummed my fingers against my forehead. *What to do. What to do. What to do.* "Chester, that's fine. Just meet me at Nina's. Dylan can take me." My driver was more than capable.

"Yes, I know. But—" Chester drew in a loud breath.

Then . . . there was that pause I hated. My spine stiffened. My blood boiled. "Let me call Sam. I'll see if he can get someone else to cover you."

"Don't be stupid." I yanked a jacket off a hanger so hard my hand shook. "I'll be fine."

"Gemma," Chester snapped. "I'm calling Sam. Stay put until you hear from me or him."

Ugh! This was ridiculous. Before I could argue, he'd ended the call.

I stormed into my bathroom and threw toiletries into a bag, then grabbed a few clothes for Kyle and stuffed them into his overnighter.

Two minutes later, Sam rang.

"Gemma, are you still at home?"

"Yeeees." Just like the good little girl I was supposed to be and doing what I was told. It irked me to no end.

"Good." Sam's deep voice rumbled, full of calm, composure, and clarity. "I'm with Kyle, Hunter, and Hayden. We're caught in a gridlock near One World. We're two blocks from the store. Mick had to drop his kids off at school; he's just left Stamford. He's at least an hour away. The rest of my team are on assignments, so I'll leave the guys with Mick, jump on the subway, and come to you."

I clenched my teeth to stop myself from screaming. I had to go to Nina's, get my dresses, come home. I wasn't going off to wander around the streets of Manhattan by myself. "Sam. Stop. Please." I ripped another T-shirt off a hanger and tossed it onto the bed. "Dylan can take me to Nina's. Chester will meet me there."

"Gemma." Kyle's voice shot down the phone. *What did he do? Rip the phone out of Sam's hand?* "Just call Nina and arrange another time before Tuesday."

"I can't."

"Why not?"

I sliced my fingers into my hair and pulled on it. My throat choked with frustration and fury. Should I tell him the truth? About the dress for today?

No. I wanted to surprise him. I wanted to see his face light up when he saw me. "I'll be okay." I sank onto my bed. I was so over all this bullshit. "I'm not an invalid. I love you. I'll see you soon. I gotta go."

I ended the call and threw on a pair of skinny blue jeans and a DKNY T-shirt, ignoring Kyle's incoming calls. He tried five more times before he stopped. Then he sent me several texts. I ignored them. He had to trust me.

As I loped down the stairs, the intercom rang. Dylan was here. I grabbed my purse and cell phone and headed for the elevator.

I walked across the foyer and out of the building. The moment Dylan saw me; he opened the car door. I dashed toward him and slipped into the back seat. I rested my head against the soft leather. My heartbeat eased as Dylan drove off and headed for SoHo.

Everything was fine.

Everyone had to stop fucking worrying.

Chapter 16

GEMMA

At Nina's, I stood in front of the gilded mirror in the huge upstairs private dressing room. Nina peered over the rim of her gold-winged glasses, examining her beautiful creation. My wedding dress was gorgeous. Just what I wanted. Luxurious, silky, and sexy. But the Swarovski straps were too long and kept falling off my shoulders.

I'd been to a fitting before today. They'd been fine. Maybe I'd lost weight from being stressed about the wedding and the threats. Not what I needed to do.

Nina, with little white gloves on her hands to protect the delicate fabric, grabbed her pins and made the alterations. "Have you got half an hour? I'll take them up for you straightaway. Save you coming back. You can wait in our lounge."

I glanced at my watch. 12:45 p.m. Two hours to go. I'd gotten here ten minutes early, but could I wait, get home, change, and still make Richard's by three o'clock?

Yes. Plenty of time.

It only took ten minutes to get home.

Chester still hadn't arrived. Dylan was waiting down the street by the park for my call to pick me up. "Sure. I'll wait."

"Excellent." Nina unzipped my gown and pulled it over my

head.

As I tugged on my jeans and T-shirt, my cell phone buzzed with a message from Kara.

Kara: Still in meeting. Soooo long. But good.
Won't make it to your place. Sorry.
Meet you at Richard's.

Fuck. That sucked. We'd planned to get ready for this afternoon together. I texted back, my fingers flying across the screen.

Me: OK. See you there. xG

As I pulled on my Vans, excitement flitted through my stomach. I couldn't wait to marry Kyle this afternoon, spend a luxurious night in a fancy hotel, and indulge in some fine food and champagne. But I'd love to add to it. Give him something special for the occasion. Leonard's—the jeweler we often borrowed items from for gala events and award shows, or grabbed the odd birthday gift from—was three shops from Nina's. I could duck in there while I waited and pick up something for Kyle. He'd eyed a titanium chain bracelet and onyx ring when we'd gone there to choose our wedding bands. Hell, maybe I'd just buy him both.

Yep. Do it.

I had time.

"Nina, I'm just going to Leonard's quickly and then I'll be back. Fifteen, twenty minutes tops."

"Actually, Gemma . . ." Nina held her phone in one hand and read the screen as she hung my dress on the change room door. My other dress for today, the short cream party dress with a box-pleated skirt, waited next to it, ready to go. It had fit perfectly when I tried it on before my wedding dress. "I've just got an urgent message from my daughter's school. She's sick, and I need to pick her up. Just take the dress for today, and I'll courier the other one over to you tomorrow morning. Is that okay? I don't want to do a rush job."

"Sure. Can you send it to Kara's place? I won't be home, and I don't want Kyle to see it. If there are any issues, I'll call you on

Monday."

"Perfect." Nina grabbed my other dress. "Let's get this bagged up for you to take."

I grabbed my purse and followed Nina down to the ground floor.

While Nina placed my dress into a garment bag, I ambled around the showroom, scanning the gorgeous wedding gowns on the racks, and the blingy tiaras and sparkling shoes displayed on glass shelves.

I hesitated by the front door.

Going to Leonard's wasn't foolish, was it?

It's three shops away.

I was safe.

I glanced out at the quiet cobblestone street lined with trendy renovated apartments that had fire-escape stairs zigzagging across the facades. Only half of the ground level retail spaces were occupied—a dry cleaner, an optometrist, and an accountant. The other stores had 'For Lease' signs in the windows. The occasional person with their head down and their eyes glued to their cell phone scurried past Nina's entrance. There was no one standing around staking out the place. There were no paparazzi in sight.

Chester hadn't turned up, so I gave him a quick call. "How're you traveling?"

"I'm still stuck outside the tunnel. A massive collision had blocked every lane. It's clearing now. I should be there soon. Where are you?"

"I'm just finishing up at Nina's." I scanned the street, taking in the parked cars and vans. Nothing looked suspicious. "I'm going to Leonard's Jewelers; it's three shops down. I'll be quick."

"What? Wait. Where's Dylan?"

"He's parked down the street. I'll call him when I'm ready to go."

"No. Call him now to go with you."

I checked up and down the street again. "There's no place for him to park. Every space is full. Leonard's is really close. I'll be fine."

"Gemma?" A gravelly scalding rasped through Chester's tone. "I'm not happy about this. But fine. Don't go anywhere else."

"I won't. Just meet me at my place. I'll see you there."

I dropped my cell phone into my purse and pulled out my baseball cap. I jammed it onto my head and tugged it down low. I slid on my big sunglasses. Wiping my clammy palms on my jeans, I was set.

I got this. Leonard's, then home. Done.

After Nina handed me the dress, I took a big breath, pushed open the glass door and walked out onto the street. I hugged the gold garment bag close to my chest, kept my head down, and hurried along the sidewalk.

I made it ten yards.

Ooph. I crashed hard into the person in front of me. *Shit.* My heart clambered into my throat. I hadn't seen them. I'd been too busy looking at the ground, trying to ignore the niggling nerves gnawing like a rat at the base of my neck.

"I'm sorry," I apologized and went to weave around the woman, but she didn't let me pass. She stepped and blocked the way.

Keeping my cool, I looked up, ready to excuse myself again. But my mouth fell open. My eyes widened. I struggled to comprehend who stood before me dressed in bulky black jeans, a big black hoodie, and an oversized floppy black broad-brimmed hat.

"Vicki? What the fuck?"

Chapter 17

GEMMA

"You scared the crap out of me. Why aren't you at work?" My heart beat like Led Zeppelin's Bonham on the drums. I grabbed Vicki by the arm, drew her out of the way of pedestrians, and stood by the brick wall of a vacant shop.

"I'm sorry." Vicki's hand shook as she toyed with her earring. "I'm meeting my brother. He's late." She kept her head low. Her eyes were red, like she'd been crying. Her face was flushed, no doubt from being too hot in her thick clothing—it was a warm day. A hoodie wasn't necessary. But as Vicki wiped her brow, a few fine strands of hair stuck out from underneath her floppy hat.

"Oh wow. You dyed your hair? Black?" I reached out to touch a strand, but Vicki slapped my hand away.

"Yeah. It was time for change."

"Cool." I glanced up and down the street. Two men standing by a tree fifty yards away were having a cigarette. They didn't look my way, but it was time to get off the sidewalk.

What had made Vicki upset, though? She clearly wasn't herself.

"Hey." I stepped closer. "Is everything okay?"

"No."

Screeeeech.

A cab slid to a halt at the nearby traffic lights. My pulse shot shockwaves through my head. The car's horn blasted and echoed off the surrounding buildings. I glanced at the intersection and up and down the street again. I placed my hand over my chest to steady my racing heartbeat and catch my breath. A couple of clueless people jaywalking across the road had caused the commotion.

Fuck! I hated being so on edge. I didn't need to be so wired now I was with Vicki.

As a puff of smoke and the foul stench of burned rubber filled the air, Vicki yanked her purse high on her shoulder. "You want to know what's wrong? Everything. I got fired from my job. Life is shit. I never get a break. I've had enough."

"You lost your job?" My jaw dropped. Vicki had worked as the receptionist at the same office equipment company since high school. "What happened?"

"As if you'd care."

"Of course I do."

"No. You. Don't." Vicki spoke through tight lips. She tugged on the cord of her hoodie, twisting and twirling it around her finger until the tip of her pointer turned blood-angry red.

I adjusted the dress bag draped over my arm and pushed my sunglasses higher on my nose. "I understand you're upset. I'm really sorry, but I don't have much time. Can we catch up soon? Um . . . I'm not sure when." Fuck, I was the worst friend in the world, but I had to go get married.

Vicki folded her arms and tucked her clenched fists under her armpits. "Why . . . why did you cancel tomorrow night's show? Why did you do that? Why?"

I straightened my shoulders. I hadn't seen Vicki this upset in years. "Um. We had to. Management thought it best. Security was an issue."

"I wanted to see you guys play."

"I'm sorry. You should've told me. I could've got you passes. We're not playing back here until December."

Vicki clenched her teeth and seethed. "I can't wait that long."

"Wait for what?" I jerked my chin back.

"It doesn't matter anymore." Vicki closed her eyes and swayed on her feet. Then she froze. Her gaze fell to my dress bag. "Oh. My. God. Is that . . . your wedding dress?"

"No. No. It's a dress for something else."

She mumbled under her breath, but I couldn't make sense of what she'd said.

Then, like the wind changing direction, a new Vicki appeared.

Her gaze softened as she pleaded. "I've had a really rough day. I could use a friend right now. I know you're busy, but would you have time for a quick drink? I'd really appreciate it."

Shit! The mood swings. The haze in Vicki's eyes. *Fuck.* Was Vicki on something? Or were my nerves playing havoc with my head? I wanted to make sure she was okay. I twisted and fidgeted with my watch. 12:51 p.m. I thumbed toward the jeweler. "Um . . . I actually want to go into Leonard's. Come with?"

"Noooo. No shopping." Vicki's hand trembled as she held it out flat. "I really want a drink."

Did I have time? As long as I was home by one forty-five, I'd be fine. Alcohol might do us both some good, and take the edge off wired emotions. I gave a nod and held up a finger. "One drink. But it has to be quick. I have a busy afternoon." I didn't want to turn up to my wedding drunk.

"That's all I need." A sharp edge sliced through her tone. But she'd just lost her job; she had every right to be snarky. She waved up the street. "There's an old sports bar over there. Will that do?"

Diagonally across from the traffic lights stood an old white building with blue trim. It looked more like a Greek restaurant than a sports bar, but it was close and easy to get to. I scanned every direction. Nothing suspicious. No obvious paparazzi. "Sure."

Vicki tilted her head. "Where's Chester?"

"He's stuck in traffic. Dylan's down the road waiting for me."

"Cool." She shrugged and took a step toward the bar. "Let's go."

One drink. Kyle's present. Home. "Okay." I was with a friend. I was safe. I'd text Dylan when I got to the bar.

But as we walked along the street, Vicki hobbled beside me.

"What happened to your foot?" I pointed to it.

"Oh, it's nothing. I tripped on the stairs at home."

"Lucky the bar isn't far."

The bright blue sports bar on West Houston Street was surrounded by old apartments and a closed pizza shop. It wasn't on the busiest of intersections for foot traffic. I walked inside and pulled off my sunglasses. The onslaught of sports commentary blaring from the gigantic TV screen mounted above the bar pummeled my eardrums. Other TV screens hanging on the walls displayed different sports. Old chipped and stained wooden tables and chairs were scattered randomly around the two small open spaces. Despite the bar's abundance of flat screens, it held a ton of old New York charm—copious bottles of liquor lined the mirrored shelves, warm lighting lit the rooms and rustic dark wooden beams ran across the ceiling.

The stench of beer and deep-fried food hung in the air like a dangling carrot. My mouth watered. My belly grumbled. After all, it was lunchtime. But there was no time for food; I'd grab something to eat at home.

A couple of men in construction gear sat at the counter, eating loaded fries and having a beer. One barman loitered behind the serving area, his eyes on the big screen, watching football. He didn't even notice we'd walked in. Otherwise, the place was empty.

Vicki waved toward the pale red booths to the right. "Let's sit over there. I know you want to avoid fans and the paparazzi like the plague, right?"

I winced, but nodded. That was only half true. I didn't like paparazzi invading my privacy or being harassed by fans in my free time. But being photographed by professional photographers and meeting fans for work was an entirely different story. I loved that. But now wasn't the time to argue. "Thanks." I nodded my head toward the bar. "Let me grab you a drink. What will it be?"

"No. No. I asked you. My treat," Vicki insisted and scurried over to the bar.

I slid into the far booth, hung my dress over the seat, and placed my purse beside me.

"YYYEEESSS!" The barman roared so loud the roof left the

rafters.

I jumped two inches off the seat. My heart slammed against my ribs. *Fuck.* This was a bad idea. I needed to go home.

The barman pumped his fists and clapped at the TV as the other two guests hollered and cheered. *Football.* The replay showed the touchdown from every angle—forwards, backwards, in slow motion , then at normal speed.

Football was okay in small doses, but not today.

The barman made our drinks and placed them on the countertop.

Vicki paid, then was on her phone, texting. The barman returned to the football.

I tapped and strummed my fingers on the table.

Shit. I don't have time for this.

Just when I was about to call out to Vicki to move her ass, she grabbed our drinks and strolled over to the booth. She slid into the opposite seat. "Sorry. That was my brother, Anthony. He'll be here soon." Her hands quivered as she passed me my drink. Droplets of perspiration zigzagged down the side of her neck.

Take your fucking hoodie and hat off if you're hot.

Folding her arms and hunching her shoulders, Vicki kept her head down, peering up at me from beneath the broad brim of her hat.

I leaned forward and rested my hands on the table. "Vicki, are you okay? You don't look well."

"I'm fine." She stirred her drink with the straw. By the smell of it, she'd grabbed her favorite poison—Bacardi and Coke. She raised her glass. "Cheers. Drink up, bitch."

I clinked my glass against hers and took a sip. I winced and licked my lips. Hmm . . . it tasted funny. "Is this JD?"

Vicki rolled her eyes. "Yes. I wouldn't dare get you anything else."

"Just checking." I shrugged and downed half my drink. Maybe the bartender poured from the wrong bottle. Gave me a different whiskey. He was rather distracted by the TV. "So, tell me. Why did you get fired?"

As I sipped my drink, Vicki rattled on about her dismissal being unjustified and unfair just because she turned up late, lost her cool at customers, and stole office supplies.

Yeah. All valid reasons for being sacked.

Vicki put down her drink, and a coy grin slid across her lips. "But I don't care about my job." Her voice rippled with the calmness of a lake. She placed her palms on the table and smoothed them over the wooden grain. "My future is about to change. I'm going to get everything I want. What I deserve. And no one is going to stop me."

Woozy dizziness swam through my head. Hazy fog clouded my brain. I knocked back the rest of my drink. My arm fell onto the table. The glass slipped from my hand. *What the hell?* But Vicki wasn't making any sense. "Stop you from doing what?"

Vicki's gaze turned icy cold. "I'm not going to let anyone stand in my way. Not anymore."

"Good for you. You go girl." I swayed, wanting to put oomph into my voice, but failed. *What's wrong with me?* My gut sank as if loaded with cement. My bones grew heavier and heavier. *Shit! I haven't felt like this before.*

No, wait.

Vegas.

Panic clambered up my throat. I tried to get my brain . . . to talk to my hand . . . to reach for my cell phone. *Shit.* I forgot to message Dylan. I needed to call Kyle, Chester. *Shit. Shit. Shit.* My body wouldn't work.

A man walked into the bar, caught sight of Vicki, and charged over to our table. He took a seat beside her. "This is your plan?" He spoke in a rushed, hushed tone. "In broad daylight in SoHo. Are you fucking crazy?"

"I'm not crazy," Vicki said through clenched teeth. "Just a few more minutes." Vicki whipped her head around to face me, her eyes squinting. "You remember Anthony?"

He had beady eyes like a mole. A mop of short blond dreadlocks spiked out from underneath his cap. He had grayish, gaunt skin like a vampire in desperate need of a drink. He was tall and skinny, like Mick Jagger. Oh yeah, I remembered him. He had a reputation for being the biggest drug dealer in high school. Looked like he still sampled the goods too often.

Wait.

Oh no. Oh shit.

My head lolled back. Anthony scuttled around to sit beside me and hooked his arm around my shoulder. Every instinct told me to push him away, but I didn't. I couldn't.

"Looks like it's worked." Vicki's face lit with a sinister smile.

Fear clambered to every extremity of my body. I wanted to get out of there, but my limbs wouldn't cooperate. Wouldn't work. As if intoxicated, my arm fell from the table to my side, knocking my garment bag and purse to the floor. Tears stung my eyes. *What's happening?*

I licked my lips, my mouth dry. My voice failed. *What was in that drink?*

"Gemma, it's okay," Anthony whispered, stroking my hair back from my eyes. "We're going to get out of here. I'm gonna help you. Okay?"

No. I didn't want to go with him. How come I had no control over my body? I needed to get out of there. Needed to get away. Needed to marry Kyle. I couldn't be late.

"My car's outside. I'm double parked." Anthony said to Vicki. Then, in a low voice, he hovered near my ear. "Let's go."

No. No. No.

His hand slid over mine. Cold, skinny, bony fingers wrapped around my wrist. Couldn't the barman or the guys sitting at the counter see I needed help? *No.* Their eyes were glued to the TV.

Fuck.

I should've listened to Kyle. Had someone with me. Waited for Chester. Texted Dylan. Every muscle in my body ached, and I slumped against Anthony's bicep.

"I need you to stand." Anthony slid me to the end of the booth, hooked his hand underneath my arm, and I drifted to my feet. With Vicki on my other side, we headed out the door. My eyes drifted shut.

No. No. No.
I don't want to go with you.
Kyle.
Help.
I'm in trouble.

Chapter 18

KYLE

In the tiny, half-full Italian restaurant not far from Richard's office, aromas of herbs, garlic, baked bread, and mozzarella cheese wafted from the small kitchen. I leaned back in my chair, my stomach full after a late lunch of chicken pasta and salad. Hunter and Hayden had demolished a massive serving of Bolognese and two pizzas.

The waiter cleared away our plates and left us to our icy-cold beers. Stretching my legs out, I couldn't hide my grin. One hour to go. Time to chill, have another beer or two, and calm my nerves before getting married.

"So, you ready to get hitched?" Hayden straightened and smoothed his hand over his silk tie. "Always knew you'd be the first to tie the knot."

"What?" I fidgeted with my gold cuff links; the bass guitar-shaped ones Gemma had given me for my birthday. "What made you think that?"

"You love love." Hayden shrugged his shoulder. "You're sensitive. A crooner. Girls dig that."

A crooner? Maybe I was. Singing songs about love and longing came easily to me, dealing with other emotions, not so much. I'd lost Gemma once for not being honest about my feelings. I'd never do that again.

The thought of losing her terrified me. I hated my concern for her safety had come across as controlling. The idea of turning into my father scared the shit out of me. I'd sworn never to be like him. I'd never be an alcoholic, abusive, power-tripping asshole. I vowed to spend the rest of the days making Gemma happy. Being the man she deserved. That dream was about to become a reality.

A waiter scuttled past our table, carrying large white plates, one loaded with ravioli, one with a mouthwatering steak for another table. It smelled so good, but I couldn't possibly eat another thing.

Hayden slapped Hunter on the back. "Hunt will be next down the aisle. Now he's hooked up with Kara, it's just a matter of time."

Hunter choked on a mouthful of beer. "Dude, I've been dating her for a few months. I'm not ready to get married."

"You've already moved in together." Hayden chuckled over the rim of his beer glass. "I mean, what the fuck?"

"You wait." Hunter waggled his finger at Hayden, a playful smile curling across his lips. "Your turn will come."

"No girl will tie me down." Hayden shook his head, then held up three fingers to a passing waiter and ordered another round of beers.

"Yeah. That's what I said." Hunter drained the rest of his glass.

"You're just jealous." I placed my hand over my heart. "I'm lucky I've found the person I want to spend the rest of my life with. I can't believe I'm marrying Gem this afternoon."

So surreal. So cool.

As the waiter placed three fresh beers onto the table and cleared away our empty glasses, Hunter grabbed his phone, took a photo of our drinks, and spoke as he texted. "Beer with the boys."

"Do you have to post everything to Instagram?" I grabbed my drink and downed a mouthful.

"Yep." He flicked his long hair over his shoulders. "That's why I have twice as many followers as you."

I cracked a smile. Twenty-one million followers on Instagram was nothing to be shy about. But I didn't feel the need to post something every day.

My cell phone rang. I grabbed it from my suit pocket, grimaced at the caller ID, and answered it. "S'up Dylan?"

"Sorry to bother you, Mr. McIntyre. Has something changed? I've been waiting for Gemma for half an hour past her appointment's scheduled finish time, and she hasn't called. I've tried phoning her, but it keeps going to voicemail."

I drew my eyebrows together. "What? No. Nothing's changed." *Shit.* Did she have her phone on silent? I glanced at my watch. 2:06 p.m. "Where are you?"

"At the park down the street from the bridal shop," Dylan said.

"Is Chester with Gem?" I doubted her final fitting and picking up a dress would take this long. She'd said it wouldn't even take an hour, not go for longer than ninety minutes.

"No. He got delayed by an accident in the tunnel. Last message from him said he would meet Gemma at home."

"What? You mean Gem's by herself? Without security?"

"Well . . . she's with Nina at the shop."

I closed my eyes and rubbed the back of my neck. Fittings could blow out and go over time, but Gemma would've called Dylan if she was running late. "I'll call Nina's and see what's taking her so long. I'll phone you back."

I hung up, my mind spinning. *Fuck!*

"Kyle?" Hunter leaned forward; worry filtered through his eyes. "What's happened?"

"It's Gemma." My leg jiggled underneath the table. With each passing second, my blood pressure spiked higher and higher. "She's late calling Dylan for pickup. He's worried. She should be finished at Nina's by now."

I hit the Contacts button on my cell phone and rang Gemma's number.

Fuck. It went through to voicemail.

I sent her a text.

Me: Call me. URGENT.

Hunter's face blanched.

Hayden gulped his mouthful of beer and wiped the corners of

his mouth with his fingertips. "Shit. I'm sure there's an explanation. Don't worry yet."

Too late for that.

The waiter walked over to our table. "Can I interest you in the dessert menu?"

"No." I didn't even look at the waiter as I gave him a flick of my hand. "We're fine." I didn't want to be rude, but now wasn't a good time. I had to find Gemma.

"No worries. Let me know if you'd like anything else." The waiter bowed and scuttled away.

"Hunt, can you call Kara?" My hands shook as I Googled Nina's number. "Find out if she's with Gem and see if they've run off to do something without telling anyone."

"I can, but she got held up at Tom Ford's and is meeting us at Richard's. I told you that."

I rubbed at the tension building in my brow. *Shit!* Yes, he did . . . when we were goofing around trying on our suits.

Hunter grabbed his cell phone and called Kara, anyway. "Hey babe, are you with Gem? . . . You heard from her?" Hunter shook his head, and the blood drained from my face. Hunter strummed his fingers against the table, listening to whatever Kara was saying.

I dialed Nina's number and put the phone to my ear. I scrunched and crushed my napkin into a ball as I talked to Danielle, Nina's shop assistant. She didn't believe it was me. It took some sweet convincing for her to put me through to Nina. "Nina, it's Kyle McIntyre. Gemma's fiancé. Is she still with you?"

Nina hesitated before speaking softly. "I'm sorry, I can't help you. My client base and any information about them is strictly confidential."

Fuck client privacy. "NINA." My desperation bordered on a growl; my politeness veered close to cracking. "I know she went there at twelve-thirty. Her driver's waiting for her. Just tell me, is she still there or not?"

Silence.

For Christ's sake.

"Please, Nina." I yanked my necktie from side to side. "She's not where she's supposed to be. I'm concerned about her safety. It's urgent."

"No," Nina whispered, soft and meek. "She's not."

My heart hammered out a fast tempo, slamming against my ribs with each beat. "Did she leave with someone?"

"As far as I'm aware, no, she didn't leave with anyone. She said she was going to Leonard's."

Leonard's? What was she doing there? Picking out different jewelry for the wedding?

She had to be there. Had to be. "Thanks Nina. Appreciate it. Bye."

I dialed the jeweler. The shop assistant said Gemma hadn't been into the store. They hadn't seen her. *Fuck!*

I tried her cell phone again. No answer.

Where are you, Gem? Oh God, please be okay.

My gut rolled like surging waves; my lunch threatened to return. I scrolled through my cell phone and opened our tracking app, even though I hated doing it. I hated having to check where she was. The loading icon circled round and round. What felt like minutes was in reality only a few seconds.

Gemma's icon appeared on the screen.

What the hell? She was at a bar? Down the street from Nina's?

What was she doing there?

Wasn't she coming?

At what point did I fucking panic?

Chapter 19

KYLE

"Kyle, let's get out of here." Hunter waved urgently at the waiter for the check. "Before we make the headlines on TMZ."

"Good call." I downed the remains of my beer. Hunter clearly sensed my escalating state of frenzy. My mind raced as I charged out of the restaurant and slipped into the waiting stretch limousine with Hayden, Hunter, and our security. My gut rocked and rolled with so much nausea it could be mistaken for the biggest wave pool in North America. The guys did their best to keep me calm, making jokes and reassuring me that Gemma would still make it to Richard's on time. But nothing worked.

Gemma was cutting it too damn fine.

I just wanted to hear from her. Make sure she was okay. But something tugged deep down inside the pit of my stomach, telling me she wasn't.

As our driver headed toward Richard's office, I googled the bar Gemma was supposed to be at and dialed the number.

Some chick with a Reese-Witherspoon-like voice answered. "Hi, this is The Edge Sports Bar."

Loud sports commentary, music, and people's hollers reverberated through the speaker. I could hardly hear the lady. I covered my other ear and concentrated on my conversation. "Can you see if Gemma Lonsdale is there, please?"

"Are you joking?" The woman shrieked with a disbelieving laugh. "You mean Gemma? From Everhide?"

"Yes."

"Yeah, right. As if she'd come to a bar like this."

"Just . . ." I clenched my jaw, my hands, and my teeth. "See if she's there. Please?"

"We had sixty people rock up for some guy's birthday at two o'clock," she yelled over the background noise. "It's super busy. But hold on, I'll check." Her shout rattled my phone. "Is there a Gemma Lonsdale here? . . . Gemma? . . . Gemma Lonsdale? Nope. Can't see her. It's hard to be sure, though. Lotta people watching sport and stuff."

"Okay. If you find her, tell her to call Kyle. It's super urgent."

"Kyle? As in McIntyre? *Holy crap.* Yes. Yes. Um . . . Sure. Will do."

"Thanks." I hung up. Well, that didn't help. *Totally freaking useless.*

I was about to call Dylan to check the bar, but Chester's name lit my screen.

I hit the answer button. "Please tell me Gem's with you." I tried to remain calm, but panic had crept into my voice.

"Um. No." Chester's hesitation sent my worry up another notch. "I've just got to your place after being held up by an accident in the tunnel. She told me to meet her at home, but she's not here. I've called her, but she's not answering. Dylan hasn't heard from her. The tracking app says she's at The Edge sports bar. Do you know about this?"

"She shouldn't be at *some bar*." My voice shook. "I rang them, but they couldn't find her in the crowd. Something's not right. She should be home by now, or on her way to meet us."

"Kyle." Hunter grimaced and scratched at the red rash breaking out on his neck—the telltale sign he was freaking out. "You know Gem. She probably ran into someone she knew, had a drink, lost track of time, took off in a rush and left her phone behind. She'll make it. Everything will be fine."

But it wasn't.

She wasn't with Dylan. Or Chester. She wasn't at home. Nothing was fine.

Chester cleared his throat. "The bar's not far from here. I'll go there and find her."

"That'd be great. I was about to get Dylan to do that."

"I'll touch base with him and meet him there." Chester's voice came out in a breathy rush, like he was running. "Give me fifteen minutes. Your doorman can contact us if she turns up."

"Excellent. Please hurry." I hit End. So much had happened in a few minutes. But there was still no word from Gemma. I wiped my hand down my face and rubbed it across my mouth. As I caught Hunter's and Hayden's gloomy gazes, I'd reached the edge of my sanity. "Fuck, I hope she's alright."

Sam rested his arm on the windowsill and tapped his index finger at sonic speed. "I should've gone back for her. Damn it."

There was no doubt the threats played on repeat at the forefront of everyone's minds. The very thought of them becoming a reality curdled my stomach.

Had the stalker gotten to Gemma?

I hated waiting. Waiting for Chester to call. Waiting for this nightmare to end. Waiting for Gemma to make contact. Her silence was killing me.

The limousine pulled up near the wide sidewalk outside Richard's building. Men and women, dressed in suits, dashed in and out of the rotating glass doors. The planter-boxed trees along the edge of the curb showed the first signs of fall, their leaves tinged with shades of yellow and orange. Tourists with maps in hand glanced up and down the street with *I'm-lost* looks on their faces. But the one person I hoped would miraculously appear . . . didn't.

No Gemma.

The compression crushing my chest was so hard I thought my ribs would crack. With fumbling fingers, I loosened my tie and ripped open my top button. *Just breathe. In. Out. In. Out.* "Come on, Gem," I mumbled. "Where are you?"

"Stay in here." Sam ordered as he and Mick slipped out of the car. They stood at opposite ends of the vehicle, looking foreboding in their black suits and dark sunglasses. So much for being discreet.

Sweat trickled down my spine and soaked the small of my back. It had been twenty minutes since Chester had called. Why the hell was it taking him so long to get to the bar?

In front of us, Kara and Lexi rushed down the street, the skirts of their similar pale blue dresses swishing in the breeze.

"The girls are here." I shoved the car door open. We piled out and dashed over to greet them. "You heard from Gem?"

"No," Kara panted, catching her breath. "She still not here?"

"Phew." Lexi fanned her face. "We made it in time, then." She joked, but concern hooded her eyes.

I glanced at my watch. It was nearly 2:45 p.m. There was still no sign or word from Gemma.

A pedestrian walking by grabbed her friend's arm, pulling her to a halt, and pointed in our direction. Her mouth fell open and her frizzy black hair flopped about as she jumped and squealed. "OhmyGod. It's Kyle. And Hunter. From Everhide. OhmyGod, OhmyGod, OhmyGod."

Great. Not the distraction I needed today. We shouldn't have gotten out of the car. I forced a smile, gave the girls a wave, and paced the sidewalk.

Gem. Call me. Just call me. Let me know you're okay.

Luckily, the gawking girls just took some photos and scurried off, too shy to come over and say anything. Maybe my *I'm-not-in-the-mood* vibe scared them off.

Kara, Lexi, and the guys huddled in a circle by the car. With their help, I ran through a list of places where Gemma could be. Nowhere seemed feasible. As each second passed, I drew closer to the worst conclusion. I dialed Gemma's number for the twentieth time. It felt like I was doing something to find her. But yet again . . . it went to voicemail.

Fuck!

I hung up.

"She's still not answering." Panic lodged between my ribs. Cloudy thoughts, thick and dark and stormy, hurtled through my head. With the force of a hammer drill, another what-if scenario rammed into my skull. It throbbed and ached and pounded. What if all the stress and pressure of the wedding had gotten to her? Had she had enough? Of me? Reached breaking point?

Shit.

My breath hitched hard, ripping my lungs to shreds.

She wasn't coming.

SHE. WASN'T. COMING.

No. No. *No.* This was what we'd wanted. She wouldn't do this to me. Would she?

Tears burned my eyes.

Oh God. No.

Bile bubbled in my throat. I gripped my cell phone so hard I thought it might shatter. I halted in front of Hunter. "I'm losing my fucking mind."

"Yeah, I kinda got that impression. I know you're worried. Everyone is."

"WHY ISN'T SHE HERE?" Fire tore through my soul.

"I don't know." Hunter's voice caught in his throat. "She was so excited about today. In that *I-don't-want-a-big-wedding* kind of way. There has to be a valid explanation."

Yeah. And it terrified me.

I closed my eyes and tilted my head back. Every drop of blood drained from my face. My breath seesawed in my lungs. I had no idea what else to do.

People walking by slowed when they recognized us. With the guys and I decked out in matching suits, and Kara and Lexi wearing similar blue dresses, it wouldn't take any fan too long to piece together what we were doing here. The only element missing was Gemma.

This is fucked. So fucked.

I strode over to Sam at the front of the limousine. My jaw ached, and so did every muscle in my body. "When am I allowed to panic?"

Sam's expression didn't move off neutral. His dark glasses hid his eyes. "I think you started a half an hour ago."

I fisted my hands. I was in no mood for Sam's smart mouth. "Do something."

"Let's wait until Chester calls with an update."

Freaking useless. Well, I couldn't stand around and do nothing. I stormed back to my friends. "Guys, help me contact everyone. See if anyone has seen her or knows where she is."

I divvied out names, and we jumped into making calls—to friends, Bec, Sophie, other team members, our backup band, and regular road crew. Ten minutes later, no one had found her. My friends' faces had grown paler and paler with each failed attempt.

Shit.

My cell phone buzzed, and my heart skipped a beat.

A message.

No caller ID. The number withheld.

I swiped the screen open and time stopped. Pain speared my heart. My knees buckled. I staggered back three steps and sat on the edge of a planter box. A burning tear slipped down my cheek.

"Kyle?" Sam charged forward; his hand outstretched.

Hunter dashed to my side. "What is it?"

My hand shook as I held up my phone for them to read the message. The message that destroyed me.

GEMMA: I'M NOT COMING.

"What the fuck? No way. Give me that thing." Hunter snatched the cell phone from my grasp. He re-read the message. His eyes glassed over and he shook his head. "No. I . . . I don't believe this."

My vision blurred, and a high-pitched ring pierced my ears. Gemma didn't want to speak to me. Didn't want to marry me. Hurt exploded like an erupting fissure, burning through every blood vessel. "She's not coming. She's NOT FUCKING COMING."

Stunned, Hunter's jaw dropped. Kara's hands shot over her mouth. Lexi's eyes flooded with tears. Hayden stood frozen.

I stood and grabbed Hunter by the lapel of his jacket. "Get me the fuck out of here. NOW."

No one moved.

"I said NOW." I stormed toward the car. I punched the side

of the limousine, hurt the crap out of my hand. "Shit." I yanked the door open and jumped inside. I pummeled the fuck out of the leather seat. The others scrambled around me, giving me space to vent.

Mick hopped into the front passenger seat and ordered the driver to take off.

I punched the seat again. "FUCK! FUCK! FUCK!"

Kara, with tears zigzagging down her cheeks, clutched Hunter's arm. "This can't be true. This isn't Gemma."

I'd thought so too. I'd thought our love defied the universe, that we'd survive anything. I didn't want to believe that message. But the alternative . . . that something might have happened to her . . . was worse than being stood up. "If she didn't want to marry me, why couldn't she tell me to my face? Call me? Instead, I get a fucking text."

Wait.

The text.

Oh shit!

I ripped my cell phone from my pocket and stared at the message. My hand shot over my mouth, then fell like a dead weight into my lap. "This message. Gem didn't send it. She never sends a message without '*xG*', kisses Gem, at the end."

Sam half-turned toward me. "Are you sure? Even if she's a no show?"

"Even if. Guaranteed." My lungs hurt. Breathing buckled my bones. "I'm a fucking idiot. I flipped out, thinking she'd stood me up, but she wouldn't do that. I know Gem. She wouldn't leave me. Since Dylan's call, every cell in my body has been screaming at me to face the truth." Nausea flooded my stomach in squalling waves. "It's the stalker. They've gotten to her. Haven't they? They sent this message."

"Let me make some calls." Sam jumped on his cell phone. He talked to someone in his office, then Jones.

"Where to?" Shell-shocked, Hunter asked.

"Let's go to that bar." My voice scraped my vocal cords and lodged in my throat. "We'll find out what they know. And call

Richard." I winced like an arrow had been plunged through my chest. "Cancel the wedding."

Hayden gave a solemn nod and grabbed his phone. "I'll do it."

The fear in Hunter's eyes reflected exactly how I felt . . . totally fucking terrified. He shook his head slowly. "Bud, you really want to go to the bar?"

"Yes. I do." Not the 'I do' I'd expected to be saying right now. "I need to find her. It's the only place I can think of where to start."

"If Gem's missing, shouldn't we leave it to the police?" Hayden softened his tone.

"I can't do that." Tears singed the rims of my eyes and threatened to fall. "They don't care about her like I do."

Hunter leaned forward, resting his elbows on his knees. "I know you, and I know her. Do me a favor. Let's go home, change, take a breath, then we'll try to find her."

"Are you fucking serious?" *Did he not know me?*

Lexi fidgeted with the hem of her dress. "Maybe she was so nervous, she got drunk and lost track of time."

I hoped that was the case, but the tightening knot growing between my shoulder blades told me otherwise.

Hunter splayed his hands. "It's possible. She's been stressed about the threats and the wedding. You don't want to storm into that bar, find she's there, and say something you may regret."

I took a deep breath and shot him a don't-fuck-with-me glare. "Do you honestly believe she'd do that? Get drunk and not turn up to our wedding?" I hated myself for even contemplating that path for a second. That wasn't Gemma.

Hunter sank into the leather seat. "No."

"Exactly." I snapped. "I'm going to that bar with or without you."

My cell phone rang. It was Chester. Everyone kept calling but Gemma. I swiped the screen and put it on loudspeaker. "Chester, did you find her?"

"Ah. No. We have a problem." Chester's voice quaked. "She's not here at the bar. But I've found her purse and a dress bag. They'd fallen onto the floor, underneath the booth I presume she'd sat at."

Oh shit.

My stomach hit the asphalt. I closed my eyes and rubbed my fingers against them. She wouldn't go anywhere without her purse. And her dress was there? *Her wedding dress? Fuck.*

That voided all options but one. My breath shuddered through my chest. I shook my head, over and over again. "Oh my God. She's been taken."

Chester's voice was barely audible over the background bar noise. "Let's not assume the worst yet."

Too late for that. I didn't want to draw any horrible conclusions. Her standing me up was heartbreaking; her being kidnapped, hurt or killed, would destroy me.

I gripped the edge of the seat. Hissed through my teeth. "I trusted you to look after her, and now she's gone."

"I'm so sorry." Regret loomed in Chester's voice. "I won't rest until we find her."

"She shouldn't be missing in the first place." My heart lurched, not knowing whether to break apart or freeze with fear.

"I talked to the barman." Chester spoke at one hundred miles an hour. "He saw two girls come in and have a drink. Said they seemed to know each other. They weren't here long. Some guy joined them and then they left."

"How long ago? She could be anywhere by now." Kara's ashen face was a mirror image of Hunter's. Hayden and Lexi stared at me; worry set in their eyes.

"The barman is getting me a copy of the security footage," Chester added.

"Good." Sam leaned forward and spoke into my phone. "We're on our way."

Fifteen minutes later, I stormed into the bar. Everyone else followed. Sports blared on TVs and patrons' heads turned. A few eyes lit with surprised recognition, but no one rushed over to greet us. Seemed like beer and sports were more important. *Thank goodness.* But this was not the type of place where Gemma would hang out. Sam and I charged through the crowd and weaved around some men gawking at the television screens. We made our way over to Chester sitting at the far end of the bar, hunched over a laptop.

My heart stampeded like a herd of wildebeest. I slapped him on the shoulder. "What have you found?"

"This." Chester swung the laptop toward me and hit play on the security footage.

As I watched the two videos, one angled down from the far end of the bar and one at a distance overlooking the tables, my pulse roared like a waterfall in my ears, louder and louder. Sweat beaded on my brow. In the footage, it was definitely Gemma.

But the other person? The girl?

Was that Taylah?

Her head was constantly down. Her big hat hid her face. Her back was always to the camera. And she'd walked with a limp. Taylah didn't limp. I didn't know anyone with a limp. Not once did she glance upward. It made it impossible to confirm her identity. It looked like the same person from the SummerStage and Brooklyn captures. *Shit.* And the guy? Tall. Super skinny. Head down. I couldn't tell who he was either. *Damn it.*

Sam took a seat in front of the laptop. Mick and Chester stood beside him, and they watched the videos over and over again. I paced behind them. Hunter, Hayden, Dylan, and the girls sat at a booth. They kept making calls to find Gemma, but had no luck.

The video kept flickering through my mind. *Girls walk in. Sit. Get drinks. Chat. Guy joins. Then they leave.* I stopped in my tracks. My gaze jumped back to the video Sam had on repeat. I stepped in behind him and pointed to the screen. "Gem's walking funny. That's not her usual drunken stagger."

Sam cleared his throat and nodded. The hard lines drawn on his face sent an icy shudder through my bones. "I agree. I've watched you three for years. I know the way each of you move. How you run, skip, jump, and dance. Sober or drunk and disorderly. That's not her usual stride." Sam twisted the laptop toward me. "And look here." He pressed play on one of the other videos and pointed at the screen. "On this video, when the girl gets the drinks, she places her bag beside them, digs inside it for something . . . and there . . . see? She covers the glass with her hand." He loaded the next video and hit play. "Then in this video at the table, Gemma gets groggy a few minutes after having her drink." He looked up at me and swallowed hard. "Kyle, you can definitely hit that panic button now. Ramp it up to full throttle. I think she's been drugged and kidnapped."

My heart stopped.

My knees buckled. I caught the edge of the bar to steady myself.

Kidnapped?

My instinct had been right.

They'd gotten Gemma. They'd fucking gotten to her.

FUCK.

Every muscle in my face twisted and contorted. My eyes stung with burning tears. I keeled over and howled. "No. No. *No.* Not Gemma. Oh God, no." I straightened and grabbed him by the shoulders. "Sam, please? I don't care what you have to do. Just find her. Fucking find her. Find her now!"

Chapter 20

GEMMA

The blanket covering my body from the waist down lay heavily against me, like it had been made of lead. *Why can't I move? Shit!* My mouth, dry and gritty, struggled to form saliva. The musty odor of dirt, dust, and dampness assaulted my nostrils. The flat, uncomfortable pillow beneath my head wasn't mine. I forced my eyes open, and my heart clambered to my throat.

Holy fuck! Where am I?

Nothing looked familiar.

In the small bedroom lit by a lamp on the nightstand, the faded mint-green walls were lined with posters. Old pine shelves, stuffed with CDs, albums, and old magazines, bent under the weight of their burden. Faded, warped photos pinned to the corkboard above the desk had seen better days, but they were too far away for me to make out the people in them. But the pile of pale pink envelopes and paper in a tray on the desk chilled me to the bone.

Oh shit.

Sick, nauseous, and unable to roll off my side, I did a double take of the shelves and wall. Shards of ice crept beneath my skin, crippling me even further. Everything—every picture, every poster, every piece of paraphernalia—was of Kyle. Hunter and I had been cut out or torn off all the photos. There was only one printout of me, stuck to a dartboard on the closet door . . . with five darts rammed through my head.

Fuck. I gotta get out of here.

But my legs and arms couldn't move more than an inch. Every attempt left me exhausted and weaker than before. How did I get here? What time was it? I stared at my immobile hands. *No wedding ring.*

Oh, no. Kyle. Our wedding.

Tears stung my eyes as I wriggled on the lumpy mattress, turning my head just enough to glance toward the end of the bed.

Vicki sat on an old wooden chair by the door, dressed in a black tank top and cut-off shorts. Her new gothic-black haircut curtained her face. As she held a glass pipe to her mouth, she lit a cigarette lighter, blazing it beneath the bulb. A small ziplock-style bag of white crystals lay on the small table beside her. *Ice? Fuck.* Vicki sucked in a deep breath, held it, then exhaled a puff of smoke. She looked up, and a wicked smile drew across her face. "Good. You're awake."

"Vicki?" Grogginess swung through my whispery voice. "Where am I? What are you doing?"

Clutching onto her pipe and lighter, Vicki dragged her chair around the end of the bed and plonked down on the seat before me. "You're at my place. Enjoy your sleep?"

Stabbing pain shot through my head, speared my temples, and ached behind my eyes. The worst hangover and nightmare clawed through my brain. I'd only been to Vicki's house a handful of times over the years, but had never seen her bedroom—her shrine to Kyle. Short, sharp breaths shredded my lungs. "Oh my God. It's you. You're the one who's been sending the letters?"

A twisted half-smile tugged at the corner of her mouth. Satisfaction glistened in her eyes. "Like them?"

I fought the tears welling in my eyes. Vicki was my friend. Why was she doing this? "Please," I begged, fighting the panic seizing every inch of my body. "Let me go. You don't know what you've done."

Vicki leaned closer, her eyes cold and dark. "I know exactly what I've done. I stopped Kyle from making a huge mistake. You're not going anywhere. Not until I get what I want." I tried to sit, but Vicki pinned her hand against my shoulder. Her voice, curt and short, sliced through the air. "Stay down."

Nausea swirled like a squalling sea in my stomach. A cold sweat shivered across my fevered skin. "I'm gonna be sick."

Vicki spun on her chair and grabbed the trash can from beside her desk. With all my might, I lurched over the edge of the bed and vomited into the waiting bin. With nothing in my stomach, bile burned my throat, leaving a bitter taste in my mouth. Collapsing back onto the pillow, I didn't have any strength left to wipe my lips. "What did you give me?"

Vicki lit and sucked on her pipe, then blew a mouthful of rancid smoke in my face. "Just a roofie." She shrugged as if it were an everyday occurrence and placed her pipe on the nightstand.

A roofie? Oh shit.

Vicki grabbed the glass of water and shoved the straw into my mouth. "Drink. It's just water."

What if the water was drugged? Don't drink it. Don't drink it. But thirst overruled. I sucked down small sips to rinse my mouth, but it did little to revive my dry lips. My brain rattled for answers. "Why did you drug me?"

There had to be a logical explanation. Surely my friend wasn't a drug-addicted psychopath.

Vicki put down the glass, folded her arms and rested them on the mattress. One thin eyebrow arched like the blade of a scythe. "Because time's up. I want Kyle. I need you out of the way."

"What are you talking about?" None of this made sense. Vicki wanted Kyle? She hadn't been with him since high school. She couldn't have obsessed about him for that long. "Kyle doesn't love you. He loves me."

Red rashes licked like flames up the sides of Vicki's neck. She hissed through her clenched teeth. "No. He. Doesn't. He loves *me*. You've brainwashed him. Made him forget what we used to have. It's time for me to get him back. Make him realize *I'm* the one he's meant to be with."

"Vicki, stop." I tried to move again but couldn't. "You're sounding crazy."

"I'm not fucking crazy." She stabbed her finger at my face. Her words were like a booming bass drum, pounding inside my head. She tilted her head to the side. Shards of ice flared in her deep blue eyes. Her voice took on a chilling tone. "But you'll be out of the picture soon. When my brother and I meet our next shipment offshore on Sunday night, you're coming with. You'll have a little accident on-board the boat, fall into the river, and be gone. When the harbor police find you, Kyle will be devastated. And guess who'll be there for him? To console him? Nurse his broken heart?" Triumph rippled through her malicious smile. "*Me.*"

My heart rate tripled, thudding and clawing at my chest. *Fuck.* Vicki was going to kill me. *Oh God.* I had to get out of there. Vicki was deranged.

But my body wouldn't work. It felt like it weighed ten tons. "Kyle will be looking for me. So will the police and our security." Why hadn't they found me yet? It was dark outside. Why was it taking so long? I'd been so stupid wanting to go to Leonard's. Even more of a fool for having a drink with Vicki. I should've called Dylan. Waited for Chester. This was all my fault.

A tear slipped across my temple and soaked into the pillow. My heart ached, and every breath hurt my ribs. Kyle would be heartbroken, gutted. I'd missed our wedding. He'd be tearing Manhattan apart trying to find me. Or . . . doubt seeped into my brain . . . or did he think I'd left him? Think the stress and threats had gotten too much? *No.* He wouldn't think those things. Our love ran too deep. It had been a rough few weeks, but I wasn't a quitter like my parents. They had walked away from each other and me when things had gotten tough. I'd never do that. I'd never leave Kyle.

I closed my eyes and said a prayer. *Kyle. Please. Find me.*

The fire in my spirit hadn't been extinguished. There was no way I'd let Vicki take me down without a fight. I needed these drugs to wear off, and then I'd be out of here.

Vicki smiled a thin-lipped smile. "Kyle is looking for you.

He's already called. He's *very* upset you didn't turn up for your wedding. Oh yes, dear Gemma, thank you for telling me that in your druggie state. I told him I hadn't seen or heard from you." She placed her hand over her heart and smeared on the sarcasm. "I've been nothing but a concerned friend."

I sobbed and curled into a fetal position. I hugged my arms against my chest, partly to see how well I could move, partly to hide my fear. With my body laced with drugs, I couldn't get out of bed. Not yet. All I could do was think. I had to think clearly. Strategically. Not succumb to panic. With all my band's security measures in place, never in my wildest dreams did I think I'd be kidnapped. Least of all by one of my friends. Betrayal cut my heart like a knife. But I had to play this right, play into Vicki's hands. Keep her talking. Somehow appeal to her humanity. "Vicki, why are you doing this? You're my friend."

"No." Vicki shook her head. Her black bob flicked her cheeks. "We were never friends. I used you to stay close to Kyle. I can't stand you. I hate you." Spite dripped from her tongue like venom. "People like you make me sick. You're so wrapped up in yourself, your success, your high life, you don't see what's right in front of you. It took you years to even notice Kyle. You don't deserve him."

There were many times I didn't think I was worthy of someone as amazing as Kyle. But his love had changed me. I was, without a doubt, a better person because of him. *Fuck.* I'd let my stress and worry taint the things I treasured about him. His protectiveness. His leadership. His ability to get things done. How safe and loved he made me feel. How in tune we were—mind, body, and soul. I didn't have that connection with anyone but him. "Yes, I do." I licked my dry, cracked lips. My mind clouded. My voice trailed toward nothingness. "I love him."

Vicki slapped her hand on the nightstand. The glass and pipe jumped under the force. "Don't say that. If it wasn't for you, Kyle and I would be together."

"Me?" My body grew more weary. *No.* I shook my head. *Stay awake.* "What did I do?"

Vicki inched forward to the edge of her chair. "You've always been in the way. In high school, when I tried to make amends with Kyle, you told him not to come near me. You said I would cheat again. I wouldn't do that. I made a mistake. And you've made me pay for it every day since."

"What?" My head ached. "You cheated on every guy you dated."

"Most, yes. Because no one was as good as Kyle. He was mine. I had to get him back."

High school was so long ago. Kyle had been heartbroken when their relationship had ended, but he was glad it was over. She'd wanted to get serious, move in together, get married, have babies. None of those things were on Kyle's wish list back in our high school days. And . . . she'd cheated on him.

"Just when Kyle and I were getting close again at the end of senior year, you had to win that fucking contest and land that record deal. You moved to the West Village with him and Hunter." She stabbed her finger at me again. "You took Kyle away from me."

My head spun like the reels on a tape recorder. My pulse throbbed in my temples. "We had to move for our music. We were just friends back then."

"That's right," Vicki hissed. "You haven't loved him as long as I have. I've always been there for him. Let him chase his dreams. I've had to watch and wait while you toured, while he was with other girls, listen to every song he wrote about me."

Vicki was truly insane. There was no way Kyle had written songs about her. Unless they were the ones about cheating, skanky bitches. Thank God those songs had never made it onto one of our albums.

Vicki's top lip twitched. "When you got together at your birthday party two years ago, you were only supposed to fuck him for a while, then break up. Not get engaged. Not marry him. I had to act. Had to stop you. You don't get him. I do. Kyle's mine."

Like hell. I'll take you down, bitch. When I can move. "Vickiiii, enough." My voice slurred; grogginess pressed against the insides of my skull. "Where's my phone? Let me call him. He can come over. We can talk. Forget this ever happened."

Vicki snarled and shook her head. "I'm not stupid. Your cell phone can be traced. We left it and your bags at the bar."

Oh no. How would Kyle find me?

"Who's *we*?" I searched through the fog growing thicker in my mind, backtracking through my day. I'd gone to Nina's. Run into Vicki. Offered to have one drink. Listened to her talk about losing her job. Then ... blank. Nothing. I couldn't remember a thing.

"Wow." Vicki folded her arms and leaned back in the chair. "You don't remember Anthony coming into the bar? That's so cool. I'd never used roofies before testing one on you in Vegas."

My gut cinched. Yet another low blow. So that was what had happened to me at my bachelorette party? Vicki had been planning this for weeks? Months? *Oh shit.* Since the first death threat arrived after my engagement to Kyle twelve months ago? Vicki was beyond sick. My body shuddered, shivering despite the lack of cold. Being drugged horrified me, but what scared me even more was how anybody would find me? I had to throw Vicki off-guard. Find a cell phone. Plan my escape. "Vicki, I don't want you to get into trouble. Let me help you. When they find my purse, the police will look for me."

"I know. But I'm not a suspect, dear sweet Gemma." Vicki's tone turned condescending. "I've worked with my brother selling drugs in SoHo for years. We know where the cameras are. Anthony's license plates are fake. He knows which routes to take. We dress in disguise. We've learned how to be invisible. He doesn't exist; neither do I."

I closed my eyes. My throat tightened as if Vicki held her hand around my jugular and squeezed it. "How did you know where I was?"

"I'm your *friend*. I have your cell phone number. A tracking app. I can find where you are at any time. I've been following you since you got home from tour, waiting for that perfect moment when you were alone."

I clutched the edge of the pillow to hide my hurt at the betrayal. I'd hated it when the paparazzi and fans followed me; I'd never expected a faithful friend to stalk and hunt me down. After this, how could I ever trust anyone?

Drowsiness set into my eyelids. My body sank deeper and deeper into the polyester sheets. I wanted to sleep forever. *Oh no. The water.* Had Vicki doped me again? *Fuck. Fight it. Fight it. Don't fall asleep.*

I gripped onto a fine filament of hope. I wasn't dead yet. But how much time did I have? Sunday . . . there was something about Sunday.

My bones ached. My muscles failed. God, I wanted to sleep. I fought the urge with every ounce of my willpower. Could I get to the bathroom? Lock myself inside? Climb out the window? Vicki's place was only two stories. I'd beat these drugs. I would . . . hopefully . . . maybe . . . *shit.* Shivering and shuddering, I glared at Vicki. "Kyle will never love you."

"Yes, he will." Vicki never faltered. "There's nothing I wouldn't do for him. Nothing. You're the only thing standing in my way."

My eyes fluttered shut. Tears slipped down my cheeks. "What's . . . wrong . . . with . . . me? I don't want to go . . . to sleep."

Vicki sighed and brushed my hair off my forehead with soft, gentle strokes. But her touch was like ice against my skin, making it prickle and crawl. "The water I just gave you was laced with enough drugs to knock you out for days. If you rouse, I'll tip more down your fucking throat. Then . . . on Sunday . . ." She twinkled her fingers. "It's ta-ta, Gemma. The world will be a better place when you're not in it. Guaranteed."

She's fucking mental. Truly unstable.

I closed my eyes, turned my head, and let my tears soak the pillow. My brain grew foggier and foggier. No matter how much I fought, I couldn't beat the drugs.

No. No. No.

I don't want to die. Please. I don't want to die.

But there was nothing I could do.

Even though I tried to come up with a plan, I'd failed.

This was it.

The drugs coaxed me, lured me down into the depths of the unknown.

Kyle's smile flickered behind my eyelids. I remembered the

taste of his kisses, the warmth of his touch, the magic of his love.

Kyle.

I'm so sorry.

I love you.

My heart broke.

Unable to fight anymore, I drifted toward the darkness.

Chapter 21

KYLE

The bright fluorescent lights in the precinct's meeting room hurt my eyes. Looking through the glass wall over the open-plan office made me feel like I was in a fishbowl. My head ached from drinking too much whiskey last night. This was taking too long. I should be out trying to find Gemma. My chest had never felt this hollow. I hadn't recovered since my heart shattered on the sidewalk downtown when she didn't show up to get married. *Kidnapped.* I'd never been this terrified. This scared. Giving Detective Marshall my statement to report Gemma as missing had crushed me even further.

The last twenty hours had been a nightmare. I hadn't eaten or slept. Every hour that ticked by slimmed our chances of finding her.

Slouching in my chair, I jiggled my leg. Marshall's questioning dragged on and on like Guns and Roses' "November Rain" stuck on repeat. *"When did you notice Gemma missing?" "When was the last time you saw her?" "Does anyone new come to mind who could be a suspect?"*

I rubbed my palms against my tired eyes. *This is such a waste of time.* I dropped my head back and stared at the ceiling. Hunter was in the room next door, giving his statement to another detective.

Sam and Mick waited on chairs in the corridor.

"Are we done?" I'd been here for half an hour, going around in circles.

"Almost." Marshall clacked away on his laptop.

Movement outside the office caught my eye. My pulse surged through my veins like a tsunami; I felt every rising wave. *Taylah!* Detectives Jones and Morris escorted her down the hallway toward the building's entrance. I shot forward in my chair. "What the fuck is Taylah doing here?"

Marshall didn't look up. "Jones brought her in for further questioning following the new lead."

"What?" I leaped from my chair. "What new lead?"

Marshall looked over the rim of his black-framed glasses. "They think they identified her off the bar footage."

I rushed for the door and charged into the hallway.

"Kyle. Wait." Marshall clambered after me.

Striding toward the detectives and Taylah, I yelled, "Jones, what the hell is going on?"

All three turned. A steely snarl twitched across Jones's lips. Morris gave me a curt nod. Taylah's hand shot over her mouth. Her eyes, red as a blood moon, glistened with tears.

"Oh my God. Kyle." She sobbed and hooked the sleeve of her baggy T-shirt back into place over her shoulder. Her black hair, tied into a ponytail, was a mass of knots. Loose strands framed her cheeks.

Detective Jones clutched his pile of folders to his chest. "Kyle, everything's fine. Miss Anderson is free to go."

My heart clambered to my throat. "Did you find Gem?"

"No. We haven't." Jones said through stiff lips. "Do not interfere."

Taylah rounded her shoulders. Sorrow darkened her eyes. "Kyle, I'm sorry I can't help you."

Marshall fell in beside me. "Kyle. Come on. Let's go finish your statement."

I wasn't buying Taylah's innocent act. Desperation clawed at my brain. I stepped toward her. Fire licked through my veins and

I stabbed my finger toward her face. "What have you done with Gem?"

"I don't know anything." Tears welled in her eyes and she shook her head a fraction. "I haven't seen her since Vegas."

My gaze bore into her like Superman's lasers. "Bullshit. Where is she?"

Sam's hand appeared on my shoulder. "Kyle. Come on, dude. Let Jones do his job."

I shrugged Sam's hand away and straightened my denim jacket. "Not if he's going to let her walk out of here."

Jones threw me a frosty glare. "Our analysts identified someone with short black hair from the bar footage yesterday. We went to Taylah's, did a search, and brought her in for further questioning. But nothing ties her to recent incidents. Her story checks out."

She was lying. She had to be lying. "I don't believe you."

Taylah wrapped her arms around herself. "Kyle, Jones showed me the pictures. It's not me. I was at work, on day shift at the hospital."

I pointed toward Jones's folders. The photocopies of our death threats and printed images from the bar protruded from the sides. "Show me them. Prove to me it's not Taylah."

"Fine." Jones's eyes drilled into me. "But Miss Anderson may leave."

Taylah sucked in a jagged breath. "I can stay. I said I'd do anything to help."

If Jones couldn't get a confession out of her, maybe I could? It seemed unlikely, going on my past performance, but I'd give it my best shot. "She stays."

A low growl rumbled deep in Jones's throat and he jutted his chin toward the meeting room I'd come from. "Get in there."

I stormed into the room, followed by the detectives, Taylah, and Sam. Everyone took a seat around the boardroom table. Jones and Morris next to Marshall. Taylah, two chairs away from me and Sam.

Jones sifted through his folders, grabbed the printouts, and handed them to me. "This is what we got from the bar footage. Enhanced imaging shows black hair sticking out from underneath the hat. Going on physique and Taylah's recent activities, we thought it was her."

I examined the five photos, feeling Taylah's wary but star-struck eyes on me. God, the pictures looked like her. Black hair, slender shoulders, same shaped jawline. *It is her.* Whatever bullshit she had spun, I had to get to the truth. I slapped the photos on the table in front of her and stabbed them. "This is you, isn't it? You shoot through on your lunch break? Come here for Gem?" *Time to fess up, bitch.*

Jones hit me with a hard glare. Morris, with a half-smirk on his face, seemed to be enjoying the show.

Taylah jerked her chin back. "No. I don't know who is in these pictures, but it isn't me."

Liar! I clenched my fists, dug my fingernails into my palms. What did I have to do or say to get her to confess? For her to tell us where Gemma was?

Jones picked up his pen, spun it, and clicked it against the table, like he had during our first meeting. Every *click* twisted tension into the back of my neck like a tightening clamp. Clenching my teeth, I snarled at Taylah. "You're lying."

Her eyes welled with tears again. "No. I'm not. It's the truth. I don't know why you think I have something to do with her disappearance. Is this more serious than the detectives have let on?"

"Beyond serious." I blurted. "Where did you take her?"

"Take her?" Taylah's eyes widened. "You mean as in k-k-kidnapped?" she stuttered. "Oh. My. God. Is that what's happened?"

Frustration got the better of me as I turned on Jones and Morris. "What the hell did you question her about? What she ate for dinner?"

Morris kept his poker face in place. "Kyle, we asked her regarding her whereabouts yesterday and checked their validity. She has been cleared. So stop. Now."

There was no way I'd do that. I tilted my head toward Taylah.

Acid dripped off my tongue. "Are you jealous of her? Delusional. Think you and I should be together?"

Taylah gaped as she rubbed the tattoo of my face on her forearm. "What? No."

"Did you hurt her?" My chest seized at the very thought.

Taylah shook her head. "God no. She's awesome. You two look amazing together."

I slapped my hand on the table and shot her my most chilling stare. "Then where is she?" My voice cracked. "What the fuck have you done with her?"

Jones shoved his chair back and shot to his feet. "Kyle, enough. Do you want me to haul your ass out of here?"

As I meet Jones square in the eye, my blood hit boiling point. "No, I don't. But I will *not* calm down. Not until Gem's found."

Taylah held her hand out toward Jones. "It's okay." There was a shaky edge in her voice. "I deal with distraught people all the time in Emergency at the hospital. He has every right to be upset. Who wouldn't be? I've seen every online video and interview of Kyle and know this isn't his normal self. He's a softy at heart. Just overly emotional right now."

Who was this chick? Mother Fucking Theresa?

She swiveled on her chair to face me. She still had that star-struck haze in her eyes. "Kyle, please believe me. I don't know where Gemma is."

You're full of shit.

Hunter burst through the door with Mick tailing him. "What's going on?" His face blanched at the sight of Taylah.

"What the hell, Collins?" Jones spat. "I don't need you in here too."

Hunter shrugged. "Sue me."

I jumped from my seat and paced the floor, filling Hunter in on what had happened. Jones folded his arms and his eyes bored into me the whole time. Taylah's mouth hung open as her eyes, welling with a teary and bedazzled gaze, stayed on Hunter and me.

She took a deep breath and placed her hand on her heart. "Wow . . . both of you are here. For real. Like . . . in person. So surreal." She drew her shoulders back and wiped her damp cheek. " Wow!"

I'd had enough. I stormed toward the table and smacked my palms onto the surface. I shot icy daggers at her. "For the last time. Where is Gem? What the fuck have you done with her?"

"Nothing. I swear. I love you guys. And Gemma."

Jones's face reddened. His eyes bulged. He stepped toward me and pointed to the chair beside Taylah. "Kyle. Sit down and shut up, or you're gone. Got it?"

Marshall and Morris stiffened, ready to assist Jones.

As I clenched my fists, my breaths came hard and fast, like a dragon ready to spit fire. I burned from the inside out, my hold on control slipping. I wanted to pick up the chair and smash the glass. Throw the files across the room. Upend the desk and break it into a million pieces. *No.*

Stop.

Shit.

I turned and stepped toward the back wall. I closed my eyes and covered my mouth with my hand. Flashes of my father in a rage hurtled through my mind. *Don't be like this. Don't be like him.*

I glanced at Hunter standing nearby. An *I'm-just-as-worried-as-you* look was written all over his face. Knowing Hunter and our security team were as concerned about Gemma as I was, earthed my fuse. I needed to draw on Hunter's control and Gemma's strength, wherever she was, to get through this.

Nope.

No chance.

Without Gemma, the restraint on my temper had worn paper-thin.

This chick would pay.

I spun back toward the table and gripped onto the edge so tightly I thought it might snap. "If you're such a fan, and love us so much, why have you been sending us sick, fucked-up letters?"

"Letters?" Taylah smoothed her hand over her hair and furrowed her brow. "You mentioned something in Vegas about letters. But I don't know what you're talking about."

I snatched the top folder off Jones's pile, grabbed the copies, and slapped them down in front of her. "These."

Jones lunged after the paperwork, but I yanked them out of his reach.

Fire burned in Jones's eyes. "She doesn't need to see those. We'll handle this."

My insides screamed. "Like you have been until now?" I handed Taylah the letters, my eyes pinning Jones. My hands shook. I wanted to punch the shit out of the guy. But being thrown in jail wouldn't help Gemma. "You waited until Gem was kidnapped before you acted."

Morris stabbed his finger against the table. "That's not the case, and you know it. We are, and always have done everything we can. We've followed every lead. Whoever is behind these threats knows what they're doing and has been very elusive."

My nostrils flared as Taylah read the letters.

Nausea pooled in my gut knowing this sick chick wrote them. That she hated Gemma so much. That she was obsessed with me. I didn't want to be near her, but I had to suck it up so I could find Gemma.

"Last warning, Kyle." Jones's jaw ticked. I could almost see the steam coming out of his ears. "Sit. You're here to discuss Miss Anderson's innocence, not pass on evidence."

Sam gave me a stern nod.

I drew in a deep breath, rolled and stretched my neck from side to side. Stepping around Taylah, I grabbed my chair and took a seat, angled sideways. I stretched out my legs and propped my elbow on the table. I gave a quick flick of my hand at Jones, encouraging him to proceed. *Hurry up. Let's get on with it.*

Jones grumbled as he sat.

Taylah shuffled through the pages again, reading each one. Her lips mouthed every word. Her fair face paled, turning ghostly white.

I counted each letter. *Wait.* We'd received five letters. Why were there seven? I grabbed them after Taylah finished and scanned the words. More sickening death threats. I flipped the pages around to Jones. "When did these two turn up? Why haven't I seen them before?"

Hunter dashed over from leaning against the wall and read them. "Jesus. There are more?"

Morris's brow furrowed. "Both were delivered to Sophie's office. She sent them to us after she'd told Miss Lonsdale about them."

Why didn't Gemma tell me about them? Why had she lied? And Sophie was in on it too? My sworn oath with Gemma was to never keep secrets from each other. So why had she? *Why?*

But none of that mattered right now. I had to turn this city upside down to find her.

Taylah shed a tear; the papers trembled in her hands. "I've never seen these letters before in my life." The fear in her eyes caught me off-guard. *No . . . don't fall for her games.* Her voice shook. "Death threats? On Gemma? Who'd do this?"

"Um . . . Someone crazy like you," I mumbled under my breath, loud enough for her to hear.

"I swear, Kyle." Another tear fell onto her cheek. She brushed it away with her fingertips. "I didn't send these. I'd never hurt Gemma. Never stop you from marrying her."

My heart constricted with every beat. *I should be married.*

I shot forward to the edge of my seat. One more inch and I'd be down on my knees, begging. "Then please, if you know anything about where she is, tell me. I need her to come home. Safe."

I needed Gemma more than oxygen. I'd lost my family; I couldn't lose her too. What would I do if something horrific had happened? I couldn't bear the pain. Even the mere thought crippled me.

Taylah picked up one letter and then another. "Kyle, I didn't do this. I can't help you. I'm so sorry."

My heart hit the floor. I hung my head. This was useless. God, even I believed in her denial.

She picked up another page.

I looked up, scrutinizing her every move as she concentrated on each letter and read them again.

I pointed to the pages. "You know something, don't you?"

Taylah shook her head but remained focused on the letters. "No. I mean . . . these words. This line. I know it. I've seen it. It's always on someone's comments on my Ringers Fan Club posts or . . . could be on my personal Facebook page. I have thousands of followers on each. Any time I post about you, they always reply with *'Kyle's mine. Mine. Mine.'*"

My heart kick-started. "You know who it is?"

"Not off the top of my head. But they're always active on my posts." Taylah's gaze flitted from me to Jones, to Morris, to Marshall. "Search my Facebook pages. You'll find the person I'm talking about."

Holy shit. My gut hit the floor. Did we have the wrong person? Or was this just another diversion? If Taylah was right, saying sorry would never rectify what I'd accused her of. But this wasn't over. Not until we'd found Gemma. I wouldn't let her off the hook yet.

"Didn't you search her social media?" I directed my snarky tone toward Jones. Wouldn't they have done that when she was a suspect?

Jones remained unmoved by my challenging glare. "Taylah was cleared after our first interview. There was no need. We analyzed your social accounts but found nothing abnormal." He waggled his pen at Marshall. "Let's move on this. Can you issue an emergency request to get Taylah's data from Facebook? See if we can find the comments and link them to a profile?"

"Yep." Marshall nodded. "But it can take up to twenty-four hours for Meta to respond."

"What?" I was over slow processes and no outcome. How did any case ever get solved? "Gemma could be dead by then. We need to act. Find her now."

Taylah pointed to Marshall's laptop. "Can we use that? We can search my posts. I'll give you my data. I've got nothing to hide."

"I appreciate your cooperation," Jones nodded, "but we have procedures to follow."

I clawed my hands and raked my fingers through my hair. "We

don't have time for procedures. Taylah's here, willing to help. Let's do this."

Jones's eyes narrowed into razor-sharp slits. Clearly, he'd had enough of my outbursts. I didn't care. I wasn't afraid of him.

He sighed and jutted his chin toward Taylah. "Are you sure?"

"Yes." She nodded. "I said I'd do anything to help."

Jones tapped his pen against his folders. Everyone's eyes were on him, waiting for his response. He flicked his hand. "Fine."

Marshall spun the laptop around to Taylah. "Log into your account. I'll go grab my other laptop to run the traces and analysis."

As Marshall rushed from the office, I jumped to my feet and paced the width of the room. I racked my brain. How had we gotten this so wrong? Who was it if it wasn't Taylah?

Hunter tapped my arm. Dark circles loomed underneath his tired eyes. "Hey? This is good."

I leaned in close so no one else could hear. "God, I hope Taylah's onto something. She has to be. I can't shake this awful feeling Gem's in real danger." The feeling had been gnawing inside my gut like a rat on a rope since she'd gone missing. And it grew worse by the hour.

"Yeah. Me too."

"I should've done more to protect her." I should've canceled picking up my suits and gone with her to Nina's. I'd lost Gemma over wanting to wear a new fucking tie to our wedding. How stupid was that?

"No. We did everything possible. This isn't your fault." He clutched my shoulder and gave me a gentle shake. "Hopefully, you've just gotten the breakthrough we needed. If you hadn't gone all desperado and shown Taylah those letters, we wouldn't have this lead."

True, but I shouldn't have lost my temper.

This had to be the right step.

I had to trust Taylah.

I'd gone from despising her to putting Gemma's life in her hands.

Taylah looked up from typing, and her hand shot over her

chest. Her puffy eyes darted back and forth between Hunter and me. "I know you're worried, and I wish I was with you under different circumstances. I know it's not a good time to go all fangirl on you, but wow. Just, wow! Kyle, seeing how much you love Gemma makes me adore you even more."

She really was wearing rose-colored glasses, a truly devoted fan. But right now, I was grateful she'd turned a blind eye to my poor behavior.

"Yeah. Thanks. I'm sorry I got all apeshit." I pointed at the laptop. "If you help find Gem and have absolutely nothing to do with her disappearance, I'll make it up to you. Just do whatever it is you have to do and find who made those comments."

Marshall came back into the room with another laptop and sat beside Taylah.

Jones pulled his chair closer toward Marshall. "You got this?"

"Yep." Marshall's fingers clicked on the keyboard as he typed. His eyes stayed glued to his screen. "Let's see if we can find our stalker-come-kidnapper."

God, it was like watching two gaming geeks go into battle as Taylah and Marshall worked side by side. Sam hovered nearby, watching their screens.

Taylah threw me an encouraging smile. "I know this tagline, Kyle. We'll find her." She turned back to the laptop and gawked. "My God. I knew it. There are hundreds of comments with that phrase. They're on my profile page, not the fan page. Those posts aren't public. The person's name is . . . *Forever Mrs. McIntyre*. Well, if that isn't a dead giveaway, I don't know what is."

"Now what?" I stepped in behind Taylah.

Marshall pointed at Taylah's screen. "Click on that name. Open the profile page."

"On it." She clicked the name.

I held my breath, scanning the screen. A cartoon avatar was the profile picture. No personal details were on the information page.

Shit.

Nothing.

Marshall's voice took on a sense of urgency. "Go into your Facebook settings and download a date range of six months of your posts' data. I'll run it through our diagnostics, see if we can find who it is via an IP address, or a device ID, or some other unique parameter."

Fuck. This will take forever.

My patience wore thinner and thinner. I hated standing here, doing nothing. Waiting. But what else could I do?

Data was downloaded. The USB drive was ripped from the laptop in front of Taylah and inserted into Marshall's device.

"Just running through diagnostics now." Marshall's fingers glided over his keyboard.

I stood, peering over his shoulder, chewing on the edge of my thumb. My heart thudded harder with each passing second. *Please. Please. Please. Find her.*

Taylah clicked on the photo album on Mrs. McIntyre's profile page. "Let's see if she's got anything here." She scrolled through the albums. They were all just pictures of me from my band's photo shoots and events we'd attended. They weren't personal photos; just images anyone could have saved off the Internet.

I stared at Taylah's screen and half-heartedly listened to Marshall's rambling. "Looks like they used a VPN. I'll see what else I can find . . ."

Losing hope, my heart filled with lead. Another dead end.

Then . . . an image caught my eye.

"Wait." I tapped Taylah on the shoulder to stop her scrolling through the photos. "Go back a bit . . . stop." There, on the screen, was another picture of me. But it was a personal photo. On Hunter's balcony. I sifted through my brain. That suit. I'd worn it to my engagement party. Who'd taken that photo of me outside? I swiped my hand across my brow, then rubbed the back of my neck. My pulse pounded inside my head. *Come on . . . think.*

Marshall hollered. "Aha! They always stuff up somewhere. I think I have a cell phone ID . . . It's not a burner phone . . . Checking records, and . . . Gotcha."

I turned to Hunter. The blood drained from my face. "I know

who took that photo. I know who it is—"

Marshall gloated. "The cell phone is registered to—"

My mouth ran dry. I could barely say her name. "It's Vicki."

"Yeah . . . Vicki Rogers." Marshall nodded, but then comprehension hit. "Shit . . . as in your friend?"

"Oh, fuck!" I keeled over and clutched my knees. My vision tunneled toward darkness. "It's Vicki."

How had I been so blind? I remembered her in Vegas. The way she'd disregarded my concerns about Gemma passing out. How she'd begged me not to leave the club. My skin crawled, recalling her touch on my arm. *Fuck.* I'd wanted to invite her to the wedding. What an idiot. What the hell had she done to Gemma?

Hunter shook his head. "You're kidding, right? Vicki?"

A ringing noise burst inside my head like ear-splitting feedback from a speaker.

I had to get out of there.

I had to get to Gemma.

"We have to go. Go now." I waved at Hunter, Sam, and Mick, and charged toward the door.

"Whoa." Jones stood. "You're not going anywhere. This is a police matter. With the threats made, we have to take precautions."

My veins scorched with fire. I had no time for logic. I needed action. "You think I'm not taking this seriously? You can follow your procedures, but I'm going. You can't stop me."

Sam leaped from his chair and blocked the doorway. "Kyle, I agree with Jones on this."

"Vicki has Gem." Agony sawed in my voice. "I have to go. With or without you."

"Don't be a fool." Sam's sharp tone was like a clip to the back of the head. "If Vicki's crazy, she could be armed. Dangerous. Don't try and be a hero. You could put Gemma in more danger. Risking your life is not worth it."

My eyes stung. Every muscle and tendon in my body screamed. "Gem is worth risking everything for."

"Bud." Hunter grabbed my arm. "Please, let's do this the right way."

Tears burned the back of my eyes. My chest ached. "If she's hurt…"

Hunter's eyes flickered with as much pain as I felt tearing my body apart. "Let's not go down that path."

"I have to be there." I swallowed, my throat dry and scratchy.

Jones gave me a stern glare. "You need to follow our procedures. We'll go to Vicki's home, analyze the situation, and question her. You can wait down the street. If she has Gemma, her safety may be compromised if Vicki sees you, or … she may not even be there."

She'd better be.

After running through the processes of what was to happen and the way the detectives would handle the situation, Jones glared at me. "You do not come anywhere near Vicki's home until we give the all clear. Got it?"

I closed my eyes and gave a reluctant nod.

After picking up Chester, we headed for New Jersey. Dylan drove the Suburban as fast as he could.

We stopped a couple of houses down from Vicki's place. My heart raced. The pale blue two-story townhouse with plantation shutters looked unimposing from the outside with its mowed lawn and trimmed hedges. But if Gemma was in there, its veil of innocence would be stripped away.

"Okay," Sam said from the front seat. "We wait here until Jones calls."

Jones and Morris pulled their cruiser into Vicki's driveway. Adrenaline spiked through my veins like shockwaves on steroids. I wiped my sweaty palms on my jeans. The detectives stepped out of the car, straightened their gun holsters, buttoned their suit jackets, and headed up the pathway.

Tapping my heel and fidgeting with my watch, I inched forward on the center rear passenger seat. I leaned closer to the windshield as the detectives approached the house.

At the top of the steps, Morris turned in our direction, gave a short nod.

Jones rolled his shoulders and stretched his neck from side to side.

He raised his hand and knocked on the door.

I held my breath. My heartbeat hammered like a drum.

Oh God. Gem, please be in there.

I need you.

Please be okay.

Chapter 22

GEMMA

I woke, shivering and shaking in Vicki's dark bedroom. The gag around my mouth was new. So were the binds around my wrists and ankles. I tried to move but couldn't. My heart clambered to my parched throat. *Somebody, please help.* Pictures of Kyle stuck to the wall stared back at me. My heart hurt. My eyes stung. *I don't want to die!* I needed my fairy fucking godmother to turn up and get me the hell out of here.

I wanted to go home. To Kyle. Chilling perspiration coated my skin, dripped into my eyes, ran down my cheeks and clung the loose strands of my hair to my face. The putrid smell of pot, crack, and ice hung thick in the air. And was that vomit? In my hair? *Ew!*

A sliver of afternoon light came in from the narrow window above the bed. How long had I been asleep? What day was it? Drugs fogged my head. The effects made my limbs feel even heavier, rendering me immobile with the binds. I needed water. My mouth was as dry as deadwood. The gag had absorbed every droplet of moisture. My body was weak from lack of food. *They're going to starve me to death.* I hadn't eaten since I'd been kidnapped. The glass of water on the nightstand called to me. But everything I'd drunk had been laced by Vicki with God only knew what to keep me comatose. I doubted that water would be any different.

Not that I could remove my gag and reach it anyway. I didn't have the strength.

There was a knock. Downstairs. At the front door.

My pulse jumped so high my head spun. The door to Vicki's room stood slightly ajar. I could hear people talking, just.

"Good afternoon. Are you Vicki Rogers?" A man's voice drifted up the stairs.

I closed my eyes to concentrate and listen. *Who is it? Can they help?*

"Yes." Vicki's tone held no care.

"I'm Detective Jones; this is Detective Morris. We'd like to ask you a few questions about Miss Gemma Lonsdale."

"What's wrong with Gemma?"

"We have a report that she's missing."

My heart jackhammered against my ribs. *They're here.* I fought to find a droplet of moisture in my mouth to call out. *Help.* But my frail voice was nothing but a muffled whisper against the thick wad of fabric tied across my lips. I didn't possess the energy to formulate a scream. Fear scrambled up my throat. I had to let them know I was here. How?

Vicki's voice wafted up to the bedroom; her tone was embedded with innocence. "She's missing? Kyle rang yesterday and asked if I'd seen her, but I didn't know she was missing."

"Can we come inside?" Jones asked. "We'd like a few minutes of your time to ask some questions."

I wriggled on the bed, too weak to move more than an inch. My eyes burned, but no tears formed; they were too dry and gritty from dehydration.

Please, please come inside. I need help.

What could I do to attract attention?

Vicki took on a sheepish tone. "My place is a mess. Can we talk here on the porch?"

"We'd really like to come in so we can get a formal statement."

That must have been Morris, the other detective.

"Sure." There was no hesitation in Vicki's voice. How could she sound so calm? "Please, come into the living room."

The living room? That was on the other side of the hallway. They wouldn't hear me from there. Would they? I needed to make noise now. But how? Twisting my head to look around, desperation grappled my brain for ideas. I could hear the detectives asking questions. Vicki played along, acting upset. *Ugh. That bitch.*

I needed to rattle something. Hit something. Break something. Forcing my limbs to move, I slid my hand across the mattress toward the nightstand. Each finger felt like a leaden nail. Each inch took seconds. Each breath sapped my energy. Biting into the gag and gritting my teeth, I thrust my hand onto the flimsy nightstand. Panting, and with the last fragment of my strength, I pushed the ceramic lamp toward the edge. It took the glass with it and smashed to the wooden floor.

Crash.

Yes! I held my breath, hoping they'd heard.

"What was that?" Morris asked.

I swallowed, trying to find my voice again. My lips were dry and cracked. My tongue had swollen. My throat begged for moisture with every breath. "*Help. Please.*"

God, I could barely hear myself over the gag, let alone someone downstairs. Weak from the exertion, I slumped against the mattress. I had nothing left. *Oh God, please help me.*

"Mind if we check it out?" Morris said.

I prayed. *Yes. Please. Come.*

"It's nothing." Vicki's response was quick and flippant. "Probably just the cat."

Cat? There's no fucking cat. Come.

"Sounded like broken glass," Morris said. "Better make sure your cat is okay."

Footsteps. There were footsteps on the wooden floors. *Yes.* My heart raced. Drawing my hand above my head, I grabbed the metal frame of the bed and tried to rattle it, but it didn't make a squeak.

More footsteps.

Vicki's voice jumped. "The sound didn't come from up there. It was outside."

"Then you won't mind if I take a quick look." Morris's voice drew closer.

"Please," Vicki pleaded. "Don't go up there. My room's a mess."

"Miss, I'll be quick."

"NO!" Vicki screeched. There was a scuffle of footsteps. "Don't touch me. Get your hands off me."

"Ma'am, please stop." Jones groaned as if wrestling Vicki. "Before I arrest you for assault."

Loud thuds ascended the staircase.

I moaned and whimpered, anything to make noise so whoever was coming could hear. The rock goddess was gone; a frantic innocent on death row took her place.

Through the curtain of my messy hair and my sore eyes, I stared at the doorway. *I'm in here. Come.*

A man appeared. With his plain navy suit, white shirt, and jaw squarer than Rami Malek's, he was no sparkling, glittery fairy godmother, but I'd fucking take him.

Too weak to do anything, my eyes fluttered shut. A lone tear slipped from the corner of my eye.

"Jones," Morris hollered. "She's here. Bound and gagged. You right with Vicki?"

"Yep."

"I'll call the paramedics." Morris rushed to my side and removed my gag and binds. "It's okay Gemma. We got you. You're safe now."

Oh. Thank. God.

I sobbed. Relief seeped into my heavy bones like thick tar. I drifted in and out of consciousness. I had no idea how much time passed. Was it seconds? Minutes? Hours? Then I heard familiar footsteps downstairs. My heart pounded. *Kyle. He's here.*

"Kyle. No." Vicki's screech hit my ears as if she were standing right beside me, not downstairs. "No."

"Where is she?" Kyle yelled.

Jones's voice drifted up to the room. "She's upstairs. Morris is with her. Paramedics are moments away."

"NO!" screamed Vicki. "Kyle. Stay with me, not her. Don't go up there. Please don't."

Thunderous footsteps charged up the steps.

"Oh fuck. Gem." Kyle rushed to my side.

My angel had arrived. My eyes fluttered open and shut. I wanted to speak, cry, and fling my arms around him, but weakness rendered me useless.

He sat on the bed, stroked my face, kissed and hugged me. "Babe, I'm here. I'm here. Oh God, please be okay." His hands trembled against my face. "Shit. You're burning up."

I breathed him in. He smelled so good, like whiskey and spice. Dizziness rushed through my head. *He's here. Kyle's here.*

More footsteps. Hunter and our security team barreled into the room.

Hunter's voice hovered overhead. "Holy shit. Look at this fucking place." He glanced at the walls, then fell onto his knees beside my head. "Gem. We're here. We found you." His fingertips felt cool against my hot skin as he stroked my forehead.

Hey Hunt.

They'd found me. Relief should set in, but it didn't.

My vision blurred. My eyes fluttered closed. My heart rate skyrocketed, and I panted, struggling for each breath. Everything was hot. Too hot. I clutched at the sheet.

Burning. Everything's burning.

Sam and Chester and Mick ordered each other around to get towels, get water, get ice to reduce my fever.

Kyle hooked his arm beneath my shoulders to help me upright, but my body slumped. My head lolled back. "Gem, baby, please wake up." His voice, soft and shaky, pleaded. He stroked strands of sticky hair off my face and placed me back on the pillow.

Regardless of how hard I tried, I couldn't open my eyes. Not again.

Sirens wailed and screamed down the street.

Thank fuck.

I'd be okay.

Everything would be okay.

It had to be.

Muffled sounds drifted around me. Oxygen mask. IV needle.

Flashes of light in my eyes. Lifted onto a gurney, carried, placed into the back of an ambulance.

Kyle stayed by my side, never letting go of my hand. Hunter mirrored his actions on my other side. These guys were my life.

As the ambulance raced toward the hospital with sirens blaring, my eyes flickered open. Kyle's eyes were rimmed with red. He clutched my hand to his lips. His cool touch soothed my blazing hot skin.

"I'm sorry," I whispered. "For everything. I love you. So much."

Some alarm beeped above me.

"What's that?" Hunter jumped, clutching my hand tighter.

"Her blood pressure's dropping." The paramedic by my head flicked a switch or two.

I couldn't keep my eyes open any longer. I just wanted to sleep.

"Move," the paramedic snapped.

Was that directed at Kyle? Or Hunter? I couldn't tell.

Another alarm sounded.

"What's that one?" Panic gripped Kyle's voice.

"Her heart rate's dropping."

"Gemma … Gemma … what are you doing? Stay with me." Kyle squeezed my hand, but I couldn't squeeze back. His voice sounded close, then far away. Close, then far away. "Gemma. GEMMA?"

The oxygen mask reappeared over my nose. Another needle pricked my arm. I didn't even flinch as I was prodded and poked.

Fog consumed my brain.

Numbness washed over me.

Darkness set in.

"Gemma. GEMMAAAAAAAAAA."

Kyle's cry was the last thing I heard.

Chapter 23

GEMMA

Lights flashed overhead. A frenzy of whizzing wheels and fast footsteps clattered over the floor. My eyes opened to barely-there thin slits. Everything was blurry. Fuzzy. People in teal scrubs rushed around my gurney.

A voice rambled. "Blood pressure seventy over fifty. Pulse forty-three. Possible drugging with GHB, fentanyl, and ketamine."

Sticky monitors and tape pulled my skin. Fire burned beneath my flesh. I wanted to rip and scratch at it, but my limbs wouldn't work. My breath sliced through my lungs. Nausea heaved and swelled in my gut like a boat on a wild ocean. Bitter vomit filled my mouth. I spluttered and spat. *Bluuugh.* Someone wiped a cool cloth across my lips. My eyes fluttered closed. I slipped into darkness.

***

Crisp sheets itched my skin. Cool air enveloped me. Cackling laughter on low volume filtered from a nearby TV.

I sensed Kyle beside me. Ignoring the scratchiness in my dry eyes, I pried them open slowly. His hand lay beside mine on the mattress. His woodsy scent filling my head. My body ached to touch him, have him hold me.

"Oh. Thank. God." He lunged forward from the chair and kissed me. Tears escaped down his cheeks. "You're awake. You're awake." He kissed my lips, my forehead, my cheeks, again, again, not letting me go.

His warmth seeped into every cell of my body. "Hi," I whispered, my throat sore and arid.

Sitting on the mattress beside me, he pressed his forehead to mine and stroked my hair. "You okay? You scared the hell out of me."

My head ached, my body ached—everything ached. But I was alive. "Where am I?" With an IV in my arm, an ugly nightgown covering me, and bland surroundings, I could easily guess. But how did I get here?

"You're in hospital." Kyle sniffled, rubbed his nose.

My pulse shot upwards. Random images flickered through my mind. *Vicki's room. The drugs. The hate in Vicki's eyes.* Was it real or had it been a nightmare? Nothing made sense. My voice came in a staggered whisper. "Vicki . . . wanted to kill me."

He lowered his chin; anguish contorted his face. "I'm so sorry. I never suspected her. Never knew she felt that way. She'll be in jail for a very long time."

I sobbed. Tears slipped from my eyes. "She was my friend." My trust in those close to me had been shattered yet again. Only Vicki made the awful things others had done look like child's play. Vicki was pure evil.

Kyle wiped my wet cheek with the pad of his thumb. "She had us all fooled." He entwined our fingers and kissed the back of my hand.

I stared at our ring fingers. The absence of wedding bands crushed my heart. "We didn't get married."

He shook his head in slow motion. "*Shh.* Don't worry about that now. We'll sort that out later. When you're better. You're safe. That's all that matters."

The evening sunset threw a golden glow through the venetian blinds. I had lost all sense of time. "How long? . . . What time is it?"

"It's Sunday afternoon. You've been in here nearly twenty-four hours."

Sunday. What? It felt like a couple of hours had passed, not days. "How did you find me?"

Kyle ran his thumb over the back of my hand. "You won't believe this, but Taylah—we ran into her at the police precinct. She recognized a line on the letters was the same as some comments on her Facebook page. It was a freakish lucky break. But it was the one that saved you."

Our psycho fan helped find me? The one who'd stressed me out for weeks? I couldn't unpack that information right now. Nothing made sense. "I don't care how you found me. I'm just glad you did." Otherwise, after tonight, it would've been pointless. I would've been dead.

Kyle scooped my hair back and cupped the side of my face. "Just so you know, I never would've stopped looking for you."

There was a distance in his eyes. I sensed he wanted to say so much more, but he didn't. Was he mad at me for not listening to him? Was he blaming me for what had happened? Had he found out about the other letters? *Shit.* My palms turned clammy and I fidgeted with the sheet. None of this would've happened if I hadn't felt like a caged bird, confined to my home, and being told what to do. Sinking deep into the pillows, I closed my eyes. I didn't have the strength to talk about that now.

"You tired?" He ran his fingertips across my forehead. "You need more rest?"

"No. I'm okay." I adjusted the pillows beneath my head, grateful to move, even if only slowly. "Where's Hunt?"

"He'll be here soon. He went home to get some sleep. It's been a long couple days."

Days I couldn't remember; just snippets of horror.

Gerard Rivers—our archenemy of a reporter—filled the TV screen mounted above the end of my bed. What was Kyle doing watching *Entertainment On-Show*?

Live, from outside the hospital, Gerard delivered his story:

Shocking new details have been released from Everhide's

publicist today after recent events surrounding the band's lead guitarist. Gemma Lonsdale was rushed to the hospital on Saturday afternoon after being the alleged victim of a terrifying abduction. Speculations rose on Friday as to the whereabouts of Miss Lonsdale when she didn't turn up to what appeared to be a private wedding ceremony for her and fellow band member, bass guitarist, Kyle McIntyre, in Downtown Manhattan. Fans posted pictures of the broken-hearted heartthrob sighted outside their lawyer's office, being consoled by friends.

My heart bled as photographs of Kyle kneeling on the sidewalk flashed on the TV. His face was in his hands. Wide-eyed shock was frozen on my friends' faces.

Kyle's grip tightened around my fingers. I never wanted to break his heart, and I had.

The news continued.

It turns out the situation was much more serious than being stood up at the altar. Witnesses saw detectives entering a townhouse in Montgomery, New Jersey, believed to be owned by one of the band's close friends, Vicki Rogers, late yesterday afternoon. Moments later, band members Kyle McIntyre and Hunter Collins were on site and left in the back of an ambulance with Miss Lonsdale. Miss Rogers was arrested by police. Initial reports state that Miss Lonsdale had been drugged and held against her will. Their publicist has confirmed Miss Lonsdale is recuperating and the band requests respect for their privacy as they recover from the horrific ordeal. We wish Gemma a speedy return to health. We send her and the band our best wishes.

I drew the sheets high up my chest. *How humiliating.* I prided myself on being strong and independent. Dealing with scandals, rumors, and gossip was easy, as most of them were lies. But this was a new personal low. This incident made me out to be fragile and vulnerable, and highlighted how quickly everything could be snatched away. Every step I made fed the media wolves. Nothing was ever private. "Of course this made the news."

Kyle grabbed the remote and switched off the TV. "Yeah. We had to get Kate to send out a statement. Our cell phones went into meltdown. Kate and Bec couldn't handle all the calls."

I tugged at the neckline of the gown, digging into my neck. Nothing about my abduction had been sugarcoated. But the last thing I needed was an influx of sympathy and pity from fans and the media. I just wanted to be alone, process what had happened.

Pushing my fears aside, I hardened my heart. It was best to treat this as just another fiasco. "It's been a while since we've done anything headline-worthy. Thought I better give Kate and Bec something to earn their keep. Wouldn't want them to get bored."

Kyle puffed air through his nose. No humor touched his voice. "I'd sooner have them deal with us having sex in public again than something like this."

True. When we'd first started dating, our well-constructed lies and diversionary tactics had kept our relationship a secret for months. We'd kept our private lives out of the spotlight until we were ready to go public. But there was no way to cover up this nightmare. No way to control the narrative. It was as if I'd been strung up naked in the middle of Times Square for all to see. I felt weak. And I hated that. I didn't want people to see that side of me exposed.

Tears stung the backs of my eyes. Then *thump.* My stomach sank to the floor. There was only one thing worse than dealing with the media. "If we've been in the news, I guess my mother called."

Kyle scratched his scruffy chin. "Actually, no. She hasn't. Not even a text."

Welts of hurt pushed against my ribs. My life had been in danger and my mom didn't care. Either she hadn't been offered money for some bullshit story, or my kidnapping wasn't scandalous enough.

He reached inside his leather jacket. "You want me to send her a message?"

"No." I caught his arm. "Don't bother." My mother had done too much irreparable damage over the years. Best she stayed away.

"Good. She'd only upset you. But there are people here who do care." He thumbed toward the door. "Lexi and Kara are outside. They'll be stoked you're awake. You want me to get them?"

My lungs seized. My vision tunneled and blurred. Panic shot through my veins. *I was in Vicki's room. Unable to move. Couldn't scream. Couldn't fight. Vicki loomed over me. Red devil eyes.*

"No." The door to my heart slammed shut. "No. I don't want to see anyone."

"But they've been worried about you."

The tape on my arm pulled my skin. I picked and scratched at the edge. I needed to get out of here. Out of bed. Out of the hospital. Out into fresh air. Now. Now. *Now.* "I'm not ready to see them."

He placed his hand over mine. "Gem, what are you doing?"

I slapped his hand away and scratched at the tape. Harder. Faster. *Pick. Pick. Pick.* The walls grew closer. Every breath was a struggle. The room was too small. Too dark. Too pungent, like a chemical factory. It was just like Vicki's place. It wasn't safe. "Get me out of here."

He grabbed my hands and drew me against his chest. "Gem. Gem. It's okay. I got you." He kissed the top of my head, held me close.

Tears burned my eyes. I sobbed, emotion pouring from me in a rapid current. "It's not okay. I'm not okay." As I clutched his T-shirt, my chin quivered. "I want to go home."

"You can't. You have to stay for another night or two." The anguish in his voice speared my heart. The image of him on TV, devastated on the sidewalk was scorched into my brain. I didn't want to put him through heartache like that ever again. He tightened his arms around me. "God, I'm so glad we found you. I was terrified I'd lost you."

That possibility had come too close. This was so screwed up on so many levels. How would I come to terms with what had happened? Be able to trust people again? Find myself again and my strength? My mind spun out of control; I couldn't see the path forward. This wasn't like me. I'd always known what I wanted and went after it. The past few weeks had done nothing but hinder and cloud my judgment. I needed my balance restored.

I reached up and stroked Kyle's cheek. His soft stubble tickled my fingertips. "I'm not going anywhere. Not now. Not ever."

But getting out of here was all I wanted to do. I wanted to get away from everyone and the mayhem in my mind. I'd been violated, drugged, and held against my will. I couldn't see past the darkness. It grew thicker and thicker. Drew closer and closer. Somehow, I had to find my way back into the light.

Problem was, I didn't know where to start.

Chapter 24

GEMMA

For two days, I was prodded and pricked at the hospital. Blood tests, examinations, and an IV for rehydration. I was never alone— Kyle and Hunter took turns being by my side. They were the only people I wanted to see. I refused to see anyone else. The horrific kidnapping had rattled my brain like coins in a tin can. No other noise could drown it out, and other people only exacerbated my fear.

The next day at home, I still didn't feel normal. Was it the drugs wearing off? Clutching a cushion to my chest, I curled up on my sofa, staring at an unlit candle on the coffee table. I kept trying to piece together the days I'd lost. I was alive because of Kyle. He'd told me about what happened with Taylah at the precinct. I'd never had anyone like him care for me so deeply before. He loved me. Gave me his all. And it scared me. How could I do the same after being kidnapped? I feared shadows, noises, the dark, small spaces. I wasn't the same anymore. Somehow I needed to lock this fear away. Re-establish my resilience. Kyle knew me better than anyone, but if he saw how fucked up I was . . . he'd run.

My therapist would have her work cut out for her trying to fix the shit going on inside my head.

How could I get married when I was broken?

Kyle lazed on the adjacent sofa, reading a Charles Bukowski paperback. Every conversation we'd had since I'd been rescued had exhausted me. Irked me. His never-ending *"Can I get you something to eat?" "Are you feeling okay?" "Do you want to talk about what happened?"* was a constant jackhammer in my head. The things I loved about him—his love, our connection, the way he made me feel safe—smothered me again like a crude oil spill.

Something had to change before I drowned.

I wanted to blame him for what had happened, but I couldn't. It was my own stupid fault. Being kidnapped had happened so easily. So quickly. One horrid thought kept skipping through my brain . . . none of this would've happened if we weren't together.

Kyle put down his book on the coffee table and fidgeted with his watch. "Can I get you anything?"

Every muscle in my hands tensed, and I crushed the cushion against my chest. "No. I'm fine."

"Okay." He brushed his hands over his thighs and stood. "We're meeting Richard this afternoon at four. I'll just go confirm our flight for tomorrow night and send out the final invite details to our guests before I get changed."

Shit. Belize. The wedding. *Shit. Shit. Shit.*

Kyle stretched his arms above his head, flashing a strip of bare flesh beneath his T-shirt. Skin I missed touching and kissing, but couldn't bring myself to do so. What was wrong with me? I had to fix this. Fix me.

He went to step past me, but I grabbed his hand. My stomach plummeted to the floor. "Wait . . . we need to talk. About the wedding." I tugged his hand, and he sat beside me. I couldn't meet his gaze. "With everything that's happened, I think we should wait. Maybe a couple weeks. A month. Maybe even longer."

"What?" Air rushed from his lungs. "No." He swiveled to face me. "You're fine to fly. The doctor gave you the all clear."

"I know. But that's not what I mean." I closed my eyes, searching my brain for the right words. "I need time. To recover. To clear my head."

"Yeah, we can do that together. On our honeymoon."

"It's not just about Vicki." There were other issues that needed resolving. "It's about us too."

"What are you talking about?" His voice sliced my heart slowly, one deep cut at a time.

I picked at the threads of the cushion; it helped me to focus. "After we got engaged, we toured for nine months and did promo. Life isn't normal when we travel. We know that. But organizing the wedding around shows, events, and the threats—things went haywire."

"Our circumstances haven't been normal. Even for us, it's been hectic. I agree."

The show business I could handle. But the threats and my capture had changed me. "My life wasn't my own. I got frustrated by you and everyone telling me what to do. *You* were suffocating my existence."

He flinched as if I'd torn his heart from his chest. "I *what?* Suffocated you? How?"

The agony in his expression made me feel worse than I already did. But I'd opened my mouth and my stress flooded out. "All the extra security, the checking up on me, the wanting to go everywhere with me. It got too much."

"Is that why you lied?" His eyebrows pinched together as he stared toward the coffee table. "About the other letters?"

I twisted the cushion tassel tight around my finger. *Fuck. He'd found out about them.* "Things were stressful enough; I didn't want them to get worse. I felt trapped, like Rapunzel locked away in a tower. That's not me."

He took my hand in his. "I know it's not. Why didn't you tell me? I didn't know what I was doing and how much it affected you."

"I got tired of fighting."

His eyes, dark and glassy, locked onto mine. "Maybe if you hadn't been so blasé about the threats, I wouldn't have gone so crazy making sure you were safe. I could tell you were worried. But you never took things seriously. The show in Vegas got to you, yet you put on this tough front. You made out you were invincible when I know you're not. I was scared for you. We all were."

"Everything just got so fucked up."

"I know. And I'm sorry for my part in it."

I dug my nails into the cushion, hard. "You want everything to be perfect all the time, and it's not. *I'm* not perfect. You've gone loco over our wedding. You want the perfect suit. The perfect cake. The perfect day for everyone. But during the process, you lost sight of us. All I wanted … what *we* initially wanted … was for the day to be about us. Nobody else."

"I want the people who are important to us there to celebrate. What's wrong with that?"

"Because they don't matter. It's our day, not theirs."

The pain storming in his eyes tore my heart. "They do matter. They'd do anything for us. They're our family. Don't you see that?" He searched my face for my answer, but it never came. I didn't know who I could trust anymore. His shoulders slouched. "Gem, what's going on? We never usually fight like this."

I sank deeper into the sofa. There'd been too much heartache and pain since we'd gotten together. "Life's changed. We've grown up, lived for our music … fell in love." I threaded my fingers with his. "We're still finding our groove as a couple. Neither one of us likes to compromise. We're stubborn and pigheaded."

"So, what are you saying?"

"I can't flick a switch and go from fearing for my life and nearly dying to being happy and celebrating our wedding within a couple days. I'm not thinking straight. Please, can we wait at least a month or two until I'm in the right headspace?"

I heard his heartstrings snap. Furrows as deep as the Mariana Trench appeared in his brow. "Gem, I can only try to understand what you went through. I'm here for you in any and every way possible. But I don't want to delay the wedding. It will be good for you, something positive. You'll be in a safe place, surrounded by people who love you." He squeezed my hands tight. "I've waited so long to marry you. My heart broke when you didn't turn up at Richard's. I hated myself so much when I thought I'd driven you away. But you're here. And I love you so much. We need this Gem to set our lives back on the right track."

"We will. I just need some time."

"Time is so precious. It nearly got stolen away from us." Tears welled in his eyes. "When we worked out you'd been taken, I lost my mind. You're my life and you got hurt because I didn't protect you enough. I didn't do enough to keep you safe."

I ripped my hands free from his. "Haven't you heard a word I'm saying? You can't protect me every second of the day. It's impossible."

"I should be able to. With all our resources and money and tech, you should be the safest person on the planet." He stopped and the color drained from his face. "Or is there something else going on?"

I sniffled, and a shudder coursed through my veins. "Don't you feel it?" I hated the way the words tasted in my mouth. "There's this wedge between us. It's been growing and growing."

"What wedge? The few disagreements we've had about the wedding? About your safety? That's not a wedge; that's life. We haven't seen eye to eye. I know that's weird for us, but it was bound to happen. Don't draw conclusions based on a few crazy weeks."

I shook my head slowly. "This isn't a sudden thing. It's been gradual . . . over the past couple months." *Shit.* Could I crush him anymore?

"Gem, no." He edged closer, curled his hand behind my neck, and threaded his fingers into my hair. He kneaded at the knots at the base of my head. His touch normally made me melt. But not today. "We've had a few arguments; nothing we can't sort out."

My eyes stung. My heart ached like a rake had ripped it to shreds. "Then give me some time. Some space."

"Don't shut me out. Not now." Fear flicked through his dark eyes.

My pulse hammered in my ears. "How can you marry me when I'm a mess?"

He leaned closer. "Because I love you. I know you. Better than yourself. You're tough. A fighter. My Gem."

I'd thought so too. But I hadn't been strong enough against Vicki, had come too close to losing my life. I needed time to repair.

"You're all I thought about when Vicki had me. Your love kept me going. I want to marry you. Spend my life with you. I just need to feel better before we get on that plane."

His hands fell to his lap. He gazed toward the windows.

My stomach twisted into a frenzy of somersaulting knots. "I'm sorry. Please understand."

Pain chiseled his face, dug deep hollows into his cheeks. "Can you be honest with me?" He swallowed hard and grimaced. "Do you want to fucking marry me at all?"

I gasped, lost for words. How could he question that? "I do, but—"

"But nothing. We could get married and recoup on our honeymoon. I know you've been through hell. I'm here for you."

He went to wrap his arms around me, but I shied away. "I know. But I need to fix me first. You can't help with that."

I placed my hands on the sofa to stand, but he grabbed my arm. "Where are you going?"

"I don't know." My lip quivered. "Out. Away. Somewhere I can breathe."

"You can't leave."

"Yes, I can. I've lived long enough in this crazy world and in the public eye to know how to look after myself. I don't need you to father me. Or control me."

"I'm not. Gem?" A tear caught on his lashes; his agony thundered like rapids through my veins.

But I'd had enough.

I tugged my arm free, kissed him on the forehead, and headed toward the kitchen. I grabbed my cell phone off the counter and rushed for the door. "I just need to get out of here." I needed fresh air, not be cooped up inside.

"I'll come with you."

"No. I'm okay."

"Gem." He charged after me, blocking my path. His soulful eyes speared arrows through my heart. "Don't do this. Let me in." He flicked his hand toward the living room window. "You won't see anyone other than me and Hunt. You've locked yourself away from the people who care—Kara, Lexie, Hayden, our team— they're worried about you. Stop pushing everyone who loves you aside. When times get tough, we stick together. Always. You don't abandon those you love."

I grimaced and lowered my gaze. He'd just smashed and stomped my heart into the floor. Tears pooled on the rims of my eyes. *Fuck.*

I *was* just like my father.

I needed to protect myself. Protect those I loved by dealing with the trauma in my mind by myself. I needed to find my strength again. Find me again. Kyle wanted every ounce of my love, and I could only give him so much. "I . . . I have to go."

I reached for the door handle, but he grabbed me on the shoulder.

He spun me around and crushed his lips against mine. He kissed me hard. Weakened my knees. Left me gasping for breath. His hands, trembling and warm, caressed my neck. "Stay."

"No. I need to get out of here." No matter how much it hurt, I needed to be alone. Needed some space. Needed to feel *free*. With shudders coursing through my body, I pushed against his chest, opened the door, and rushed down the stairwell to the garage to avoid the paparazzi camped out the front of my building. Texting Chester, who was on duty, to follow, I burst through the door into the back laneway and headed toward the river.

Cries erupted from deep inside my chest. The *I've-lost-the-battle* look in Kyle's eyes hurt my soul. Had I done irreparable damage? Broken his heart too much? I clutched at my T-shirt. My heart bled across the cobblestones. I couldn't comprehend I'd hurt him again. But I needed time to myself. No one could help me.

Not even Kyle.

Crossing the highway and the Hudson Greenway, I hit the pier and ran. Ran as fast as I could toward the end. The wind whipped my hair. The muddy smell of the river filled my nostrils. The sun beat against my flesh. With each pumping fist, I wanted to pummel Vicki's face. With each pounding heartbeat, I wanted to fix everything between Kyle and me. With each heaving breath, I wanted to erase the nightmares from my head.

At the end of the pier, I keeled over and clutched my knees. Chester kept his distance, lingering by a park bench. As I sucked in huge breaths, my whole body shook. I couldn't think straight. Every time I closed my eyes, I saw Vicki. Her manic eyes. Panic clawed at my brain. I didn't know which friends I could trust. Those I loved knew how to hurt me the most. But I was no better. I'd just hurt Kyle.

Was he better off without me? So we couldn't hurt each other anymore?

Had I destroyed what we had?

Arrrrgh!

Vicki. Hospital. Kyle. Light. Darkness.

My mind wouldn't stop racing.

Drawing in the biggest breath, I turned toward New Jersey. The afternoon sunlight glinted golden off the water and the distant buildings. With all my might, I screamed. Screamed until tears streamed down my cheeks and burned my throat.

I wouldn't let this ruin me. Being alone was the only way I could get through this.

I needed to process what had happened. Find a way forward.

When life fell apart, there was only one person I could truly rely on.

And one person only.

Me!

Chapter 25

KYLE

I took a swig of JD straight from the bottle and stared at the headstones on my parents' graves. After a shower of rain, the damp ground beneath my knees soaked my jeans. I'd never felt so alone in my life. Empty. Wrecked. Gemma had broken my heart for the second time within a matter of days. First, when she hadn't turned up to our wedding at Richard's. Second, when she'd wanted to delay Belize. I'd hurt her too. Something I swore I'd never do again. Words could be crueler than actions.

Truth hurt even more.

She was struggling to come to terms with what had happened. Who wouldn't? I wanted to be there for her, be her life support. When things went wrong, we'd jam, thrash out our problems playing music. Write some gut-wrenching lyrics. Drown in a bottle or two of JD. That was the way we'd dealt with any issue.

We didn't walk away from each other.

She'd pushed me away one too many times.

But she'd done me a favor. I'd woken up. I had to stop being blinded by love. *I'm the problem. Not Gemma.*

I'd been a selfish prick. I'd thought marrying her sooner rather than later would be a good thing. When had I not given her anything and everything she needed?

Since I'd thought I'd lost her.

Leaning forward, I ran my fingers over the marble headstone, tracing the engraved names. *Claire and William McIntyre.* "Hey Mom. Dad." Every breath caused my ribs to shudder. "Sorry, it's been a while since I've visited. Life's been crazy. I miss you so much, Mom. I don't know what to do. I screwed up. Gem's hurting. And I don't know how to fix it. Don't know if I can."

I sat back on my haunches, the heels of my Nikes digging into my butt cheeks. "The thing is . . . it's my fault. I drove her away. She resents everything I did. Losing her would kill me." I took a gulp from the bottle and wiped my mouth on the sleeve of my leather jacket. "Maybe after everything that's happened, we should just go back to being friends." Was that even possible? I'd sooner have her in my life than destroy everything we'd built together. Maybe Gemma was right. Our problems had been snowballing since we'd first gotten together.

I sniffled and fought the sting in my eyes. "I'm just like you, Dad. A fucking control freak. An asshole. I destroyed her. Like you did to Mom. Like you did to me." I scratched my cheek, remembering the sting of my father's backhand and the anger, laced with disappointment, in his voice. *"You'll do as I say." "Turn off the fucking music." "You'll never amount to anything." "You're nothing but a puny weed."* I wasn't violent like my father, but my unrelenting determination to make something of my life, the uncanny connection with those I called family, and my obsession to keep those I loved safe had backfired. Epic failure.

I had no idea what to do next.

My cell phone vibrated in my jacket pocket. Placing the JD on the grave, I grabbed it, thinking it would be the hundredth call from Gemma I'd refused to answer. She wanted space, so I was giving it to her.

I went to swipe the screen to stop it ringing, but the caller ID displayed "Hunter". I took a deep breath and answered it.

Before I could say a word, Hunter screamed. "What the fuck have you done?"

"Me? Nothing."

"Where are you? Gem called me looking for you. She said she went for a run, came home, and you were gone. She's bawling. Something about you left. What the hell? Get back here now."

Every cell in my body wanted to rush home to her, but intuition kicked in. If I did, it would destroy us. We'd just fight and say more hurtful things. "No. She said she wants time to sort her shit out."

"You don't do this to her. Get your head out of your ass."

"She made it perfectly clear she didn't want me around." Gemma was one of the strongest, most resilient people I knew. She'd be fine. She always was. "She's better off without me."

"You're talking shit." Hunter's voice shredded through the speaker. "We came too close to losing her, but we didn't. Whatever hell you think you're in is nothing compared to what she went through. Don't be a dick." His harsh tone softened. "She may never be the same after what happened. She needs us. We are three. Not two plus one."

I closed my eyes and bowed my head. That was what we'd always said to each other before our hearts had gotten involved. Before love fucked us up.

Desperation swung in Hunter's voice. "I can't get through to her like you can. You're her rock. Always have been. Because of you, we found her. We have our Gem back." Hunter dialed down his volume. "What are you doing, Kyle? Come home. She needs you. Be grateful and treasure every moment you have with her. You're fucking lucky she's alive. I . . . I wasn't lucky with Ryan. I lost him."

Fuck. I was such a prick. I wasn't the only one who'd lost loved ones. Hunter had lost his son. Was it different that Hunter had lost his baby before he had a lifetime of memories that could shatter his heart? I'd wanted to give Gemma everything. Make her happy. Give her a full life. But maybe I couldn't do that anymore. "She deserves someone better than me. I'm just someone who suffocates the shit out of her. I don't want to do that to her."

"This is how Gem deals with shit. But she won't get through this without you. Can't you see that?" Frustration directed at me swayed through Hunter's every word.

"All she's done is push me away. She. Broke. My. Fucking. Heart."

Hunter didn't say a word.

Total silence.

No bird chirped. No squirrel scuttled. No wind stirred.

There was just nothing.

Hunter's voice came out slow and deep, like a baritone trying to hit bass. "Yeah. So? Get the fuck over it. I broke Gem's. You broke hers. You slightly dented mine when you moved out of our place and in with her. This shit always makes us stronger. We pull each other through everything. And goddamn it, we're going to write some fucking incredible songs out of this shit. Our next album is going to be sick. Whatever she said, I'm sure she didn't mean it."

But what if this time was different? That the wedge Gemma mentioned was real? My care and concern had caused a rift between us. "Yeah. She did. She was right."

"Bullshit. You've always had her back. You're her best friend. I'm up there, bud, but it's nothing like what you have with her. I know you blame yourself for what happened, that you think you didn't protect her. But it wasn't your fault. No amount of security, self-defense, or staying hidden would've stopped Vicki, the sick bitch."

"How could I have been so blind?" I closed my eyes and swayed. "I never suspected her."

"No one did. Now cut the bullshit and come home." Hunter scoffed. "Gem needs you."

Nothing Hunter said cleared the clouds cluttering my thoughts. The three of us had built each other up, had reached the height of success. But falling in love had brought us crashing down. The damage was done.

Visions of Gemma filled my head. Sadness loomed in her eyes instead of their usual spark. It had first appeared when I'd blown out the details of our wedding, then when I'd upped our security and suggested getting married in Vegas, and then again when we canceled our last show. I was such a dick. Since when had I not been in tune with her? I couldn't remember the last time she'd laughed. That was my fault. "Hunt, everything I did was wrong. She changed because of me."

"Give her a break. The threats scared the shit out of her. The wedding plans didn't help. You care about so many people, and many of them are an integral part of our lives. You got caught up in wanting a ceremony to please them, to show them you cared. That's cool, but those close to us will love us no matter what. You lost sight of what was important to you and Gem. I told you that weeks ago. She did too, but you didn't listen. The day grew bigger; plans got crazier. Stop worrying about everyone else except Gem and yourself. And me, of course." Hunter never failed to throw in a wisecrack. "Just come home. Gem's going crazy."

I admired his efforts to bring me round, but nothing made an impact.

A drizzle of rain fell, splattering fat droplets onto my jacket. They reminded me of the tears I'd caused Gemma. My fingers strained, gripping my cell phone harder and harder. "She doesn't want me there."

"Stop your fucking pity party." Hunter hissed, slamming a door—sounded like the fridge. "Gem can run, scream, shout, smash shit up. Do whatever she needs to do to deal with being kidnapped. And we'll be here for her. That's what we do. Every time. Now get your ass home. I'm going over to your place, but I won't be able to stop her for long. She'll be out looking for you soon."

The ground swallowed my heart. Rotted my insides like the bodies beneath the earth. "Don't let her. We need time apart to sort things out."

"No," Hunter yelled. "She needs you. Now."

No. I stifled her. She didn't need that.

Hunter's frustration vented through the cell phone like steam from a Manhattan manhole. Hot and fuming. "We're supposed to leave for Belize tomorrow. For your wedding. Remember?"

I closed my eyes and turned my face skyward. Droplets of rain dripped from the tips of my hair, ran down my cheeks and soaked the front of my T-shirt. The reality I wouldn't be marrying Gemma as planned lacerated my heart. She'd pushed me away and wanted time to think and analyze everything. Once she sifted through her thoughts, she'd draw one valid conclusion: I was the root of our problems. "There is no wedding. Call Bec for me. Cancel the trip."

"What? Hello." Hunter tapped something hard against the cell phone. "Are you hearing yourself?"

I clenched my fist and snarled through my teeth. "Damn it, Hunt. Gem said she wants to wait. She's not ready." I wiped the droplets from my face. Looming reality sent a chill through to the marrow of my bones. "I'm not sure if she ever was or ever will be." Had my dream of marrying her, with sunset vows and dancing, champagne, and stars, washed away with the rain? *Yep.* "The wedding is off."

"Fuck." Hunter's voice plummeted.

"No shit."

"Okay. But it's only temporary. She wants to marry you. She loves you."

"I know. But sometimes . . . love isn't enough." My heart splintered the moment the words left my mouth. The gasp from Hunter added an extra cut. But it was time I woke up and stopped living in a daydream. Love destroyed everything in its wake. "There is no wedding. Now she can have all the fucking time in the world. I'll be out of her way, giving her space. That's what she wants. So fuck it. I'm going to the beach house for a few days."

"Oh. No. You. Don't."

Hunter wouldn't change my mind. I slouched my shoulders, exhausted from fighting and trying to keep it together. "Don't you see? Everything I do is for her."

"Then get back here."

"No. I have to go."

"Kyle—"

I hung up.

Snatching the bottle of JD off the ground, I stood. Love had done nothing but hinder me. I'd loved my mom but hadn't been able to protect her from my dad. I loved Gemma, but had failed to keep her safe. She was my soul mate, my best friend, the rhythm in my heart. I'd become so reliant on her I couldn't live without her. I'd never stood on my own two feet. Maybe it was time I did.

I'd been terrified of losing her, like I'd lost my family. Every effort I'd taken to protect her and ease her worries had poisoned her. Left her afraid of being honest. Made her think I was controlling.

Fuck.

How could I have done that to her? I was an asshole, just like my dad.

My whole body shook, shivering in the rain.

Gritting my teeth, I tightened my grip around the belly of the bottle. With all my might, I threw it at my father's gravestone. Glass shattered into a million shards; whiskey trickled like amber tears down the marble. "I hate you. All you did was hurt me and Mom. I wasn't strong enough to stop you from drinking and beating us. I hated being afraid of you. Afraid you'd kill us. You're the only one who should've died in that accident. But you took Mom with you. You heap of fucking shit. She deserved so much better than you."

I never want Gemma to be afraid of me. Not ever. I didn't want to be controlling, or overprotective, or limiting in any way.

Before I lost her forever, was it best to walk away from our relationship? Be a better man than my dad?

Gemma deserved to be happy. It killed me to think that once she came to her senses, we could be over. *No . . . Don't go there.* I wasn't thinking straight. My head hurt. My heart hurt. "Fuuuuuck!"

I hated myself right now.

I needed to get out of the city. I needed to get away from friends. From Gemma. From myself.

The ocean called me.

Drawing my jacket tight around my chest, I headed for my Range Rover. I flicked the rain from my hair, slid into the driver's seat, and revved the engine. Spinning the wheels, I took off.

Swerving through traffic, I sped. Headed east.

Time to reset. Time to escape.

Long Island, here I come.

Chapter 26

GEMMA

Sitting with my back against the wall in my music room, I stared at the wooden floor. My tears wouldn't stop falling. My throat, dry and sandy, had burned raw from crying. I didn't care. I didn't care about anything anymore. Kyle was gone. He'd left two days ago and hadn't come home. He wouldn't return my calls or texts. My need for some alone time had blown up in my face.

Venting on the pier, and screaming at the world, had been therapeutic, just what I'd needed. But coming back to an empty home had driven a sword through my chest.

He'd left no note. No message. *Nothing.*

He had every right to take off. I'd broken his heart and pushed him away.

Closing my eyes, I hit my head back against the wall. *Thud. Thud. Thud.* I'd been in here all night, trying to eradicate my demons on the guitar. But music wasn't the same without Kyle. Silence was all I wanted to hear with him gone.

Drawing my knees closer to my chest, I wrapped my arms around them and let the waterfall of tears continue.

Love had brought us together; now, it had torn us apart.

He'd never understood my need for space. He always needed to be surrounded by people, and hated being alone. He clung onto friends, and called them family. It didn't matter whether or not the people you cared about were blood-related; everyone hurt you. My track record proved it. My parents, Ben, Hunter, Vicki and now Kyle, had left me scarred.

Music was my life; creating, performing, being on the charts and having millions of fans was a dream come true. I couldn't imagine doing anything else. But I needed downtime. I missed being alone. Walking the streets at night, finding some park to sit in, or pier or rooftop to escape to, where I could savor the silence, the stillness, and the calm, had often helped me rejuvenate. Refocus. Re-energize.

But I couldn't do that anymore. Paparazzi often followed me. My home, my haven, had changed too. My sanctuary was no longer just mine. Kyle had encroached on every corner. His bass guitars sat on the rack next to my Fenders and Gibsons. His laptop sat on the desk next to mine. His drums were crammed into the space near my piano. He'd taken over. I closed my eyes. Breath charged in and out of my lungs. The room grew smaller and smaller. My head thudded and thudded.

It was like being kidnapped all over again. Confined. Restricted. Trapped.

I couldn't move without Kyle. I'd lost myself in him. What had happened to me?

I could look after myself.

I didn't need anyone to hold my hand.

And when I did . . . he'd left.

I couldn't blame him after the way I'd treated him. I didn't deserve his love. I was just like my father; I ran away to be alone when things got tough. I was just like my mother; I never let anyone get close, and used them to get what I wanted. God—was that what I'd done with Kyle and Hunter? Used them to become a success? Vicki was right. I was a self-absorbed bitch.

No wonder Kyle had taken off.

The door burst open. My heart leaped, hoping it was Kyle. But it wasn't. It was Hunter.

"Oh no, babe. You still here?" He rushed to my side and

squatted. He'd left me here late last night; I hadn't moved from the room. With soft strokes, he rubbed the side of my head. "He's still not back?"

I sobbed and shook my head. I'd been inconsolable when Hunter had told me Kyle had gone to the beach house. It had crushed me even more since he hadn't come home.

"He'll be fine once he cools off. Trust me." Hunter swatted his hand through the air, but he couldn't disguise the doubt in his voice.

"I don't think so. Not this time." The blood drained from my heart. "Hunt, I can't do this anymore. I can't keep fighting with him. Hurting him. It's exhausting. It's sucking the life out of me. Out of us. It has to stop."

He sighed and sat beside me. He hooked his arm around my shoulder, and drew me against his chest. As he rested his cheek on top of my head, I sobbed against his T-shirt. "I hate seeing you like this, Gem. Hate what Vicki did to you. But we're here for you. Always will be. Kyle crazy loves you. Not psycho Vicki cray cray; more like I'll-do-absolutely-anything-for-you crazy. Everything will work out. I promise."

My heart squeezed against my ribs. "Stop. Fucking. Saying. That. It hurts too much."

He just held me closer, tighter. "Been there, done that."

I clutched a handful of his T-shirt like it was a stress ball. I'd had a similar conversation with him about Kara. But this was different. This wasn't a take-a-chance-on-love moment; this was an if-we-don't-stop-we'll-destroy-each-other situation.

"I really hurt him, Hunt. He hates me. I hate me." I jumped to my feet and paced beside the rack of guitars. How could I have been so cruel? Blood surged through my veins like a raging inferno. Grabbing a fistful of my hair, I pulled.

"Gem, stop. Please." He held out his hand, but I ignored it.

"No." My mind spiraled. *The kidnapping. The drugs. Vicki.* I'd been scared. Afraid. Terrified. Contradictions clouded my every thought—I needed Kyle, I needed space. There was no way I could have both. My breath seesawed, hard and fast. The pain inside me needed to escape. I reached for my acoustic guitar and swung it above my head. "I almost died. I hate that he's not here." With one big swing, I smashed the guitar against the floor. *Thwack.* The wood exploded in splinters. Strings twanged and snapped. I lifted it over my shoulder and smashed it again, and again, and again. "I hate him for leaving. Hate myself for hurting him. Hate it. Hate it. Hate it."

Hunter leaped to my side. "Stop. Jesus, Gem. No." He caught my arms and pulled me to his chest. "You're so going to regret that."

I stared at the shattered guitar my father had given me and gripped onto Hunter's arms. Tears streamed down my cheeks. "Why? Why is this happening? I love him so much."

He stroked my hair. "Babe, I know you do. And he loves you. More than anything. He took off because you wanted some space. He's self-torturing himself just as much as you are. He thinks he's not good enough for you. That he's changed you. And that he's not able to protect you."

"But he can't." I pulled out of Hunter's arms and plonked onto the piano stool.

"You know Kyle is extreme when it comes to you." He rested his elbows on top of the piano.

"Since when did you become the expert on relationships?"

"Me? Never." He smirked. "I just love you two. I'll always be like your younger, super-cool, goofy, favorite brother."

"You got goofy, right." I sighed, scanning the awards and plaques and mounted platinum records lining the shelves and walls. Life was so good. Until our hearts had gotten tangled. "What am I going to do?"

"Snap out of it. You haven't lost him. You just need to talk it out."

That was one thing I could always do with Kyle. We could sit up all night talking, often losing track of time. We could even finish each other's sentences. We knew what the other person was thinking and sometimes didn't have to say anything at all. We could just feel and tell what was on each other's mind. What happened to that connection? "I told him he was controlling and suffocating."

Hunter eased around the piano and sat beside me on the stool. "You did pull out the big guns."

"I broke his heart." I rested my head against his shoulder and sniffled.

"Yeah, you did. But you can fix it. Gem, you're a kickass queen. You've always gone after what you've wanted." He swiveled to face me and tapped his finger above my heart. "Your spark is in there; it just got snuffed out for a while. But it's time to fire it up again. It's time to come out saying, 'Don't fuck with me, bitches.'" He took my hands in his and gave them a gentle shake. "You're alive. You have me. Amazing friends. And Kyle. He loves you so fucking much."

I stared at the photo on the desk of Kyle and me at our engagement party. The gorgeous one Lexi had taken. A black and white closeup of him holding my hand against his chest, kissing my forehead. My ring sparkled, even in monochrome. That night had been magical. Had it all gone up in smoke? "I love him. But I'm terrified I've lost him. Pushed him away too much."

"Then fight for him." He shook my hands again. "You know him better than anyone. Better than me."

"What if he doesn't want to marry me anymore?"

"The question is, do you want to marry him? Kyle would do anything for you. That's all he's ever done. He's written way too many songs about you. He let you follow your heart until it found his home with him. He organized the wedding. Tried to keep you safe. Turned the world upside down to find you. Can't you see that? He's not controlling you; he's so under your thumb it's ridiculous."

"What?"

"You were so stressed, trying to keep everybody happy. You stopped being you. Stop letting Kyle get carried away with the wedding plans. Stop listening to my girlfriend go off about your simple dress and low-key service." His gaze softened. "Please don't be mad, but I made Kara show it to me when it was delivered. Gem, it's beautiful. It's so you. So stop getting lost in all the noise. The minute you did that is when things went wrong."

"So I can blame Kara for this?" I laughed through my whimpers. "You're going to have fun if you ever marry her. Your wedding will be bigger than all the Kardashian weddings combined."

He stretched the collar of his T-shirt and gave a nervous laugh. "I'm not rushing down the aisle, Gem. No way. But if I ever do, you can rest assured, I will have the largest fucking wedding ever. It will be big, bold, and totally lit. Forget the Kardashians. You ain't seen nothing yet."

"You're a nutter."

"Yep."

My shoulders slumped. "I never wanted a big wedding. So much bullshit."

Hunter chuckled softly. "Gem, you and Kyle made some compromises. Your wedding guest list isn't big. But if it's not what you want, you're going to have to stand up to him or bite the bullet and think of it as just another day in the spotlight."

I never wanted that. "I just wanted it to be him and me. You, Kar, Lexi, and Hayds. A day away from the limelight. He wanted that too, initially."

"Then remind him of that."

"I'm not sure what can be salvaged out of this mess." I'd hurt Kyle too much. Hunter was doing all he could to make me feel better, but nothing worked. "Thanks anyway. You're the best."

"I know." He crinkled his nose. "But you chose Kyle."

I thumped him on the arm. "Yes. I did."

Love had done nothing but hurt the three of us. Hurting Kyle would be something I'd always regret.

I looked at the broken guitar on the floor. Some good had come out of it. There were no more ghosts in my past. I was no longer worried about my father—he was dead . . . gone. My gold-digging mother could flit around the world from one rich man to the next—she was out of my life. But Kyle I couldn't live without. What did our future look like? Could we get past the hurt and get married? Or was going back to being friends the best option?

"You want some help to clean this up?" Hunter pointed to the shattered guitar on the floor.

"No. Leave it." It was my past. No more holding onto strings of hope.

"You gonna go see Kyle?"

A tear fell from my eye. All our wedding plans had been ruined. Thanks to me. "No."

"Damn, you can be stubborn."

"Me?" My voice jumped two octaves.

"Go. See. Him."

"No."

Hunter groaned, slapped his hands on his thighs, and jumped to his feet. "You're being a fool. I've sat around wallowing with you for long enough. I gotta go. Kara's waiting. Do you want to come to brunch, since we're not in Belize?"

Ow! That stung.

"Thanks. But no thanks." I wrapped my arms around myself and jutted my chin toward the door. "Go. Have fun. I'll stay here. I need to be alone."

"No. You don't." He bent down and glared at me. Shards of silver flashed through his azure eyes. "You need to be around people you love."

"I'll be fine. I'm going to get some sleep." Not that I could do that. Too many nightmares filled my head.

He puffed through his nostrils. "You are one cantankerous chick sometimes." He stood and kissed the top of my head. "But I love you. I'll come see you later."

He turned to leave, but I caught his arm. "Hey . . . I love that you're in love with my best friend."

"So do I." A saucy grin flashed across his face, then it warped and transformed into a frown. "And you love my best friend. The sooner you and Kyle sort your shit out, the better." He ruffled the top of my head and headed out the door.

Dragging my footsteps, I ambled up to my bedroom. The place was so cold and empty without Kyle. With clouds fogging my thoughts, I opened the walk-in closet. It smelled of him, all woodsy and spice. I trailed my fingers over his suits, shirts, and jeans hanging neatly on the rack. Piles of his hoodies, T-shirts and shorts were stacked on the top shelf. I grabbed one of his old T-shirts to wear to bed. As I pulled it down, a letter-sized box tumbled to the floor, scratching me on the arm as it fell. "Ow!"

Notebooks, pieces of paper, and music sheets spilled onto the carpet. *Shit.* I'd thought this box was full of old ties, belts, and cuff links he didn't wear anymore.

I dropped to my knees and picked up a single sheet covered in Kyle's handwriting. It was lyrics. I stared at the date. The first day of high school. The day we'd first met.

I skimmed Kyle's words.

> *The moment you walked in the room*
> *I knew my life had changed*
> *You stole my breath right then and there*
> *I knew I'd never be the same*

I'd been the newcomer, totally out of place. I'd walked into the music room, and they were there—Kyle and Hunter. Geeky, lanky, pimply teens. I'd felt an instant connection with them.

I grabbed another crumpled music sheet. Going by the date, it was senior year, post prom, a few weeks after Vicki had broken his heart.

> *The night I left broken-hearted*
> *And thought I was all alone*
> *I looked up and saw you there*
> *Your smile and touch felt like home*

Another piece of paper. This one was dated a few months after Kyle's parents had died.

> *In my darkest hours, when I'd lost everything*
> *You were there, helped me breathe again*
> *Your arms around me showed me the way*
> *Your heartbeat made me want to stay*

Another one. Dated shortly after I'd broken up with my ex,

Ben.

> *You ran so fast, you ran so far, I could feel the rip in your*
> *heart*
> *While you bled, while you cried, I just stayed by your side*
> *Held you close, wouldn't let you fall, wouldn't let you end*
> *it all*
> *You deserved so much more, as you lay broken on the floor*
> *Knew I'd be a better man, give you everything I had*
> *Can't you see, my love is true; I'd do anything, just for you*

Shit. The horrific night I'd found out Ben had sold naked photos of me to the tabloids, I'd cried so hard and had felt so humiliated. Kyle had just held me in his arms as I'd bawled on my bed. He'd told me he'd somehow get naked pictures of himself posted online to draw the spotlight off me. A few days later, he'd done that. He'd jumped, butt-naked, into a hotel pool.

I half-giggled—half-cried—at the memories, and wiped the tears from my lashes.

He'd done that for me. To get the gossip mongers off my back.

I'd taken him for granted for too long.

Fuck!

Kyle had loved me . . . forever.

He'd told me his feelings for me changed after his parents were killed, not that he'd loved me since he'd first met me in high school. I might be wrong; these lyrics could be about someone else. But I remembered every one of those moments he'd written about.

He loved me.

He *fucking* loved me.

It was stupid that two people so in love could hurt each other so much. I'd never comprehended being cared for. Never felt worthy. But time had proven that every experience had brought us closer and made us stronger. He kept my head out of the clouds while I made him chase them. I hadn't lost myself in him; I was everything because of him. He didn't smother me; he gave me strength, inspiration, and solidarity. Our friendship had blossomed into something magical. I couldn't picture my future without him. I couldn't face writing another song or going onstage without him.

I loved him. So fucking much.

I had to fix this mess.

I'd been stubborn and foolish long enough.

After stuffing the papers and notebooks into the box, I put it back on the shelf. I rushed to the hall cupboard downstairs and pulled out the shoe-sized box from my father. Sifting through the trinkets, I grabbed the one tucked inside an old black velvet pouch and hugged it close to my chest. *Yes.* This was perfect. Just what I needed.

Grabbing my purse, cell phone, and keys off the kitchen counter, I rushed out the door.

It was time to grab my future. No looking back.

It was time to get Kyle.

Chapter 27

KYLE

The salt air pressed against my face, and the sun beat into my skin. From the front deck overlooking the endless ocean, I breathed in sync with the rise and fall of each rolling wave. Since I'd left home two days ago, the ache in my chest had remained constant.

It was as if life was stuck on repeat like a broken record, unable to move on to the next track. The wind rippled through the dune grass, seagulls circled the sky, and bugs zipped this way and that. The same shit happened over and over again. Like me and Gemma. We kept hurting each other. A vicious cycle. It had to stop. We didn't need to delay the wedding; we needed to call it off.

Not marrying her would be like living with no heart. I'd be numb. But at least I could move past this constant pain. It would be hard to contemplate not kissing her, making love to her, or sleeping next to her. I'd loved her for so damn long. It had simmered beneath the surface from the moment we'd met and had burst to life after the death of my parents.

All I wanted was to be hers, love her, and make her happy. Put our troubled upbringings behind us. But it had all gone horribly wrong.

I pushed my sunglasses higher on my nose and rested my head back against the cushioned deck chair. I'd fucked up. I'd never wanted Gemma to feel suffocated. But that was exactly what I'd done.

For our music, I was a perfectionist. I'd always sought the perfect lyrics, the perfect tune, the perfect melody. I'd always wanted to deliver the best performances. We'd spent hours rehearsing and practicing, ensuring our shows went off without a hitch. I'd fallen into taking the lead in our business deals and contract negotiations. *Fuck.* Gemma was right. I was controlling. When did the power go to my head? When had I become oblivious to what others were feeling? Especially Gemma.

I'd always been the sensible one. The one who kept Gemma and Hunter from chasing overzealous dreams and ridiculous ideas. I'd thought I was helping; instead I'd been an anchor dragging in the sand, holding them back.

Shit.

Love had blinded me. I'd seen too much hurt. Experienced too many broken hearts. Eight years had flown by since we'd won that YouTube contest. Five albums, four tours and two labels later, we had a lifestyle beyond our wildest dreams.

But maybe we'd burned ourselves out.

Maybe it was time we took a break. A decent one.

Maybe . . . permanently.

Without Gemma, there was no music. It would be impossible to just be friends again. It would kill me to see her move on, be with other guys. I'd watched that happen for too long before we'd gotten together. It had slashed my heart every time.

Fuck, I had no idea what to do.

For early October, it was hot. The sun burned like I'd been thrown into hell. Reliving what had happened to Gemma tortured my brain, sickened me to the core. *Kidnapped. Fucking kidnapped.* She'd been taken so easily. It had shattered her soul . . . just like I had.

Fuuuuck!

Wiping the dampness from my eyes, I sniffled. I'd lost my sense of judgment. I'd trusted Vicki. I'd held those close to me next to my heart. From Hunter and Gemma, to our team, to Hayden,

Kara and Lexi, and a handful of other people who'd been with us—Everhide—from the start. I'd considered those people family. But, just like my own flesh and blood, they could hurt me. Destroy me. Take those I loved away.

I clenched and unclenched my hands; locked my jaw. I'd never forgive Vicki. Sick, psycho bitch. How had I not seen her obsession?

Forgotten memories of Vicki rose from the dark depths of my mind. Her hysterical tears and begging for forgiveness after she'd cheated on me in high school—I'd been upset, hurt, but was over our relationship anyway. In the couple of years following, she'd slithered up to me at parties—I'd ignored her advances. There were too many other hot girls on the scene to take notice of her. At my engagement party, she'd joked, *"Remember, I was your first love."* Nope—Gemma was. Back then, I'd been too young and naïve to know better, too focused on our music and career, too distracted by easy girls. Underneath the rush and ride of fame and success, there was and never would be any doubt about my love for Gemma.

But someone had to call *it's a wrap*.

We'd hurt each other more times in the past three years than I cared to remember. My jealousy, the lies, her pushing me away. She had one of the most beautiful souls. She shone when it soared. Her talent needed to be heard. She cared for so many people without knowing it. Gemma was tough, a survivor. She'd always said to hell with anyone who put her down, or had said she couldn't do something; she went out and proved them wrong. I'd been by her side every step of the way, but I'd been on the ride for long enough.

I didn't want to hinder her future. Especially if she felt I suffocated her.

I loved her so much. It was time to set her free.

Loneliness returned, resting on my shoulders like a lead blanket. It was like the nights during our first tours. Once the partying stopped, the girl of the night left, and the music switched off, I was alone. I hated it. But I had to find some resilience. Be prepared to face a future without her.

A young couple walked hand in hand along the shoreline. The blood in my veins congealed. I'd miss moments like that with Gemma. Leaning forward, I rested my head in hands and fought the sting in my eyes. I needed to do something before I totally self-destructed. Something to get out of this rut. My head ached and throbbed. Seattle loomed through the clouds in my mind. *Yes.* I hadn't spent a lot of time with my cousin Kade, thanks to my tour schedule. Catching up in Vegas had been too quick. Chilling out with him and spending time with relatives would help me mend.

But I had to do the right thing and talk to Gemma first. One phone call would be enough. Once the tie was severed, I'd take off. That sounded perfect.

Except it wasn't.

I hated myself for destroying what we'd had.

Digging my fingers into my thighs, I shoved my pain, hurt, and anger into a metal case. Locked it away, deep inside my heart. *Done.*

I dragged myself out of the deck chair and headed inside.

It was time to pack my bags and get the fuck out of here.

I'd give Gemma all the fucking space she needed.

Chapter 28

GEMMA

I pulled my Mini Cooper in beside Kyle's Range Rover and killed the engine. It was mid-afternoon and the sun's rays flashed like laser beams off the metallic black paint and windows of his car. Checking in with Chester, I assured him I'd arrived at the beach house safely. I'd learned my lesson. Tossing my cell phone into my purse, I rested my forehead against the steering wheel and took deep breaths. I had no idea what I'd say to Kyle. Sorry wouldn't cut it.

I jumped out of the car and dashed up the old, rickety wooden steps. Using my set of keys, I unlocked the sliding glass door and stepped inside. An empty JD bottle on the kitchen counter and Kyle's backpack lying next to the stairs were the only signs someone was here.

I was about to call his name when he came in from the front deck. My eyes locked onto his and my heart imploded. He wore the same Nickelback T-shirt I'd last seen him in. His hair was a tousled mess, like he hadn't combed it in days. Dark circles underneath his eyes highlighted his scruffy, unshaven face. I wanted to run to him, throw my arms around him, tell him I was sorry, but something about the cold hardness in his eyes froze me to the spot.

He threw his sunglasses onto the coffee table. "Gem? What the fuck are you doing here?"

"I've come to talk. To say I'm sorry." I dumped my purse on the floor and closed the door behind me.

"There's nothing to be sorry about." He stuffed his hands into the front pockets of his jeans and shuffled back to lean against the wall. "You've saved me a phone call. I was about to call you. I'm the one who's sorry."

"For what?" I ambled through the living room toward him, but he held up his hand for me to stop. *What the hell?* "You didn't come home. Didn't return my calls. I've been worried sick."

He shrugged his shoulder. "You told me to stay away. So I did."

I placed my hands over my heart, hoping that it would lessen the pain, the regret. "I said some awful, awful things I didn't mean. I never meant to push you away."

He lowered his gaze, his blond hair flopping forward. "You should've done it a long time ago. I've been an asshole."

"No, you weren't." I gave a flippant toss of my hand. "You got a little overzealous about the wedding and anal about protecting me."

His brow pinched tight. "Don't downplay it, Gem."

I stepped in beside the coffee table, knocking my knee, tipping the pile of beer coasters across the wooden surface. As I drew closer to him, the air prickled. Every muscle on his face tensed. He was like a geyser about to explode. I could feel every rumble. I stopped a few feet away from him. "We took precautions and things went wrong. There's only so much you, me, and security could do. If it wasn't Vicki, it could've been someone else. I won't let her or any other psycho come between us."

"That's the thing, Gem." He shook his head. "Something always comes between us. We should've stuck to the oaths we made in high school. Do you remember them?" He spoke through clenched teeth. "We'd remain friends forever. Never become involved with each other. That no girl or guy would come between us. We've broken every one of those rules."

"No, we haven't." My nose wrinkled. "You forgot to add that music would be our life. We'd take on the world and leave the hellhole of Montgomery behind."

"Someone from Montgomery nearly killed you." The anguish in his voice shuddered through every cell in my body. "I don't want you or any of us to go through that again."

"Neither do I." I took a half-step closer, but he flinched as if he was about to run out the door, so I stopped. "I haven't handled what happened well. I know that. And I'm sorry. One thousand times, I'm sorry."

His jaw locked. He stared out the window over my shoulder. "This isn't just about Vicki. It's about us too."

"I know." The strings in my heart pulled tense like an archer's bow. "What scared me most about being kidnapped was not coming home to you. Knowing how devastated you'd be. Over the past couple nights without you, so many of my delusions have shattered. When I lived by myself, my home was my sanctuary. But now, in every room, I see and feel your presence all around me. At first, I struggled to adjust, but now I love it. Without you there, I was lost. Because it's *our* home. All ours."

"Not anymore." He swiped his hair back. His brown eyes were cold and lifeless. "You want space? I'll give it to you. I'll go to Seattle and see Kade." He swiped his sunglasses off the table and went to storm past me, but I caught his arm and turned him to face me.

"No. We don't do this to each other." I jabbed my finger against his chest, fighting the sting in my eyes. "We stick with each other through everything. I was wrong to push you away. What has been so hard to deal with is that I don't remember the kidnapping, just snippets, flashes of images. My life was in somebody else's hands. I hated I had no control over what happened to me. I've always looked after myself." I flattened my hand against his chest. He sucked in a deep breath. It was as if even his lungs and ribs tried to keep me at bay. "But you look after me, too. You've always been there for me. Always had my back. Losing three days of my life made me realize how much I depend on you. How much I love you. I have people who care for me. I'm not alone. We've achieved so much because of the love and support we give each other and get from our friends and our incredible team. The people around us are our family."

He calmly took hold of my hand and lowered it to my side. Letting go, he shuffled back a few feet. He leaned against the fallboard on the old upright piano by the side wall. "Yeah, well . . . family only hurts you. Love blinds you. You changed because of me. I suffocate you, remember?"

Those words I'd said still left a bitter taste in my mouth. "It's my fault for not being honest. As the wedding plans and the threats grew worse, my frustration and fear snowballed."

"You were afraid to tell me how you felt?" His voice shook. Torture swirled in his eyes as he thumped his chest. "What kind of man does that make me? I never want you to be afraid of me. That's not love. That's sick. That's my father all over again."

"I am not afraid of you. Never have been. Never will be. You're so not like your dad. You aren't violent. You wouldn't hurt a flea. You avoid walking on ants on the sidewalk." I drew a foot closer to him. He gripped the edge of the fallboard, his knuckles turning white. This wasn't like him. I had to get through his thick skull. "I know you're protective. That's something I love about you. You make me feel safe and adored. You put up with my idiosyncrasies. You've stood by me through every issue with my mother, my father, and Vicki. You're always there for me. And I'm here for you."

"No. You've pushed me away one too many times, Gem." Bitterness dripped off every word.

I caught the back of the sofa to stop my knees from buckling. I'd hurt him too much. Over and over. *Fuck.* "I just needed time to process what had happened. You need to understand and respect that sometimes I need to be alone."

"I do." He flicked his hand. "But you keep putting up this wall to stop letting me in. I have given you every ounce of my heart. You have seen every raw part of me." White-hot flames burned deep in his dark eyes. "But with you? I won't deny I've seen you through a ton of tough shit. We've had some intense moments. But most of the time, you fight so hard to keep your feelings bottled. You keep me at a distance." He shook his head slowly and flexed his jaw. "I won't put up with it anymore." He turned the volume up, anger shaking his voice. "I wanted all of you. Every pain, heartache, nightmare, dream, hope. We should work on what you have gone through together. You should lean on me. Not push me away."

Fog swirled through my head. "I know. And I'm sorry. I'm dealing with what I went through in the best way I can. You've always been my shoulder to cry on. We deal with shit by jamming out music. We write therapeutic songs. You have stood up for me, encouraged me, lied for me, been my strength . . . and you've saved me. In the very literal sense of the word, you've saved me. You didn't give up on me. So don't give up on us now. Stop fighting this because I know you love me."

"That's not the problem." He leaped to his feet. Red crept up his neck. "You're still holding back."

A tear caught on my cheek. What more than my love did he want?

"The wedding plans made me realize you've still got issues you haven't worked through." He took a step toward me, towered a foot in front of me. "Tell me, what the fuck are they?" His voice fired like a gun. "Why can't you let me in? What the fuck are you so afraid of?"

This. I was afraid of *this.* Every cell in my body burned under his lethal gaze. "Losing you."

"Why?" He staggered back three steps and bumped into the piano. "Tell me why or I walk away." His voice was like an arctic chill, ripping through my bones.

"You can't." I clawed my brain for a handle to grab to stop me from crashing to the floor. "We have our music."

"Maybe we should stop that, too."

"What?" My heart screamed like a siren. The ringing in my ears deafened me. "No. Never. We can't." My bottom lip trembled. I wanted to sock him in the ears, knock some sense into him. "I won't let you. Are you that pigheaded you want to end this? End what we have?"

He clenched his fists at his side and stared through me as if I were a ghost. Stood there like I was nothing.

I shook my head, not wanting to see the end in his eyes. "You want to call it quits? Go back to being alone?"

The air warped with the force of a sonic boom. His pupils dilated to pinpricks. His red-rimmed eyes welled with tears. His teeth ground so loudly I could hear them.

I'd hit a nerve. *Yes.* I needed more ammunition, more firepower, to penetrate his heart.

My tears stung like acid as I glanced around the living room. So many memories of vacations here after grueling tours and promotional schedules. The countless hours on the deck playing tunes on our guitars. The parties. Our friendship. His light had gone out, and I needed to reignite it.

I took a deep breath. I felt like I was about to plummet off a cliff, but I wasn't ready to give up the fight. No way. I sniffled and softened my tone. "At home, I found something in our wardrobe. A box. Full of your old notebooks, journals, and songs. I read some of them."

There it was . . . a flicker of life . . . or was it hate in his eyes? He slammed his eyelids shut.

"Those songs aren't about other girls, are they? They're about me. You've loved me since we first met. We've weathered everything together. Sworn oaths and survived hell. Now stop being foolish. Come home and marry me."

Lowering his chin, he shook his head.

Fuck!

"Kyle, please?" I closed the gap between us and caressed the side of his head, stroked my fingers through his soft hair. What could I do to break through his defenses? I knew him. What would work? Closing my eyes, I took a deep breath to stop the chaos swirling in my head. I focused my thoughts on him, our love, and everything we'd shared. Songs flooded my mind. *That's it.* I clutched the pendant on my necklace, the one he'd given me on my birthday, out here on this deck. I licked my lips, swallowed hard, and recited the lyrics to "All Wound Up," the first song we'd written together. He'd immortalized the first note into my pendant.

You've got me all wound up

And I'm thinking crazy thoughts
You've got me all wound up
Because I want to be yours

He lurched to his feet and turned to face the beach. "Gem, stop."

Yeah—the lyrics were bad, but we were fifteen when we'd written it. I stepped in behind him, rubbing my hands down his arms. Rested my cheek against his back. Thank God he didn't push me away. "What about 'Horizon'?"

Let's aim for the horizon
Let's touch the stars
Sail across the oceans
Follow our beating hearts

With you by my side
We're gonna touch the sky
Gonna love you forever
'Til the day I die

He spun to face me. His eyes were wet with tears. His voice was barely above a whisper. "Enough."
Shit. We're so alike.
He wouldn't give in. I wouldn't give up.
My heart threatened to explode, shuddering against my ribs. "Every magical moment in my life is because of you. From finding you and Hunt, to writing songs, our first gig, and winning the YouTube contest. The albums, the tours, the awards. Our first kiss. Do you remember? It was right there." I wiped a tear from my cheek and pointed outside to the deck. My twenty-fourth birthday would be one I'd never forget. "The first time we made love." I waved upstairs toward his bedroom. "Proposing to you. Everything has led us to being together. I want to spend the rest of my life with you."
His shoulders rounded as if his lungs had collapsed. He

clasped the side of my head, his eyes locking onto mine. "Then be honest with me. Even now, you're holding back. You're using lyrics and moments to hide the truth. Every time the shit hits the fan, why do you push me away? What are you afraid of? You want a future with me? Then let me in."

My chin quivered. "You want to know what I'm afraid of?" I closed my eyes, swayed on my feet. I dug to the bottom of my soul. I took a sledgehammer to the wall around my heart and smashed it into a gazillion pieces. I drew my shoulders back and trembled.

I lifted my chin and met his gaze. He wanted every piece of me; I'd let him have it. "I don't have any grounds to base our future on. I'm afraid of becoming a family, that I won't meet your expectations as a wife. I have no clue how to be one. I'm afraid of having my heart broken again. It hurts too much. I'm afraid if I give you my everything . . . you'll leave. Like my dad did. And that would destroy me. Because I've never, and will never, love someone as much as I love you."

He let me go, staggered back, and connected with the fallboard again. A tear slid down his cheek, and his hand shot over his mouth. Anguish contorted every muscle on his face.

What the fuck?

This was why I hated opening my heart. It hurt too much. I'd just bared my fucking soul to him. But it was too late. I'd shattered him beyond repair.

No. No. *No.*

This was not the end.

No fucking way.

How the fuck could I fix this? Fix us?

Chapter 29

GEMMA

"Wait! I have something for you." I rushed to my bag and dug out the velvet pouch I'd grabbed before I'd left. Running back to him, my fingers fumbled as I tipped the pocket watch into his hand. "This was my grandfather's. It was in the box of my dad's stuff. I don't remember much about him other than he stank of cigarettes."

"Gem, I can't take this." His hand shook within mine.

"Take this as a symbol of timeless memories." I closed his fingers around the watch and held his hand tight. "I would sooner go through hell every day than not have you in my life. I've been a screw-up, not knowing where my dad was. Wasted too much time looking for someone who didn't want to be found. I won't lose another second worrying about my past. My dad left because he was a coward. You're not. I want to spend every second with you. We have a lifetime of amazing memories. Our love is timeless. Time nearly got taken away from us, so let's not waste another moment of it. I want to love you, make music with you, be with you." I tightened my hold on his hand. A tear caught on my lip. "You have my whole heart, own my soul, have all of me. Please come home and marry me."

He closed his eyes and clutched the watch.

The clock on the wall ticked. Each second took an eternity.

The rolling waves took their sweet time to crash onto the shore beyond the dunes.

My heart dared not beat, afraid it couldn't take one more devastating blow.

He sucked in a deep breath and wiped his hand over his mouth. Shaking his head, sorrow rippled through his eyes.

Oh. My. God. I've lost him.

I've fucking lost him.

I sobbed, clutching at my chest. "Kyle. No. Don't do this. I love you. You hear me? I. Fucking. Love. You."

Before I could blink, he reached behind my neck and crushed his lips to mine. My knees weakened under the force. Threading my fingers into his hair, I drew him closer, gripped him harder, kissed him deeper. His tongue lashed out to meet mine, fed on me like he was a starving animal. Each kiss sent an inferno coursing through my veins.

"Don't scare me like that." I whimpered against his lips, collapsing against his chest. "I thought I'd lost you."

Closing my eyes, I breathed him in, forcing life back into every cell in my body.

His breath skipped across my face. "You had me when you walked through the door, even more so when you said you'll never love someone as much as me. That I have your whole heart. It's all I've ever wanted. You've had mine for a very long time. I'm so sorry. I thought I could walk away, but it's impossible."

"You're a stubborn ass." I stroked his cheek and ran my finger down the line of the scar I'd given him on his chin. The one I'd given him at an early gig, where I'd smacked him in the face with my guitar.

He wrapped his arms around me and hugged me tight, my head buried against his chest. He combed his fingers through my hair. "I'm so sorry about the wedding. It wasn't you who changed; it was me. Everything bigger sounded fun, but you were right. It wasn't what I wanted. You never left the page; I did. Please forgive me."

"Just say you'll marry me."

He fell to his knee and took my hand in his. He ran his thumb over my engagement ring. "Gemma Lonsdale, without a crowd of people, just you and me, Hunt, Kara, Hayds, and Lexi, on the beach, at sunset in Belize, will you please do me the biggest honor and become my wife?"

Tears blurred my vision, but not my mind. "Yes. Yes. Oh my God, yes."

He stood and planted a soul-reviving kiss against my lips. The taste of whiskey and spice lingered on his breath. Life and my love for him flooded through my veins.

With one quick swoop, he picked me up. I hooked my legs around his waist. As I kissed him, he headed for the staircase. My need for him burned like a fire in a furnace. Tilting my hips, I pressed my crotch hard into his groin. He groaned and tripped. Halfway up the steps, we fell into a pile of arms and legs.

"Ow!" The stair rammed into my spine.

"Shit. Are you okay?" Kneeling on the step below me, he scanned me up and down.

"Yes." I didn't care about my back. I wanted him. "Here. Now."

I ripped off his T-shirt and drank in every inch of his glorious body. Every muscle, scar, and piece of ink. He buried his face into my neck. Goose bumps darted across my skin as he kissed and licked and sucked. Every touch was like a new sensation, a heightened experience, just like it had been our first time together. I'd nearly lost him, but this . . . this was why we belonged together. Nobody had ever made me feel like this.

Wrapping my arms around him and drawing him closer, I trailed kisses across his shoulder and up the length of his throat. The faint smell of soap and the taste of the salty ocean on his skin made me crave more. The soft groans coming from deep within his throat sent rapid-fire reverberations straight to my core. The ache, growing, throbbing, pulsing.

His hands caught the edge of my T-shirt and tore it over my head. "I love you so much."

Snaking my hands around his neck, I weaved my fingers into his short hair and tugged on it. Fair warning played in my breathy whispers. "Never think of leaving me again."

"I promise. And you, never push me away again."

I still had a truckload of being-kidnapped shit to deal with, but with Kyle by my side, I'd get through anything.

"Deal." My heart beat with so much love, my head spun. We'd struggled to admit our feelings for each other, took a chance and fell in love, and finally stopped our pasts causing problems. Lies had hindered us. Covering up our fears had caused a truckload of heartache. Now, the truth, trusting him and exposing the vulnerability in my heart paved a clear path forward.

His mouth and body molded to mine. The timber tread creaked as he moved. Making a line of kisses, he worked his way down my neck, over my collarbone. He nipped each breast through the lace of my bra, blew streams of hot air through the fabric to my nipples, hardening them into tightened peaks. *Damn, that's good.* My little "mmm" of delight made him smile; I could feel it on his lips. Meandering lower, he kissed my tummy, the arch of my hip, down toward the top of my jeans. I circled my fingers through his hair, each strand slipping through my fingertips like soft cotton.

He looked up at me; his bedroom eyes shimmered with a hungry glint. "Do you know what I want to do to you? Right here on the stairs?" Holding my gaze, he lowered his mouth between my legs and forced his breath through the seam of my jeans, setting my insides alight.

Oh, yes please.

I slid forward an inch. Giving him a devilish smile, I leaned back on my elbows. I lifted my butt and wiggled my hips. "While I'm sure you could make me come with my jeans on, I'd prefer you take them off."

"Gladly." Practiced fingers popped open the buttons of my fly. He tore the jeans from my legs quicker than a hot wax strip. He flung them into the air, and they caught on the handrail. My panties and bra followed. So did the rest of his clothes. He tore them off and kicked them down the steps.

The timber was cool beneath my bare butt, hard against my back. But all I cared about was the way Kyle hovered over me, scorching me with the heat radiating off his naked body. All I ever needed was to be wrapped in his love.

His lips sought mine, warm and delicious. God, I wanted to touch him, taste him, take away the hurt I'd caused. Sliding my hand down his side, I swept over the smooth skin of his hip, across his belly and downward to take hold of his cock. As I rubbed his hot, velvety skin, he murmured against my ear.

"I love you touching me." He thrust his cock through my hand, drove his hips forward. "But stop. I want to keep my promise."

My pussy pulsed with anticipation.

He grabbed my hand, entwined our fingers, and pinned it beside me on the step. His other hand skimmed over my blazing flesh and nestled between my legs. His fingers stroked and played and slid along my slit before he dipped into my wetness. My eyes fluttered closed, and my head dropped back as he thumbed my clit. Around and around. Up and down. I grabbed onto the balustrade like it was a lifeline. A moan erupted deep in my throat. "Ohhh."

Over our kisses, he whispered, "I've missed this. I've missed you. Love that you're wet for me."

With smoldering eyes, he wriggled down my body. Kissing. Licking. Nipping my skin. Then he nestled between my legs. His mouth claimed me. Clutching the edge of the step, I dug my fingernails into the wood.

He drew his tongue up the length of my slit, teased and circled my clit, and set the motion on repeat. *Oh, yes.* Heat shot through my core and charged up my spine. If I was any hotter, I'd melt onto the floor. Clutching onto his shoulders, I pulsed against his mouth. He lapped and nipped and sucked. His fingers swirled and teased. His touch made my body sing, rock like Bon Jovi, soar like Mariah Carey, scream like Metallica. He made oral an artform. Every part of my body throbbed and clenched. It wound higher and higher, tighter and tighter like a jack-in-the-box waiting to pop. He didn't relent. With a firm flick of his tongue and a strum of his fingers inside me, I exploded. A kaleidoscope of color swirled behind my closed eyelids. Tingles skipped across my skin. Every nerve, charged with electricity, quaked and quivered. "Holy fuck."

I clutched his head between my thighs to stop. A goofy grin of satisfaction played across his slicked lips as he kissed the soft flesh on the inside of my leg.

I'd almost lost this. We were both fools. A tear slipped from my eye. No two people could love each other as much as we did. No two people had been through hell like we had. No two people deserved to be together more than we did. We'd come too close to throwing it away.

"Hey? You okay?" He crawled up and brushed his thumb across my cheek.

"Yeah." My heart raced like a roadster. "I just love you. Love the way you do it for me."

He stood, pulled me to my feet, and carried me up to our room. "Good. Because a fuck load of make-up sex is calling."

"Bring it." I giggled as he tossed the bed covers aside.

Laying me down onto the soft pillows, he crawled over me. I drew his body against mine. Hip to hip. Flesh on flesh. Heart to heart.

Wisps of gold. Flashes of light. Stars burst behind my eyelids as he entered me.

He thrust and rocked and drove his cock into my pussy. Each movement was deep, slow, and languid, hitting me in all the right places every time. His eyes glimmered, capturing every beat of my heart. "Gem, you're the best thing that has ever happened to me. No more mistakes. No more hurting. I just wanna love you forever."

"Same." I wrapped my arms around his shoulders and drew his lips to mine. There was nothing we couldn't survive together. Nothing could keep us apart. Being kidnapped and the aftermath of that ordeal had come close. But we'd prevailed. We always would. "So there's only one thing we have to do to start our forever together." I gave him my most wicked grin. "Let's get married."

Chapter 30

KYLE

October sunshine sparked on the crystal waters surrounding the private island in Belize. Palm trees swayed in the gentle breeze. White sand stretched along the edge of the water for a couple hundred yards before it hit a rocky outcrop, the white-railed jetty, and the helipad. I placed my hand on my fluttering stomach and inhaled the salty air. The day I'd thought would never come was here . . . my wedding day.

As the sun slowly dropped in the west, I stood barefoot on the beach, waiting for Gemma. I glanced at my watch for the hundredth time. She was late. But only by one minute. My toes twitched in the sand.

Hunter and Hayden stood beside me, dressed in beige linen suits that matched mine. The top two buttons of our white button-down shirts hung open. It was too hot for ties and vests. Single red tulips pinned to our jackets wilted in the humidity. We had to have tulips. No other flower would do. The special delivery of Gemma's favorite flower had been worth it. The smile on her face when they arrived this morning was priceless.

I glanced toward the main house beyond the stretch of lush green lawn. Still no sign of Gemma and the girls. *They were here. Everything is fine. Just chill.*

Hunter wiped the perspiration from his forehead, then tousled his fingers through his loose hair. "What is taking them so long? They crack the champagne without us?" He fidgeted with his collar and stretched his neck from side to side, looking more nervous than I felt.

I patted him on the shoulder. "Looks like you could do with another drink." Having him and Hayden, my two best friends, by my side on my wedding day meant the world to me and brought a smile to my face.

Following a couple of days of recouping at the beach house, Gemma and I had revised our original plans. She'd requested only one small change. Her incredible idea still had my heart swelling with love, pride, and astonishment. Today, we'd say our vows and sign our certificate. Today would be the official day we got married. Just like I'd wanted. Once our friends left tomorrow night, Gemma and I had the place to ourselves for ten days. After everything that had happened, we'd only lost a week of our three-week vacation. We'd still have the perfect honeymoon.

"I'm fine. The few JDs at lunchtime helped." Hunter straightened the collar of his shirt for the tenth time. "Are you ready, bud?"

I wiped my clammy palms on the back of my jacket. "Yep. I've been waiting for this day for over a year."

"Good. Because here they come." Hayden pointed toward the main house. With camera in hand, he snapped pictures of Lexi and Kara walking toward us. Their long, strapless, blood-red dresses blew gently in the breeze. They held a small bouquet of red tulips in their hands. Their eyes sparkled like the sun's rays on the ocean's gentle waves.

"Sorry if these photos turn out to be shit," Hayden mumbled from behind the lens. "Lexi's the photographer, not me."

I grinned. I had every confidence some shots would be fine. While they'd help capture the memories, I'd remember every moment, every second, of this day, for the rest of my life. The best thing was that there were no paparazzi, no fans, and no crowd in sight. A day out of the spotlight. *Perfect.* Just like Gemma wanted.

The girls stepped past another camera mounted on a tripod a

few yards away that Lexi operated by a remote and halted beside me and the guys.

"She's on her way." Lexi smiled at me as she relieved Hayden of her camera.

"Thanks." I ran my hands down the lapels of my jacket and fidgeted with my cuffs.

I looked back toward the house just in time to see Gemma appear at the top of the stairs. My breath hitched. From sixty yards away, she stole my heart all over again. Her sparkling smile hit me in the center of my chest, filling me with radiating warmth.

In bare feet, she stepped onto the sand. Her smile broadened with each step along the water's edge. The flyaway strands falling in soft waves around her loose updo danced in the breeze. Her dress . . . simply wow! Absolutely breathtaking. The long, cream-colored silk slip dress flowed over her petite frame, hugging her body like a second skin. Rhinestone straps draped sexily over her shoulders, matching her glittering eyes. A single diamond glinted at the hollow of her throat. Her gorgeous lips were the same color as the small bouquet of red tulips she clutched in her hands. I blinked away the tears pooling in my eyes. She was perfect.

Fuck! I was the luckiest man alive.

She glided over the last few feet of soft sand and stopped before me. Happiness shimmered in her teary eyes.

"Hi," she whispered.

"Hi." I took her hand and kissed her cheek. "You're so beautiful."

"Hey." Hunter thumped me on the shoulder. "No kissing until after the vows."

I grinned, unable to wipe the smile off my face.

"Let's get started." Hunter stepped in front of us. An *I'm-the-coolest-officiant-ever* expression rippled across his face.

When Gemma suggested Hunter register and conduct our wedding, I nearly fell off my chair. I was beyond overwhelmed when Hunter agreed. Thanks to New York's All Loved Up officiant registration website, Hunter had signed up to marry us.

Hunter cleared his throat, pulled out a piece of paper from his pocket, and read. "Kara, Lexi, and Hayden. We've gathered here today to celebrate ..." Hunter sniffled. "... the union of my two best friends, Kyle, and Gemma."

"Shit, man, are you crying already?" I rubbed Hunter's arm.

"No ... now fuck off." Hunter swatted my hand away and drew his shoulders back. "I'm honored to stand here before you and do this, so shut up and let me continue."

"Okay. I'm sorry. Please." As I glanced at Gemma, my heart thudded harder than an auditorium full of feet-stomping fans. I was so in love with her it hurt. Hurt in such a good way.

"Since no one here objects to this marriage, let's get down to business." Hunter took a deep breath and swept his hair out of his eyes. Gemma handed her flowers to Kara, then turned toward me. She entwined her hands with mine. There was no shaking, no clamminess, no fidgeting. Everything about this moment was right.

Hunter cleared his throat. "A ceremony of marriage is many things to different people—tradition, religion, a symbolic ritual. Not for us. We don't believe in any of that shit. This ceremony marks a moment in time. This moment is not the start of something new; the seed for this love was planted a long time ago, back in high school. This moment in time isn't about growing into something beautiful. She already has. My girl, Kara. You all lucked out. She's mine." He winked and blew Kara a kiss.

I shook my head and chuckled. Hunter was such a goof. I loved him to death.

"This moment in time is not a beginning or an end, but a time to acknowledge and celebrate. Kyle and Gem, your love has evolved over the years into something that is truly fabulous. You are the best of friends who have had an incredible connection, off-the-charts chemistry and have created magic for many years. Our string of global number-one hits has proved that. Your love can only grow stronger in the years ahead. And finally, this moment in time is simply a requirement by the state of New York—and providing I get on a plane and hand your damn signed certificate into the Marriage Bureau within the designated timeframe—to declare you legally wed."

I leaned in and kissed Gemma on the forehead. Today would always mean so much more than that for me. We'd declare our love in front of the universe. Become a family. And promise to spend the rest of our lives together. My dream come true.

Hunter flicked his page. "Kyle, do you come here of your own free will? To promise to love Gem every day for the rest of your life? Because if you don't, I'll beat the shit out of you."

"Me too," Hayden added, nudging me on the shoulder.

Grinning, I gazed into Gemma's gorgeous green eyes and dipped my chin. "I've been under Gem's spell for so long, I lost all trace of free will and sanity years ago. I love her like crazy. But for legal purposes, I say, I do."

She bit her bottom lip but couldn't hide her smile.

Hunter continued. "Gemma, do you come here of your own free will? To promise to love this douchebag for the rest of your life? Because if you don't, I won't be able to put up with his whiny ass."

"Hear, hear." Kara raised her flowers and her eyebrows.

Lexi clicked away on her camera.

Gemma's eye glinted as she nodded. "I'm addicted to him in every possible way. I lost all trace of free will and sanity the moment we kissed. I'll never stop loving him. But for legal purposes, I say, I do."

"You're both fucking crazy, if you ask me." Hunter chuckled softly and shook his head. "Okay, moving on. You've prepared some vows. So, let's hear 'em."

I licked my lips and swallowed hard. This was it. Declaring my love for Gemma in front of my dearest friends, the heavens above, and all the galaxies. The moment I'd been waiting for.

I squeezed her hands gently, just savoring her touch. That she was here. "Gem, there aren't enough words to describe how much I love you. You are my titanium, my kryptonite, my universe. You . . . are my everything. You own my body, my soul, and my heart. Music binds us. I live and breathe for you. Always have. Always will. More than once you have brought me out of the darkness, and my future is bright because of you. I will love you for all time, in this lifetime and every one after it. With that, I promise myself to you."

Gemma wiped a tear from her cheek, then reconnected our hands. "Kyle. We had a beginning, but there is no end. My love for you grows stronger and deeper each day. You have stopped me from living in the past, taught me to treasure the present, and to look forward to the future. Your faith and trust and belief in me has made me a better person. You are my grounding, my solidarity, my foundation. The flame we ignited grows brighter every day. Life is wonderful because of you. Your love has saved me on countless occasions. You have shown me that love conquers all. I want to be everything you deserve and more. My heart beats in time with yours. Music runs through our blood, unites our souls. You . . . rock my world. Here, in front of the universe, I promise myself to you."

Tears swelled in my eyes; my heart filled my chest. There was and only ever would be Gemma.

After an exchange of platinum rings and a blessing, Hunter said, "With the authority vested in me thanks to New York's All Loved Up website, I now declare you husband and wife."

My heart soared. I cradled Gemma's face between my hands and kissed her. Kissed her with all my being. Her warm lips on mine sealed our lives together.

Finally, she was mine. Finally, we were a family.

"I love you," she whispered over our kisses.

"Love you more." I pressed my lips to hers. My love for her filled my smile. My soul. My heart. I entwined our fingers again and took a step back. Her cheeks had flushed red from our kisses. *Nice.*

Hunter slapped me on the shoulder, pulling me out of my daze. "Congratulations."

"Hunt?" Gemma giggled. "You're crying."

He wiped his eyes with his thumb. "I may be a little emotional. Yes." He hooked his arms around our shoulders. "You guys are the best. You two may be married, but we will always be three. No matter what. I promise you that. I love you both. Always will."

"Thanks, Hunt." Gemma kissed him on the cheek and slipped

from his embrace.

The girls and Hayden rushed forward to congratulate us.

"Those vows were beautiful." Kara wiped her eyes with her fingertips. How she could do anything with such long nails baffled me. She stepped in beside Hunter and slid her arm around his waist.

"I can't believe we're married." Gemma's voice soared like an eagle over the ocean waves lapping gently against the shore. "We did it."

Lexi gave us a hug and a kiss. "You two are amazing. Congrats."

"Makes us all have faith in finding the one someday." Hayden slapped me on the back, his eyes diverting to Lexi.

"It will happen, dude. I'm sure." I grinned, shook Hayden's hand, and turned back to my gorgeous wife. She radiated as the sun set. Her hair blowing in the soft breeze caught the golden rays. I slipped my arm around her slender waist. "Let's get photos and get on with the celebrations."

A dirty, devilish smirk slid across Hunter's mouth. "You just want to practice making rock star babies."

Gemma's eyes widened. "Sex, yes. Babies, no. The only things we'll produce are more hit singles."

I couldn't agree more.

"Fuck yeah." Hunter pumped his fist.

Lexi took copious photographs of the six of us with the camera set on the tripod, and a zillion more with her handheld of me and Gemma on the beach, by the house, in the gardens and on the pergola. The shots had looked awesome on the preview screen.

By the end of the evening, my cheeks ached from smiling so much. With our four friends by our side, marrying Gemma in this spectacular setting had been truly magical.

As everyone lazed around on the outdoor sectional by the pool, fire torches threw a soft glow over the lawn. Gemma sat with the girls, sipping champagne. I couldn't take my eyes off her as my fingers slipped down the steel strings of my guitar. My acoustic was an extension of me as much as my bass, and much nicer to play on vacation alongside Gemma. I stopped and waggled my finger at her. "Gem. Come. I have a song for you."

"For me?" She brushed her fingers down her throat.

I couldn't wait to trail kisses down her neck, to feel her pulse beneath my lips. Her in that dress—it was hard not to think of anything else.

"Yeah. Come sit." I patted the cushion beside me.

She drifted to her feet and floated over to me. Her cheeks were rosy, no doubt from the combination of sunshine, champagne, and the sexy buzz that hovered between us. She sat and gave me a quick kiss. "Love you."

"Always." I strummed the strings louder. Everyone turned to listen. But Gemma was the only one I focused on. As I gazed into her gorgeous green eyes, I sang:

> *As long as the moon rises*
> *As long as the sun sets*
> *As long as my heart beats*
> *As long as there's air to breathe*
> *As long as there's fire in my soul*
> *With you, I know I've found my home*
> *Best thing is now and forever*
> *I get to call you mine*
>
> *I want to touch your long hair*
> *I want to taste your sweet lips*
> *I want to give you the world*
> *Fill your life with happiness*
> *I'll do anything for you*
> *Make all your dreams come true*
> *Best thing is now and forever*
> *I get to call you mine*
>
> *I love the way you stand on tiptoe*
> *When you want to kiss me*
> *I love your little smile lines*
> *When I touch and tease you*
> *I love waking up next to you*

Each and every day
Best thing is now and forever
I get to call you mine

There is not one thing
That I want to miss
My heart belongs to you
And everything I possess
You're my fire, my light
Own my soul for life
Best thing is now and forever
I get to call you mine
Now until the end of time
I get to call you mine

Tears gleamed in her eyes as I struck the final chord. I set down my guitar beside me and she leaned in to kiss me, soft and sweet. "You're mine too. Until the end of time. Love you."

Kara placed her hand over her heart. "Oh, that was beautiful." She turned toward Hunter and thumped him on the arm. "Why don't you write songs like that for me?"

"Because I'm not a sap." Hunter grabbed the champagne from the ice bucket on the low-set table in front of him. He refilled Kara and Lexi's glasses, and his own.

Gemma held out her glass for Hunter to fill. "Yes, you are. I've seen some of the stuff you've been working on. You're a real romantic at heart, Hunt. Our next album will be badass and sexy as hell."

"Oh, yay. Image revamp." Kara clinked her glass against Gemma's.

"Let's not talk about work." Hayden dug into the cooler next to his chair and grabbed a beer. Swiping the Bluetooth speaker remote off the table, he turned on the music. "We're here to party."

The Ed Sheeran and Justin Bieber duet "I Don't Care" came on.

Lexi, sitting next to Hayden, held up her hands and swayed to the music. She sang so off-key it hurt my ears.

I leaned over and kissed Gemma on the shoulder. "Wanna dance?"

She took a sip from her flute, then put it down. "I'd love to."

I took her by the hand and walked over to the lawn just beyond the outdoor sectional. Drawing her into my arms, I held her close. I inhaled the sweet scent of her floral perfume. Her heart beat against mine. *Perfect.*

As waves crashed rhythmically against the shoreline and the string lights, wrapped around the palm trees and the pillars of the house, twinkled gently, I swayed in time to the music with Gemma. I held her hand over my beating heart. "So, my beautiful wife, we did it."

She lifted her chin. Her eyes sparkled, reflecting the firelight. "Husband. Yes, we did. It was perfect."

Under the sliver of moonlight, I kissed her, tasting the sweet champagne on her lips. The millions of stars in the heavens above were better than a stadium full of fans, better than accolades and awards, better than music itself. I had Gemma, now and forever. I wanted nothing more.

I hooked a loose strand of her hair behind her ear and skimmed my fingertips down her cheek. "Can we stay this happy forever?"

She toyed with one of the undone buttons on my shirt. "We have it good. Won't be hard."

Movement caught my eye. Hayden had grabbed a six-pack of beer and wandered off down the beach with Lexi, who swung a bottle of champagne between her fingertips. No doubt they were trying to get away from Hunter and Kara getting hot and heavy on the outdoor sofa.

I ran my hands slowly up and down Gemma's waist. The silky fabric of her dress was cool beneath my fingertips. I eyed the rhinestone straps on her shoulders. I was sure—one little nudge and the whole dress would slip to the ground.

She stood on her tiptoes and brushed her lips against mine. "You wanna get out of here?"

"I thought you'd never ask."

I swooped her into my arms and carried her up the steps into the house.

"Go get some loving." Hunter hollered.

"Planning on it," I said as I swept Gemma through the open French doors, and headed toward the ground-floor master bedroom.

By the time I kicked the door closed, she had my shirt half off. I yanked it over my head and tossed it onto the floor. Her hungry lips found mine. God, I wanted her. Loving her was so easy.

My cock ached, straining against my pants. As she rubbed me, I grabbed her hands to stop . . . Well, at least slow down. I panted, breathing her in. I wanted to embed this moment into my mind.

The dim lights shimmered against her dress and danced off her fair skin. In the middle of the huge bedroom decorated with dark wood furniture, corner lamps, and an enormous ceiling fan with rattan blades, I drank in every inch of Gemma's beauty. Her eyes, her body, her soul. "Gem, for the next ten days of vacation, and for the rest of our lives, I'll make love to you hard and fast, in any and every way you want to, but tonight, let's not rush." My heart had other ideas. So did the blood rushing to my groin. I wanted to make love to my wife. All night. Slowly. Tenderly. Lovingly.

I glided my fingertips up her arms, leaving goose bumps in their wake. "I want to touch every inch of your skin." I trailed kisses across her neck and nibbled on her earlobe. "I want to taste every piece of you." I slid my hands around her waist and lowered the tiny, concealed zipper at her waistline. "I want to take every part of you in."

Her eyes darkened, wicked and inviting. "We can do slow."

I skimmed my hands up her bare back and circled the tips of her shoulders. "Ever since I saw you in this dress, I've wanted to do this." I hooked my fingertips beneath the rhinestone straps, slid them off her shoulders, and let them go. The silk fell to the floor like a sheer scarf floating on the breeze. It pooled at her feet like liquid gold. At the sight of her in only a pair of sheer white panties, my dick hardened even more. "God, you do it for me."

"Good. Because you're stuck with me forever." She stepped forward, wove her hands around my neck, and drew my mouth to hers.

I moaned against her lips. Her peaked nipples pressing against my bare chest sent heat storming through my body. I hooked my hands beneath her ass, picked her up and headed for the grand four-poster bed. After ripping the covers off, I laid her down in the center of the mattress. Kicking my trousers and boxer-briefs off, I crawled over her and settled between her legs. I teased my nose against hers, breathed her in. "I love you. So much. You rock my world."

She scraped her nails up my back, threaded them into my hair. Tingles skipped across my scalp and shivered down my spine. "You got it wrong. You're my rock. My world."

I tormented her mouth with light kisses. "You are mine ... Mrs. McIntyre."

She wrinkled her nose and giggled. "That sounds so weird. But I love it. I love you. Now ... make love to me."

"Gladly."

With playful nips and kisses, and sweeps of my fingertips, I teased, taunted and tickled her skin before I eased off her panties. Every little moan and groan that escaped her lips embedded deep inside my heart. Every taste of her lips and flesh branded into my brain. Every lock of our gazes united our souls even more. I worshiped her tits with my hands and tongue. Then did the same to her pussy. Her hot arousal made me crave more. I'd never get enough of sucking her clit and fucking her with my tongue.

Her thighs quaked. She arched off the bed and came. Panting. Clawing at the sheets. Shuddering.

"Kyle." She moaned as I lapped and licked her harder. "Fuck, that's good."

Yeah, I'd never tire of this.

She tapped me on the shoulder, tugged on my hair. We were nowhere near done.

I rolled onto my back and drew her over with me. She wasted no time in straddling my lap and mounting my cock. My pulse quickened as she drove me deep inside. As I clutched her hips, I thrust into her. Over hot, searing kisses, I got lost in her touch. She rocked and rode me until our bodies were licked with sweat.

So much for going slow.

I tugged her forward and penetrated her hard and deep. Heat surged through my veins, coiled across my skin. My blood pumped and pulsed inside my dick.

"Gem." Every muscle in my body tensed, chasing, begging, burning for release.

As the waves broke lazily onto the shore beyond the French doors and my breath entwined with hers, she drove me over the edge. My cock throbbed, spilling inside her as she clenched around me. *Heaven. Pure heaven.* Buried deep inside her, I convulsed and quaked beneath her. "Fuck, I love you."

I'd never forget how lucky I was to have her. How grateful I am she came into my life. That she was here. Alive.

I kissed her sweet lips, drew her down beside me and held her against my chest. My heart raced in time with hers. My dick throbbed. The scent of our love-making filled the air.

"I'm yours forever, Gem."

"Forever and always," she whispered. "That was only round one, right?"

"Absolutely." I touched my lips to hers. "The night is still young."

She was the only one who I had such a powerful, uncanny connection with.

She would always be the one in control of my heart.

I loved her. More than anything. I was totally rapt.

I was hers.

Forever.

Epilogue

GEMMA

I slipped my transmitter into the pouch on the back of my leather pants and hooked my in-ear monitors over my shoulders. My heartbeat pummeled my ribs. I closed my eyes and stretched my head from side to side. Taking a deep breath, I focused. It had been just over a month since my honeymoon. New York was sinking under the weight of Thanksgiving paraphernalia. Corncobs, pumpkins, dried leafy arrangements, and oversized stuffed turkeys decorated every store window. I was about to go on stage at the Prudential Center in New Jersey with the guys. My first performance since Vegas. The first time as Kyle's wife. The first time since being abducted.

I got this.

Backstage, in the dressing room, the electric vibe in the air had everyone in a buzz, but the frenzy of butterflies wouldn't settle in my stomach.

Kyle, rocking a pair of ripped red jeans and a black button-down, slipped over to my side the second Carla finished styling his hair. His bedroom eyes roamed over my sequined halter top, my red pants with rhinestone trim, and my face plastered in stage makeup. A gravelly groan rumbled deep in his throat as he swooped in to nuzzle my neck and whispered into my ear, "Damn, you're sexy."

Heat flushed my cheeks. "You're not so bad yourself." I slid my hands around his waist, clutched his ass, and pulled him closer.

"Kyle," Hunter buckled up his belt. Dressed in red jeans covered in large white stars and a shimmery black button-down, he walked toward us. "Stop eye-fucking Gem. We have a show to do."

I hooked my arms around their waists and drew them into a tight-knit hug. My knees jiggled. My nerves shook. "I didn't think I'd be this anxious, but with you guys beside me, I'll nail it."

"You've got this, Gem." Hunter nudged his hip against mine.

"Once that music starts, you'll feel right at home." Kyle kissed my temple. I inhaled the smell of his delicious woodsy cologne and let it fill every corner of my soul, calming my mind. *Yeah. I was home. These people were home.*

"Let's do this." My voice boomed with confidence, but my insides skipped like a scratched CD.

Sophie tapped me on the shoulder, and I jumped. "Sorry," she winced and rubbed my arm. "It's time."

I smiled a nervous smile. *No need to be on edge.*

Sophie had done an incredible job rescheduling our canceled show. It had sold out in record time. Every cent of the profits would be donated to the Victims of Crime Center which supported those affected by stalkers and domestic violence. I widened our circle and formed a huddle with everyone present.

"This night is extra special." I spoke from the depths of my heart. "I'm grateful to be here. Grateful to have each of you in my life. Over the years, we have grown and have become a family. You are my strength. You all hold a place in my heart." Pursing my lips for a second, I fought the tears stinging my eyes. "Let's show the world that nothing can tear us apart. We are one. We are Everhide. Let's give this crowd one hell of a show."

Kyle thrust his hand into the center of the circle. Everyone followed. "This one's for Gem."

"Yeah!" Together, they chanted and flung their hands in the air. "Woohoo!"

Sophie clapped her hands and pointed toward the door. "Let's go."

Careful not to smudge my eyeliner, I dabbed tears from my eyes with the tip of my finger. I followed the guys and Sophie through the white concrete maze of corridors toward the stage. Like in the movies, every step I took played in surreal slow motion.

Entering the darkened backstage area, I glanced up at the huge black curtains that hid us from the auditorium. My heartbeat hit a vivacious tempo. The loud screams from the fans hummed in my ears. Crew—sound engineers, lighting specialists, equipment technicians, and stagehands—scampered in all directions to take their stationed positions. The vibrations coursed through my veins like a high-voltage electric wire.

Fuck, it's so good to be here.

As we neared the stage steps, I grabbed Kyle on the arm and drew him aside.

Worry skipped through his eyes. "Is something wrong?"

I shook my head and rubbed my hand over his chest. The smooth fabric of his button-down slipped softly beneath my fingertips. In a short couple of hours, his shirt would be nothing but a sweat-drenched mess, but for now, it cooled the crazy in my head. Just feeling his heartbeat eased my anxious pulse. "I just wanted to say I love you."

He grabbed me around the waist and pushed me back against the metal railing. He kissed me hard. Hard and deep and hungry. My tongue met his in fiery flicks.

The crew mumbled their objections as they shuffled past. *"Get a room." "Isn't the honeymoon over?" "Um, guys. Showtime, not playtime."*

No doubt they rolled their eyes. But I needed this. Needed Kyle. He was my strength. I couldn't get on that stage without him.

I threaded my fingers through his hair, messing up Carla's styling. "Thank you. I needed that."

"Anytime." Throwing me a mischievous grin, he pressed his forehead against mine. "You want to take this back to our dressing room? I will gladly delay the concert for ten minutes and show you how much I love you."

Hmmm. Him fucking me on the countertop in our dressing room. My legs wrapped around his waist. His kisses covering my face. *Oh yeah.*

But no. Reining in my lust-fueled thoughts, I stroked his cheek. "Later. It's time to get onstage."

"It is." He winked, then grimaced as he readjusted his crotch. "Thanks for the semi."

"Sorry." I winced, but I loved having that effect on him.

Hunter stepped over to join us and placed a hand on each of our shoulders. Shards of concern flickered in his azure eyes. "You guys good?"

I straightened my in-ear cords and realigned my transmitter. I set my resolve in place. Music was my life. Nothing and no one would take that from me. "Yep. Let's go."

Lucas, our production manager, tapped his headset and scanned the monitors before him. He sliced his hand across his throat, the signal for radio silence. The lights lowered to near pitch-black. The noise from the auditorium erupted and slammed into my chest. He shone a torchlight in front of his face, held up one finger and mouthed, *"One minute."*

I blew out my breath slowly. The chill of the air-conditioning shivered across my skin. I had performed thousands of times in front of audiences of all sizes, but the nerves had returned with a vengeance. My last performance in Vegas had rattled me. The possibility of more threats and crazed fans loomed in the back of my mind. Being abducted had scarred me for life. I'd been in therapy for weeks. Nothing had erased the nightmares. But I was determined not to let being kidnapped stop me from living life. I trusted my team to ensure our safety. Trusted myself and my experience to put on a kickass show. Trusted these guys beside me.

The fog machine came alive, spurting smoke across the stage like a dragon's breath. Adrenaline surged through my veins with the hiss of the noise.

Crew shone their flashlights to show the guys and me to our

positions.

It's time. I gave Hunter and Kyle one last reassuring nod as we grabbed our mics off the equipment table. Wiping my sweating palms on the back of my top, I stepped toward the metal stairs. They led up to the stage, hidden behind the mounted video screens that opened for the start of the show.

With wobbly feet, I took the first step. Then another and another. Climbing the stairs seemed dreamlike. It felt like a lifetime since I'd done this.

The countdown began. *Twenty seconds to showtime.* With the guys standing on either side of me, waiting for the screens to open, I whispered a silent prayer. *Let this be an awesome show. We know the songs. We've rehearsed. We know our shit. Let's kick some ass.*

The torchlights went out.

My heartbeat thundered louder than the screaming and stamping crowd. I shoved in my in-ears. The stage lights blazed to life. Our backup band played.

Here we go.

Three. Two. One.

Pyrotechnics blasted. The three of us struck our poses. The screens slid apart. Stage lights flashed down on us. Music flooded my ears. We rushed toward the front of the stage. The whole auditorium took to their feet. Through the sea of cell phones, many people waved banners of all sizes and colors above their heads that said, *"I love Gemma," "Gemma Rocks,"* and *"Live life to the fullest."* Oh my God, that was the tattoo on my inner bicep. Several signs were printed with *"#GLADTOBEALIVE,"* the hashtag I'd used on my social media posts.

Holy fuck. I never expected this. Our fans are freaking awesome.

A blanket of warmth and overwhelming gratitude enveloped me and filled my chest. My eyes pricked with tears. *This is amazing.* Millions of fans adored me. I had to remember that. I absorbed energy from everyone present.

I glanced at Hunter, then at Kyle. I gave him a wink and held my mic to my lips. With a deep breath, I pointed and hollered at the crowd, "Yo, bitches. We're back. Who's ready to rock?"

The crowd roared as Kyle and Hunter stepped in beside me. We hit our first song, "Phoenix." It was full of raw fighting attitude.

> *I've been lying on the ground*
> *I've been beaten, knocked around*
> *You can kick me when I'm down*
> *You can fight me, steal my crown*
> *But you forgot just one thing*
> *I'll come back again and again*
> *I'll come back again and again*
>
> *Because, baby*
>
> *Like a phoenix, I'll return*
> *Fire won't ever keep me burned*
> *From the ashes, I will rise*
> *I am beautiful, let me shine*
> *Like a flower in the sun*
> *I stand tall; I am one*
> *I'm determined and strong*
> *Have always known what I want*
> *Don't fuck with me, you'll get burned*
> *Stand in my way, you'll get burned*
>
> *I've been up, I've been down*
> *I've run wild all over town*
> *You've seen me at my worst*
> *Scared of truth because it hurts*
> *You think that you've won,*
> *And believe I've had my run*
> *But you forgot, just one thing*
> *I'll come back again and again*
> *I'll come back again and again*

For two hours, the guys and I sang our hits, slayed a set on our guitars, and had the crowd dancing on their feet. As the confetti cannons fired at the end of the show, and gold pieces of foil rained down on my head, I closed my eyes and let the soft paper tickle my face.

I did it. I'm back.

I joined hands with the guys, and we bowed to the audience. We blew kisses and waved to the sea of screaming fans. I covered my heart and tapped my chest. Overwhelming gratitude washed over me. This is where the three of us belonged. This was our dream. And we would follow it forever. With a skip and a jump, we rushed off the stage into the arms of our crew, ready to celebrate the end of an incredible show.

But they could start the party without me and Kyle. I pulled him into our private dressing room and hauled him into the shower. There was nothing like a hot fuck heightened by performance adrenaline. It intensified every sense and sensation—the scent of his skin, every touch of his hands, every thrust of his cock inside me. Every time he slammed into me, shudders shivered up my spine.

Oh yeah. So, so good.

Hard and fast, just the way I liked it.

After we showered, I ripped on fresh jeans and a T-shirt. The heat of lovemaking still blazed in my cheeks. "That was incredible. The show and the sex."

"You nailed both." Kyle grinned, tying up his bootlaces.

Holding hands, we rushed into the room next door and joined the party. Music blared; alcohol flowed. Laughter filled the air.

Through the crowd, I caught sight of Taylah. Kyle had tracked her down after our honeymoon and kept his promise to thank her for her help in saving me. He'd offered her two VIP tickets to every concert we performed in New York City . . . for life. I dropped Kyle's hand, dashed over to her, and threw my arms around her neck. Took me a minute to let go.

"Oh my God, Gemma." Tears welled in Taylah's eyes. "What was that for?"

I clasped her hands. "I will never, ever be able to thank you enough for helping everyone find me."

She sniffled and bobbed her head. "You're welcome. I'm just glad you're okay."

I wiped the tears from my cheeks, but they weren't sad ones; they were tears of gratitude and happiness.

Kyle veered around me and gave Taylah an enormous hug. He lifted her off her feet. "My number-one fan."

"Absolutely." Taylah laughed as he placed her back on the ground. She flicked her black bob off her face and blushed. "I knew you were nice. I never doubted it for a second."

He eased back to my side, and a heartwarming smile lit his face. "Yeah, just don't mess with my wife, and I'm cool."

I slid my arm around his waist and cuddled into his chest. "So true, my sweet, overprotective husband." I reached for Taylah's hand once again and held it tight. "Taylah, from the bottom of my heart, thank you. We have to mingle. Please enjoy the rest of the evening, and we'll see you at our next show."

"I'll be there." Taylah nodded. "Front and center."

"Catch you soon." Kyle drew me into the crowd.

As we made the rounds, talking to everyone, my heart beat to a new rhythm.

For so long, Kyle, and Hunter had been my world. I'd kept everyone else at bay. But over the past few months, most of the people in this room had shown me the true meaning of family. Family wasn't just about DNA. It was about the people who loved and supported you, the people who'd do anything for you, and who were there in a crisis, no matter what. It had taken me too long to learn and accept that.

As I scanned the room filled with our closest friends, our security team, our backup band, and crew members who had been with Everhide for years, I truly felt safe. Comfortable. At home.

This was my family. This was living.

Kyle entwined our fingers and drew me near a group of people dancing in the middle of the room. I laughed as crew members swung their arms over their heads and downed beer in races. I fell into Kyle's embrace, resting my head against his chest.

As we swayed to the music, he stroked my hair, rubbed my back, and kissed my head. "Can we do this forever? Make music. Make love. Make magic."

"Yeah. I'd like that." I tucked my hands into the back pockets of his jeans. Cupped his ass. "Life is pretty darn good, isn't it?"

"It's better than good. It's fucking awesome . . . because I have you."

I tilted my head back and gazed into his dark espresso eyes. "I love you."

"Always." He pressed his lips to mine, deepening our kiss with a flick of his tongue.

Since we were gangly high school teenagers, we'd become best friends, bound by our love of music and our shitty home lives. We'd chased our dreams, had toured and had experienced the many ups and downs life had thrown at us—all those things had brought us to this place. We were married. In love. Ridiculously happy. The things we'd feared and craved had united us. *Trust. Love. Family.*

Kyle was my rock. My soulmate. My forever. He had hold of my heart. I loved him with every ounce of my being. He'd taught me it was okay to be vulnerable. He let me shine. He never failed to love and support me. And I did the same for him. Honesty had brought us closer and made us stronger. For so long and from this point forward, every song I wrote, every scale I sang, every sound from my beating heart would now and always be for my one true love . . . Kyle.

Thank you for reading **RAPT – The Price of Love.**

Kyle and Gemma finally got their happily ever after.
But what about Hayden and Lexi? Do you want to find out how they fit into the Everhide world? He's a drummer with a dream. She'd given up on hers. But one kiss change everything.

Did Hayden regret kissing his best friend? . . . *Hell No!*
Did he regret losing his best friend? . . . *Hell Yes!*
Continue the series with Book 4: **REGRET – The Price of Truth**

Available on Amazon and Kindle Unlimited.

P.S. If you love **RAPT - The Price of Love**, would you kindly take a moment and leave a quick product review on Amazon. They are music for an author's soul.

Thank you.
Tania Joyce

BEFORE YOU GO.

Would you like a BONUS EBOOK for FREE?

Find out how my world of rockstars began with the Everhide Rockstar Romance series.

ROCKED – The Price of Dreams is the origin story to my bestselling Everhide Series. Find out how the band met in high school, experience their heartbreak and hardships, and follow their journey to stardom. It is the pre-romance to the adult relationships that develop, evolve, and change throughout the six books. (Three standalones, three follow-ons—all happily ever afters, no cliffhangers).

This series will have you falling in love, shedding tears, and laughing out loud.

Read the prequel, **ROCKED – The Price of DREAMS,** for **FREE** when you subscribe to my newsletter. I only send emails about once a month, so your inbox won't be inundated with my news. Please subscribe here: https://taniajoyce.com/subscribe.

OTHER BOOKS BY TANIA JOYCE

Rockstars, bad boys and billionaires . . . something for everyone. For eBooks visit Amazon. Paperbacks are available at all good online book retailers. Author Signed Copies and Bookplates are available from my website.

The Flintlocks Series

The Everhide Series

Billionaires and College Romance

NEWSLETTER

For information about my new releases, bonus content, and special offers, please subscribe to my monthly newsletter.
Join at: https://taniajoyce.com/subscribe
REMEMBER: You get a BONUS BOOK if you join.

***

FOLLOW TANIA JOYCE

You can follow and find me on the following social media platforms.

Amazon: https://amazon.com/author/taniajoyce
BookBub: https://www.bookbub.com/authors/tania-joyce
Facebook: https://www.facebook.com/taniajoycebooks
Goodreads: https://www.goodreads.com/taniajoyce
Instagram: https://www.instagram.com/taniajoycebooks/
Pinterest: https://www.pinterest.com/taniajoycebooks
TikTok: https://www.tiktok.com/@taniajoyce
Web: http://taniajoyce.com

ABOUT TANIA JOYCE

Tania Joyce is an author of rockstar, contemporary and new adult romance novels. Her stories thread romance, drama and passion into beautiful locations ranging from the dazzling lights and glitter of New York to the rural countryside of the Hunter Valley.

She's widely traveled, has a diverse background in the corporate world and has a love for sparkles, shoes and shiraz.

Tania draws on her real-life experiences and combines them with her very vivid imagination to form the foundation of her novels. She likes to write about strong-minded, career-oriented heroes and heroines that go through drama-filled hell, have steamy encounters and risk everything as they endeavor to find their happy-ever-after.

Tania shuffles the hours in her day between part-time work, family life and writing. One day she hopes to find balance!

She loves to hear from her readers.

Visit: www.taniajoyce.com
or email her at: tania@taniajoyce.com

***

MORE BY TANIA JOYCE

Visit Tania Joyce on Amazon.Com